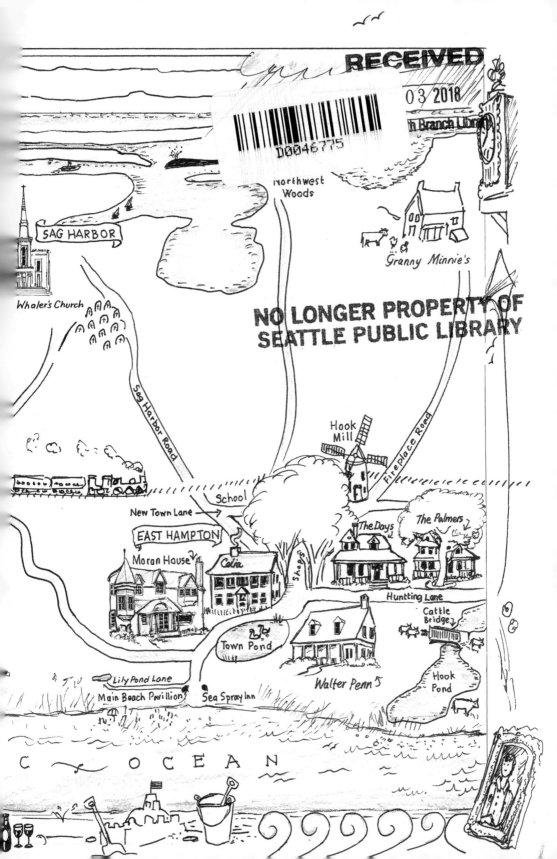

RECEIVED
03 2018
h Branch Libr

D0046775

NO LONGER PROPERTY OF
SEATTLE PUBLIC LIBRARY

A DAY LIKE ANY OTHER

A DAY LIKE ANY OTHER

THE GREAT HAMPTONS HURRICANE OF 1938

A NOVEL
GENIE CHIPPS HENDERSON

ILLUSTRATIONS BY CHARLOTTE SHERWOOD

PUSHCART PRESS
WAINSCOTT, NEW YORK

Copyright © 2018 by Genie Chipps Henderson

All rights reserved. No part of this book may be used or reproduced in any manner whatsoever without written permission from the publisher, except in the case of brief excerpts embodied in critical articles and reviews.

ISBN 978-1-888889-91-8

Illustrations by Charlotte Sherwood
Cover and book designed by Mary Kornblum

Cover art:
Waves—Hato Zu, woodcut by by Uehara Konen (1878-1940)
Courtesy of Library of Congress
Interior art:
Bathing Beach, Courtesy of the East Hampton Library, Long Island Collection, Harvey Ginsberg Postcard Collection
Calm, Gary Felton photographer

Published by Pushcart Press
P.O. Box 380
Wainscott, NY 11975

Distributed by WW Norton & Company, Inc
500 Fifth Avenue
New York, NY 10110

FOR BILL

Our Town

Amagansett

Jack Burns. An artist living in an old converted chicken coop for the summer.
Mitch Grindle. A fisherman.
Nettie Kitchin Grindle. His wife.
Eddie. Their 12-year-old son.
Also in the Grindle family:
Bette & Jo (high school girls) and *Baby June* (age 5).
Lottie Kitchin Foss. Nettie's sister.
Herb Foss. Her husband, proprietor of a general store in Amagansett.

Bridgehampton

Judy and Chip Tate. A young married couple who summer on Dune Road.
Alice. Their 4-year-old daughter.
Raleigh. Their houseman.
Emmaline Hartley. A wealthy New York socialite also living on Dune Road.
James Hartely. Her financier husband.
The Hartely children:
George (15), *Violet* (12) and *Peter* (9).
Mrs. Sternhoffer. The Hartley housekeeper.
Virgil Cobb. Farmer and weather watcher.

East Hampton Village

Wilma Harding Palmer. A lifelong villager, housewife and horticulturist.
Jim Palmer. Her husband, owner of Palmer & Day Insurance Company.
Lewis Palmer. Their 7-year-old son.

Margaret Day. The Palmers' next-door neighbor
and Lewis' babysitter.
Mrs. Sweeny. A veteran high school English teacher.
Celia Dowling Slade. Wilma's frivolous best friend
since childhood.
Harry Slade. Her husband, a boisterous blowhard
from away.
Walter Penn. A preeminent art critic dividing his time
between East Hampton and New York.
Mrs. Cunningham. His English housekeeper.

Montauk

Hannah Wood. A high school girl from the fishing
settlement.

Napeague

Crazy Tom. A hermit who lives on a wild stretch of beach.

The Springs

Granny Minnie. Nettie & Lottie's mother, a farmwoman.
Old Man Burl. A self-proclaimed "Bonacker"
and eel monger.

Washington Weather Bureau

Will Foster. A rookie forecaster new to the Weather Bureau.
Victor McGraw. His boss.

wind

AIR IN MOTION. *Moving around the earth, cleansing, cooling, furling sails, spinning mills, lifting kites – but not all winds. In the Sahara Desert ill winds are born; hot winds that rise up from the burning sand. In Africa they have names for these troublemakers. Sirocco is one. A blistering wind that travels north, crossing the Mediterranean where it skims off moisture and then cloaks the cities and villages of southern Europe like a wet-wool blanket on a sweltering day. When the Sirocco blows, men and animals go mad.*

Yet worse, far worse, is the wind off the Sahara that travels west. Hermattan is his name and he shows no mercy. Hermattan scoops up grit and sand, parching fields, killing animals and babies with air so fetid that the people on the western edge of Africa can only gasp for breath. When Hermattan finally moves out to sea he will perhaps die. Or, perhaps he will join in with the trade winds over the Cape Verde Islands. If this happens the potential to create a giant cyclone is ripe but the journey across the southern sea is a long one and no one can predict the outcome.

*People think of history in the long term
but in fact, it is a very sudden thing*

PHILIP ROTH

September 21, 1938
THE SOUTH FORK OF LONG ISLAND, NEW YORK

1

Mitch and Nettie Grindle
Before Dawn, Amagansett

On the morning of the hurricane, Mitch Grindle lay in bed listening to the deep resonant chimes of the clock strike three, filling the still night around him and his sleeping family. It was an old clock. Come down through the family from way back. Mitch didn't really know how far because he had never paid much mind to details like that but hadn't he and Nettie been tickled when his mother awarded it to them when they married. A little over two feet tall and made of mahogany – two brass keys hung inside the glass door – one for the time, the other for the chimes. Mitch wound the clock every night, the last thing he did before bed.

He could hear the ocean not far from where he lay and feel her big, restless soul calling to him. "What'cher doing in bed?" she hissed, the long wave of her arms rolling over sand, "Come out here and get to work." Sometimes when he wasn't heading out on the boat he might allow himself the luxury of staying warm next to Nettie until four. But four was his limit. Even that time when he and Nettie was on their honeymoon up to Boston he had been up at four peering out the window down seven stories to a silent street below wondering what the hell he was supposed to be doing in a big city hotel room at that time until Nettie had waked up and teased him back to bed. He grinned now in the darkness, remembering.

Nettie was a sound sleeper. She went to bed later than Mitch because there was always something more that needed doing – dough punched down in the rising bowl, a school project for the kids, a cake to be frosted for the church, mending and darning (she darned every one of his wool socks until the threads got so weak in the heels she'd give up and unravel the sock, wrapping the good yarn in a tight ball for her knitting basket). Some nights she'd be out late over to her sister Lottie's, then she'd tiptoe into the bedroom around nine trying not to wake him. Mitch slept in fits and starts like a dog, always just a little awake around the edges but Nettie? Once her head hit the pillow, she was out. She had a little snore that signaled she was deep into it, but it didn't bother him. He probably snored too.

In the kitchen he put a match to the fire to heat the coffee before splashing water on his face. Nettie got up too, yawning and pulling her bathrobe tight around her. This was their time – a time to talk, quietly so as not to wake the kids. Nettie called it "dream time" and often she would actually tell him about a dream she'd had, more often about something she had overheard the day before telling him in detail while she made his lunch.

Mitch looked up at the calendar hanging next to the sink. He saw Nettie had circled the day – Wednesday, September 21 – and he nodded at it.

"What's on," he said.

Nettie glanced at the calendar. "Oh it's nothing. Circle One at the church is going cranberry pickin' out to the dunes in Napeague but I sent word I wasn't going. I think I'm going back over to Mom's today. She was acting funny when we were out there yesterday."

"Funny? How?"

Nettie frowned. "Can't say, really. She'd be fine, you know slicing fruit, stirring the pot and then she'd just stop, like she couldn't quite remember what she was doing. I asked her if she was OK and she just shook it off. Lottie noticed it too."

"Well, she is getting old, you know. Maybe she can't remember what she's doing. If you're worried take her to see the doc."

Nettie snorted. "You take her to see the doc. She hates doctors. Hates medicine. Why it's gotten so she won't even leave the farm."

Mitch reached over and touched her hand. "You go see her if you're worried. Stay over if you want to. I'm likely not coming in tonight."

"Oh?"

"Yeah. There's cod off Block Island. Lotta guys hauling good out there."

Nettie shook her head. 'Well, why didn't you tell me. I'd have fixed up some stew…"

Mitch stood setting the chair carefully back to the table. "We're OK. One of my guys is a real good cook. That new fella from up Gloucester…he's got it all in hand."

"Well he sure hasn't got any pie in hand. I baked two yesterday just to use up those peaches. You're taking them with you." And with that she got up and started pulling out some butcher's paper kept carefully folded in a box. Mitch watched her as she tightened her blue chenille robe around her, setting a determined hand on the paper and string. "You go over to your mom's tonight. OK? Tell the girls and Eddie to head that way too after school. I think there's some weather coming in."

Nettie frowned. "No! After this last week? I haven't seen such a spell of pretty days all summer. And that's the truth. Worse summer I can remember with all the rain. Near rotted out my garden. You really think so?"

He shrugged. "Smells different out there." He leaned over and pulled his boots on and took an extra shirt down from the hook. Nettie watched him. Mitch picked up the pies. "Sure hope these make it all the way to Montauk. It's a long ride."

Nettie smiled. "You better go then or it'll be high noon before you get out. But Mitch," she shook her head like she was trying to stop herself, "you won't go if the weather looks bad." She said this almost by rote but it made her feel better. She feared the ocean and knew what every fisherman's wife knew deep down – that no man was in full charge out on the water. It was a job filled with danger and risk and it was stupid for anyone to think differently.

"Nope." He leaned down and kissed the top of her head, which was what he did every morning and then he headed out the door.

About an hour later on the docks loading his gear onto his boat *Kitchin Girl*, some of the other guys joined him. 'Wadda

ya think, Mitch?" Mitch had what was known as "weather eyes."
He could predict the weather better than any radio forecaster and
that was a fact. They could all see an uneasy sky and an agitation
that could mean a blow. The trick was to figure how much of a
blow, how much of a risk. Mitch wasn't all that concerned. Sure
– it could get rough but like most of the fishermen who gathered
on the docks that day, he decided it was worth the risk.

Hannah Wood came out of her dad's bait shop and watched
Kitchin Girl pull out into Fort Pond Bay. Though it wasn't something she normally did, she waved, and a couple of the guys working to secure their lines, paused and waved back. Hannah chewed
on her lip watching the trawler as it headed for the ocean.

2

Will Foster
7:30 a.m.
Washington, D.C.

"You're up, Foster. You make the noon report today."

Will Foster clamored off his stool, upsetting a glass holder with all of his pencils in it to the floor. "Yes, sir," he said feeling almost as if the breath had been knocked out of him.

The noon report. Every trainee in the bureau vied to be assigned the noon report, and he, Will Foster, had never before been tapped. This was the report picked up by every radio station and newspaper on the east coast and served as the official weather word for 24 hours. His boss gave a tired little grunt and glared at the glass pencil holder still rolling on the floor. "And pick up that mess," he barked before striding off.

Will, along with a dozen or so bright young men – the Juniors they were called – arrived for work as part of the vast bureaucracy located in the block long Department of Agriculture building at 7 a.m. sharp. Juniors were told to submit practice forecasts based on what they could "dig up" and a senior, more experienced forecaster would compare these with the official outlook. It was a stern office – as stern as any military post and a newcomer better look sharp or face humiliation from the higher ups if he didn't pass muster.

Charting the weather was done by hand, with information culled from as many sources as could be mustered – relay stations, weather watchers, ships at sea, even – some joked – an 80-year-old Civil War veteran with a bum leg garnered in the Battle of Bull Run. After consulting his leg, the old man would make his forecast, beating out the bureau's predictions more times than anyone cared to admit.

Truth was, weather forecasting was more of a best guess than a scientific discipline. That "best guess" had proved disastrous three years before when a complacent Miami weather bureau had failed to warn residents of the Florida Keys of a killer storm with winds gusting at 200 miles per hour until too late with no evacuation possible. The storm had killed over 400 people, many of them war veterans hired to work on the rail lines, their clothes sandblasted from their bodies. The public outcry had been loud, demanding vigilance.

Never again, declared the Weather Bureau and to that end the forecasters from Miami all the way to Washington had been monitoring this new storm formed in the Cape Verde Islands and traveling across the southern seas for over a week – a massive storm hitting Puerto Rico with unprecedented force and now heading straight for Florida. Warnings had been issued to all of southern Florida and every weatherman in the nation was following its track.

Will Foster was not only a Junior in the Bureau, he was the newest Junior, having badgered the appointment via his Senator from Vermont, and he was passionate about the weather. An eager trainee, he was filled with an encyclopedic recall of weather related passages found in literature and history – a conceit that was noted with dismissive disdain by his superiors. His questions and opinions were often peppered with quotes from *The Tempest* and *King Lear*; he might reference the Spanish Armada defeated by a storm, Napoleon saved by the sun, and, Will always noted proudly, the last entry in Thomas Jefferson's diary written the day before he died, was to record the weather. He wanted more than anything to tame the tempest, to figure it all out, to know why and how it could be predicted.

This then was what confronted him that morning as he bent to the task of the noon report. The threat to Florida was over. The storm they had followed with mounting alarm had turned north in the night, brushed up against Cape Hatteras before looping out into the Atlantic. As storms go, it was following a familiar pattern. Heading out over the ocean it would dissipate and disappear.

Will sifted through his facts. The reports from ships at sea as well as the relay stations in the Caribbean were grim. *Nothing like it. Gusts at 185 miles per hour. Unpredictable. Unstable. Moving at tremendous speed. An out-of-control megaton of vicious energy.* Yet in turning north it had entered colder waters – waters that traditionally slowed these tropical monsters hungry only for warm seas. It appeared to one and all to be set on a classic route to oblivion. The senior forecasters all agreed – this storm would fade by afternoon. Rain would be the worst of it for the eastern United States. That was the bulletin that had gone out early this morning. That was the conclusion Will was expected to make at noon.

And yet...and yet? Will pored over his charts checking and rechecking the data he had at hand. Every indication supported the prevailing opinion that the eastern states would get rain but there were niggling variables that bothered him. For one thing, the weather all over the area, from the Alleghenies to the coast was curious, if not unstable. It could mean nothing – but it bothered him. There was a front over the Blue Ridge Mountains that was stalled and *that* bothered him. One of the ships at sea had reported a discernable shift in the Bermuda high. So much so the captain was changing his course so as to delay his arrival in New York. *Too dangerous,* came the cryptic transmission. Too dangerous to come in to New York waters?

And then there had been the morning report called into the bureau from that old weather watcher out on Long Island. Corn Cob, the Juniors called him because he was a farmer and his last name was Cobb. He was old and cranky but Will had become somewhat of a fan of old Corn Cob mainly because he took his daily report so seriously. Cobb and hundreds like him were part of a nationwide network of volunteer weather watchers. Anyone could do it – housewives, shopkeepers, teachers, farmers.

Day in day out, come rain or come shine, Virgil Cobb gathered data for the weather service using only a rain gauge, a weather vane, two thermometers and a measuring stick in winter when it snowed. Mundane information mainly – high and low temperatures of the day, wind direction and speed, rainfall. The Cobb's were farmers, had been farmers for generations past and had every intention of remaining farmers for generations to come. And one of the underlying facts of farming was "You don't cut hay today to dry in the field if you know it's going to rain tomorrow." This one caveat plus a strong sense of civic duty had led Virgil Cobb, senior of the Bridgehampton clan, to become a weather watcher, a job he took very seriously. He was seventy-years-old and had been a watcher since he was a young man. Virgil went about his every day milking cows, tending chickens and recording the weather. And every day through drought, flood, fog, nor'easters, planting in spring, harvesting in fall, the advent of children and then grandchildren, and even on the death day of his wife, he went to the wall telephone in his kitchen and put his call through to Washington to transmit his numbers.

Today was different. Today when he called Washington and spoke to Will, he didn't give him figures. "Sonny, take care," he said, his voice grave. "Whatever's goin' on out there is no good. Measurements make no sense." And strangely enough, that bothered Will most of all.

3

Judy Tate
8:00 a.m.
Dune Road, Bridgehampton

Rain. Again? Judy Tate reached across the table and flipped off the radio. It had been a long, bleak summer of rain, so hot, humid, and wet that beach towels never seemed to dry and houses took on a permanent smell of mildew. Yet just a week ago the weather had at last turned balmy. Blue skies, powder puff clouds, a gentle soft breeze lifting joyous displays of flapping linens on clotheslines – children dashed onto the beach where the lovely sweep of waves topped with white foam made swirling eddies for them to jump in. And everyone from town folk to summer people greeted one another beaming in the euphoric air.

At the eastern end of Long Island the land jutted out into two forks – the North Fork within distant sight of Connecticut and the South Fork stretching some 26 miles of beach, farmland and villages along the Atlantic Ocean. The villagers had long ago, and wisely, built their houses away from the ocean but not so the summer colony and on this day in this delicious and long awaited sublime weather, the mistresses of the large rambling ocean front houses were delaying departure dates so that they could enjoy its perfection. Judy Tate among them. Young and prosperous, the Tates seemed an ideal couple. Chip Tate had done all right for himself in marrying Judy. When they stood at the railway station just after Labor Day, they might have been models for an advertisement in a magazine. He had gone through the motions of regret that he would miss the big fourth birthday party for their daughter but in fact he was glad to get away having long since wearied of summer with its endless parties and infernal social obligations. Judy prattled on about the pony and the clown she had hired as if it were her own party and not the little girl's. Chip half listened to his wife hoping the train wasn't late.

And now here it was September 21 and the birthday had arrived. The house and deck on Dune Road were festooned with balloons and colored streamers. Judy eyed the scene, willing the rain to hold off until late afternoon. With any luck the children would have this one last day outside in the sun. Well, so far so good. The sun was pale but shining. The white caps on the water set a beautiful backdrop. The balloons snapped in the breeze.

In nearby East Hampton, Harry Slade had just returned from the post office bearing a hefty package. He was glad his wife was busy elsewhere in the house for she was irrational over his hobby of collecting nautical paraphernalia. "You come from the Midwest," she said in exasperation. "You've got our whole house looking as if we're part of the British Admiralty. And you, you'd hardly seen an ocean before you married me." Now he carefully unwrapped and mounted his new Fitzroy Storm Glass barometer in his study. It was a beauty on order for months from a dealer in London and one he could ill afford. But Harry never worried about affordability, ever the optimist he saw prosperity just around the corner. Eight years of the Depression had done little to dampen his theory and this irritated his wife even more.

He lifted the heavy brass barometer, which was encased in an oak box fitted out in rich royal blue velvet and stood back to watch the mercury level. It sank lower, then lower still – the lowest he had ever seen. In dismay he took the fixture down. Damn thing must be broken.

Three miles away in Amagansett, twelve-year-old Eddie Grindle walked to school along Atlantic Avenue chafing in the restrictive starched clothes. School had been back in session for two weeks but he was far from settled in to the rigors of the seventh grade. From his desk in the new two-story brick school building he could see the ocean, smell the sea air. Eddie had been out over the summer with his dad fishing and to be cramped in behind a desk listening to boring stuff about the Battle of Long Island and the Revolutionary War…geez…it was all up the island anyways, all the way to New York even. Eddie had never been to the city and neither had any of his friends. New York might as well have been London or Paris. Eddie was going to be a fisherman like his dad.

In East Hampton village some of the shopkeepers along Main Street lingered outside their stores talking to each other, marveling that almost everyone you saw was someone you knew. After Labor Day their town was returned to them. High time, too. Summer people…OK sure…they were the money, they were the jobs but it was certainly a lot less complicated when they all went home.

The people of the South Fork were well acquainted with summer people who had come in increasing droves since the Civil War – the rich and privileged scions of New York and Philadelphia, foreign diplomats and European aristocracy who even as they extolled the beauty of the beach, its cooling sea breezes, the charms of rural life with its picturesque windmills and sleepy traditions nevertheless built opulent "cottages" by the sea making sure that their verdant lawns swept majestically to the very edges of dunes, taming the landscape to suit lavish incomes. Yet despite the extravagant parties, the golf and tennis and beach clubs, the sailing boats and yachts, the high speed railroad linking them to New York, the South Fork remained essentially a fishing and farming community priding itself on its long history and traditional way of life. Well good. Now this life could resume. Summer was over.

4

The Palmers
8:15 a.m.
East Hampton Village

"Late again with the delivery." Father shut the back door where yesterday's empty milk bottles sat on the stoop. "Third day in a row."

"His wife is in the hospital," said Mother who always knew what was going on in town.

Father's mouth formed a tight line of disapproval. Lewis, age seven, sat between his parents at the breakfast table. He looked down at his bowl of oatmeal and wished he didn't have to go to school. Second grade, all two weeks of it thus far, was not at all like first grade. There was hardly ever drawing and no games at snack time. The lined paper they were handed every day had to be filled with pencil strokes of numbers and letters copied off the blackboard. And they had to be neat and inside the lines. And… what else didn't he like about second grade…oh yeah, the older kids pushed him in the hall.

His mother smiled at him and he smiled back and now he was thinking about his Civil War soldier set. Twelve uniformed men, Yanks and Rebs, the blues and the grays, each in a different pose: some holding their guns, others flat on their bellies, and on each side there was one soldier holding a flag. Best of all were the two cannons. It was a present from his grandmother all the way from Connecticut. There was no reason for the present. It wasn't his birthday or anything but Grandma was like that. *Oh, she's full of surprises* Father said and Father didn't much approve of that either.

Wilma Palmer glanced at her husband. She wished he would hurry up and leave for the office. She had a dozen things to do before Celia was to pick her up. Today was one she had been anticipating for months and now here it was and Jim was dallying over his breakfast. The Garden Club luncheon in Southampton was an annual highlight and this year the guest speaker was none other than Leonard Pinckney, Central Park's renowned expert in arboriculture. It was a big day for Wilma.

As the newly elected chairwoman of the Tree Committee for the Ladies Village Improvement Society she was now firmly on the list of invitees to this coveted annual lunch and lecture. Heading up the Tree Committee was quite an honor and one she had worked hard at these past few years. She knew the condition and position of every important tree in the village and that, of course, included the prized Dutch elms on Main Street. East Hampton was justly famous for those trees and she, Wilma Palmer, took enormous pride knowing their care and maintenance was in her hands. The sheltering arms of the elms formed a canopy on the broad main street of the village and when LIFE Magazine named East Hampton the 'prettiest town in America,' Wilma privately considered her elms the reason why. Of course, the windmills, the 18th century salt box houses, Town Pond with its swans all helped but the trees, her trees... Wilma wondered if she might not persuade Mr. Pinckney to come here next year to speak. Surely, he knew of the elms.

Jim poured himself another cup. He was against this outing of Wilma's for a number of reasons. For one thing he did not approve of Celia Slade even though she was Wilma's oldest and dearest friend. She was far too flashy for Jim's taste, driving around town in a new car. To buy a new car in 1938 was a shocking display of pretense. A new anything was simply not done and it was certainly not done in the Palmer household. Why, imagine trying to sell insurance to someone while sporting a new overcoat or driving to the Rotary in a spanking new car. Selling insurance in these times was hard enough – seemed so many felt this was the first thing they could give up when in reality insurance was the only thing that could save them if things got worse.

And another thing that rankled Jim about Wilma's all-day outing was the fact that Lewis along with all the children in the lower grades were being let out early today because of a teacher conference and he, who would be spending his day in Sag Harbor assessing that fire in the back of Benson's hardware, was not on hand, as he had been on many occasions when Wilma was bound up with "The Ladies," as he liked to call them, to collect Lewis from school and usher him the four blocks home. Wilma's careless – yes, that's what it was – careless assumption that Margaret Day would pick Lewis up did not sit well with Jim Palmer – not by a long shot.

The Days lived next door. Old Mrs. Day was the widow of Jim's partner in Palmer & Day Insurance. Actually, Jim had bought the business outright in 1927 but Mr. Day had stayed on as a 'consultant' if only to have a place to go every day, driving Jim crazy with his meddling and tinkering with the new business models Jim had meticulously built into a once thriving business now suffering in the Depression. There could be no meddling when it came to claims – and no soft-heartedness either especially when it was easy enough to set fire to a foundering business.

Margaret was their daughter. Never married, which was no surprise as she was about as bland a person as you would ever meet. Margaret, near 50 years old by now, was a perennial do-gooder serving tirelessly on church and civic committees, tending the old, the sick, and, as she was doing today, the children. "You can always count on Margaret," the Ladies said.

"You can always count on Margaret," Wilma was saying and Jim's mouth all but disappeared into its fine line of disapproval.

"We'll be home by four," Wilma assured him for the tenth time, "and you like Margaret, don't you Lou-Lou?"

Lewis ducked his head and blushed. His mother wasn't supposed to call him that. It was a baby name but he secretly liked it when she did. "She's OK," he said. Then, glancing at his father, quickly added, "She doesn't make the right kind of sandwiches for lunch and…and she has funny breath." He ducked his head again as he saw his father light on the comment.

"And another thing, Wilma. You tell Celia, in that big new car of hers, to watch the curve just before Wainscott. That's the most dangerous spot on the road. Why last year alone…" but Wilma had heard it all before. Jim could give you a rundown on every dangerous and potentially dangerous aspect of every imaginable situation – she supposed that was what the insurance business was all about or maybe Jim was in the insurance business because he had such an obsession with disaster. Whatever it was, she fully expected him to one day declare her precious trees a liability.

The house on Huntting Lane was a pretty house in keeping with the style of East Hampton village. Cedar shingled, trimmed in white, a wide front porch, its ceiling painted pale blue with the big Victorian rockers for sitting out on summer evenings, a garden filled with bright blue hydrangeas that Wilma picked every fall and dried in the attic for Christmas. Their car, a purposeful, black 1928 model A Ford sat in the driveway under a large shade oak; in back was an expanse of lawn with a flower border in the English style and a high hedge shielding the Palmers from their neighbors.

It was this pleasant vista that the Palmer trio, silent now, could see from their breakfast nook set into a bay window just off the kitchen. Jim, his annoyance with Wilma aside, was contemplating the last of his coffee and his meeting in Sag Harbor. There was a wily side to Harv Benson and, he, Jim Palmer, would have to look sharp at that fire damage. Wilma inexplicably was thinking of an editorial in last week's *East Hampton Star* which chastised the editors of *The New Yorker* for an article they ran painting a silly view of "club" women. "Sensible shoes, no nonsense coiffeurs, purposeful stride, buxom…" Wilma supposed she was just such a woman. She had been an LVIS clubwoman for almost twenty years now. She glanced down at her best silk blouse neatly tucked into the waist of her tweed skirt…at least she wasn't buxom. Suddenly, without any indication that such a thing was about to happen, the large center glass pane in the bay window of the breakfast nook exploded. Just plain shattered into a million pieces.

For a split second – father, mother and child froze – then all three jumped from the table away from the shards of glass that now lay on the cloth, on the floor, in the food, on the ground outside. They scrambled back into the kitchen dumbfounded but when nothing else seemed to happen, Jim stepped forward and bent to look at the broken window peering out as if a culprit were there to be found.

"Must have been a bird," he concluded when finally they had swept up the glass. But there had been no bird. Wilma was sure of it. It was as if some unseen fist had deliberately punched the window from within.

5

Jack Burns
9:00 a.m.
The Coop, Amagansett

He came back into the converted chicken coop and lit a match under the tin pot. Disappointed…frustrated…he poured the dregs of the coffee he had been drinking before his early morning beach walk through a crack in the floor. At least four or five times a week he walked the beach hoping for a glimpse of the beachcomber. On the few occasions that he had actually sighted him he tried to approach but the old fella could disappear faster than smoke.

No one knew how old he was but the long white beard and hair made him look as old as time itself. His name was Tom – just Tom, though the kids called him Crazy Tom out of earshot of their elders. No one could recollect him ever having a family. Some said he was Indian, others just shook their heads and shrugged. He was a hermit for sure but mostly he was known as a beachcomber and the things he found and dragged up the sand to his hut were often wonderful things lost off of ships and aged by the sea. Sometimes he bartered these treasures for coffee and sugar, other times he would walk himself the mile or so down the beach to the Amagansett dunes where the fishermen's shanties were and help bait traps or mend nets taking his pay in tobacco or even tattered and worn clothes.

He lived out in the wild dunes of Napeague in a shanty built out of old planks and driftwood washed ashore. The back half of his lean-to was wedged into the bank above the high water mark in the dune. The roof was corrugated tin and in summer the door was a tattered grey canvas that flapped in the wind. He lived with a dozen or more cats that came when he called them though they had no names. Mainly, he foraged off the land and knew every plant that was edible. Mushrooms were a big part of his diet and he brought them back in sacks and dried them on his tin roof in summer for the long winter ahead. He caught fish, fed the heads and tails to his cats while boiling up the fleshy parts for himself. He rarely spoke or looked anyone in the eye but he was no threat. People who knew him knew he was harmless and to leave him be.

All these things Jack had learned about the old man over the summer but try as he might, he couldn't hold the man in his sights long enough to get a clear picture of him. Jack tried to sketch him over and over from the image he had in his mind but in the end, the renderings were shallow and without meaning. It was driving him crazy.

He had rented the coop in the early spring, having heard from a pal at the Art Students League that out on the end of the island the living was cheap and the natural light sublime. If you liked the outdoors, which he did, then this was the place to paint. Land surrounded by water plays tricks with the light casting a clear yet soft, golden glow permeating the woods and farm fields and tree lined villages. And for a painter, it was special indeed.

Jack was crazy for the wildness of the beaches and dunes, the drama and sheer beauty of the ocean, the wind as it played through the marsh grasses and salt hay on the bays. In New York he was known as an excellent draftsman but out here, in the open air, in the spell of that glowing light, he had simplified and stylized his figures and landscapes almost to the point of obliterating familiar features for something else. Something he had not yet quite defined.

This summer had been meant to give him answers…and direction…but as he poured himself a scalding cup of coffee and lay back on his bed, Jack could think of no answers worth anything to him. Instead he was filled with frustration bordering on dismay. Soon enough he would head back to the city. Did he want to go? There was a big job circulating around New York and he was one of two maybe three commercial illustrators being considered for it. He was broke. The job would give him enough money to fund another summer yet there was nothing but an overwhelming lethargy in him.

His eyes traveled about the coop. It had been his home since boarding the Long Island Railroad one breezy day in March and three hours later finding himself in a village called Amagansett. The rest of it had fallen into place so easily he might have believed, if he believed such things, that the unseen hand of Fate was guiding him. From the station he had walked to the ocean following the smell of the sea until he stood on a bluff overlooking a wide expanse of dunes and beyond a swath of pale sand with long rolling white capped waves washing ashore. Dotted throughout the dunes were tarpaper shanties draped in netting with wooden traps and large steaming kettles. Jack had felt himself go very still.

In short order, thanks to a local farmer, he found his own kind of shanty to rent. It had once been a chicken coop, but fixed up years earlier to house summer farm workers. It was a long room with a bed at one end and stove and table at the other. Windows lined either side so that light flooded in. No electricity but oil lamps. No running water but an outhouse and a big red handled pump. No garden but the promise of wild roses climbing over the weathered grey boards of the coop. Jack took it without a moment's hesitation. The farmer thought maybe he would want to get more furniture and other household items and suggested the general store on Main Street or maybe the junkman over in Springs who always had usable things in his yard but Jack wanted no clutter. A bed, a stove, an old rocker, a table for his paints and brushes and he was in business – for the summer anyway.

And in all that time, despite his efforts he had not come one step closer to the old beachcomber. Crazy Tom had come to represent more than a subject for drawing, he seemed to be the embodiment of everything that eluded Jack – something just out of his reach.

In frustration he threw the covers off, managing to spill coffee all over the sheet. He paced down the length of the coop, viewing a stack of his paintings leaning one by one against the wall as if they might speak to him. In his present mood, they looked tired and dull. But damn it – there had been moments of real clarity. He reached for the pot on top of the burner and poured himself another cup. The coffee had been reheated many times and was bitter, burning his tongue. Now laying back on the bed, the springs squealing in protest, he felt listless, uneasy. Maybe it was the muggy air, he thought staring out the window. The sky was a pale strange ochre color.

6

Judy Tate
10 a.m.
Dune Road, Bridgehampton

Sitting in the hallway of her house she held the telephone in her hand not wanting to put the receiver down. Chip had hung up first after a hasty goodbye. He was busy. He was always busy. *And, no darling, I can't come out on a Wednesday. If you had planned it for the weekend...* the rest of the sentence was left unfinished but it said volumes to Judy. Of course that's what she should have done. Why hadn't she? A four year old doesn't know, a four year old doesn't care... but Judy cared. Your birthday was your day and four years earlier hadn't it been the most important day of their lives?

She could hear the dead air over the wires – wires that stretched from their house, down Dune Road, around Mecox Bay to the highway. From there, strung pole to pole, the wires traversed in precision relay the entire 100 mile length of Long Island, somehow frog jumping the East River, burrowing through mid-town shops and department stores, down Madison Avenue until reaching the tall grey building at 36th Street – up and up the twelve floors to Chip's office where Miss Stanley ruled, fielding all of Mr. Tate's calls with uncompromising rigor. Judy always felt her spine stiffen slightly when having to deal with Miss Stanley, like in school when the headmistress was about. She called her Miss Sternly behind her back but Chip said he couldn't live without her. "She's a professional," he said, as if that said it all, and Judy wondered what in heaven's name a professional was? Probably something like a grown-up.

"You alright, Miss Judy?" Raleigh peered down at her, the question hanging over his face. He had changed from his dark green work apron into his white jacket, entirely unnecessary, Judy thought, for a children's birthday party but Raleigh was, in addition to everything else, unimpeachable when it came to dress. He had once been a porter on the Silver Cannonball – the Southern Railroad's streamlined luxurious train from Washington, DC to Miami, which is where her daddy met him, then stole him away to come to the apartment on Fifth Avenue to take care of the family. Judy could never remember life before Raleigh.

She laughed now, a breathy girl's laugh, and hung up the receiver. "Are we ready for this?" she said making a face. "Eight little brats, a pony, a clown, AND rain?" She turned and walked into the living room, her face gloomy. "Oh, Raleigh, I so wanted this day to be perfect."

Though he knew the discouraged tone probably had more to do with her conversation with her husband than the probable advent of rain, Raleigh chose to take the weather route. "Sure looks like rain," he said matter-of-factly. "But mebbe not. This don't mean much…most likely blow over."

She gave him a bemused smile. They both knew the problem wasn't that the party would have to be moved inside and it would be bedlam with these kids. It wasn't about that at all but it was easier to talk about the weather than to talk about a husband who had lost interest in his wife. There it was. She had as much said it but to Raleigh she said, "These poor children have had a summer of wet weather, indoor games, canceled picnics, and I don't know what else. Maybe it will hold off until this afternoon." She laughed again, a bright, quick laugh as if to say, *See what a brave little person I am?*

Judy walked into the living room thinking how much she didn't want sticky hands all over her pretty furniture. This was her room – the room she had designed and had built onto the house the summer before, paying for it out of the trust left to her by her grandfather. Not that Chip hadn't grumbled about it. *Building in 1937?* But Judy had countered *giving people jobs!* And Chip retreated. Unlike the newer summer estates that populated Dune Road, her house was solid and stocky, weathered cedar shingles, a gambrel roof, white trim, and an expanse of lawn down to the water. Her grandparents had built it with no notion of creating a showplace and in doing so had neglected the most obvious attribute of the property – the view – a beautiful view especially at dusk with the sun setting over the bay.

And so she had built on a room of large glass windows that framed this view. Because the lawn inclined to the water the room sat on pilings cleverly disguised so as to merge with the landscape thus from a distance it looked as if it floated in air. And this "floating" room lifted the house out of its square and serviceable lines and gave it a sort of grace.

Judy loved the bay. Though the ocean was only steps away across the road and over the dunes it was a vast mysterious territory to her, its surf and tides controlled by an inexplicable force; but not so on the bay where tall grasses and cattails edged the shoreline, where egrets and swans and whole platoons of ducks swam in the calm inner water. There were no rip tides in the bay or ocean creatures lurking below. On the bay, the ever-changing light seemed to transform the landscape hourly as if an unseen artist was in a constant state of creative transformation.

The telephone rang and Judy rushed to answer it but heard Raleigh's sonorous, "Tate residence," after the first ring. There was a silence, then "Sure enough…yes, sir…ain't that something…I'll tell Miz Tate right away." He hung up and turned to her standing in the doorway. "That's the man with the pony. Says she won't get in the truck…something got in her and she's acting up. Says he can't come."

7

Emmaline Hartley
10:30 a.m.
Villamere, Dune Road, Bridgehampton

Not far from the Tate house, the Hartleys were in another turmoil altogether. The Hartleys moved at a different pace than the more conservative Tates but Emmaline Hartley liked Judy well enough – if only during the summer months when the strict social circles of New York were more relaxed. *Liked* was actually not quite how Emmaline felt about Judy Tate because Emmaline never liked people. She either adored them or couldn't be bothered, but Judy Tate seemed to fall into a category all her own – she was tolerated. She had her uses; something Emmaline Hartley was good at exploiting.

Villamere was one of those gilded age beach houses, the last on Dune Road, commanding the full sweep of the point and built to accommodate elaborate parties and reckless fun – midnight revels, dancing around the pool, fireworks on the beach on the Fourth of July, martinis, crisp and cold and dry at 6 o'clock on the stone terrace. Though the Depression had certainly curtailed much of the free-spirited life at Villamere, the parties went on. Emmaline was a clever and inventive woman and few could tell that the Hartley fortune had been bruised.

On this day, however, Emmaline was in no mood to be clever or inventive. There was much to do. The house was in disarray. Trunks and dustcovers littered the rooms and packing was in earnest. Her eldest son had left early that morning, his bags bulging with all the regalia a returning sophomore would need at Andover. No, it would not do for him to be escorted thus by his father insisting he must go by train to New York with another boy of whom Emmaline knew nothing. They would catch the afternoon Bostonian from Penn Station giving George a good four hours on his own in the city. He was a mischievous boy, prone to giving back smart answers and always reliably to be found where he shouldn't be.

She was thinking about those four un-chaperoned hours when she glanced out her bedroom window in time to see her younger son and twelve year old daughter flying by on the bay in one of the small sailboats. The water, which most days was as glassy as a skating rink, today was choppy with the flag at the end of their dock snapping angrily at its pole. There was no way they could sail the little boat back and her daughter was due at the Tate child's birthday party before lunch. Violet was to be Judy's "helper" organizing the children in games and she was immensely proud of her responsibilities and the handsome wage of fifty cents an hour. Emmaline drummed her fingers irritably on the windowsill and then decided to ring Judy to see if Raleigh could drive around to the far end of the bay and pick the children up. What a bore it was not having the full staff of servants as she once had.

Judy's line was engaged so Emmaline went down to the study and tapped on her husband's door. James had elected to stay on at the beach long after the other men had returned to the city, which had done nothing to endear him to his wife. James was fussy and demanding and Emmaline relished the days he was elsewhere.

"Violet and Peter are out on the water in the Beetle Cat," she announced. "They'll never get back in time for lunch and now I have to find someone to go fetch them." She picked up a pair of binoculars and peered out the window, finally finding the children who appeared even through the strong lens as small specks on the water.

"Well, I can't go for them," James grumbled. "I should have gone into the city this morning with George. Where are my papers...I swear that woman comes in here in the night and hides things." That 'woman' was Mrs. Sternhoffer, who served double duty as housekeeper and cook. "Send her for the children," he muttered while rooting through a stack of files on the sofa.

"She doesn't drive," Emmaline said still glued to the specks through the lens. "Oh, for goodness sake, James, stop fussing!"

She abruptly left, crossing the hall to the living room, an expansive room in pale blues and whites facing the sea. At the far end, two large Victorian leaded glass doors opened onto the terrace. Emmaline turned the knob and the door flew open, her grip on the handle wrenched from her hand. A warm, sticky wind rushed in, taking possession of the room blowing magazines and papers off tables and catching up the curtains in a demonic dance. In front of her was the panorama of the Atlantic Ocean. The waves were enormous and beautiful. She watched as one crashed onto the shore, the other immediately behind. The water line was higher than she had ever seen it. It must be high tide she thought.

She stood there for a few minutes, undecided as what to do next but then another gust of wind whipped stinging sand across her face and she turned back into the house. Closing the door was a struggle. "All right," she said as if the door had demanded an answer from her, "I'll go myself." Her handbag was nowhere to be found but a scarf and the keys to the runabout were on the table. By the time she had given Mrs. Sternhoffer instructions to serve lunch immediately upon her return, a truck had turned up Dune Road and into their drive. Out jumped the two children flushed with excitement over their runaway ride followed by their rescuer, the beach boy at the club.

Bursting with the adventure, ten-year-old Peter declared it had been a thrilling ride. "The best of the whole summer," and no, he never thought for a moment they couldn't turn and sail back but then Danny had seen them career by the club dock and had given chase on land in the manager's truck finally waving the two children into an inlet where they tied the boat to someone's dock. Danny would sail the boat back that afternoon he said suddenly remembering he had to get going or his boss would have his hide. Emmaline surmised the manager of the club had no notion his truck was in the hands of a fifteen-year-old boy whose job it was to put up umbrellas and run errands.

Emmaline tucked a few dollars into the boy's shirt pocket. "You have a good winter Danny. We'll see you next spring and thank you for rescuing my naughty children." He blushed, embarrassed by the money and the praise.

8

Chip Tate
11 a.m.
New York City

Chip Tate hung up the telephone and breathed a sigh with Judy's plaintive voice still in his ear. His mood mirrored the day outside his window and he got up now and walked to it staring down Madison Avenue. Already the sidewalks were a mass of black umbrellas as the first drops of rain fell – the weather forecast right on the mark. And here at Delany, Osborne and Fox the business of turning product into sales was well underway. On his desk were renderings of ebullient travelers boarding a Pan Am Clipper for the islands in the Caribbean. Escape. That's what he dealt in. The fantasy that you could buy a ticket, or a car, or even a laundry product and... escape. Escape the humdrum of your life, escape the problems and the fears and, he felt a sharp intake of breath, the guilt.

He examined a scar on his palm. It was a rough welt, the redness diminished over time, one he picked up as a boy working the farm fields outside his hometown of Ames, Iowa. They were called "volunteers," not the boys themselves who worked row upon row of whatever crop the farmer had growing. No, a volunteer was something that was out of place – say a stalk of corn growing in a bean field. The farmers organized gangs of town kids during the growing season to walk their fields pulling up those volunteers, those wandering strays who didn't belong. Now sitting on the twelfth floor and staring out into the grey day, Chip thought about the boy he had been who found nothing profound in the never-ending furrows. He thought about his father, a dry goods salesman, traveling all over the mid-West from town to town selling everything from ribbons to sheets, towels and baby clothes. At best it had been a slim income because he was bored with his job and spent time and more money than he could afford on diversions – the horses, mainly, and poker – women too. He thought about his mother crying in the kitchen and about his sister who went to work after high school as a secretary giving him all the spare money she could just so he could go to college. He thought about the jobs he worked in college and paying for his classes by the week. They let him do that – maybe other students did too, he didn't know but Monday mornings he would show up at the Dean's office and pay for the week – if he could.

There had been nowhere for him to go after graduating. He couldn't go home for it wasn't there anymore. His family had been in a Depression long before the rest of the country and when his father died in a car accident on some back road – the car rolling over and over until it landed hood down in a muddy ravine – his mother had moved out to California where she had relatives. His sister married and did rather well for herself if you can call marrying an Iowa feed store merchant doing well.

He thought about the day he arrived in New York, feeling painfully like the rube he was until one day soon after he realized that this place was choked with "volunteers" – a city of strays from all over the world transplanted to this fertile urban field. The scar on his palm is like a spur of a bone and it sometimes itched. For some reason it was itching something terrible right now at eleven o'clock on the morning of September 21, 1938.

"But Mr. Tate, you are expected for lunch at the club." Miss Stanley pursed her lips. He had always been a little intimidated by that pursing of the lips. It meant that some procedure had not been correctly followed; some loose end was threatening to unravel the orderly rhythm of her day.

"Yes," he said vaguely. "Tell them we'll have to postpone. Tell them...oh, hang it, tell them anything you like." And then he was gone out the door, like a man with a train to catch which was precisely who he was.

And now he was in Penn station, the domed glass cavernous structure echoing with announcements for arrivals and departures. For the life of him he couldn't think why he was here, what he was doing but it hardly mattered. He rushed to the gate only to be told the Montauk train was delayed by some 20 minutes. He turned away, a newspaper? A coffee? What was the delay? The weather? It was now pouring rain outside and he wondered if it was raining on the birthday party. He hoped not. He wouldn't get there in time for it he knew, but at least he would get there on the day.

He spotted a florist and headed toward it.

"Mr. Tate?" A voice said at his elbow. Chip turned and for a minute couldn't put a name to the face of the boy who said his name. Did he even know him?

"It's George, Mr. Tate. George Hartley." Chip exhaled. "George indeed! You never expect to see anyone you know in New York. For a second I had no idea…Say, you got caught in the rain, didn't you." It was pretty obvious. George stood before him like a wet puppy, drenched hair, sodden school blazer and, Chip took notice, a very wet new Mark Cross leather satchel.

"Yes, sir. My friend and I were in Times Square." He gestured to another boy, equally wet who was buying a bag of peanuts from a vendor. "We were walking, but then it started to pour…"

Chip didn't know why but he was immensely glad to see George. As if this kid, a cheeky kid in his opinion, was some sort of talisman on this day. He didn't know him well beyond the casual encounters on the beach or at some of the more formal parties he and Judy had gone to at Villamere (he hated that name – such a conceit of the rich to name their houses) but he had certainly seen him in action, playing tennis, sailing on the bay in his very own sailboat, charming his mother, teasing his sister … all the usual things for a boy of fifteen but there was something else about George Hartley that Chip had observed, if not admired. He had, even at this young age, an assuredness that comes only to those who have no doubts whatsoever about their place in life. What a luxury, Chip thought, aware of the insecurities of his own childhood. Well – he wasn't about to be intimidated by a fifteen-year-old boy. "Heading back to school?" He asked knowing full well that he was.

"Yes," George smiled politely. Or was it condescendingly? It was pretty obvious given the school blazer, the satchel...

"Ah," said Chip. *Well, jolly ho, have a ripping good time, hooray for the home team and someday you're going to grow up to be as pompous as your father.* "What train are you on?" he asked mildly.

"The Bostonian, so I guess that means we'll have to hang around here for another three hours." He pushed his wet floppy hair off his brow, a startling version of his mother, too beautiful for a boy. Chip who intensely disliked Emmaline Hartley softened and stuck out his hand. "Have a good term, George. Andover isn't it? We'll see you next summer."

"Yes, sir." George shook his hand. For an instant they seemed to connect almost as if there had been some divine reason for them to bump into one another, but it quickly passed and George gave a small childish laugh and turned to find his friend.

The Long Island train lurched through a series of tunnels and finally came out onto a grey bridge making its way across the East River in the murky day. Despite the gloom, Chip felt good, light-headed even. He imagined the surprised look on Judy's face when he arrived. He would take a taxi from the station hoping that the one lone woman who drove the one lone taxi was available. This made him smile.

Unfolding the Times, he began to read the headlines about the tension in Europe. The threat of Hitler, now shaking Nazi sabers at Czechoslovakia, giving the Brits and French a real turn. In no mood to delve into the fine print of European politics, he leafed through the paper not seeing much else of interest. A small article on the back page reported that Miami was now spared the threat of a hurricane giving kudos to the Weather Bureau for their vigilance and caution but it was of little interest to him.

The rocking of the train lulled him and he nodded off thinking about his sudden impulse, thinking about the birthday party, about the tiny baby he had held in his arms four years before, now a beautiful child whom he adored. He was dreaming now and in his dream he was lost in a cavernous room, his arms and legs heavy so that try as he might, he could not move but then a pretty girl with blonde hair, a doll-like girl with a smile on her lips, floated in front of him. She took his hand and led him to a window but it wasn't a window, it was a large painting in a frame and he was in the echoing halls of the Metropolitan Museum and the pretty girl was laughing. "It's my favorite painting too."

And now he jolted awake. Now he knew why he was on that train in the middle of an important work week. Innocent, trusting, believing Judy. He would have to tell her – he would have to tell his wife about Maggie.

9

Will Foster
12 noon
Washington, D.C.

"Foster," the chief stood in front of his desk. "Ready with your report?" Victor McGraw was a short, stocky man in his forties but he stood as tall as any man in the weather room. The Juniors were terrified of him. He wore his suit and his hair in military fashion and had no time for this eager, young, questioning man with *theories*. Theories were for dreamers. Weather forecasts were built out of facts. McGraw was at the top of his form now that the threat of this storm was over. This cub Foster, no matter how filled up he was with youthful enthusiasms, had been handed a foregone conclusion – the storm was now safely out to sea and breaking up.

Will nodded his head, gathered his papers and was on full adrenaline when he mounted the podium at the end of the long room. Somewhere in his mind he knew he wasn't much liked by his boss but he respected him and he wanted more than anything to make a good and knowledgeable impression. He pinned his charts to the board and took the black pointer from its holder.

"Gentlemen," he cleared his throat of the nervous squeak threatening to come out. "Until a few hours ago I had full appreciation of the forecast as sent out over the wires from Miami. This morning we sent a bulletin forecasting rain and that was correct. It is now raining in New York…"

McGraw leaned back in his chair already bored with the proceedings. He'd never much liked this young Foster but now he seemed to be falling in line as well he should.

"…for the moment." Foster continued. "Indeed this storm seems to be following the typical pattern of these tropical storms when it turned out to sea but with all due respect I think we have a problem on our hands. You can see by the chart that something unusual and unsettling could be in the making." Everyone in the room shifted uncomfortably.

"My calculations are based on the very full report of," Will consulted his notebook, "Captain Craig from the ship Carinthia issued at 3 a.m. this morning. Ships log records the barometer at sea in the path of the storm to have registered the lowest reading ever recorded in the North Atlantic. The captain will not bring his ship into New York area waters until clear of this storm. The Bermuda high has shifted and is pushing west and the Blue Ridge front is pushing east and if neither one gives way, then this storm now at sea," his pointer circled the large mass of lines indicating the storm, "will be caught in a trough putting it on a dead heat due north. Given the velocity of which it was last calculated, it is not only packing winds well over 150 miles per hour, but will, if caught in this trough, be like a toboggan in a greased shoot. A storm like this with nothing to stop it can move at tremendous speed *and* it is heading into the most populated part of the country." His pointer tapped ominously along the coastal outline. "As we know, hot weather has been a problem all summer and coastal water along the eastern seaboard is uncharacteristically warm – a good temperature for a rogue hurricane to feed on." He wondered if he should mention the old farmer's morning call but thought better of it. "My conclusion, gentleman, is that a warning of severe hurricane weather conditions should be issued to New Jersey, New York, Long Island, Connecticut, and Rhode Island."

He stepped back from his chart, confident of his presentation, laying down all the paraphernalia, perhaps a trifle too dramatically. The room was silent. McGraw and the other seniors glanced at one another. Then McGraw rose to his feet, thanked Will, and stepped up on the dais. "A very interesting and thorough report," he said mildly, smiling. "Yes – we've already noted these highs and fronts with initially some concern but there are many other considerations that Mr. Foster has not taken issue with. Only two tropical storms of any magnitude have ever reached New England in the last 200 years. Hurricanes don't come this far north. Any such kind of storm is extremely unlikely and so unlikely that to extend a hurricane warning to an area of dense population has the earmarks of causing panic. You can make some sort of hypothetical case but this is certainly not the mission of the Washington Bureau." McGraw's voice was terse with measured control. "For us to issue a dire warning to hundreds of thousands of people, alarming whole cities on the *possible* theory of a frankly inexperienced trainee is hardly the basis for doing so. I commend you, Foster, for your creative thinking but we will stick by the forecast arrived at by my colleagues and myself earlier today. Rain. Rain will be the worst of it. And rain will be the afternoon forecast. However, to be prudent we will add *heavy at times*. Gentleman, that will be all." And he strode from the room. "Damn upstart," he muttered to no one. He would have him on the carpet yet.

10

Emmaline
12:30 p.m.
Dune Road, Bridgehampton

Emmaline went down the passageway to see that Violet was dressed for the birthday party. She was. Violet was a most efficient child. Not only dressed she was packing crayons and small squares of paper she had precut into a variety of shell shapes into a canvas beach bag.

"For a treasure hunt," she informed her mother's inquiring eye. "I don't think Mrs. Tate has really thought this party through. She seems to think a clown and a pony are enough but children need games." She said this with all the authority as if a seasoned teacher. "If it rains and we're inside, they'll be very disappointed so I think a treasure hunt for seashells would be fun." Violet patted the beach bag presumably filled with shells.

Emmaline nodded, not really listening, appraising instead the dress her daughter was wearing which seemed too tight in the bodice and definitely too short. Violet was growing up, getting tall, leaving childhood behind. For perhaps the millionth time she wondered why so many girls inherited their father's looks. Both of her boys looked like her but Violet took after James. James was not a bad looking man, though with age he had gone soft in the jowls and paunch but his looks did not settle easily on a girl. Violet was losing the soft protection of childhood and now the prominent chin, narrow eyes and broad shoulders of her father were emerging all too clearly. Poor thing thought Emmaline as she ushered her daughter out the door and watched her walking down the drive, the large beach bag of shells bumping awkwardly at her side.

She could hear her mother's voice – *There are only three things that open doors for a woman – beauty, wealth and family*. How well Emmaline had been schooled in that but her mother had been wrong. Emmaline had brought beauty to the table and to the unknowing and unsuspecting, she had succeeded admirably but only she knew of the effort and compromise, the prodding and downright plotting that had gotten her to this moment. Watching Violet as she rounded the hedges and disappeared, she wondered what, if anything, was in store for her. If only... but she wouldn't go there. Shutting the door firmly she turned back into the house. It was lunchtime.

James appeared with their youngest son Peter whom he was lecturing on the irresponsibility of taking the Sea Cat out on such a windy day. Though warm outside, the wind was too high to sit on the terrace and it was too depressing to sit in the sunroom with all the packing going on, so Emmaline led them into the more formal dining room normally used only for dinner parties. Mrs. Sternhoffer came through the swinging door from the pantry with a clattering tray of food. She set this firmly down on the sideboard. It was a poorly put together meal from food that was perishable and needed to be eaten or thrown out before closing the house. Emmaline, who could be surprisingly thrifty, had instructed her housekeeper to make-do on the lunch especially with no guests that day. Mrs. Sternhoffer inspected her meal with disapproval but she made no move to serve it to the waiting threesome at the table. She was an excellent cook and housekeeper but she *did not serve* and had made this clear to her employer from the first. Now both Peter and Emmaline rose from their chairs to serve themselves. At that precise moment James turned ashen, clutched his chest, and slumped over the table.

"James? James!" Emmaline went to him, tugging first at his arm then lifting his head. His eyes had rolled back in his head.

He was a big man but somehow she, Peter and Mrs. Sternhoffer managed to get him from the dining room, across the hall, into the living room and onto the sofa. Emmaline grabbed a bottle of brandy off the drinks table and forced a shot of the liquid down his throat. It seemed to revive him. She felt for his pulse but she knew little of first aid and besides the color seemed to be coming back into his face. He blinked blearily and then let out a soft moan. Emmaline waved the bottle of brandy towards Mrs. Sternhoffer for her to pour another glass but Mrs. Sternhoffer was worse than useless. She had thrown her apron over her head and was whimpering into its folds. Peter looked on, horrified, thinking somehow it was his sailing escapade that had distressed his father. Emmaline barked at Mrs. Sternhoffer to bring her a cold towel and when she did, she placed it on James' forehead instructing Peter to hold it in place. Emmaline squeezed her son's shoulder as she walked by him to the telephone. "The doctor will be here soon," she said.

As she dialed, she thought, *God! Could anything else go wrong today?*

11

Walter Penn
1:00 p.m.
East Hampton Village

All morning, people had been heading down to Main Beach to witness the grand and beautiful spectacle of the ocean waves. "You won't believe your eyes. They're beauties," they said. "Twenty footers, I'd say." "A nor'easter?" some asked. "Naw. Wind coming from the south."

At his house on Town Pond, Walter Penn rummaged in the front closet.

"Mrs. C, come with me down to the beach."

"Why in heaven's name would I want to do such a thing?" Mrs. Cunningham bustled in from the library where she was dusting. "Mrs. C," a name she preferred over her given name Mary, had perfected the "bustle" to a fine art of efficient motion at all times and he often wondered if that was why he liked her so much. Over the years her common no nonsense even bossy nature served as a touchstone for him – a reminder that not all was about line and form and the endless erudite language of museum curators and art critics. Here in East Hampton, Walter could forget the constant pressure on him to give authenticity to the very thing that had no business being authenticated. As if art, true art, needed the likes of him to give it meaning.

"Why not? You like to walk with me and the ocean is playing up a very dramatic show for us or so I hear. Come on now. The rain is holding off. What better do you have to do?" He enjoyed sparring with Mrs. C.

She gave him a withering look. "It's a daft idea that's why. Walking out in the face of a storm just to see some waves. I saw plenty coming across in '22 and believe me those were waves. Like mountains they were only made of water and that's not much of a laugh when you're out to sea. We bobbed about like a cork. Captain said he'd never seen the like and while we're on the subject what is this nothing better to do?" She waved the duster towards an overhead light. "And wear your Anorak if you must go. I can feel the rain coming."

He did as he was told. Mrs. C looked on, secure in the knowledge that she was right, had always been right and would continue to be right on matters of outerwear.

"If I were you," she said at the door, "I would head up to Main Beach. Least ways you can get under the roof when the rain comes." Walter nodded agreeably having no intention of joining the crowds. He turned instead down a lane that led to Hook Pond, a long and narrow fresh pond that nudged against the ocean dunes at one end wending its way into the village at the other. There it ended at the Hook Windmill standing as it had for hundreds of years where once upon a time corn and wheat were ground not now in use of course, but an icon of East Hampton village and its heritage.

Yet historic windmills were not the reasons for Walter's route to the ocean. He often walked this way if for nothing more than to stand on the stone bridge that crossed over the pond. You could travel all over the world, as he had, drink champagne with Manhattan's most distinguished hosts as he had, dine in the most celebrated restaurants in Paris, and gaze on works of art in private collections, as he had more times than he could count, but there was never anything quite like breathing in the air over Hook Pond and letting its magic envelop him in the warm cocoon of a long ago memory. This was where his life had changed so many years ago.

Today the wind was almost more than he could handle but he was determined to see those waves…if for nothing more than for her. The woman he had loved so much. So he pressed on.

• • •

Up at the high school, Mrs. Sweeny could see the class was restless, their eyes darting to the windows as the tops of the trees twisted and turned seeming almost ready to take flight. Being a small woman, she stood on a foot high box behind the podium at the front of the class. Now she rapped on the podium with her pen.

"Blow, winds, and crack your cheeks! Rage! Blow!" The class squirmed uncomfortably. "Who can tell me the source of those words? Frank Wood? (She paused) Anyone?" Bette Grindle hid a grin on her face. Frank made it a point to never speak in class as proof of his superior intelligence and masculinity. Bette had nursed a secret crush on him since freshman year, so far unrequited.

Mrs. Sweeny rapped again.

"Seniors. Pay attention. Those are the words of Mr. William Shakespeare, the greatest writer in the English language. King Lear, Act Three, Scene two. King Lear is about hubris and fall from grace. Who can tell me the meaning of the word 'hubris'?" Inwardly she wondered, as she did every year, what of Shakespeare, indeed what of literature, of poetry, of history, would these children take with them into the world ahead where fishing, farming, marriage, and children were the norm. As suspected, the class looked blank over 'hubris'. She told them to write it down on their vocabulary page and 'look it up'. Bette dutifully wrote the word down noting that Frank did not.

No one saw it coming – a weathervane flying headlong through the window, shattering the glass, hitting the inkwell on Mrs. Sweeny's desk and splattering black ink on all the students in the front row. No one moved.

Mrs. Sweeny stepped around the pool of ink as if this were a normal everyday occurrence and in a steady and calm voice said "Class, form a line and proceed to the hall immediately."

Kids were coming out of other classrooms – some orderly, some in disarray. You could hear glass shattering and shouts and crying. They were herded to the gym which was bedlam until the principal got up on a bleacher with the bullhorn he used at football games and bellowed them into order and silence.

"No one will leave the gym until this storm has passed. No

one under any circumstances." His voice ricocheted off the high walls creating even more of a panic in its echo.

Bette saw Frank nudge a few of his buddies. "Let's get outta here guys," he whispered. "I ain't missin' this for nothin'." And sure enough, a few minutes later, she saw them sneaking out through the boy's locker room.

Outside the world was in chaos.

September 21, 3 pm. *From open seas it comes in a howling roar like hundred pipe organs playing in mighty discord. It comes without warning. It comes fast and hard and deadly. In winds at 145 miles per hour, windows break in storefronts, barns implode. Cars skew and roll, their paint sandblasted to dull steel. Trees topple and debris torn from roofs and shingled houses shoots through the air like deadly weapons. Then it gets worse. Those who see it can't believe their eyes. Walter Penn on the dunes sees. Judy Tate, surrounded by eight children, sees. Crazy Tom sees. Perched on his tin roof, his white beard flying, abandoned by his cats, long since gone from his shack to the high ground of the bluffs, Tom cackles with laughter. Is it a fog bank? A mirage? No. What Tom sees, what they all see through the wind and the driving rain is the Atlantic Ocean rising up as one solid green and foaming mass — a single towering wall of water surging onto the gentle flat land of the South Fork.*

Until now, the storm had been just that — a storm — a bad one but now the land and its people know they are caught in the jaws of a nightmare.

Three Months Earlier...

In summer the song sings itself.

WLLIAM CARLOS WILLIAMS

June
THE SEASON BEGINS

IT IS JUNE. *Crops are planted in furrows that run to the ocean dunes; nets are mended and the cod, flounder and mackerel are running. In the empty salt marshes the great blue herons rise above creek banks. The harsh winter with its nor'easters and frugality is over. Summer has arrived on the South Fork.*

From the Shinnecock Hills to Montauk Point, 26 miles along a single road, the villages and hamlets that line the Atlantic Ocean hang like jewels on a necklace each bearing a marked difference from the other. In time it will be known collectively as The Hamptons, a term shunned by the locals who know each town, village and hamlet for their own particular quality. Southampton, an elegant dowager; Water Mill with the water wheel to prove it; Bridgehampton, its backside to the prehistoric moraine, the place where the last Ice Age came to a halt before receding back into time. Sagaponack and Wainscott, Indian place name meets English settler on topsoil so deep and rich they say it's the finest farmland in North America. The road curves through East Hampton with its handsome old salt box houses and quaint windmills. Due east is Amagansett, home of the haulseiners, sea hearty men and women from Sussex and Kent who settled along the shore generations ago. Follow the road out onto a flat sandy stretch called Napeague before rising up into the Hither Hills of Montauk. Here the island ends in a burst of wild beauty, surf against high cliffs, tall grasses, stunted trees, hidden ponds, and tiny coves, once the hiding places of pirates and buccaneers. And at the very eastern, most point stands the Montauk Lighthouse, commissioned by President George Washington, the last outpost on Long Island.

But above all the charm and beauty of the South Fork there is only one real siren call to summer – the beach. And here it is – an endless unbroken swath of dunes, pale fine sand and the eternal sea.

13

Wilma Palmer
East Hampton Village

"Why is it," thought Wilma as she stood gazing down Main Street at the avenue of elms, "that the trees go nubby soft along their branches in the promise of leaves to come, holding off for a maddeningly long time before in the blink of an eye they unfold into a canopy of green just in time for the summer people." This had always annoyed her. As if even Mother Nature herself felt obliged to hold back until the paying customers arrived.

Summer people. Wilma did not relish their return even though all around her she could feel a heightened sense of movement, of anticipation, of excitement. She didn't like the way summer swallowed up the town, upset its harmony, the city people layering themselves like a fancy Persian carpet over the homespun fabric of village and rural life. When the summer got seriously underway the things Wilma so loved about her town, its unity and fine meshed workings, suddenly seemed to clog up in a snarl of nervous energy. But she was, if nothing else, realistic knowing full well that summer meant work and income for hundreds of locals many of whom had eked by in the winter holding on and making do.

Wilma Palmer and her son Lewis were on their way home down Main Street at the end of the closing ceremonies on this the last day of school. There was a palpable hum in the air. Workmen were brushing fresh coats of paint around doorsills and store windows. Shopkeepers were stocking more trendy wares and window displays had forgone the practical and serviceable for color and whimsy. White's Drugstore now carried a new line of ladies' cosmetics; Marley's News shop was ordering in city newspapers; Epstein's Department Store featured a new line they called "resort wear" and over at The East Hampton Star, the Want Ads were flourishing. High school students were already signed up for summer work at the tennis and golf clubs, as caddies, babysitters, lifeguards and beach attendants. One enterprising boy had started a lawn mowing service, "Perfect Lawn Care," and had mimeographed flyers in the school office to distribute door to door. The summer largesse fed into professional coffers as well. Doctors and lawyers knew they could count on being paid and even Wilma's husband Jim had a decided spring in his step as he wrangled increased insurance policies out of frugal customers.

Well, so be it, she thought. She herself was counting on generous donations to The Ladies Village Improvement Society for their tree preservation program. The summer fete, always a high mark in the season was almost totally dependent on the summer colony and her friend Celia was riding high this year on plans to bring in something startling and new for the event. "A camel, Celia?" Wilma had exclaimed at the last meeting of the Fair Committee when Celia laid out her plan. "Yes," Celia crowed, "isn't it divine? Harry, god knows where he finds these people, is in some sort of business deal with a traveling circus and they said they would lend us their camel. For a price of course but well worth it. We can have the camel for two hours and think how stunning that will be."

Wilma gave Lewis' hand a little tug. She heard the whistle of the afternoon train.

• • •

Hannah Wood pulled her dad's old black Chevy up to the train depot, glad she had made it off Montauk and all the way to the station before the Cannonball arrived from New York. Summer was here at last. She could see her brother and his friends lining up on the platform to unload trunks and supplies onto pickups hauling them up to the big houses along the ocean. Sure bet – you could pick up a nice bit of jingle meeting the trains from New York.

Like most of her friends, Hannah entered willingly into the prosperity of summer. She liked the hum and excitement of the new season and wished she could work at the jobs so coveted by her classmates but Hannah was stuck working in her dad's bait shop on the fishing wharf in Montauk. Wilber Wood didn't hold much with summer people and cautioned his kids to "steer clear of those loons." Advice they mostly ignored.

Hannah Wood had precious little time of her own and at 16 thought maybe she had worked every day of her whole life. Ever since she was twelve she had worked after school and summers in her dad's shop. Before that, as eldest girl, she had helped her Ma take care of the younger kids. They lived in the fishing settlement clustered at the edge of Montauk's Fort Pond Bay. The bay and the docks appealed to the fishermen because here on the inner waters was protection from the ocean and boats large and small could ease into the turbulent sea from safe waters in the bay. The houses were small and weathered. They had peaked roofs with lightning rods and flat facades with only a rough stone step leading to the front doors. There were privies in back propped up by mounds of fish boxes and traps and nets.

Hannah's house was no different with little room for the burgeoning Wood family. Seven kids now and Ma's tolerance near gone. *For the love of God stop havin' em'* Hannah thought, more than once, but she kept her tongue. Her Ma was a querulous woman with little patience and a quick hand for a back talking daughter. The bait shop wasn't much better. It was freezing in winter and in summer the smell of fish was enough to knock you sideways.

High on the cliff behind the settlement was a big, rambling hotel called The Manor and sometimes after work Hannah went up to visit her friend Gloria, who worked as a maid cleaning rooms. The world inside the Manor was a world apart where ladies dressed in tennis whites by day and long skirts in the evening; girls and boys, her own age, sat around the pool looking bored and men hired charter boats to take them out fishing. Gloria grumbled about always being asked for clean towels and fresh linens but Hannah envied her friend and the smell of the fresh towels and the nice sweet smelling soaps on Gloria's supply trolley that Hannah sometimes tucked into her pocket.

She watched as the train pulled into the station, the passengers exploding onto the platform, ladies in bright dresses, men with city ties loosened and jackets slung over their arm. With a lot of good-natured calling out to friends and waving down cars sent to collect them, Hannah thought it looked like a movie where any minute they would all burst into merry song. Then a sharp tap on the roof of the car reminded her she was there to taxi people and she rolled down the window.

"Hey, Mr. Slade. You just off the train?"

"Sure am. Mighty crowded today but when the city calls," he patted his briefcase, "Harry Slade answers. Say now, Hannah, my wife was supposed to meet me but she's nowhere to be seen. How about giving me a ride home?"

"Sure, Mr. Slade. Glad to." Harry Slade was already around to the passenger side sliding onto the seat. He smelled of whiskey and cigars but it was a nice smell, a manly smell.

"Yep. The wife is off on a toot I suspect. Seems everyone goes a little crazy this time of year. School out?"

"Yes, sir. Ended for me a week ago. My dad needs me in the bait shop."

He looked at her and winked. "And I expect you'd rather be here in town where the action is. Not that your dad's shop isn't a fine establishment. Mighty fine." His eyebrows lifted.

Hannah giggled. That was the nice thing about Mr. Slade. He always knew what was up. He was like that with everyone, like he was your best friend and he knew everyone's name and what their business was. Hannah had heard things said about Mr. Slade that weren't so nice. That he was a blowhard, that he lived off his wife, that you had to watch it or he'd try to sell you the Brooklyn Bridge, that he was 'from away' like that was something bad but Hannah figured people always had too much to say anyways. Still, one thing was true, she knew she wouldn't get a fare from him.

Pulling up in front of his house near the pond on Main Street they could both see that the car was in the garage. It was a nice house, not grand like the south-of-the-highway crowd, the preferred address of the summer people, but a two-story white colonial with a pretty side porch and lots of rooms inside. This she knew from people who had worked for Mrs. Slade – "A real driver" they said. "Nothing pleases *her*." And it got so no one wanted to work for her at all.

Mr. Slade looked a little downcast for a minute but then slapped his knee and let out a bellowing laugh. "Darn if I didn't tell Mrs. Slade I'd be on the late train. Say now, Hannah, since she's not really expecting me until later why don't you just drive me on down to the Sea Spray. I'd like to have a look at that fine ocean of ours."

Hannah bit her lip to keep from snorting. She knew where he was heading – the taproom at the Sea Spray. But she didn't say anything just put the car in gear and drove on down the main street and onto Ocean Avenue.

Perched on the edge of the dunes, the venerable old Sea Spray Inn seemed disinclined to acquiesce to the buzz of the season. Its sagging roof and weather worn porch sat as it had for decades, rocking chairs and wicker swings a welcome relief to beach goers in the heat of the day and a place all locals knew in winter for the best chowder on the Eastern seaboard. It also sported a dark paneled bar, the drinking place of choice for gents about town. Women not allowed.

"You tell your dad hello for me and tell him if he ever wants to get some of his pals together and talk property why I've got half a dozen good investments for him and his friends. Montauk is the place, I tell you. Carl Fisher sure knew that. Montauk is like panning for gold. Pure gold."

He grinned and Hannah grinned back. She'd heard him before hot airing about Montauk but to her mind Montauk was a dead end place where nothing happened except fish. Montauk had once been the dream of speculators – a man named Carl Fisher decided to make it "the Miami of the North" with big ships coming into harbor and fast trains to New York. Golf courses, polo grounds, gambling casinos, big hotels had been part of the plan and to that end he built The Manor up on the hill and a seven story command post down by the ocean. *Sticks out like a sore thumb,* said the likes of Wilbur Wood and his cronies noting with relief that Fisher's dream had died in the '29 crash, and soon after Fisher himself. And that was that. Montauk resumed its quiet ways with only the Manor and the 'sore thumb' to remind people of what might have been. And here in his office overlooking the ocean, Harry Slade alone had determined he was going to keep the dream alive.

He winked at her and bounded out of the car and up the steps to the porch. Hannah watched him swing his briefcase and push his hat back on his head before entering the inn. Mr. Slade hadn't sold any property in Montauk in years and people just laughed at him.

Turning the car around Hannah figured she had missed her chance at any paying customers and decided instead to drive down Lily Pond Lane. Here, life was lived on a scale that boggled her mind. Grand summer houses running up to thirty rooms or more hid behind privet hedges with swimming pools, stables, and carriage houses.

Yet as Hannah and all local people knew despite all the grandeur these people ran around town like they were having a nonstop party. She had grown up with the stories told all winter in places like the bait shop with everyone gathered around the wood stove. Like the story Homer Cuddeback the soda jerk at the drugstore told about the two girls driving their sports car down the sidewalk on Main Street in the village and then nudging it right through the big double doors into the store and ordering themselves an ice cream cone. Or Peeky Thompson who worked the marina down at the Devon Yacht Club. He could tell you about what landlubbers they were, how they rowed their dories sitting down and ran sailboats onto sandbars. Or Mack Handy who worked over to the Maidstone Club. He had been out mowing the greens when someone flew over in one of those two-seater airplanes and dropped about a million golf balls down like hail and hadn't there been a chatter and fuss over that. Yeah. Crazy stuff and now, like flocks of geese here they were again – and here to serve them were gardeners and maids, cooks and laundresses, tradesmen and shopkeepers, delivery boys and caretakers. The busy song of summer hummed in every corner – and nowhere else was there more polishing of silver, dusting of shelves, airing of blankets, ironing of linens, and buffing of floors than at Villamere, the Hartleys summer beach house on Dune Road.

14

Emmaline

Villamere commanded an arresting view. Positioned at the end of Dune Road, a road hardly more than a spit of sandy land jutting out from tree lined streets and farmland further back towards town, there were nevertheless a number of fashionable residences. The older (and smaller) houses such as the one Judy and Chip Tate owned were on the bay side of the road, the newer more extravagant houses fronted on the ocean. Villamere however enjoyed the best of both. Built in the Gilded Age of 1910 it was probably better suited for the Mediterranean with its red slate roof, arched windows, striped canopies and stone balustrades sitting grand and alone at the end of the road beyond which the sand narrowed and ocean and bay met through a narrow watery ravine prosaically called "the gut." Gut or no, it afforded water views from every room.

Standing in her bedroom silhouetted against the afternoon light, staring out the window Emmaline was not thinking of the house or its spectacular view, she was thinking of her soon to be fortieth birthday. Opening the window she let the air wash over her. *Not that anyone really knows* she reasoned– not even, she thought, James, her husband, but there it was anyway. Forty. Four-oh. Emmaline shuddered. Death.

She turned to the full-length mirror to gaze at her figure removing the robe she was wearing. Not an ounce of fat. Were her breasts sagging? Yes… no… she couldn't tell. But her legs, those long legs that had so intoxicated the fashion photographers, as lean as ever. A breeze off the ocean made her shiver and a million tiny goose bumps rose on the white smooth skin. She turned again to the window feeling the sensual pleasure of her nakedness exposed to the outside world wondering what it would be like to walk naked through her house, down onto the beach and into the spray of the ocean. Why not?

Emmaline wondered what exactly was happening to her life. She knew she was much in demand, she knew she had a great deal of influence, but the beauty she had once been? She found herself avoiding bright lights, staring at much younger women, wanting to reach out and touch their skin the way one would stroke a fine kid glove. Worse was the vividness of youth, its brightness and reckless abandon as if tomorrow didn't count. As if the days and months weren't ticking bombs adding up to grim realities. And love? What she wouldn't give for one more rollicking love affair. One she could then tuck into the secret most parts of her and carry into the grey-haired future. But who? It had been ages since she had met anyone of real interest. Young men treated her like some sort of icon, their flattery and obsequiousness more annoying than anything else. Older men were either tiresome bores or looking beyond her to the fresher faces on down the line. Endless parties – a thousand nights and yet she never had fun anymore. There was too much drinking, too much hard talk and cynicism, too much pretense at not caring. But fun? Real gaiety and spirited fun? Where had all that gone?

She stood at her window staring out over the bay and all she could see was that much younger self, sent to Paris as a model for *Vogue*, sailing out of New York's harbor to France on the Mauretania in 1921. Had anyone had quite so much fun as she? Turning heads in Paris and on the Riviera? The feature photograph taken of her on the beach in a striped swim suit (horribly itchy she now remembered) and a large straw hat, with that expression she herself had made famous – the young American, the new face, the restless eyes and dark hair cropped short with a sassy American personality to go along with it. The 1920's were a good time to be young and daring and American providing you were pretty. That prettiness could go far, and further still if you had family and money behind you, which she hadn't. Not then when it might have made all the difference. Her family credentials were as hazy as were her funds but Emmaline had an ambitious mother ready to exploit her smart and beautiful daughter who was quick and game. Borrowing more money than she could ever hope to repay, her mother urged Emmaline to stay on in Paris even after *Vogue* had packed up their cameras and returned to New York – to go everywhere and to meet everyone and to come out of it having made a brilliant match.

Could there have really been so many parties and all with absurd themes attached to them – masked parties, Wild West parties, parties where you had to come as your favorite villain, parties where you wore only white, swim parties, picnics and bacchanals, tea parties that turned into all night revels. Emmaline raced headlong into the circus of Paris as if there would be no end to it.

It had been inevitable that they would meet. Freddy Langdon perhaps the most notorious of a pack of self-indulgent young Englishmen who had come to Paris that year, so good-looking, so long on charm. One day he would inherit an ancient title and the estate that came with it but for now he was happily broke – almost as broke as she. Emmaline remembered seeing him for the first time watching her from across a roulette table and even now, so many years later, she could recall the magic of him. The sort of magic that happens once in a lifetime…if you were lucky. And they were lucky. That night they pooled their meager resources and miraculously won more money than she had ever imagined possible. And nothing would do but that they spend it lavishly, carelessly and as foolishly as they could. Infatuated? Swept off her feet? She neither knew nor cared. She was in love and that was that. Their *affaire de coeur* caused a sensation and they were feted and fawned over wherever they went. It seemed everyone wanted to celebrate the two beautiful young lovers. Fool that she was, she had believed that Freddy would actually marry her. Freddy who fell into oceans of despair when she flirted with other men. Freddy who once told her that she was a Grecian goddess come alive, that he would lay his entire life at her feet if only…if only…. Oh how cool she had been, how cleverly she had played her hand. There was nothing she couldn't have from him with a mere nod of her head. That very same Freddy had run home to Mama at the first hint of family disapproval where no amount of beauty, brains, lies, and wiles could transform her into a worthy contender. American brides need be heiresses before they could become the wives and mothers of future English heraldry not pretty models who could offer nothing more to fortune than high cheekbones and slender bodies. Astonished, humiliated, and brokenhearted, Emmaline's never-ending party ended without fanfare or reprieve. Ahead of her lay a mountain of debts and her now hysterical mother.

And then, providence had provided – literally – in the form of James Hartley, a man from Providence, Rhode Island who had made a small fortune in military uniforms in his textile factories. He was 20 years her senior and provincial to the point of dullness but was, according to her mother, "your last chance." No doubt he was.

As Mrs. James Hartley, Emmaline set to work retooling her husband, tailoring his clothes and polishing his manners molding him little by little into the likeness of a gentleman. Her command post was now a penthouse on Fifth Avenue, a showplace from which to muster her battle plans from a terrace filled with exotic trees. People said admiringly, "Where did you find it?" "It's so unusual!" And it was, too. She made sure that the Hartleys always did the smart new thing, lending her time and his generous donations to all sorts of charitable causes, securing invitations to dinners and house parties that were fitting for the dazzling Emmaline Hartley. It all cost money of course, a great deal of money, but James had done himself proud on Wall Street and he enjoyed indulging his beautiful wife, so neither of them worried. There was no reason to – the money kept pouring in. Curiously, for there was nothing remotely maternal about her, in all of this Emmaline produced three children. Despite the inconvenience of pregnancy she found that children brought a whole new dimension to her empire building. They were the future – her future – and she was extremely aware of what security her progeny could bring to the equation. With the advent of her second child, the penthouse had to go – a townhouse on Sutton Place was secured and with it an entourage – baby nurse, nanny, cook, various maids, and a chauffeur. James bought her the beach house, Villamere, in 1927 where she reassembled the entourage in lavish display in the summer months. And now here it was the summer of 1938. She was the mother of three growing children, the wife of an old poop, a few discreet affairs notched in her belt and ...forty! She was practically a relic.

It took her a number of beats before realizing she was watching a motorcycle with a sidecar attached to it coming down Dune Road – making quite a racket too. It came nearer, then nearer still until... damn, it turned down the Tate drive. Emmaline immediately lost interest. The Tates had little appeal and that goody two shoes Judy Tate actually irritated her. If Judy Tate had one ounce of fire in her she could actually be a real beauty but as it was she was determined to play out her life the devoted wife and mother dressed in those off the rack clothes from B. Altman's.

When did I get to be so negative, she wondered. Perhaps I always was but no, there had been a long stretch of her life when she felt all the promise of the future.

She should be nicer but everyone was so tedious and predictable. Why should she be nice? Where had she heard someone say that hate shows up on your face once you turn forty?

The motorcycle disappeared behind the privet hedge.

15

Judy Tate

"Guess what, Mommy."

Judy put down her teacup. "What, darling?"

"I'm a girl." Alice crowed.

Judy laughed nodding, "Yes, you are."

"Are you a girl, Mommy?"

"Yes. I am a girl,"

"Like me," Alice squealed. Judy and Alice were on the lawn near the water's edge having a tea party. All of Alice's dolls and Teddy bears were invited and the table set with a lace cloth and real china teacups, the same tiny teacups Judy herself played with as a child. Raleigh came across the lawn with a small tray and on it were tiny tea sandwiches.

"Yayi," Alice could not say her "r's" and "l's." "Guess what? I'm a girl. Are you a girl?"

"No, ma'am." He drew himself up. "I'm a boy."

Alice was wild with delight. "A boy. Yayi is a boy. Is Daddy a boy?" And so it went. Until everyone they knew including the dolls and Teddy were declared girl or boy. And by now they were all laughing and making such a fuss that they didn't hear the motorcycle coming into the drive.

He came across the lawn taking his leather helmet off, wearing tall boots and golf trousers, a plaid vest, his hair floppy and dark and he was grinning. "I hate to interrupt your party but..."

Alice rushed up to him. "Are you a boy?"

"Yep. I reckon I am and I'm also your cousin, Jack Burns."

Judy's mouth formed a great round look of surprise. "Oh my – today is Sunday and you said you would stop by. Jack, I'm so terribly sorry but...well...," she gestured at the dolls and tea table. "I'm afraid I simply forgot. Can you forgive me?" She leaned forward with a conscientious expression – then she laughed, an absurd, charming, breathless laugh, and held out her hand, a delicate hand as childlike as her daughter's.

"No apologies, please. I can certainly see why taking tea with Teddy is far more delightful. I'm sorry to burst in like this but I had to come over and say hello before the summer gets seriously underway. Do you know it's been over three years?"

Judy and Jack were related by some circuitous route known only to his mother and her father through marriage ties long obscured by years, but cousins they were and Judy was delighted to see him.

"Stay for dinner, Jack. It's just us and we're still unpacking so I can't guarantee anything. I'm longing to know all about you. Where are you living?"

"In a chicken coop in Amagansett." He saw the look on her face. "Terrific really. Very basic but I love it. You and Alice must come over someday and...uh, Chip?" He looked around as if Chip might suddenly appear.

"Chip's still in the city. He's not coming out until next weekend and then I guess only weekends all summer really. Maybe I can persuade him to take a week here and there. Endless work, I'm afraid. Ever since Daddy...," she trailed off. She couldn't remember how much Jack knew about her father but he nodded with a look of concern.

"Yes. So I heard."

"I'm sorry we've been such strangers in the city, Jack. It just seems one thing after another – the baby and then my father's illness...and then..." She flapped her hand in the air, "Oh I don't need to go on and on. You know how it is. Let me show you the house. It was my grandfather's – he built it long before anyone else was out here on Dune Road... quite the hinterlands which is how he liked things..."

Judy kept up a patter telling him all about designing and building it the summer before and how Chip was wildly disapproving but the townspeople would drive by to watch the construction because so little had been built locally since the start of the Depression and how one old gent came with his camp chair just to sit saying how much he liked smelling new cut lumber. She had seen a picture in a magazine, couldn't remember where but it stuck in her mind and she knew, just knew right here (hand on heart) that this was *her* room. By now they were sitting on the deck drinks in hand.

"The house has always been so stuffy and closed in, just like the grandparents," she rolled her eyes and shrugged, "but I've always wanted to open up the view. Why live in such a beautiful place if you shut it out?" A breeze blew through the room, catching the curtains so that they proudly billowed their excess of floral chintz.

It was all too frilly and girlish, thought Jack, but sipping his bourbon, a big hug from Alice before being put to bed, the aroma of Raleigh's cooking scenting the air, Jack made every effort to appear interested in whatever Judy cared to talk about, sinking into the comforts of home and the feminine patter with ease. Indeed Judy's idle chatter was welcome after almost two months of local living and, until this very moment, his only social life had been amongst the fishing and farming families of Amagansett. He was getting desperate.

It was a custom among the families to spend two or three evenings a week gathered in one kitchen or another after supper. The chicken coop once part of a local farm somehow qualified Jack as a candidate for inclusion in such gatherings and he immediately understood it was a solid acceptance of him in this tight knit community. He had appreciated the novelty of it all, even welcomed it back in his first few weeks of residency in the early spring but soon found it stultifyingly dull. With evening chores completed, chairs at one house or another were gathered from the various rooms into a circle. Coffee, maybe a cake of some sort was served followed by what passed for lively chat about people and things Jack knew nothing of – local news, tidbits of the day, the price of fish, farm machinery repair, bake sales, church comings and goings, a new teacher up at the high school, a sick neighbor. He was treated no more, no less than anyone else, and except for a few questions sent his way about the comforts of the "coop" or inquiries about the inner workings of his motorcycle, there seemed little interest in him as an artist. But here on Dune Road with his drink in hand and Judy so pretty and accommodating, Jack relaxed into more familiar territory.

Judy now tucked up on a cushioned outdoor divan, her gold hair cut short almost like a boy's, a cardigan around her shoulders and her slim long legs comfortably stretched out with a plaid throw against the cool night air, exuded sweetness. She always had. Years earlier when he had first arrived in New York fresh out of college with only the vagaries of family ancestry to introduce him, Judy's parents had welcomed their distant southern cousin into their comfortable though stuffy life. Judy at seventeen was a polite, dutiful and amiable girl much as she was now. Marriage, a child and a few years had not greatly changed that girl of a decade ago.

She got up to refill his glass, returning it to him with a breathless little laugh. "Bourbon and branch, right?" She laughed all the time, he noticed. It was the kind of laugh that people found charming until perhaps they had heard it once too often – then it might sound childish, even meaningless as one might find Judy herself. Indeed, it was hard not to think of Judy as anything but a sheltered girl grown into a sheltered woman.

Still, Jack owed much to his New York cousins who had shepherded his entry into city life with agreeable results. Judy's father, Bill Delany was in advertising. Introductions had been made. Jack was talented with a knack for commercial illustration. His portfolio, tweaked by Delany, was sent to all the major design studios. Within a year, Jack landed soundly on his feet with an offer from J.C. Lyendecker to join his stable of illustrators.

Lyendecker was a legend. His illustrations, filled with patriotic sentiment and healthy idealism graced magazine covers, advertisements and kitchen calendars across America and Jack quickly caught on to the Lyendecker style drawing strong, athletic men and lithe, feminine women with equal ease. Work provided income and income provided Jack a whole new take on New York. He fell in with a crowd of jazz-fueled clever young things and soon enough the Delanys became familial social obligations that ran to Thanksgivings and occasional dinners.

Judy stopped her chatter about builders and architects mid-sentence. "Look, Jack. This one's going to be spectacular." The sun had begun its final descent into the western shore of the bay. The undersides of the clouds caught the glorious fire of rays and for a few minutes the water, the sky, even the deck on which they were sitting became a shock of burning red and gold before easing into an astonishing palette of magentas, purples and deep velvet blues. They were both silent.

"Chip and I have a game rating the sunsets on a scale of one to ten but I would say that's an eleven. Beautiful isn't it?"

"What I wouldn't give to be able to paint that light," Jack said quietly. "In the late afternoon I set off on my motorcycle and drive all over the place chasing the light. It's extraordinary everywhere I go. Sort of a gold gossamer netting falls over the land and everything on it seems to swim in the light as if the air itself has gone to liquid. They tell me it's being surrounded by water with no hills and valleys to cast shadows but whatever it is, I want it." He paused, looking at the last of the spectacle as it drifted into the muted tones of deepening night.

Judy let out a deep sign of contentment. "I love it here. All of it," she gestured to the bay. "There's something about this whole place that makes me think of...I don't know...it's a sort of paradise, isn't it? So calm and safe. All this beauty. Sometimes when I go back to the city after the summer I feel like Eve banished from Eden." She giggled self-consciously.

Jack leaned forward. "Would you mind if I came here to work some afternoons? I won't get in anyone's way."

Judy clapped her hands. "Of course not. Anytime. Really ... we'd love it. And we won't bother you but promise you'll make our house your second home. I mean it, Jack. I'll be on my lonesome during the week. By all means, the view is yours but I didn't know you painted landscapes. What happened to all those beautiful people you do for the magazines?"

"Ah, that's the me in New York in the clutches of gainful

employment. I want to move as far away from all that as I can – at least for the summer. I thought if I had to draw another tanned young man on the tennis courts or a foxy girl in an evening gown I would go insane. Who knows," he said, looking over at Judy with a quick smile, "by the end of the summer I might be an artist. I mean a real artist, not just a hack."

"No, Jack. Your work is wonderful. I've admired it for years. It's all so...so dashing and sophisticated," Judy protested, but Jack held up his hand.

"That's just what I mean. All that 'dash' is wearing me out. This summer in that chicken coop in Amagansett I want to re-discover or maybe reinvent myself. I'm twenty-eight you know, and that means no more excuses. Time is marching on." He said this with a dramatic flair knowing full well he still looked like a college boy.

"But Jack, I had no idea you weren't perfectly content with what you did." Judy was leaning toward him attentive to his every word.

Jack frowned. "I'm probably a fool to give up such a good paying job when so many are out of work but the truth is I'm bored. I go to work and sit in a room full of other guys, all just as talented, and no matter how agreeable and easy it is for me, I know that a few more years of commercial art will end any hope I have of serious work as an artist."

Judy looked perplexed. "What does that mean?"

"Most of the time I don't really know what that means but I look at the greats, Van Gogh in particular. Did you see the show at the Met? I saw it...god, I must have lived there for weeks. He figured something out, something indescribable, and I want to, too." He said this with an intensity that startled them both.

But he was on a roll now. "As an illustrator, I've idealized how things look. Now all I want to do is play with color and light and find out how things move within a painting, even past a painting." He saw the look on Judy's face. She was impressed and Jack liked the sound of his words. He had never really articulated exactly what it was he was trying to do. Perhaps he had never even known but now this began to sound like something interesting.

"You see by definition commercial art is a way of enhancing what is real and manipulating it into an ideal. What I'm trying to do is take what is real and deconstruct it, find out what makes it tick so to speak, and then paint that. Or try too." His voice trailed off uncertainly. *What the hell was he talking about?* But Judy was rapt, her eyes shining.

Jack laughed to break the sudden serious mood and Judy bounded off the divan. "I think supper is almost ready," she said pulling Jack to his feet. "Oh, I wish Chip were here. He will be so happy you've come back into our lives."

Jack nodded. There had been a time when Chip and Jack had tried to make a friendship of it but after a few beers together, even a baseball game or two, it had more or less petered out. Chip was too serious for him, too careful but Judy... Jack smiled at her, with her small slender frame and her arm now linked in his, her bountiful table and generous liquor cabinet, her devotion to 'family' – all this might be a welcome addition to his summer.

"I mean it Jack. Anytime. You'll be such company for me. I need a friend out here." And there she was with that breathless laugh again as if she had said something witty rather than poignant as she led him to the dining room.

16

Jack Burns

Life came easily to Jack – always had. This "ease" was by no means economic. The Burns family having fallen on hard times since the war – the War for Southern Independence, the Freedom War, the War of Northern Aggression, the War Between the States – *that* war, the only war ever referred to in the Savannah lowlands. But whatever they chose to call it, the Civil War had lost the Burns family their property and prosperity forcing them to the small house on Henry Lane just south of Savannah's old Victorian district. It had not however lost them their pride. Here on humble terms the Burns lived as if still the lofty landowners of the antebellum glory days – a dim photograph of the manse taken by an itinerant photographer before the war prominently displayed on the mantelpiece. Born John Adolphus Delany Burns, Jack was the only male in a house full of women – his grandmother, mother, a maiden aunt and Bessie, the ebony housekeeper and real major domo of the family. Jack's father had long since departed, choosing to die in a hunting accident before Jack turned five.

Surrounded by women, Jack learned early that charm and a winning smile, however insincere, opened doors. His artistic ability added further appeal. Caricatures had always been a specialty and he often made flattering quick sketches to impress the girls. At the University of Virginia where he excelled in gambling and parties, his sharp and irreverent drawings often appeared in the college humor magazine. He was encouraged to take an art class. "You have a talent," declared the instructor holding one of Jack's studies of an afternoon picnic held on the lawn of Monticello. The instructor had once studied at the Art Students League in New York. So, thought Jack, would he.

It was late afternoon when he stepped into the high echoing dome of Pennsylvania Station and out into the clogged streets of the city. The crush of people moving around him seemed to know who they were and where they were going and Jack fell in with them as if born on a swift stream. At some point he found himself on the edge of Central Park across from the Plaza Hotel. The dusky sky held a single bright star suspended over the famed plaza fountain like a talisman to be wished on and he found himself wishing with all his might that he might find his place in this extraordinary city.

He signed on to classes at the Art Students League and took them seriously too, joining in with a large and dedicated, if boisterous, group of young artists like himself. They picked up menial work during the day and took night classes at the League then met in automats and cheap working class diners downtown, stretching a cup of coffee and a bowl of soup into all hours of the night with talk, egging each other on, infatuated with themselves and their lofty ideas. And for a time this life suited Jack with all its attendant fervor and depravations, but thanks to his Delany kin and the rare novelty among his fellow League artists of a steady paycheck in the Lyendecker stable, his early passion was soon eroded. It was just too easy to forego night classes for nightclubs and way more fun to dress the dandy squiring pretty girls about town than drinking coffee in a dingy automat.

He might have sailed indefinitely along in this bubble of ease and relative solvency except for two very significant events that by coincidence or grand design came hard on each other's heels. Jack had been at work on an advertising layout fine-tuning a cherub of a child in orgasmic delight over his bowl of cereal when the great Lyendecker himself came strolling into the studio. This was not uncommon but always cause for a stir especially if you had been slacking off in your renderings. Lyendecker strode by Jack towards another fellow's drafting table, the tall, thin, laconic Yankee with such a sentimental bent that Jack found his colleague insufferable. This fellow, Norm, seemed destined for calendar art and nothing more. He drew characters and scenes from small town New England life – shopkeepers and matrons, schoolboys and yapping dogs. The best he could do with an attractive young woman was to give her lank hair, a pencil behind her ear and a stack of library books on her desk. He watched Lyendecker approach Norm's desk, his hand stretched out, his face florid with pleasure.

It seemed Norm Rockwell's work had been picked to adorn the next three issues of *The Saturday Evening Post*, the most widely circulated magazine in America, at the unheard of sum of $300 per illustration. Jack felt a rush of envy and disbelief. Worse, he felt doubt – in himself. And this was something new indeed.

That night in a bar, bourbon and its balm may have assailed the green-eyed monster inside him but two days later on a business call on Wall Street, Jack was again confronted with doubt. It was a cold January day but the sun was out and the air invigorated him. Jack stood on the Battery and let the wind seep through his Madison Avenue suit, his kid gloved hand holding the large portfolio he was carrying full of sketches just shown to a client.

Nearby the old Customs House caught his eye and he strolled up the stairs into the musty government building. Here a group of artists were painting a large mural on the wall of the lobby. He could see in an instant they were part of the WPA program set up by the government to give artists work in these lean times. And here among the mural painters was his teacher from the Art Students League, Guy Dambrose.

They greeted each other warmly and Jack suggested coffee at a nearby diner where Dambrose proceeded to order a large meal on Jack's tab.

"So, how is it a young fellow like you is so prosperous, "Guy asked leaning back after the spread and lighting a cigarette.

Jack laughed. "It's all smoke and mirrors I assure you." But he could feel himself redden thinking he probably did look prosperous in his suit and carefully combed hair next to Dambrose who was wearing coveralls and a flannel shirt spattered in paint.

"I'm making out OK," he continued. "I'm doing some advertising work…illustration…just a little here and there."

"Sounds good." The older man looked pointedly at the large portfolio. "Is that your work?"

Jack waved it off. "Oh this is nothing. Just some sketches I was showing a client. My work, my real work is back in my studio. Well, studio is stretching it a little, just a small loft in Chelsea..." but Dambrose was holding out his hand for the portfolio, pushing his coffee cup to the edge of the table to make room. Reluctantly Jack handed it over.

Dambrose leafed through the binder slowly, pausing here and there and peering closer at some of the images. Jack winced when he seemed to linger unnecessarily long over a woman in a flaming red dress dancing with a sleek tuxedoed man for the glory of After Eight Chocolates. Dambrose smiled as he closed the book and looked at Jack. "You were always a good draftsman. One of the best I ever taught. God, that seems years ago now? Are you still painting?"

"No." Jack's bravado withered. "The truth of it is I'm not. This commercial stuff pays the rent and more. It's just too easy."

Dambrose was no idealist – at least not anymore. Back in the day he had been the man to watch both in New York and Paris but the Depression had dried up his escalating fame and any thought of success, real success in the art world, had all but disappeared. Yet success had never really been his passion. It was all about the work – and yes, eating too, which is why he was grateful for the mural work and grateful now for this extravagant meal. He couldn't remember the last time he had eaten meat – he, the dashing young man of less than 20 years ago now grateful for a full meal? Well, such is life.

He sat for a while smoking then he looked at the younger man across the table. "You do what you have to do. I think that's the right answer. I really don't know but what I do know is if you leave it off too long, it will die. Talent is only a small part of it. You've got to be pent up inside, urgent, even desperate, to do great work. You've got to say to hell with it all including your luxuries. If you don't think that's the way to go, then," he shrugged, "make your peace with whatever you do but just remember, my friend, you go around once, then its over. So whatever you decide, make it work."

Jack felt a knot in his stomach. "You were a great teacher."

Dambrose gave a slight bow. "And in return I say, you were once a promising student. You are now a very talented illustrator. Let's leave our evening at that."

But Jack couldn't leave it. God damn it! He was no longer a kid with talent to burn and years to burn it in. He had saved no money. He had made no plans.

Some weeks later when a friend told him about this dream place on the tip of Long Island, where the light settled in golden waves, where the beaches stretched into infinity, where the living was cheap and the natives welcoming, Jack bit.

• • •

One look at the Amagansett double dunes with its weathered fishermens shacks dotted along the shore, the dune grasses waving silver and green against the white sand, the salt air deep in his lungs, he knew he had found redemption. But it wasn't until Jack had stumbled on the old beachcomber sitting atop his tin-roofed shanty in the dunes of Napeague that he felt the first flicker of that passion Dambrose had described.

The sight of the beachcomber, the gulls wheeling overhead, the turbulent ocean roaring against the shore awakened Jack to something wild and uncivilized deep within and in one clarifying moment he was certain that he and the old man shared a mysterious destiny.

This epiphany had come to Jack on a warm day in March soon after he had secured his "coop" and settled in but by mid-April the mild air had turned cold and wet with harsh winds coming in off the ocean. Spring, Jack would learn, came in fits and starts on the South Fork, more an absentminded concept than a full blown season, where locals knew that the tease of a warm day could easily change and drive the chill of winter back into the bone. None of the blankets and outerwear he had brought from New York sufficed and the coop, even with the wood-burning stove, was freezing. Worse, the roof had sprung a few leaks. Jack pulled on his anorak and walked the quarter-mile to Amagansett's tidy, white picket fenced Main Street and the general store.

There he got little to no sympathy from one Herb Foss, the proprietor. "Yep, cold spell. Not unusual in April. Already spring I 'spect up island but we're at least a month later out here. 'Course it goes the other way in the fall. Never knew why the summer folks leave in September just when it's getting nice. You'll be needing some blankets I 'spect, how about some canvas for the windows and maybe a few buckets for the leaks?"

"Yes," Jack agreed. He looked around the store which seemed to sell just about everything – food, tools, whiskey, candy, paints of the household variety, work clothes, bait and the aforementioned blankets and buckets. Jack started carting things up to the counter. "You wouldn't know where I could get some dry firewood, would you?" he asked.

"Sure thing," said the obliging Mr. Foss. "Out back, take all you need. Load it onto the back of the pickup out there and Eddie and I will bring it around. No charge for delivery." Jack ducked out back. The wood was stacked up in a shed but Jack paid it no mind. What he saw instead was just about the most beautiful thing he had ever seen. A sleek 1924 Harley Davidson motorcycle complete with a sidecar. He had only seen one other like it when he was a boy down in Savannah and had loved it then. As he ran his hand over the handlebars and onto the soft leather of the seat, he fell in love all over again. Jack let out a low whistle.

"Yep, she's a beauty," Mr. Foss stood in the doorway to the shed wiping his hands on the long apron he wore. "In good condition too. I've had it ever since rum running days. This little gal can do better than any car on the road. Why she outran those Feds time and again. Wife won't let me take her out anymore. Too many accidents says the missus but she sure is fun."

Reluctantly Jack stepped back from the cycle. "I've wanted one of these all my life. Don't reckon she's for sale?"

Foss scratched his head. "Don't reckon she is...at least I never thought to sell her. Let me think about it. Say...how much firewood you need. Let me get my helper to load up the truck."

His "helper" was his nephew, 12-year-old Eddie Grindle.

Eddie loaded the truck and Herb, Eddie and Jack drove it around to Jack's place where Eddie and Jack unloaded while Herb scouted out the coop noting the leaks and chuckling under his breath.

For the next week Jack could think of nothing but the Harley. In his rush to leave New York, he hadn't given much thought to how he was going to get around in the country but transportation was only a secondary advantage to owning the cycle. The real reason was freedom – man alone on the road, unencumbered, open to the elements and …damn, he wanted it like he had wanted no other thing.

Jack dropped into the store just about every day to pick up a few supplies and every day he went out to have a look at the cycle and nudge Herb Foss about selling it to him. Herb chuckled and would not be nudged. Sighing, he said he couldn't part with it because someday he was going to take it out again and have himself some fun. But then again…. maybe. He'd scratch his head and shrug and then go about doing something else in the store. While this scenario was playing itself out, young Eddie Grindle and Jack struck up a sort of friendship.

Eddie was a likable kid and seemed to have a maturity that Jack envied. Here was a kid who knew what he wanted out of life – to be a fisherman like his dad. And no one disputed that notion. This was a good thing in the Amagansett community where generation after generation had produced men of the sea. Eddie, for his part found in Jack a grown up who was fun. He didn't normally have much to do with summer people but Jack was different.

"What'cher drawing," asked Eddie one late afternoon finding Jack down in the dunes with his campstool and sketch pad.

"An old, old man," Jack said, "with long scraggly white hair and tuffs of white beard." Eddie watched in admiration Jack's deft hand and the shade of grey from the charcoal pencils. He saw a tall skinny man in ragged clothes, the wind blowing his hair. Jack put a few extra flourishes on the figure to impress Eddie but even as he drew, he knew it was no more than a caricature. Nothing like the real man, the way he moved, almost as if his feet weren't touching the ground, almost as if he floated in the salt air...and then poof, like a magician he would be gone.

"You're drawing Crazy Tom," Eddie exclaimed.

"You know him?" Jack turned to Eddie.

"Sure. Everyone knows Crazy Tom."

"Is he crazy?"

"Sure is. But don't let Ma catch me saying that. We're supposed just to call him Tom. He's been out there in his shack for a long time. Forever, I guess. My dad remembers him from when he was a kid. No one knows much about him. Dad says he came up out of the sea. Ma says that's nonsense and that he's Indian. But no one really knows. Ma sends him food sometimes and once or twice he let me poke around his place. He's got some swell stuff, old things he's found on the beach from ship wrecks."

Eddie could see he had his new friend's full attention and decided to embellish his story. "Some people say he's even found Captain Kidd's treasure and that he keeps it up there in his shack buried in the sand." But when Jack asked him to take him out to the shack, even Eddie, so eager to please, knew that was off limits. Eddie knew to let Tom alone. He tried to explain this to Jack.

"No one bothers Tom. If he comes to do some work, like he might help with the baiting or mend nets, no one asks him how he is or says 'nice weather' kind of stuff. Tom don't talk unless he really, really has to. Ma says..."

But Jack hardly listened. For days afterwards he pressed the boy to take him out to where Tom's shack sat half buried in the Napeague dunes. Finally Eddie struck on the idea of bringing Jack to Ma. She would know what to do about Tom.

The Grindle family lived on Atlantic Avenue – a road leading down from the bluffs into the dunes, their house not fifty yards from the water. To Jack's eye it looked as if it had started out as one room and been added onto as needed. Outside was a chicken coop for about twenty-five chickens and a privy set back from the house over sand. There was also a fruit cellar built on the side of a knoll covered with eelgrass. Inside the cellar were shelves stacked with Eddie's mother's handiwork – glass jars filled with all kinds of fruit, jelly, jams, pickles. The fruit, Eddie said, came from his grandma's farm in Springs. There was also homemade ginger beer kept cold in the root cellar and Eddie poured Jack a drink into one of the clean Mason jars. Delicious, Jack agreed. Inside, the kitchen was the main room. Here the Grindle's cooked, dined and even, said Eddie, took their Saturday night baths in one of the three big basins set in the corner. There was no electricity but many kerosene lamps for light and a hand pump over a large sink.

"Here comes Ma," said Eddie, "and my Aunt Lottie." The two women came through the door each one talking and Jack did a double take, his mouth actually dropping open. Nettie Grindle laughed. "Newcomers always do that," she said good-naturedly. "Been happening all our lives."

The two sisters were identical twins, mirror images of each other. He turned to Eddie, "How do you tell them apart?"

Eddie shrugged. "We don't have to tell them apart. We just do what they both say and everyone stays happy." They all laughed but as Jack would observe in the coming weeks, it was true.

He would learn much about the 'Kitchin girls', as they were known to one and all, that summer but mostly about Nettie, whom he grew to love. Lottie was a pleasant woman though not given to overt friendliness. Married to Herb Foss, she had met Jack at her husband's store in Amagansett and cooked him a few breakfasts wishing him a good day as she parceled up his goods and rang up his money but she never engaged in conversation with him. Nettie, however, took a particular shine to Jack from the start.

The sisters lived in a world dominated by the traditions of men and women who lived off land and sea. Stalwart people who had fished and farmed for generations, one generation folding into the next, passing along their skills and customs and expectations – hardworking people, strong-minded and determinedly independent.

Into this unchanging mix had come these startling twins. Nettie and Lottie Kitchin – indistinguishable one from the other.

Born in the hamlet of Springs, the Kitchin girls were something of a legend amongst the locals. Maybe they had once been pretty – yes, Jack could see it – but now in their 50's with 9 children between them and the sapping toll of hard, unrelenting work, they were simply women – shop keeping women, fishermen's wives, good stocky pillars in a tiny community. Still, even in the ordinariness of their days, they evoked an aura of mystery – they were simply impossible to tell apart.

Jack marveled at their efficiency. Nettie cared for a household of six, baked cakes and muffins for Herb's store as well as one or two of the food stores in town, managed her husband's accounts and sold produce and preserves made by her mother to local restaurants and boarding houses. Lottie and Herb lived about a mile away and while Herb tended the store, Lottie, when not helping him, ran the dairy farm and grew vegetables enough for three families. This along with raising four children. Both women went regularly to their mother's farm in Springs to help there and were active in the church and social clubs. Even with all they had to do, hardly a day went by that one or other of the sisters wasn't coming through each other's door. If Nettie was baking when her sister arrived, she might stop her mixing to tend to another chore and Lottie would step up to the task knowing exactly where her sister had left off adding sugar or eggs in the exact right amount as needed and without asking. The children responded to both sisters as if there was only one authority. The twin mothers seemed to be thinking the same things at the same time and one or the other could easily pick up and finish a story in such a seamless way that the listener was hardly aware of the change in storyteller.

As alike as the two sisters were, they had married men who were entirely different. Nettie's husband, Mitch Grindle, was a fisherman and every part of him from the rough calloused hands and the raw leathered skin proclaimed his trade. Conversation was something he rarely engaged in, deferring to Nettie on almost every subject requiring more than a few words. Not so for Lottie's husband. Herb Foss was plump and pink-skinned and looked as if he had sampled too much of the enormous wheel of "rat" cheese he had sitting on his store counter. He was a jolly sort, talkative and quick with the jokes but behind those jokes was a shrewd man who never missed a penny of profit. Jack wondered if the two husbands ever got their wives confused or, more mischievously, if the ladies might have at one time snuck into each other's marital beds. But he doubted it.

Nettie handed Jack a cup of coffee and a fresh baked slice of blackberry pie and Lottie asked him how it was going at the chicken coop.

"Well," said Jack, "it would be a whole lot better if I could convince your husband to sell me that motorcycle. I don't have any way to get around and I want to explore the area – really get to know it. I've never even been to Montauk."

Lottie let out a snort. "That man is teasing you, Jack. I shouldn't be the one telling you this but he's been trying to sell that infernal machine for years and no one wants it."

"Those things are dangerous and you shouldn't want one either," continued Nettie in the same tone and then both sisters laughed. "Herb's a sly one, isn't that right."

"Yes. But you out-sly him, Jack. He'll sell fast enough." They both grinned.

The next day Jack went to the store to buy food and as he paid, Herb asked if he didn't want to have a look out back at the Harley. Jack shook his head. "You know, I figure I'm better off with a car. I heard there's one for sale over in Bridgehampton, a real bargain too. I've got a ride over there this afternoon to see it. If it's half as good as they tell me it is I'm going to buy it on the spot." Patting his coat pocket as if the money were already there Jack smiled his most carefree smile. "This time tomorrow, I'm a man with wheels."

Herb frowned. Jack picked up his goods and gave a jaunty wave as he started for the door. Herb called him back. An hour later Jack was on the telephone to his bank in New York. The beautiful black Harley was his.

Everyone in the village enjoyed the joke on Herb, who soon

enough enjoyed it on himself, and that alone seemed to open the communal door for Jack. He might be from away, he was certainly different with his sketchbooks and paints and sparse life in the chicken coop but he was embraced and no more so then by Nettie Grindle. It seemed Jack reminded her of her oldest son Jarvis who had gone out West a few years back and it was obvious that Jarvis held a special place in his mother's heart. She was always quick with advice or information for Jack when he set up his easel on the bluff overlooking the Amagansett dunes declaring he looked the image of Jarvis. He could buy eggs and fish from her and even a pie or two though she was happier when he would sit on her stoop and eat a large slice fresh out of the oven. "I declare this was Jarvis' favorite pie too," she would say approvingly.

"Where is he now?" Jack asked with a full mouth.

"Oh, lord. Last time we heard he had settled in Oregon of all places. He sells machines. Of all my children, he was the only one who just couldn't take the fishing life," she said with a sigh.

"How about you, Eddie?" Jack asked. "Have you got the wanderlust?"

Eddie shook his head vehemently. "I don't want to go away – no sir. This summer I'm old enough to go fishing with my dad and uncles and cousins...."

"Not so fast, young man," Nettie shook the big spoon she was about to stir with. "The short hauls, maybe, and only in good weather." She looked at Jack. "He's like his dad, that's for sure. Why he was born right here in this house as close as you can get to the water. The doc held him up to an open window and his first breath of air was off the ocean. I swear he was crawling in the surf before he could walk. Even now, I wake up some nights and sure enough, Eddie is out on the beach in the dark. He'd rather sleep out there than in his own bed."

"That must be why he's a friend of Tom's," Jack said.

Nettie frowned then lay the spoon down on the draining board. "Eddie's told me you want to meet Tom," she said slowly, "but I don't know. Tom is an odd bird, that's for sure. No one really knows much about him. Some say he's Indian and I reckon he is. He knows more about these parts and plants and ways to catch fish and birds than anyone. He's been on the beach ever since we was kids is all I know. I send Eddie with food from time to time but Tom doesn't want company. We leave him alone. You should too, Jack. There are some folks that should just be left to themselves and Tom is one of 'em."

Jack nodded agreeably but determined more than ever to try and capture this elusive character and to paint him – to paint the elusiveness. In his eye he pictured Tom in some sort of swirling fluid way – a figure, yes, but without definition. And that image was just as mysterious as the man himself. There, clear in his mind and then…gone, like a dream.

17

Judy Tate
Mid-June

Mondays were always a letdown for her. The weekend over and Chip gone back to the city, the week stretching ahead with little more than outings at the club and maybe a shopping foray into East Hampton, sometimes a movie. Alice had more of a social life than she did – birthday parties, swim parties, play school, arts and crafts – the four-year-old world was a swirl of activity. Judy stood on her porch looking out at the night sky. Jack's sudden reappearance in her life had been exhilarating but two weeks had gone by and he had not reappeared either to paint or to visit. The Kitchin girls, the motorcycle, the coop, the old beachcomber and Jack's exuberant telling of each story had regaled Judy all through their impromptu dinner and she found herself hoping he would call or come by almost as if she were a lovesick girl again. She could remember her big crush on her handsome, effusive cousin when Jack had first appeared in the Delany household. He had seemed larger than life then, his infectious laugh, floppy dark hair that begged to be smoothed off his forehead, lovely large dreamy eyes, and, like a movie star on the big screen, he filled a room with seductive flirtation. Even now she felt a sort of giddy rush of pleasure thinking about him. His surprise visit had seemed like a party. With Jack maybe this summer would actually be fun for her.

She could see lights on at the Hartleys ablaze as always. With a sigh, she supposed it would be another summer of parties over there and even though in the past Emmaline had sometimes included them, Chip actively hated those evenings, grumbling about the noise and the excesses and whatever else he could think to grumble about.

Still, it was nice to be invited. Nice? More like glorious. The Hartley parties were famous in their extravagance and celebrity

– Emmaline Hartley, an icon of fashion, her name peppering the columns – Judy had even seen her in the news reels gliding up the staircase at the Metropolitan Museum, a glittering beauty at New York's most exclusive ball. In summers past, Emmaline had merely acknowledged Judy and Chip as neighbors – a bit of casual conversation when they met on the beach or on the private road they shared. Once, Judy had invited Emmaline to come and see the new addition on the house and had been flattered when she did drop in one afternoon but it hadn't really been to see the room, though Emmaline had given it a cursory once over and declared it "charming." No – Emmaline had walked down her long drive and across the road to request Raleigh for the evening and Judy, at a loss and feeling embarrassed that she could deliver Raleigh like an indentured servant hither and yon, had faltered like a stammering schoolgirl. Raleigh had been a part of her family ever since she could remember. He must have been young when he first came to work for her parents but his chestnut face was now deeply lined and his hair gone to a steely grey. He was an excellent houseman and a fine cook. He had ferried Judy to and from school, to and from dancing classes, birthday parties, circuses and goodness knows what as she grew up. In that respect he was an excellent nanny as well. Yet here she was expected to dole out his time and services like some lady of the manor. Judy finally stuttered that Emmaline should ask him herself and Emmaline immediately took charge and disappeared into the kitchen where she and Raleigh spent an inordinate amount of time talking – and laughing. Apparently he was eager to oblige and duly dispatched himself that evening in a dark suit and tie complete with a chauffeur's black-billed cap. Where in the world had he got that? Raleigh often drove Judy to the shops or to various social events but never in a cap! That first request from Emmaline had opened wider the neighborly doors and intermittent invitations to the grand events at Villamere but what Judy never quite understood was that these social gestures were merely to increase Emmaline's access to Raleigh and her ultimate goal of hiring him away permanently.

She stood on the porch for another few minutes breathing in the briny ocean scent but far from invigorating, it made her sad.

She and Chip entertained rarely now. In New York he was often out with clients and seemed happiest on the evenings he was free just to come home and relax. Well, of course, he has a lot on his mind, she reminded herself, but the endless work seemed to sap his enthusiasm for everything else. Jack's ease and good humor reminded her of the Chip she had first known. The man she had stumbled on one afternoon in the Metropolitan Museum.

• • •

She was a city girl. At eighteen, Judith Anne Delany was pretty, well cared for and happy, her life one long unbroken series of flowing events – private girls schools, a tour of Europe, a presentation tea dance at the Waldorf, shopping with girlfriends, a few art, music and even cooking classes, volunteer work at whatever charity was top on her mother's list, dances and parties with boys she had known most of her life. From this carefree pool she was sure to find a mate and continue on in the unbroken chain that expected very little of her. Life circulated between the commodious apartment in the Fifth Avenue Hotel at Twelfth Street, the farm in Connecticut, the beach house on Long Island. Since graduating from the junior college she had attended overlooking the Hudson River, she had not been expected to actually get a job but she *was* required to keep busy. Which is why she went to the Metropolitan Museum as often as she could to escape her wonderful life. There was something about the venerable old museum – the cool rooms and echoing sound off the polished stone floors, the hushed voices, the enormity of the art – that made her stop having to be Judy. As if she could check herself, along with her coat, in the cloakroom and emerge free to wander through the halls as someone else…or no one at all.

From the moment she entered the gallery she was aware of him. He was looking at *her* painting – a dramatic rendering by Thomas Moran of the East Hampton beach with a storm brooding in the distance over the ocean. She watched him, watched how intently he stared at the canvas and determined right then and there to find out who he was.

"It's my favorite painting too," she said enjoying his startled look. In measured beats he looked at her, then back at the painting as if seeing it for the first time.

"I've never seen the ocean, at least not that ocean, but the sky reminds me of where I come from," he said and a pleasurable tingle ran down her spine. His voice was clear and low. They both gazed at the painting in silence.

"Where do you come from?" she finally asked.

"Iowa."

"Ah," said Judy conjuring up a mental map of the United States and trying to place Iowa on it. "Are you visiting New York?"

He looked at her thoughtfully. "No. Are you?"

She laughed. "I'm one of the very few born and bred New Yorkers you will ever meet. I've lived here all my life and spent more time in this museum than just about anyone." She continued. "I love the Met...do you?"

He smiled. "I do now."

"I live there, you know." She nodded again to the painting. "In the summer."

"On the beach?" he asked

"Well...sort of. I live in a house but the house is right next to the beach. It's out on Long Island – Bridgehampton – near East Hampton where Moran lived when he painted this. The towns are differrent but the beach is all the same. Miles and miles of it. Beautiful white sand."

"Yes," he said still looking at her. "For castle building?"

"Why yes," she laughed. "Guess I have built many a castle in that sand."

They moved along to the next painting and then another gallery and Judy found she was chatting as if he were an old friend. He was not a particularly talkative person but he was remarkably at ease and listened to what she was saying intently as if it had great relevance.

And that was how it started. They met again a few days later at the Museum of Modern Art and then planned another meeting

– and another – always at a museum or an exhibit. Once he asked her to a concert in Central Park at the band shell but it rained, so they went instead to the Natural History Museum and wandered in the darkened exhibit halls filled with the cycloramas of ancient tribes and wild animals.

He was like no other boy she had ever known. He hadn't gone to any of the Ivies for college but had worked his way through the University of Iowa, sometimes, he said, paying for his classes at the door. He was tall with brown hair and brown eyes that narrowed at the corners as if he were staring into the sun. He had a boy's face with even a few freckles but big hands that looked like they had worked out in the open, and he was lean and angular – like a cowboy out of the Wild West she said. He laughed. "You Easterners think anything beyond the Hudson River is the West. But not Iowa. Iowa is corn as far as you can see and believe me that's anything but wild."

He aspired to be a writer in a vague way or at least she thought of it as vague as he didn't want to work for a newspaper or a magazine. He didn't want assignments from editors, he said, but seemed to want only to write for himself. And to that end, he kept a journal – a small, worn, brown leather notebook. He worked for a printer on a late shift after four in the afternoon downtown somewhere in the warehouse district, not anywhere Judy had ever been. Nor had she ever known anyone who worked a "shift". It fascinated her.

His name was Chip Tate. "Why Chip," she laughed. "Chip off the old block?"

"Actually..." he paused rather dramatically, "something like that. My dad's name was Woody so it seemed natural enough I guess to call me Chip."

She found out he didn't much like talking about himself. Besides Judy did most of the talking. "I prattle," she said. "You mustn't let me go on and on." But then she would go on about her life in New York, about her schools and friends and the things she did for fun and movies she saw... and he seemed to like it. And he liked her, she could tell. That day in the rain running to shelter under a tree he had kissed her for the first time.

They met sometimes twice a week and no longer went to museums but wandered about odd neighborhoods, poking around little shops, talking to shopkeepers and street vendors. He seemed insatiably curious about the city and everything in it. They went to Little Italy and Chinatown, both places Judy had been but then they discovered a whole block of Ukrainians down a side street east of Greenwich Village where Judy bought herself a little embroidered peasant blouse which she wore when they went up to Germantown on 86th Street. They ate bratwursts with sauerkraut and both decided that sauerkraut must be an acquired taste. Once they went all the way uptown and walked across the newly opened George Washington Bridge, staring back at the startling panorama of Manhattan and river just at dusk with millions of tiny lights lighting up the skyline And that was exhilarating.

Chip asked her opinion. No other boys she knew seemed to care what she thought, or at least they never asked. She was flattered – more than that she found she had actual opinions and even some original insights, and this was a revelation to her, but all the while Judy wished he would stop his looking at things and talking to people. Now, two months after meeting him, she was aching for more than a few kisses. At home at night she would lie in her bed thinking of their bodies pressed together, imagining him naked, herself in his arms, those big hands exploring her body and then the dull throbbing deep inside her was so intense it was almost frightening.

Her mother wondered why she wasn't going out with her friends but Judy had begun to see her life through Chip's eyes and worried what he must think of a girl like her. Superficial? Privileged? She wanted to be more like him – a vagabond, a free spirit. She saw how frivolous and shallow her friends were – how narrow their world was…her world until a few short weeks ago…a world of parties and shopping sprees and no other expectations but the expectations laid down by the boundaries firmly in place for a girl of her social standing. Indeed hadn't Judy herself assumed her ultimate goal in life was to meet, marry and proceed in the same manner as her friends, changing nothing, living within a carefully prescribed life. And now here was something else, the outsider, the unknown. Here was something risky, something mysterious and just knowing him made her feel mysterious and desirable and grown up. Marvelous.

So she avoided her friends until at last her mother asked her point blank if she was seeing someone. And there it was – the rub in the whole affair. How could she tell her mother, tireless in her many charitable good works, that her only child was in love with a farm boy from Iowa who worked the night shift in a printing office? How could she face her father, who still treated her like his little girl, now that she wanted to rip her clothes off and sink into unbridled passion and desire with a boy who rambled around the city and had no proper connections and seemingly no ambition.

• • •

They got to Bridgehampton later than expected because a cow grazing on the tracks had delayed the train – something they found pleasing and rural and very funny. It was September and the village was quiet with the shops closed for the night and the only taxi driver in town, a farm woman who was not at all happy about having to drive, "All the way out there?" meaning the three miles from the village to the ocean and had to be cajoled with an extra bonus on her fee.

The house on Dune Road was dark and shuttered. Inside, dust cloths covered the furnishings – a ghost house full of echoes. She felt very small in the house, like a child again and determined to shake off the feeling – to grow larger somehow, to fill up the space and play the grown up. Dumping a bag of provisions on the large worktable in the kitchen and the overnight bag on the stairs, Judy grabbed Chip's hand leading him out the door and down the drive. "You've got to see my ocean. I can't wait another minute." At the bottom of the dune she kicked off her shoes and made him do the same before heading up a long steep sandy path edged in tall grasses. At the top, slightly panting from the climb she stretched out her arms as if showing him something she had just created herself, "Ta dah," she sang out. "Presenting... the one... the only... Atlantic Ocean!"

This was *her* ocean, the ocean in the Moran painting and now, watching his face, she knew he had never seen anything like this. The sky dipping into inky blues before the black of night, waves capped in white foam rushing up onto the pale sand of the empty beach – the ocean vast, mysterious, shimmering and gliding in eternal motion. In the sky, the first stars were beginning to shine. "I feel like we're the only two people on earth," Chip said, his voice low and Judy tucked herself in the crook of his arm. "Maybe we are," she whispered.

"Come on," he said. "Let's go down to the water. Let's walk this beach of yours." They half slid down the dune to the flat sand and ran in and out of the waves shouting like mad people knowing no one could hear them.

Soon enough the chill autumn air sent them back to the house where Judy lit candles and Chip fiddled with the flue in the chimney for a fire. Judy set out the picnic she had brought, pleased with its frugality – a large wedge of cheese, bread, apples and a big bag of chestnuts from a vendor outside of Penn Station.

She knew he had been against this idea of hers from the start but she had refused to let him talk her out of it. Chip had some deep-seated idea that what they were doing was wrong – wrong because he knew without having to be told, that the whole notion of them as a match would be considered unsuitable by her parents. Still, he could not believe his good fortune that this golden haired, beautiful, doll-like girl had come into his life. He had not known how lonely life could be in the big city. For someone barely out of college and on his own, with no introductions, a job that kept him working evenings, no concrete ambition and certainly no money after the rent and food, he was sinking into near despair. That day, the day in the museum, he had been wandering about trying to focus on the paintings when this image of an ocean caught his attention. It occurred to him that he had never seen the ocean, not like this, and the more he looked at it, the more it seemed to draw him in – and then there she was, *It's my favorite painting, too.*

Now as he watched Judy move around the room so sure of herself, and that vast and awesome ocean just outside, Chip dared not think about how and why it had all happened – only that it had. Maybe he should stop worrying about right or wrong. Maybe just for tonight they *were* the only two people on earth.

"I love this house," he said giving the doorframe a few hearty whacks and stomping his foot in the hallway. "It's so solid. Built to last. I expected something on stilts leaning into the wind." He gave the frame another appreciative once over. Judy could have told him all about the house, about her grandparents who had built it and that yes, it was solid because they were solid and stern people for whom she had always had to be on her best behavior. The house would be hers one day, she told him. "My parents prefer the farm in Connecticut though they open the beach house each summer only to spend as little time here as they can. They do it for me, I guess, because I love it. Someday when the house is mine I'm going to make it bigger, prettier ... more like a summerhouse. It's awfully stuffy now, don't you think? Just like the grandparents." She rolled her eyes teasingly indicating how unstuffy she was but Chip was still inspecting the sturdy staircase with admiration. "You can feel when a house is well-built... strong," he slapped the newel post with satisfaction and Judy quickly poured the wine to distract him. She wanted to talk about love and be loved. Why else had she lured him out here? Certainly not to talk about the nuts and bolts of a house.

But soon enough the wine and warmth of the fire, the soft cushions of the sofa, and the steady roll of the ocean outside lulled them into a contented sleep, her head tucked between his shoulder and chin, her legs wrapped around his. She awoke from time to time to feel his breath brush her cheek, to feel his heartbeat. His skin smelled of the chestnuts they had roasted in the fire. As morning edged the curtains, he began to stir holding her even closer. Still half asleep she unbuttoned his shirt and laid her face against the soft hair curling across his chest and stroked it.

"I'm going to tie you to me with a silk ribbon and then you won't ever be able to leave me. Not ever." She could feel his grin. "So I'm the leaving one am I? I thought that was what you rich New York girls were good at. Not us poor farm boys from Podunk." He tilted her chin up so that his face was very close to hers and started to say something else but instead pulled her to him and kissed her in a long, deep kiss so that Judy felt herself falling into a gulf of pleasure. His hands reached down and caressed her small breasts, one then the other, until she moaned as if in real pain. "Please...please don't stop," she begged, and he didn't.

Dragging a comb through her hair in front of the bathroom mirror, she was immensely pleased with the woman she saw in the glass grinning back at her. "She knows," Judy said, tapping the comb at the reflection. "She knows what I've been up to and she approves. At least I think she does." She put her face up close to the mirror. "You approve don't you?" Judy nodded. "You see, Chip. My friend and I are in complete agreement here." He sat in the bath, knees up, whistling. "Ask your friend if she'll come over here and scrub my back." And Judy laughed, kneeling down and lathering up the bath mitt with the only soap she had been able to find – a big bar of kitchen soap left on the drain which smelled surprisingly good, natural and clean.

The September day was sunny and sharp, a light breeze off the ocean when they set out on two big black bikes to find some breakfast. Judy thought the grocery store in town might give them coffee and rolls and she was right. Mrs. Dawson greeted Judy with a pleasant enough smile, eyeing Chip with a little lift of the eyebrow. "What brings you out here this time of year? I thought you folks closed up the house over Labor Day?" "Oh we did," said Judy, "I just wanted to show my friend the Atlantic Ocean." Then she leaned over the counter in a stage whisper, "He's from out west – he's a cowboy and he's never seen an ocean before, only cactus and tumbleweed."

Mrs. Dawson looked mildly interested. "Then I best make you a picnic. Never seen the ocean, indeed. No use wasting your time in a store when you can spend a day like this on the beach."

Biking with the picnic in the front baskets, they left the store heading to the opposite side of Mecox Bay – the other side of the "gut", Judy instructed, where the ocean met the bay through a narrow passage. Leaving the bikes sprawled in the dunes they wandered up and down the beach hopping in and out of the small waves, not saying much, not wanting to say much. They ate and lay in the sun snoozing and then tussled a bit in the sand, until Judy reckoned it was about two in the afternoon and time to start the long ride back. Judy saw it before Chip did and stopped her bike so suddenly it was as if she had hit a wall – which in many ways she had. There in the driveway of the house was her father's car and there standing on the porch was her father.

Chip slowly got off the bicycle and looked first at the man and then back to Judy. Her face told him everything. He reached over and took her hand giving it a small squeeze, then like a man being lead to the gallows, he walked with her up the drive.

• • •

It began, perhaps from that very moment as they turned to walk towards her father, the transformation of Chip Tate from "volunteer" transplant from Iowa to hedgerow establishment on the South Fork. And like so many things that go wrong in life, it had all started so right.

Thinking back on it now, her marriage almost seven years old, their beautiful daughter asleep upstairs, it seemed ludicrous how dreadful they had felt. Her father didn't bellow, he didn't even look angry but he was clearly upset. Oh yes, there had been the stern talk after the silent drive back into New York. And yes there had been the dissolve of her mother's stoic face into tears and the rushing from the room sobbing on Judy's part and even, she could recall, a few slamming of doors. She loved him, she said, and she would never give him up. "You're hoping I'll forget about him. But I won't. I won't. I love him and if you can't understand and trust my deepest feelings then... then we will elope!" And *that* had been the moment of the slamming door.

For Chip, there was the ill-fitting suit hastily bought from a second hand store and the quiet talk with her father at his club. Bill Delany was clearly playing his hand as a man of reason. Chip apparently played his well enough to be invited to dinner to meet Judy's mother. This was a formal affair at the apartment with Raleigh serving the chicken almandine to an alarmed Chip who had no idea of how to manage the curved silver serving utensils as the sauce dripped over the white damask tablecloth.

If the senior Delanys had hoped that their non-resistance to Chip might diffuse the relationship, they were wrong. Judy accelerated. When they realized that she was more infatuated with him than ever, they began to seek out Chip's better qualities. Responsible. Polite. Respectful. They could see the more they got to know him that Chip was certainly not a bad fellow and soon acknowledged to each other in private that he had distinct qualities. "Nothing wrong with solid American values," declared Judy's father. "A diamond in the rough," agreed her mother.

In due time it was settled, Chip and Judy would marry the following spring. It would not be a big wedding given the somber times and the fact that Chip had no family that could make the trip east. They offered a wedding trip to Bermuda but both Judy and Chip preferred to spend their honeymoon at the beach house. Chip was given a job in her father's ad agency. Her cousin Jack Burns, sophisticated in ways of dress and manner, was enlisted to befriend Chip and advise him on proper day wear for the office and evening wear for the many parties now planned. Judy's girl-friends were wild about this lanky newcomer and fell under the spell of Chip's "western" roots as a romantic ideal. No one knew exactly where Iowa was but wasn't it more or less out there near Wyoming, a place they had all heard of via the movies where tall, lean men in tight Levis, leather boots and sweat brimmed hats walked the boardwalks and took their drink in saloons.

Even Chip found it easier to play along with the image if for no other reason than it allowed him to be the archetypical silent type. In silence he was able to watch and learn from this effortless effervescent world of Judy's, untouched, it seemed, by the harsher realities that faced most people – people born outside the magical circle of privilege, people by the thousands in the deepening gloom of the Depression for whom there were no celebrations but only hardscrabble, bushwhacking days. Judy and her cohorts suffered none of these things. Oh yes – there had been cutbacks and tightened belts but on the surface, life skimmed along with only minor inconveniences.

Judy was in her element. She had found him, plucked him out of the din and cacophony of New York and now she was remaking him into the very image of that which she had so recently disdained. As for Chip, he watched and imitated her. He learned that this was the way you spoke to the doorman, to a waiter; this was how you talked to older people and these were the jokes you laughed at with your peers. These were the forks you used for the fish course, for salad, for the main entree. This was the gift you brought for a weekend party, for a dinner party. He wanted to know these things and he asked her questions and sought her advice. Judy was charmed by his curiosity, by his eagerness to fit in and Chip vowed he would do everything in his power, and more, to make her happy.

Happiness it seemed belonged in great part to his success at the newly attained position at Delany, Osborne and Fox Associates. The agency inhabited two floors on Madison Avenue and 36th Street where every morning Chip arrived at 9 a.m., and was greeted by his secretary.

"Good morning, Mr. Tate," said Miss Stanley handing him a typed sheet on which were the day's activities and his appointments along with a cup of strong black coffee.

"Good morning, Miss Stanley," said Chip taking the cup from her, along with the schedule, as he disappeared into his small, bright office.

The day was now launched. "Get to know the business," Judy's father had said expansively. "See where you best fit in." And so he had. Now five months later, the wedding only a few weeks off, Judy and her mother inundated in wedding showers and trousseau matters, a tiny townhouse in the West Village secured with an advance against his salary as down payment, and still Chip had not stumbled upon one concrete or even vague "fit" within the walls of Delany, Osborne and Fox.

The truth of the matter was that Chip didn't really *approve* of advertising. Wasn't the act of persuading the customer to buy the product only a brief cut above the traveling salesman his father had been? Always on the go, moving town to town, his sample suitcase in hand, his quick smile and slick patter. It was the stuff of smutty jokes and his father had lived up to every tawdry cliché about the traveling salesman. Drinking, gambling, womanizing…. fleabag hotels, greasy diners and quick getaways when he had to. Now sitting high on Madison Avenue, Chip had apparently entered into the same slippery trade; only here it was coated in respectability, in hushed carpeted offices and attentive secretaries. Lunches took place in wood paneled mens clubs or fashionable restaurants. The client was treated as a prince among men, the ad campaign a hallowed testimonial to the fine art of salesmanship. And wasn't it all a grand and unknowable mystery, said these stylish hucksters – the art of the deal, the psychology of persuasion, brand loyalty – these respectable, near patriotic words did little to cover in Chip's mind the nagging certainty that this advertising rose by any other name was essentially the same old snake oil of his youth.

A stack of successful past advertising campaigns were on his desk and day after day Chip sorted through them wondering what exactly made one ad a success while others failed. On his desk were the specs on the car Delany, Osborne and Fox were to champion. It was a sporty low-slung coupé better suited to the carefree flappers and dandies of the 20s, entirely impractical for these sober times. Most car ads touted safety features and shock absorbers and economy factors. Indeed, he had in hand one of Delany, Osborne and Fox's old ads for a Ford coupé. In it, the lady of the house sat in the back seat of the automobile while her husband and a small boy sat up front. *All the comforts of home*, said the caption and then it went on, in detail, about the shatter-proof glass and advanced braking system. If Judy were reading this, he grinned, she would stop right there and turn the page. Chip sat back at his desk and thought about it. Women were the primary consumers in America and though they might not write the checks for the big-ticket items like cars and houses, they were the ones the advertisers catered to. This sports coupé was not bad looking but the sketch of it from the art department had it lying flat on the page, inert, as if in a showroom. Chip was no artist but he had an idea and sketched it out. Then he scribbled some words down on a pad, crossed them out, and scribbled some more.

The next day he invited Jack Burns for lunch and showed him the sketch and his copy. Jack laughed out loud. "If you don't mind me saying old man, this is a wild idea. You could use a few drawing lessons though."

Chip nodded smiling. "I thought you might say that. How about mocking it up for me – a wedding present from my soon to be Cousin Jack."

A few days after that, armed with Jack's drawing and a paste-up of the copy, Chip presented his brainchild to the partners. The ad was passed from Osborne to Fox and then to Mr. Delany. Silence. Chip felt the first inkling of doubt. The ad which only minutes ago had seemed so modern and bold was now beginning to seem tawdry and naive. He began to perspire. His soon to be father-in-law put the ad down on the conference table and leaned back in his chair, his eyes half closed. The silence grew. Then he sat forward and laughed. "Son, this will either kill that car for good or sell it like no other. I think you've hit on something."

Two months later, Chip and Judy just back from their honeymoon, the ad ran full page in *The Woman's Home Companion*, *Life* and *Colliers*. It pictured a car bursting head on from the page, a young woman at the wheel alone, her hair flying in the wind against a backdrop of a distant mountain range and a long, lonesome road. The copy began: *Somewhere West of Laramie there's a lass whose face is brown with the sun. Both wild and tame, she rides the land of real living into the red horizon of a Wyoming twilight.* No detail whatsoever about the car, no mention of safety or comfort or economy or of anything practical. Only sweeping prose at the heart of which was a restless, independent young woman speeding through the untamed western landscape.

Within weeks car sales had shot through the roof, and Chip Tate, newly wed, beautifully groomed, and armed with his first professional success, had arrived.

18

Wilma and Celia
East Hampton Village

Dressed to the nines and tugging at the boy's hand, Celia Slade strode purposefully along the shaded sidewalk toward the shops on Main Street. Wilma had deposited young Lewis on her doorstep "just for an hour, Celia," she had pleaded rushing off on some Ladies Improvement tree business none of which Celia ever understood. Indeed Wilma and her trees were the source of some friction between the two friends if only because Wilma could never quite grasp how very boring it was to Celia to have to hear about ailing elms or the finer points of planting saplings. Take for instance today – a lovely June day just begging for fun. And where better than the club for afternoon tea. Oh, how Celia loved the club – the striped cabanas on the beach, the terrace overlooking the ocean, impeccably set with white cloths and gay umbrellas – the summer crowd beautifully turned out, and wasn't afternoon tea such a genteel pastime. The season was now in full gear and Celia in a smart new dress was taking Wilma as her guest. Then came Wilma breathless about some dreary old Sycamore that had to be cut down "I simply have to be there, Celia. I can't risk the men cutting the wrong tree." Depositing Lewis without further ado, Wilma had rushed out leaving Lewis in his starched new sailor suit. And then, damn it, Celia discovered her new lipstick carelessly left on the windowsill had melted in the sun into a greasy mess.

Celia fumed. It seems that's all she did these days was fume. At her husband, at her children, and now here she was fuming at her oldest and dearest friend. She had half a mind to tear off the new dress and throw it in the trash bin but then she caught a glimpse of Lewis staring up at her.

"You look nice, Cilly," he said. She turned and looked in the hall mirror. She did look nice. She simply would not let this day turn into the same mess as her lipstick.

"OK, sport," she said peering down on the small boy. "We've got an emergency. I'll leave a note for your mother to meet us at the drugstore." Lewis looked up eagerly. "A real emergency? Like in the movies? Like with firemen?"

"That's right, kiddo. But we don't need to call out the big wigs just yet. I think we can handle this ourselves." She peered again into the mirror settling a small brimmed hat over her carefully marcelled curls then put on her gloves. Her lips looked pale and pasty without the gloss. She frowned. "Ready?" She bit her lips to make them rosy.

Lewis also pulled on his hat, an English sailor cap complete with black ribbon bow. He stood ramrod straight and saluted. "Ready," he piped.

Celia laughed. She wasn't all that fond of children but she liked Lewis because he was after all her godson and Wilma's child but mostly she liked him because he was a weird little boy. Not like her own son, high school football star, president of his class, young man on the go and just like his father. And her fourteen-year-old daughter growing more beautiful every day. She could feel the crease between her eyes deepen. She mustn't. Not today.

Like every "up streeter," as the village elete were called, Celia would not dream of walking the three blocks to the shops in the village without being impeccably dressed and coiffed. Nor did she use the term 'up streeter' preferring the much more sophisticated 'year rounder' implying as it did that she had come from another place. Celia worked very hard at dispelling any notion that she was a hometown girl. Now that the summer season had started, (she loved the term 'summer season') much more effort must go into appearances. The shedding of heavy wool, the bright summer dresses and graceful hats spelled the perfect time of year for her. East Hampton in the winter might as well be Siberia. Remote, cold, dreary and, as she had so often said, you could fire a cannon down Main Street and no one would hear it. But summer was at long last here and with it the people, the real people, the fun loving people and all that they represented.

As they neared the drugstore, she heard a loud blast from a car horn and turning with irritation she saw Harry waving to her from his car. "Hey, toots, " he shouted leaning once more on the claxon horn. "Where'd ya get that hat?" Celia stiffened in horror.

"Is that a bonacker, Cilly?" Lewis said in an awed whisper. "Is it? A bonacker?"

"No darling," she gripped his hand tighter, "it's a buffoon."

The object of the child's amazement was not, however, Celia's husband cruising down the street but a rumpled, unshaven, crotchety codger unfastening the back of his truck right there on Main Street and spreading an oil cloth over the rusted truck bed which held two large tubs filled with live eels.

The man busied himself, pausing to spit, oblivious to any notion of sidewalk courtesy and Celia now directed her attention to the unfolding scene. "Shush, kiddo," she said yet she could see the old fella's eyes flickering towards them. Had he heard? Bonacker was not a nice moniker in East Hampton. It meant lazy, scruffy, poor and was freely applied to the people living out in the Springs, a hardscrabble part of town about four miles from the village towards the bay. Nice people did not use that term, nor did they allow their children to, but Celia was so angry with Harry she nodded with a nasty gleam in her eye. "Sure is," she whispered, "that's a bonacker all right. In fact I would say Old Man Burl is a bonacker with a capital B." Her eyes narrowed as she watched the man who was clearly enjoying her distain. There were those in town who thought of Burl as a colorful character, someone to be chuckled over as if he lent a sort of 'old salt' tone to the everyday life of the town. But not Celia. She thought Burl and his kind were a disgrace to the decorum of the village and an insult to the likes of ladies such as herself who were assaulted by the sight, sound and smell of him. Burl was a fixture on Main Street from Memorial Day to Labor Day – his eels, his truck and his unbridled distain of the summer folks was legendary folklore in the town.

The division between East Hampton Village and the Springs was well defined. The railroad trestle on the north end of town set the dividing line. Whereas the village was "up street" the hamlet of Springs was "below the bridge" – a local euphemism for the other side of the tracks. Springs was made up of many folks who like Burl eked out their living – digging clams, harvesting hay on the salt marshes around Accabonac Creek and getting by as best they could given the rocky soil and near treeless landscape. There was a fish factory up there that could give one quite a turn if the wind wasn't right and a smattering of small dairy farms but not much else.

Cursing a blue streak, Old Man Burl now jerked open one of two big tubs from in back of the truck and reached inside to lift out a live eel. Celia tugged at Lewis' hand but the boy seemed frozen to the spot, watching intently as the man neatly chopped off the eel's head and began to skin it, still squirming. The sight was repugnant yet Lewis was mesmerized. In all of his six, soon to be seven years he had never witnessed such a sight. Not ever. Not even when the carnival came to town with its fat lady and sword swallower. Not even...but Lewis couldn't think of another not even. People were now gathering around the truck. The eels were a big seller and Burl began his work skinning and chopping the flesh into two inch "steaks" for the housewives and cooks who were eager to buy.

"Eel rolled in flour and then fried," said a woman in cosy comraderie to Celia, "is the best tasting fish on the South Fork." And Celia froze as if she had been hurled an insult of monumental proportions. How dare this woman address her as if she was a common housewife?

Celia finally got hold of herself. "It's not nice to say bonacker, Lewis," she said perfunctorily as if only he and not she had uttered the derogatory term, and with that she ushered him into White's Drugstore. "We won't mention it to your mother. Now be a darling and go have yourself a treat. What about a nice ice cream while Cilly is over here by the ladies counter?"

She strolled away as if they had signed a pact and Lewis looked doubtfully at the tall round stools at the soda fountain. Once when he was being babysat he had been there with Grace, the sitter, and Robbie, Grace's boyfriend and the soda jerk at White's, had made them each a banana split with three different flavors of ice cream and chocolate syrup and cherries. Lewis ate and ate but there was so much of it he finally felt sick. Then he threw up all over the counter and Grace said she felt sick too because Lewis had just eaten a tuna sandwich at home and now the tuna and the chocolate, the bananas and the cherries from his tummy were all over his front and in the banana split bowl and on the counter. Then Mr. White had come out from behind where he fixed people's pills and shouted at Robbie, "You never give a kid the big split. That's why we have the junior split." And then Grace started to cry and now his mother wouldn't let anyone take him to the soda fountain at White's or any other place.

But he supposed it was all right now since Auntie Cilly was in charge. She wasn't really his auntie and she didn't like being called that so they had agreed on Cilly. A few minutes later he was back outside, a large chocolate cone in hand inching forward for a better view of Old Man Burl and his eels.

Wilma could not believe her eyes when she arrived a half hour later. Lewis, his sailor suit covered in chocolate drips, was sitting on the back of the old man's truck and Celia nowhere to be found. People gathered around seemed to find the scene very amusing – the repugnant old man and the skinny little kid in his sailor suit. "Eels rolled in flour and fried is the best tasting dish on the South Fork," Lewis piped out as if a shill and on cue Burl chopped off another head. They were quite a team. Wilma edged into the scene, nodding to Burl and lifting Lewis off the truck. "I think you've taken up quite enough of Mr. Burl's time, Lewis…" *Why if his father saw this…?* The thought of Jim passing by with his briefcase in hand seeing his son…she shuttered. And where was Celia? Really this had gone too far even for irresponsible Celia who just at that moment came out of White's. She smiled waving her hand as if nothing was amiss. "There you are at last," she said, mildly chiding her friend. "We'd almost given you up for lost. Look Wilma," she pointed to her newly glossed lips, "Bougainvillea Red."

• • •

They had been friends ever since the cradle. Celia's father, Dr. Dowling, the much beloved Dr. Dowling was the primary doctor in town. Wilma's father was the Superintendent of Schools. Dr. Dowling was short and rather plump. Superintendent Harding was tall and stern. The two men were friends, sharing a love of rare books and a keen interest in birding. So too, their wives – both members of the Ladies Village Improvement Society, that pinnacle of local good works. The girls, born within months of each other had little choice but to be best friends too.

And they were. Wilma, the more practical of the two was a studious girl who had grown into a thoughtful woman. Brown was the color that came to mind when conjuring up a picture of Wilma – brown hair and eyes, brown Oxford shoes, brown winter coat, brown cloche hat. She was slim and tall and academic. Celia, with her curly gold hair and plump figure in all the right places, was the popular one. She was full of laughter and mischief and everyone loved her.

It was Celia who initiated Wilma into the delights of sneaking out of a summer night, and how to "borrow" a rowboat so they could drift on Hook Pond with cigarettes and a mason jar of watered-down whiskey lifted off of Dr. Dowling's sideboard. There, in the middle of the pond, a million stars overhead they would dream their lives. Wilma would lie back in the boat, her sweater bunched up like a pillow and watch the spectacle of the universe overhead while Celia, perched in the bow, closed her eyes and conjured up scenes of dashing men, always in fancy dress on trans-Atlantic liners, gowns of gossamer silk and dancing – yes, always dancing said Celia.

Wilma was not entirely immune to the charms of these imagined delights but in the light of day it was she who took hold of the practical reins. Wilma taught Celia how to drive. Wilma had been driving since she was fourteen when her mother suffered a stroke and had to be driven everywhere.

Celia was Prom Queen their senior year but Wilma won the recitation prize for her heartfelt rendition of Portia's speech from The Merchant of Venice. It was remarked that old Judge Brooks, florid of face and always a trusty flask in his hip pocket had openly wept when Wilma began "The quality of mercy is not strained..."

Wilma, practical and organized, enrolled in a secretarial school up the island and upon graduating returned to East Hampton and went to work for Dr. Dowling. Celia attended a girl's finishing school in Connecticut and returned home two years later with a diamond ring and a beau some five years her senior. A big, back-slapping fellow named Harry Slade who had gone to Yale and was now in "sales". The wedding reception was a large and dignified affair at the Maidstone Club. Few local families joined the exclusive summer club but Celia had insisted that her father do so. She was like that – always reaching for more, sure that something better was just around the bend. Celia and Harry settled in Cleveland where Harry had "irons in the fire".

As much as Celia had wanted to leave East Hampton, Wilma wanted to stay. Fall was her favorite time of year. The air fresh and sharp, the beaches empty, and after a blaze of golden color, the giant elms on Main Street shed their leaves to reveal an extraordinary network of branches overhead – so majestic and sharply defined, they were to her magnificent art works patterned against the sky and Wilma often felt a real sadness to see green buds again in the spring. Often, on winter afternoons, the sky sinking into a deep electric blue, she would walk home from Dr. Dowling's office, down Main Street, past the old cemetery where the earliest town settlers lay, the etched names and dates so softened by time and weather that they were mostly unreadable. She walked past the red brick Clinton Academy, the first school on Long Island, and past the few remaining cedar saltbox houses, the architectural design of choice by 17th century homeowners. These were the things she loved about East Hampton – the oldness, the long reach of history and the people who had lived that history still here in the form of tombstones and houses, windmills and place names, ghosts of the past. In these walks, Wilma watched the stars come out through the dramatic reach of those webbed elm tree branches over head, reaching to the heavens and forming a sheltering protection to the young woman who loved them.

Wilma also loved her job. She loved running a doctor's office, greeting patients, sympathizing with the aches of the elderly, handing out lollipops to children in for their shots. She loved the occasional dramas and the challenging demands that injury and illness provoked.

She would never forget that one spring, a Sunday afternoon, when most people were at home snoozing off the big Sunday dinner. Wilma was in the office helping Dr. Dowling with a shipment of supplies that had been delivered late on Saturday and Dr. Dowling was reading his medical journals. As they worked in the quiet afternoon, she glanced out the window to see three local kids out for a lark on a warm day in May. They were pushing and shoving each other the ways boys did and tossing a ball back and forth.

An hour later she and the doctor were both startled by a pounding at the door and the stationmaster standing there in a lather. "Doc, doc...you gotta come. There's been an accident up at the icehouse. I got my car... ."

Dr. Dowling grabbed the black bag Wilma always had ready for him and with Wilma right behind, they rushed out and headed for the station. On the other side of the tracks was the Peconic Ice building and a deep water pool filled with the discharge of wastewater from melting ice. A large exposed drainpipe led from the building to the middle of the pool. Seems the trio of boys had decided to cool off on this warm day and go swimming. One of them, Billy Ryder, had walked out on the discharge pipe to the middle intending to dive in. It was slippery with algae and he had slipped, knocked his head on the pipe and fallen in the water unconscious. The other boys had tried to fish him out but the water was cold and murky and they panicked and ran for the station. By the time Dr. Dowling got there some men had found and pulled Billy onto the grass. Dr. Dowling worked over him for 20 minutes but it was no use. The boy had drowned. The doctor finally leaned back on his heels and shook his head.

The whole town turned out for the funeral held at the large, white Presbyterian Church on Main Street. Here was the church of the founding fathers of East Hampton – stern, unyielding orators on the evils of wasted life. And now here was little Billy Ryder, himself and his family descendants of those first families, a life cut short, about to be laid to rest in the old South burying ground with all his people who had gone before him.

The minister stood before the coffin in silence before speaking. "We are a community of loving people. We come together today in silence and in sorrow but we are bonded together. Together we will shoulder this tragedy – and together we will find the way to lift our hearts again."

How she loved her town then as they held themselves as one in the sorrow of the lost child.

Years passed. She joined The Ladies Village Improvement Society and took up the preservation of the village trees with a passion, reading books, attending lectures and on her holidays toured nearby parks and gardens. She helped document the trees, making note of their health and well-being yet it was the Dutch elm that earned her true love. The 18th century townspeople had loved them for the dense shade and had planted an entire avenue of the trees down the main avenue so that now these very same trees some 200 years later had grown to immense proportions, their branches reaching across the wide expanse of the street, once a common ground for livestock, now a gracious boulevard. In summer, upon entering the town, the arch of the trees in full leaf formed a dramatic tunnel. It was a marvel to behold and the entire town was justifiably proud.

Everyone said Wilma ought to get married before it was too late but she had no notion of how to go about this. Now in her thirties, there were few eligible men in town. Celia, meanwhile, produced two children, a boy then a girl, and declared herself "through" with all of that. It seemed the Slade fortunes were riding high in Cleveland or at least it looked that way whenever Celia came back for a visit decked out in fur coats and sparkling jewelry always driving some sporty little car that Harry had insisted she have. The hustle of Cleveland suited her like no small town could, of that she assured everyone. Yet as different as Celia and Wilma's lives were, there was never a moment in which the friendship faltered. They simply took up where they had left off and would go to the drugstore and sit at the soda counter as if they were high school girls again.

"Wilma, we have to find a husband for you," Celia always said as if finding a husband were a matter of buying a new hat. But who? Celia's theory was that no husband of any merit could be had in East Hampton. Words like provincial, backwater and Podunk littered her lament over Wilma's plight. She begged Wilma to come to Cleveland where Celia had dozens of likely prospects in mind, but Wilma always sidestepped the notion by promising to come for sure "later on".

Then one day Jim Palmer moved to East Hampton from Connecticut to work with old Mr. Day who was getting on in years and needed a partner in his insurance business. Jim wore somber suits and carried an important looking brief case but she was not opposed to going out with him. Movies, dances at the Odd Fellows Hall, bowling, picnics and driving – these were the past-times available to them. Wilma had her own car and she drove him about, showing him all the places she loved – the old whaling village of Sag Harbor, the rich farmlands in Bridgehampton where the potato fields stretched right to the edge of the ocean dunes, the wildness of Northwest Woods and day trips to Montauk to see the historic lighthouse. Once they had got stuck in the sand when she had taken him to see the Walking Dunes in Napeague, so called for the constant shifting of sand that covered, then uncovered, a ghost-forest underneath. Getting stuck in the sand was not new to Wilma and she knew just how to gather tall beach grasses and place them under the wheels. Jim admired her ingenuity and after much shoveling and placing of grass and rocking the car back and forth, they were suddenly released of this trap and Jim, delighted in their success, kissed her right then and there in broad daylight. Some months later, when Jim succeeded Mr. Day as full partner and chief operating officer, she brought a bottle of wine and a hamper of cheese and fruit when the new business sign went up on Newtown Lane – Palmer and Day Insurance. That evening, to celebrate, Jim took Wilma to dinner at an inn, the rough hewn rafters romantically lit in candlelight and, after much clearing of throat, running his finger around his collar and adjusting his tie, Jim proposed. And Wilma said "yes". She was thirty-five-years-old.

Then came that shocking October day in 1929 – the day Wall Street crashed and millions were plunged into financial ruin. And just as suddenly, Celia and Harry were back in East Hampton and living with her father. Harry never missed a beat in his trademark backslapping, hail-fellow routine assuring everyone who cared to listen, and the many who didn't, that "It's only a minor setback, the market is readjusting. It'll be back sooner than you think." But Harry was wrong.

Wilma was thirty-seven years old when Lewis was born – old for giving birth for the first time. "Geriatric mother" read the chart at the foot of her bed at Southampton Hospital, infuriating Celia as she and Wilma were exactly the same age. But it made Wilma laugh. Who in the world could care about a thing like that? Nothing could mar the exhilaration she felt when she looked down on her baby – the most beautiful little boy in the world.

The Depression deepened. Jim was working round the clock to keep his business together and Harry traveled quite a bit, heading out for weeks at a time on some new and brilliant idea of his, returning with all sorts of promises about deals that never seemed to materialize. Dr. Dowling, a widower for many years, deeded the main house to Celia and moved into a small carriage house on the property. After much lobbying on the part of Wilma, Celia, who had held herself aloft of the local social scene, joined the Ladies Village Improvement Society where she excelled at planning the annual summer fete.

19

Walter Penn
East Hampton Village

Jack glanced around the lobby of Edwards Movie Theater watching the big ladle in the popcorn machine lift up, swing around and pour hot butter on the popped corn. He was like a kid watching that mechanical arm. Every since he had arrived back in March, he had been making the pilgrimage from Amagansett to East Hampton Village to Edwards on a regular basis. Tonight's show, *Jezebel* starring Bette Davis, was one he had seen but no matter. Standing next to him also watching the big ladle was a tall, distinguished man, a man Jack recognized in an instant. Walter Penn. Walter Penn in the lobby of Edwards Movie Theater was about as incongruous as if Bette herself had appeared. Penn was one of three top international authorities on contemporary European art and noted for bringing the works of Vincent Van Gogh to New York in the early 1930s in a show passionately scrutinized by every young artist at the Art Students League and none more passionately than Jack. No artist in America could ignore what his European counterparts were doing and no art before had landed with the force of the Van Gogh show. At least that's how Jack saw it. And now, here was Jack's hero and legendary icon of the art world himself about to buy a bag of popcorn.

"Walter? Walter Penn?" The man turned and from the blank expression Jack knew he could not possibly remember the evening he had spent in his townhouse in Murray Hill with a half dozen fellows from the League many years ago. It was his teacher, Guy Dambrose, who had arranged the evening, meant to be a dignified exchange between young art students and the old guard, yet it had been nothing of the sort. Penn was no lover of young, scruffy artists and had been openly appalled by the argumentative freeloading students jostling for attention with high-minded views while taking full liberties at his bar.

Jack extended his hand.

Walter Penn studied him for a moment and then slowly put out his own hand. "Remind me," he said curtly.

"We met a few years back through my friend Guy Dambrose. Guy and I had drinks a few weeks ago. He came to my studio to look at my work." Jack fell easily into his fabrication. Penn shook his head. "Forgive me. I meet so many people in the city," he paused, clearly wishing to disengage. "What brings you to East Hampton?" He asked with little interest.

"I needed to get out of the city for a while. Clear the air," Jack said expansively. "Too many distractions there. No place to think."

"Are you thinking out here?"

"Well. Trying to. Intending to is probably nearer the truth. I have a little place over in Amagansett. I have my paints, pads and pencils and I have my ideas. But," and here he drew in a big breath, "it's not easy to find your muse." He laughed.

The older man gave a brusque nod. Here was a brash young man, who seemed to think very well of himself, hardly what Walter had in mind when he strolled up Main Street intent on seeing a movie. He made a motion to enter the theater.

"Well, good luck to you. I hope you find your muse. And now I think Bette Davis calls."

"Indeed," said Jack, eager to prolong the conversation. "She's one of my favorites. This is one of her best."

"You've seen it?" Walter asked.

"Yes." Jack shrugged sheepishly. "I really do get restless in the evenings. It takes place in the south – where I'm from. The movie is good, but I could have coached them all on their accents."

Walter relented. "I thought I detected a bit of the south there. Where are you from?"

"Savannah."

"Ah. Certainly one of our finer cities. I haven't been that way in years but I remember it well. Beautiful place. Don't worry, you'll adjust to the East End soon enough. Most artists do, especially if you love the ocean and appreciate the famous light. Do you paint landscapes?"

"No... figures are more my style but I'm trying to work with this light. And so, yes, I guess I am painting the landscape. Or some version of it." Jack laughed again. "Fact is I'm not sure what I'm doing."

Walter paid for his popcorn. "Oddly enough, that's often the best way to arrive at something." They had entered the theater together and now it seemed only right that they sit together. After the show stepping out onto Main Street Walter asked, "How was the second viewing?"

"About like the first. Hollywood should really take a little trip down to the land of dueling oaks and Spanish moss. They make so many movies about the south it might do them good to get off the back lot and actually see it." He looked around the quiet street. "I see this little village is shut for the night but I hear there is quite a bar scene over at the hotel. Would you ...?"

"No." Walter said quickly and firmly. "I, for one, like the quiet." He looked up at the sky and then back at Jack as if weighing something on his mind. "It's a beautiful evening. I live down by the pond if you'd care to come back there for a drink?"

Jack eagerly fell into step and they strolled down Main Street without talking, Walter clearly preferring to listen to the night sounds. Jack could hear the ocean in the distance and inhaled the sea air. As they approached Town Pond Walter stopped and gestured toward a house set back from the street with a odd rounded turret attached. "Here's a house that should interest you. Home and studio of Thomas Moran. Stands out, doesn't it. Not at all like our salt boxes and colonials. Moran had it built out of things he scavenged from buildings in New York. Built it first as a studio and then added on a few rooms for his family. Some say he did his best painting here. His daughter still lives here, you know."

Jack didn't know but Walter seemed suddenly a fountain of information. "Moran and his studio started the whole migration of artists to these parts in the 1890's and they were quite a bunch.

Called themselves the Tile Club because in the city they met every Wednesday evening in each other's studios and would paint on tiles. Then, in summer they would roam far and wide, some up the Hudson, others to East Hampton in search of the picturesque and paintable – so many of them came here, it became a joke among the locals that you could hardly get to the barn to milk the cows without stumbling over an easel. They boarded in a house over on Egypt Lane that came to be known as Rowdy Hall where late night revels led to all sorts of high jinx. But the locals took them in stride…"

"And still do," Jack added. "Leastways they've taken me in over in Amagansett. I'm in demand on the fishing circuit."

"Glad to hear it. It's a good thing to get to know the locals. Too many summer people ignore them or dismiss them but the local community is the bedrock and I like to fancy that the art community creates the bridge between the summer colony and the natives. Indeed without the artists, I'm not so sure we would have become the summer colony we are now."

"Is that a good thing or a bad one?"

"The summer crowd? Oh, I'd say a good thing though it gets a bit silly as the summer progresses. Too many parties and crazy pranks. I sometimes wonder what gets into people. It used to be only the artists that ran amok but now it seems necessary for everyone."

"I haven't been here long," said Jack, "but I'd be hard pressed to find one other painter let alone round up a circle of artists running amuck. Not that I want to. I can go back to New York for that."

"Ah. Just you wait. They'll be here in droves before long. June is a quiet month but July and August you'll be wading in artists especially in Amagansett. There's quite a crowd over there. Here we are." Walter reached for the latch on a white picket fence and led the way up a brick walkway to a two-storied weather-shingled house – the kind that exuded olden times from every nook but as they stepped inside, Jack saw a surprisingly modern interior where a large sweep of a room complete with an impressive stone fireplace ended at the far end in a series of glass doors leading to a garden.

Jack gave a low whistle of appreciation.

"I bought this house back in the twenties when one was feeling flush but until this summer only used it intermittently. Spring and autumn mainly – before and after the crowds. I usually travel in June but this year I've decided to stay the season."

The house had a slightly precious aura to it as if just attended to by servants. Every cushion on chairs and sofas was plumped, every table polished with just the right amount of objects placed in harmony and not in clutter; beautifully arranged flowers gave off the faint smell of a spring garden. While Walter busied himself over an array of bottles and glasses, Jack wandered over to a wall filled with antique prints and small-framed oils.

"Everything on that wall is a result of my days in Paris after the war. A fascinating time to be in France. Have you traveled abroad?" Handing Jack a brandy, Walter indicated a chair and Jack sank into a leather club chair as soft as butter.

"Someday and someday soon I'll get to France and to Paris. It's at the top of the list."

"Oh, it should be. Every generation should discover Paris for themselves. Of course, I've been back a number of times but for me it will never be the same as it was then. That's where I met our friend Guy Dambrose. Wonderful painter."

"Yes. Great teacher too. He taught me how to free up inside. To let go. I love his work."

"Why?" Walter gazed at Jack intently.

Jack thought for a minute, then smiling he said, "It makes me laugh."

Walter nodded. "You will have no argument from me on that score. His work is full of laughter and at the same time, he finds a depth that is quite sobering once you recognize it. Raises the art of mockery to another level. I think he had the makings of being one of the truly gifted but…" Walter let the thought hang in the air, then, "let's talk about your work. Give me the short version."

Jack took a swallow of the best brandy he had ever had. "Well…I guess the short and long version are just about the same. I had a knack for drawing ever since I was a kid and discovered there was a great deal of prestige attached to it. I could draw anything my friends asked me to which turned out to be in almost all cases, naked ladies. In college I did caricatures that got printed up in the campus rag sheet. I never really took it seriously until I studied with Dambrose. He was the one who saw something in my work. And then I saw the Van Gogh show – your show at the Met. It changed everything for me."

Walter looked only mildly interested. "Be specific. Changed what."

Jack leaned forward his brows in a frown. "Here was a guy who looked at the human face, looked at the sun on a field, looked at everything from flowers to nursing mothers to old leather faced postmen to wooden chairs for god's sake and got it. He went right to the heart of it and painted not what was there but something else. I walked around that exhibit and I felt like crying…no, not just crying but howling. I was so happy. I was so touched. I … I was so envious. And that envy, that sheer gut longing made something inside me shift." Jack shrugged. "And here I am."

"And you've been painting all this time?"

"No." Jack said reluctantly. "I got sidetracked. One of my many problems. I landed a job with J.C Lyendecker as a draftsman – ads, poster art that sort of thing. In the beginning it was just a job and steady money. I worked by day and tried to keep painting at night but I guess the good life got in the way and I fooled myself into thinking I would get back to serious work soon enough. When I ran into Dambrose he was painting a mural downtown in the Customs Building, he was hungry and I paid for his lunch." Walter winced but Jack didn't notice. "He looked at my illustrations, even admired some of the work but I could see it was hack work. He said something to the effect that if you leave off working seriously for too long, it dies. I don't want to wake up one day age 50 to a wall of women in evening gowns or chubby children hugging dogs. To hell with the steady money," he sighed, then added quickly "… so in March I quit to come out here."

Walter stood with one hand holding the bottle of brandy and the other Jack's glass. "Well, that was very…brave of you."

"Or foolish." He paused looking around the room as if to break into the doubt that washed over him. Then he brightened. "So that's it. End of short version." Walter handed him the drink, which Jack gulped down.

He found he couldn't stop talking now that he had got started. "There's an old man who lives out on the beach. He won't let me near him, he just sort of vanishes into thin air and for the life of me I can't keep his image in my mind long enough to capture what it is about him I want to draw. But he's what I'm going after – erase the line, let the light create the form. I want that fleeting thing, the thing just outside the mind's eye, the part that vanishes. I want to paint the before and the after of what's real not what's actually real." He stopped sheepish now. "Listen to me. I'm as pretentious as I was at your house that night."

Walter grimaced. "I thought maybe you had been part of that. The eager young students are not my scene I'm afraid but I'm intrigued with what you have to say. Worth thinking about."

They talked on until at last the chiming of the clock startled them both. It was midnight.

Jack started to his feet declaring that he should go but when he stood his legs were wobbly from the drink. The motorcycle, if he could drive it, was parked somewhere back near the movie house.

"No," Walter also stood. "Sleep here. There are guest rooms upstairs. Take any one you like." He waved absently towards the stairs. "My house keeper is very efficient about last minute guests. You'll find everything you need I think."

Jack stumbled towards the stairs and turned to thank his host but Walter Penn had disappeared.

Jack hardly noticed anything about the room he found until the next morning when sun streaming through the window caused him to squint painfully at his surroundings. He was lying on a big double four-poster with a canopy of lighthearted blue flowered chintz. Beside the table was a carafe of water, which Jack drank almost to the bottom not bothering to pour it into the tumbler. He had a ferocious headache and lay there immobile before an intense urge to relieve himself forced him to the bathroom. Here, thick heavy towels, a full compliment of toiletries, toothbrushes, shaving mug and razors, and a blue silk bathrobe were on offer.

He bathed, he brushed, he shaved, he splashed various spicy unguents over his body, he tied the robe securely around him and marched back into the bedroom to find the bed made, and the clothes he had left scattered on the floor, now, carefully folded and laid out for him.

Downstairs there was coffee and a sideboard of cooked breakfast. Jack was just tucking into a mound of bacon and scrambled eggs when Walter arrived through the double glass doors from across the lawn. Jack could see of all things, a windmill at the far end of the garden.

"Ah. Awake and hungry. Always a good sign," Walter observed. "I apologize for plying you with drink last night but I was enjoying our conversation. I hope you were too."

Jack grimaced " What I can remember of it. Actually, I do remember and hope I didn't bore *you*. I must have sounded so pretentious. The angst of the young artist. I apologize. It's just that they're not many like-minded people out here to talk to."

Walter held up his hand, "No apologies necessary. Angst often carries with it a rather positive message. And as for like-minded you'll be surprised at how many artists, illustrators, sketchers, scribblers and everything in between live out here. Don't let yourself get caught up in the art crowd if you want sanity and privacy. Yet, having said that, I have a proposition for you but not until you finish your breakfast."

Walter returned to the morning newspaper and Jack ate quickly. And nervously. Maybe he had walked into something he was not prepared to handle. To break the silence Jack commented on the windmill. "Does it work?" he asked.

Walter put down the paper. "As a matter of fact it does. I had it moved to the property when I bought the house. It was in terrible shape but there's a fellow out here, a master craftsman who wanted to restore it."

"They sure appear everywhere. Quite startling, really,

especially if you've never seen one before."

"Yes. The local icon I suppose. Moran painted the Hook Mill on a number of occasions as did his wife, Mary Nimmo. Unfortunately the locals have left most of the old mills to weather and decay. It's actually thanks to the summer crowd that a number have been restored. The well-heeled rather like the notion of windmills in their gardens." He laid his paper down. "Now... my proposition. Have another cup of coffee and hear me out. I'd like to offer you a job teaching art."

This was not what Jack had been expecting, worried it might be something of a sexual nature, but a teacher? Of art? To whom? Walter laughed.

"Let me explain myself. You see last year I found an old barn in Amagansett. It's not far from where you live but off the main road. You may have noticed it?" Jack shook his head. "Well, no matter. It isn't prepossessing from the outside and hasn't been in use for years. I fell in love with it and rented it from the owner for an indefinite time. I don't know why – it just spoke to me. It's a beautiful piece of work, not like any barn I've ever seen. The builder must have been an artist himself. Each beam is hewn to perfection and fitted and notched one against the other like a giant puzzle. Last fall I went there almost every day just to sit in the space. There's even a barn owl," Walter said proudly. "You don't hear them so much any more. I've been thinking about it all winter." He stopped for a moment. Jack's face was a blank.

"What I want to do is open the barn for art. Not really a school but a sort of inspirational laboratory. An Art Students League for non-artists, if you will – housewives and sales clerks and the guy who drives a milk wagon. You see, I think everyone has an artistic core, we see it in children but it's drummed out of them at an early age. The creative urge is there in all of us and I have a theory that if I can create a space for creative thought, a place that asks only that you come in and give it a try, something quite miraculous might happen. Or not. I'm certainly willing to be wrong. I want imaginative artists not so much as teachers, this is not about teaching, it's about ...well, let's see, for lack of better word, guiding. I got this idea out of watching people going through the museum. Museums can be deadening because they're so one-sided. The work of art takes center stage but the average viewer has no real idea of what goes into painting because they've never tried it. Do you know that most museum visitors look at a work of art for less than a minute before moving on? I think people would love looking at art, great art, if they felt they were on the same side as the artist. If they themselves knew something of the mysterious creative urge."

Jack knew he had a bemused look on his face. He tried to hide his discomfort behind another sip of coffee. Walter laughed again, delighted.

"You have the look of a trapped animal. Now don't think so much. As you know, I've been in this business for a long time. I've studied the great works; I've met almost every living artist of any note and many of no note at all. I've written about art, I've lectured about it. I've mounted exhibits; I've bought and sold it. I've even been called upon to lay my expert opinion on the line as to whether or not it's authentic. I've set myself up as a pretty keen expert when all is said and done but there's one thing I know nothing about, and that is where it all comes from. What I do know is that art isn't about technique but about something from within, something natural and unrefined, something innate in all of us. It's that crazy spontaneous side of us that we spend so much time trying to stamp out. I want to test this notion of mine – create a space where people are free to explore that impulse. Now you, Jack Burns, are just the fellow I'm looking for. You're young and flexible and talented and dissatisfied. You're looking for something and you're not sure of what it is. And I venture to guess you're broke. So here is my proposition – take on my barn this summer. Don't worry about how to run it, see what happens with whomever ventures in. Maybe nothing will happen and that's all right too," Walter leaned back in his chair and smiled, "But I think something will come of it."

20

The Grindles
Amagansett

Eddie Grindle lay in his bed watching the light from the moon reflect on the wall opposite the window. It was a small room but it was his alone now that his brother Jarvis had gone. Been his for most of three years. He missed his big brother and wished he hadn't left. He wondered what Jarvis was doing right now… Jarvis, the oldest of the five Grindle children, who announced the night of graduation that he was going out west. And out west he went, the very next week on the train to New York.

The walls of Eddie's bedroom were made from fish boxes – white pine, strong wood to hold 300 pounds of fish and ice. When the boxes got worn, the men would break them apart and use the best part of the lumber at home. Eddie's whole bedroom had been built with that pine and when his mother had wanted to wash his room with white paint, he begged her not to because the boards were stamped with the places where the fish were shipped. Philadelphia, Wilmington, Baltimore. His prized board said Chicago. Imagine the fish his dad hauled from his trawler going all the way out west to Chicago. He wondered if Jarvis had felt the same way about the names on the boards – maybe that's why he wanted to go out there and see for himself.

Ma had been real upset over his leaving and dad hadn't said a word just sat and stared at the fire smoking his Luckies but when the time came, they had all gone to the station to see him off – Ma and Dad, Granny Minnie, his two sisters Bette and Jo, himself, and the baby, June. No one knew what to say so Eddie told Jarvis he looked real funny in his Sunday suit carrying the valise that belonged to Granny Minnie, and Jarvis had given him one last cuff on his head. Then Ma tried to give him some money but he refused. "I got enough," he said. "I got all my savings.

Been working since I was Eddie's age for this." And that hurt Ma too – that Jarvis had been planning to leave all the way back to when he was twelve.

All that week she'd nagged at him. "But son there're no jobs out there. The whole country's in trouble. Why there are people starving. Children homeless. You can't go gallivanting around like you was someone. Stay here. Stay home where it's safe. Why would you leave a place like here? We got it easy compared to most folks."

Ma was right. Eddie didn't know much but he knew that the Depression was bad. He'd seen them pictures in the city newspapers that showed people standing in line for food. The men that came in Uncle Herb's store all had something to say on the state of things in America. The Dust Bowl? Democrats? FDR? Breadlines? All rolled into one bad and sour note. It scared him. When he asked his dad bout it, Mitch had lit up a Lucky and said, "We got all we can eat just so long as we get it for ourselves. There's fish a plenty, we got potatoes and vegetables as long as we grow'd 'em ourselves and your Granny Minnie's orchard is full of apples and peaches and there's beach plums and raspberries out to Napeague in the dunes." That seemed to sum it up for Mitch but Eddie knew his mom and dad worried. He could hear them talking in the mornings. Dad about his boat and the cost of repairs and supplies and Mom on just about everything else. She was a worrier that was for sure. The big blue and white bean pot she kept in the back of the larder, the one that had all the pennies and nickels and dimes she saved, was often just about empty.

Eddie was thinking this winter in the cod season he could start boxing up the cod tongues like lots of fellas did. You could get fifty cents a pound for tongues. Eddie had hung around the fish shanties since he was old enough to walk and the first thing he had ever learned from the old-timers was how to cut tongues from cod.

"Naw. They ain't really their tongues," he explained to Jack. They were down on the beach hidden in the tall grasses not far from Old Tom's shack. "They're the real sweet meat from under the neck of the cod." He could tell Jack wasn't listening. He was sketching the shack. He was always sketching something that had to do with Old Tom except Old Tom himself. Eddie wished he could help his friend. "I heard my Granny Minnie talking about Old Tom once. She's real old like Tom is. Maybe they knew each other back in them days when they was young. You should get my Ma to take you down to Granny's sometime. Maybe she can tell you about him."

• • •

"Isn't he the spiting image of Jarvis?" Nettie said by way of introducing Jack to her mother. Jack took off his straw hat and smiled his most engaging smile. This was his first visit to Springs and he found it another world altogether. Far from the quaint and manicure of the ocean villages, Minnie's farm stood rough and even scruffy at the end of the Fireplace Road, a single road that led some five miles out from East Hampton.

Granny gave a snort. "No. Don't look a thing like him. And what's more you got yourself all tied up in that boy and high time you stopped thinking he was comin' back."

"Oh, Mom. He'll be back. He's just trying out his wings, that's all. I know Jarvis and he…but we're not here to argue about Jarvis, this fellow wants to know more about Tom. I told him you knew Tom when you were a kid."

Granny snorted again but somehow that meant he was to come up on the porch and sit in a big wooden rocker. Nettie gave Eddie a basket and instructions to go out and pick strawberries. "I'm going down to the cellar, Mom and count what jams are left." She gave Jack a wink, poured him a glass of ginger beer from a large pitcher and then went inside the house.

Jack sipped at the ginger beer and let his eyes sweep around the porch and the view to the water. Granny rocked. Silence. "You sure have a nice farm here," he said, though the land seemed less a feature than the glorious view it had overlooking Gardiner's Bay.

Granny nodded in agreement. "We don't grow much but what we do grow is the best." The orchard was Granny's pride and a somewhat larger than usual vegetable patch, a beekeeping hutch, three cows, chickens, of course, and a goat or two. Minnie was a tough old bird living as she did alone, her husband long since gone and never much use it seemed when he was alive. The farm eked out a living mainly from the orchard. Its pear, apple and berry jams were sold in the grocery shops in the village and were well received in the big summer houses. All this Jack learned while waiting to get to the story he had come for.

Finally, somewhere between a recipe for apple butter and the price of chicken feed, he just asked. "What can you tell me about Tom? I'd like to meet him…"

"Nettie says you want to paint him. Wantin' ain't gettin'. Don't know that Tom would like it. He's not one of us."

"You mean he's foreign? Maybe off a whaling ship?" Jack prodded.

But Granny refused to be prodded. "My daddy was on one of them whaling ships out of Sag Harbor. Gone for more en' two sometime three year at a stretch. He always brought us kids back real interesting things and the stories, lor', that man could spin a yarn, and then one time, the last time, he just never come back. His boat were gone somewhere in the southern seas but we never know'd for certain what happened. My mother, bless her soul, never believed he weren't coming back. 'Till the day she died she could still see him walking up the road just as plain as your hand.." Minnie rocked on and Jack waited but nothing more seemed forthcoming.

"Did he tell you any story about Tom…?"

"Me and Tom's about the same age. I'm 88 years, I reckon." Granny Minnie was looking off into the distance.

Jack squirmed in his chair frustrated. She was telling him nothing. Minnie rocked steadily on. "Yep. My daddy could sure spin a yarn." There was another long pause "Them whaling ships weren't a good place for a family man," she finally said, more to herself than to Jack. "That's why I married a farmer." She stood up and walked to the end of her porch and spat over the side. "Yes sir," she said emphatically, "I married a farmer 'cause

I couldn't stand seeing that look on my mother's face – she was always waitin' for her sailor to come home."

Nettie laughed later when Jack told her what Minnie had said. "Well, it's a stretch to call Dad a 'farmer'. He was a loafer. No doubt about that. Loved to go out in Accabonac Creek in his old boat and lay there all day pretending to fish. Oh sure, after she'd loaded up the wagon, he'd drive uptown for the deliveries but she never could rely on him. Half the time me and Lottie would drive the cart. Minnie used to chase Dad around the farm with a hatchet saying he was only good for one thing – food for the pig. We loved him though. He liked to play his fiddle for Lottie and me to sing to. We had pretty good voices back then and we boned up on all the popular songs. Used to win the talent show down at Edwards movie house pretty regular now that I think on it. 'Course most of it had to do with us being twins – people just loved it. One of our big tunes was *After the Ball*. You know that one?" Not waiting for an answer, Nettie half humming, half singing.…*After the ball is over, after the break of day...* and we wore matching dresses with matching bows in our hair and pretended we were singing in a mirror. Dad built us the frame. Lottie and I got all the moves down so we looked like one was real and the other was the reflection. Now *that* was a showstopper." Nettie laughed and put down her dishrag.

"Now listen, Nettie, I haven't got one bit closer to Tom. You're as bad as your mother, changing the subject all the time."

"That's just the way Minnie is. She only talks about what she wants to talk about. Truth is, no one really knows about Tom but if you want my opinion…" Nettie dried her hands on a towel and sat down at the table. "I think he's an old man who wants to be left alone. And what's more I think you should stop hounding him and get on with whatever it was you came out here for. You've work to do." She got up and headed back over to the stove. "Now that I think on it, what a good-looking fellow like you needs is a girl to step out with."

Jack made a face. "That's just what I don't need. What I do need is some way to get to that old man. I don't know why but it's like he's got something I'm looking for. And the crazy part is I don't know what that something is."

Nettie stirred the pot. "Tell you what. If you really want to know about Tom, talk to Mitch. He's out on his boat now but he'll be back in a few days. Mitch has a cockamamie idea about Tom but you know sometimes I just think he might be right. Stay for supper? I got enough stew here to feed an army."

• • •

By late June the Art Barn was in full swing. Walter didn't believe in advertising because he wanted word of mouth to bring people in. He felt ads in the local paper might put people off – make them think they weren't "good" enough for the Art Barn and in the first few weeks after Jack took up his post only a few, like the two ladies who had heard about it at a lunch party, came in nervously arranging flowers cut from their gardens to render in watercolors. Jack admired the flowers and led them to tables after showing them where supplies were kept. Then he disappeared for a while reappearing long enough to ask if they needed anything.

"Well, I do," spoke up one of the women. "This is a mess." She indicated her wash of color on the paper. "I thought I had the colors right but now it's all run together." Jack complimented her colors then suggested she sketch over a few areas with a soft grey pencil redrawing just a few of the flowers." She looked dubious but a few hours later she was still at it only this time she had drawn lines first and then washed it with color and the effect was getting, if not better, at least more interesting. He showed another how to control the water paints and she was thrilled when he took a Kleenex, balled it up in his hand and blotted a swath of wet sky blue color magically creating delightful wisps of clouds. A few days later some giggling high school girls arrived who drew cartoon like fashion figures and flirted with Jack because they had all just read *Gone With the Wind* and were enamored with his southern accent. They were having a lot of fun and he let them be.

Then, in late June the warm sunny weather turned sour. Rain. More rain. Humid rain. Pouring rain. It rained as if the gods on high were disconsolate. On the days it didn't rain, the sun seemed to magnify the wetness into blankets of humidity. The world outside was sodden but inside the barn the worktables began to fill. Born of desperation over the weather, summer matrons and local farmwomen, schoolteachers and even a few retired businessmen sat side by side over their work and from this mismatched assortment came a growing sense of combined effort.

Traditional art supplies were available at the barn – easels, paper of different weights, oils, chalks, pens, even crayons – but one day an elderly woman came in with a fish caught by her husband that morning. It was a beautiful flounder about a foot long still gleaming with the vigor of its recent life. She announced that she had gutted and cleaned flounder all her life and now she would jolly well paint one. The flounder lay on the table. The woman poised a brush over a piece of paper. She put the brush down and picked up a pencil and tried to sketch the fish. Then she picked it up and laid it on the paper and drew an outline. She sat back and seemed discouraged. Jack picked up the blank paper. "Try going the other way 'round. Put paint on the fish, then press the fish to the paper before it dries."

She dipped her brush into a pool of red ink and slowly brushed the ink over the scales. Then, she took the paper and pressed it down on the fish. When she took it up there was an undistinguished red blob. Jack brought her another sheet of paper, this one much more absorbent and suggested she try again without re-inking the fish. This time the impression was…in a word, beautiful. An intricate outline of the scales of the fish, the gills, the fine lines in the tail were rendered on the paper. The class gathered around exclaiming. The woman was astounded. Jack was delighted. Here was something inspired by a hardworking trade. Something ordinary had been transformed it into something extraordinary. Everyone wanted to try a similar impression. Jack, too.

They all went outside despite the dripping moist day scavenging all sorts of things from the beach, the roadside, the general store – dune grass, shells, cast off rope, small crabs, gull feathers, paper bags, and even stale loaves of bread. Then they set about painting, pressing, joining, twisting – everyday things they had seen or held a thousand times were now objects to be rendered in new and sometimes surprising ways.

Jack was encouraged. All of a sudden it seemed Walter's crazy idea had merit. The energy now in the barn gave him renewed energy in his own work and he thought he was making progress. Maybe he didn't need the old man – leastways, he never found a time to talk to Mitch. Rising every morning in the first light he worked in the coop until it was time to open the barn. Afternoons he "chased the light" setting up *plein air* wherever the notion took him. Sometimes he worked at Judy's but more often than not he searched out remote places discovered on a whim. There was a dwarf forest out in Montauk on the cliffs that was a favorite and a long forgotten harbor and derelict lighthouse up in the place they called the Northwest Woods where he could spend hours. And in these places or even in the coop, there were moments of real clarity and flashes of insight that sometimes startled him ... but all that changed with Emmaline Hartley.

The true beginning of our end.

A MIDSUMMER NIGHT'S DREAM

July
HIGH SEASON

IN EAST HAMPTON THE BEACH IS ALIVE WITH PEOPLE. *Children squeal and race in and out of the shallow pools left by the rolling waves. Dogs too. Under the eves of Main Beach pavilion, the ice cream concession is doing a cracker-jack business. Young girls stroll casually back and forth at waters edge casting eyes on the young men in striped tank suits racing into the water. Canopied beach chairs are scattered in the sand shielding ladies in brim hats and flowered dresses, pearls in place, seated with men in straw hats and linen suits. Oh, yes —the summer season is in full swing.*

In Washington, D.C. however, buried in miles of heavy government architecture, there is, for the Weather Bureau, an entirely different season underway. The hurricane season. From mid-summer to late fall these months are officially designated as those most susceptible to severe storms. During hurricane season, the bureau routinely issues their Tropical Weather Outlook, identifying areas of concern within the tropics as well as unusual conditions that could develop into cyclones. Junior forecasters like Will Foster are immersed in their charts and reports looking for indications of trouble in the southern seas, trading teletype information with their counterparts in the Caribbean and in Florida where hurricanes happen.

Of course there is no concern for severe weather along the Eastern Seaboard. Here, rain may distress picnics, and the occasional high wind may alarm small sailing boats but for the most part, the weather is fair and the ocean moves impressively and ceaselessly — swelling, lapping, rolling in steady predictability. Of course, the sea can vibrate in fury in the winter with a full blown nor'easter underway but in summer the Atlantic is mainly playful, and today beach lovers are given to thoughts of parades and parties, fireworks and flags for it is the 4th of July. The grey-green vastness of the ocean before them is really of no consequence whatsoever.

22

Celebration
July 4th

"You got a message, Jack. A Miz Tate?" Herb Foss pointed to the telephone hanging on the wall. "Sounds important. Just tell Winnie you want the Tates. Don't need a number."

Jack had long since given up having any privacy. The telephone held a central position in Herb's store for optimal public entertainment and if Herb and his cronies weren't enough there was Winnie at the central telephone office who directed most of the calls. The summer colony had wisely converted to direct lines – a major disservice to Winnie who had been working as East Hampton's telephone operator for twenty years and now no longer had the inside track on the comings and goings of the elite. In her heyday, Winnie could hold court at any off-season gathering with her juicy tales and reenactments born from selective eavesdropping. Even so, there wasn't much she didn't know.

"Jack? Oh good you got my message." Judy sounded slightly breathless as always. "How are you?" But she didn't wait for an answer. "I know this is last minute but Chip called this morning and said he couldn't come out until Saturday and I need you to," she paused dramatically, "*take me to the ball.*" She giggled. "Not exactly a ball but our neighbors, the Hartleys, are having their 4th of July party and I need a date. It's on the beach and not formal. Do say you're free."

He was.

"The Hartleys must have some influence with God, "he commented that evening as he and Judy walked from her house across Dune Road to the drive leading up to a large house. "How else can you explain the clear night?"

The steady rain of the last week had shown no signs of letting up for America's big birthday and yet here it was a clear night. "Oh yes. I should think they have a great deal of influence with God. It never rains on this night, so Emmaline tells me. Oh look," she took in a deep breath, "how beautiful."

The house was lit with hundreds of small lanterns in a multitude of colors and for a moment they just stood admiring the scene. "I think you'll enjoy meeting Emmaline," Judy said rather grandly taking Jack's arm, pleased as anything that she could treat her cousin to such a coveted event. She could tell Jack was impressed. Entering the house, they were directed by a young man to the terrace on the ocean side and Judy pointed to the pool down a tier of stone stairs.

"Emmaline calls it a 'dipping pool'. Isn't that marvelous? But look at it." Sea nymphs and shells were painted on the walls and bottom of the 60-foot narrow strip of water. For the party, dozens of candles floating on small wooden boats cast shimmering reflections so that the water itself looked a little on fire. Surrounding the pool were tall urns with cascading hibiscus. Beyond was the ocean playing its part magnificently with a steady roll of gentle white-capped waves and a full moon near the horizon laying a golden carpet of light on the water.

Music was in the air – a man dressed as Uncle Sam was playing show tunes at a grand piano on the terrace, later to be replaced by a jazz trio imported from Harlem and later still to be replaced by an enormous wind-up Victrola phonograph complete with a giant brass horn, wheeled out on a trolley with the latest dance records. Waiters in knee britches and white ruffed colonial shirts, some in tricorn hats, busied themselves with trays of drinks on the beach where gaily patterned rugs and cushions had been arranged around a series of bonfires.

"Don't tell me." A voice close behind him commanded. "You must be the man on the motorcycle. Quite the lover's siren call."

Jack didn't actually see Judy blush but he could feel it. "Lover? Oh no," she giggled. "No, no you see Jack is my cousin. Jack, this is our hostess, Emmaline Hartley. And this is my cousin, Jack Burns." She emphasized the 'cousin' but Emmaline seemed oblivious and offered Jack her hand more as if she expected it to be kissed. Jack held it for a brief moment. "You make quite a stir, Mr. Burns, coming and going."

Jack smiled. "I apologize, Mrs. Hartley. It's an old machine and it is rather noisy. It has made me quite deaf this summer. Judy's been kind enough to let me come and sketch the bay in the evenings from her lawn."

"Ah...then you're an artist?"

"I hope so."

Emmaline stood silently and very still as if this were some sort of startling remark worthy of contemplation. "Well then...I hope so too," she said gravely never taking her eyes off his.

"Of course you're an artist," said Judy breaking in. "Jack is painting Alice and me, aren't you Jack. He's wonderful. He's really good. Not that painting us is what he wants to paint..." Judy trailed off in slight confusion. Jack turned and looked at her as if he were coming out of a dream.

Emmaline said nothing, then, as if remembering her role as hostess, waved in the direction of the beach. "Join the party." And before he could think of anything else to say, she had turned to greet another guest.

"Good lord," whispered Judy as they moved away. "That man looks just like Errol Flynn but it couldn't be. He's so drunk." Jack turned back and watched Emmaline kissing a very tall man on the cheek and slightly propping him up at the same time. He had one arm around Emmaline and the other around a pretty girl who couldn't have been more than 16 years old and Emmaline, so calm and cool, a masterpiece of composure was making the clumsy scene seem natural, even amusing.

"It is Errol Flynn," he whispered back. "I don't think anyone else in the whole world could look like Robin Hood other than Errol Flynn himself. A very drunk Robin Hood at that."

Judy tucked her arm through his. "Chip hates my obsession with movie stars but it's a thrill to see them in the flesh, don't you think? I try not to be impressed but then I can't help it. I'm terribly impressed and I really can't explain why. It must be that we see them on such big screens they become something more – like the gods on Mt. Olympus. I loved Greek mythology when we studied it in school. All the drama of love and jealousy and hate and vengeance churning up there in the clouds. Such fantastic improbable stories just like in the movies. And the movie stars... well, aren't they just like real stars," she gestured to the heavens and then laughed. "I've never really felt that way about stage actors although I wouldn't mind meeting one of the Barrymores. Did you see..." and on she chattered as they made their way down to the beach.

Drinks in hand, they wandered around, Judy admiring every detail of the lavish trays of food and the throngs of people none of whom she knew but who she maddeningly kept trying to identify. The babble of the crowd, the clink of glasses, the squeals of people greeting one another and the constant chatter from Judy began to wear on him until at last he spotted Walter Penn in the middle of a lively circle and steered Judy there; Walter greeted them and welcomed them into the group. With the promise of returning with more champagne, Jack now released from escort duty for a few moments, let his eyes search the terrace with the intent of finding Emmaline Hartley.

23

Emmaline and Jack
July 5th

"Jack…Jack… wake up you lazy boy?"

Jack rolled over in bed and peered at his clock on the night-stand. 9 o'clock. What the hell was she doing here at this hour?

"Coming," he managed with a kind of croak. Emmaline laughed. He stumbled up hitting his shin on the iron bed. He was naked and he groped around for the trousers he'd kicked under the bed the night before…not night, early morning, more like four in the morning. When he finally opened the door he saw she was perched on the wooden stool he usually took with him when he painted, her head thrown back and her eyes closed. She had kicked off her shoes.

He pushed open the screen. "Good morning,"

"Why are you still in bed?" she demanded, not opening her eyes.

"Why aren't *you* still in bed. Didn't I say good night to you a few hours ago?"

"You did. And didn't I say to you that if today was sunny we were going to the tennis matches? Well, the sun is out and here I am." She tipped her head down and put on a pair of sunglasses, "Oh darling, you look dreadful."

He glanced down. He had pulled on his work pants, thick overalls he had picked up at Herb's store. They were perfect for work, pockets and tabs and buckles everywhere to hold brushes and rags and other tools of the trade. He had no shirt on. The sun was blinding and he stepped back into the shadows of the coop. "I didn't know they played tennis this early."

Emmaline hopped off the stool and thrust her feet back into her shoes following him through the door. "I thought maybe a drive first, a swim, I know a darling little place we can go for lunch and sooner or later, we'll get to the matches." She circled around him letting her hand trail across his bare back for a brief instant all the while taking in the room. "Charming," she said dryly. "I didn't quite believe you when you said you lived in a chicken coop but here you are. Where are the chickens?"

Jack lit a match to the kerosene ring under the coffee pot. "Still asleep," he yawned. Somewhere in the back of his mind he vaguely remembered talk of tennis but there had been so much liquor and dancing and flirtation and even a bit of grappling on the terrace. "Coffee?"

Emmaline walked over to the rumpled bed and sat gingerly at the foot of it giving herself a little bounce. "Is this where you ravish all the farm girls?"

Jack grinned and then scratched his head. "Yep. All of 'em except Lula Mae. She's awaitin' for me out yonder by the barn."

Emmaline laughed. "Oh, you southern boys. Is it true what we read in *Tobacco Road*?"

Jack wondered where all of this was going. He found a clean enough cup and poured the strong liquid into it. "Oh yes. The great literature of the South." He had read both *God's Little Acre* and *Tobacco Road* the instant they had come out, as had half the young in America. The books by Erskine Caldwell were banned throughout the South as smut, but lauded in the New York literary world as luminous works of art. They were also considered the best sex manuals around by everyone under 20. Even he, proud as he was of his prowess with women, had picked up a few eye-popping pointers. "We used to be all about dueling oaks and Spanish moss now we're the back of beyond filled with sex-starved women and hot-headed men."

"Or hot blooded. Makes you think…" Emmaline leaned back on the bed on her elbow. She was wearing a red cotton sundress with tiny white polka dots in it. The material was as thin as a handkerchief and the scooped neck and short sleeves fluttered every time she moved. It was the kind of material more suited for a child but there was something very alluring about that dress and about the woman in it. Last night she had been the perfect image of a woman who was never ruffled or windblown but sleek and feline like a fashion drawing come to life as she glided in and out of clusters of guests. Now, here was that elegant, magnetic beauty, giggling in a most provocative way, lounging on his bed dressed like a schoolgirl ready for a lark. Jack could feel himself growing very interested in this surprise visit. He turned to put his cup down and saw Eddie Grindle riding up on his bike.

"Oh Christ. I forgot. Today is Tuesday."

"I suppose it is," Emmaline stretched out one leg to let her shoe drop to the floor.

"No. I mean I have something planned for today. I'm sorry, Emmaline. I'll have to take a rain check on the tennis, the lunch, the drive in the car. I promised a friend of mine I'd go fishing with him." Eddie was now leaning the bike against the fence.

"But I don't want a rain check, Jack dear. It's been raining far too much." She stretched herself off the bed. "Make an excuse, darling. The fish will be there tomorrow and today is too perfect to waste. I'll come back for you in an hour. I have some shopping to do in the village. Now don't be a bore...I simply won't take no for answer." And with that she was out the door waving him a kiss just as Eddie opened the gate.

"Thank you, young man," she said as she swept by him. Eddie blushed a deep red.

Jack watching her get into her car, a sparkling yellow convertible, which, as she drove off left billowing dust in her wake, saw that indeed she was not a woman you said no to.

Eddie came up the walk. This was the long planned day Eddie and Mitch were taking him fishing off Gardiner's Island, after which they would deliver fish to the island and Jack would get to see it first hand. The island, less than a mile offshore, stood like Shangri La, an earthly paradise virtually untouched save a Manor house and a few barns. Privately owned for hundreds of years by the Gardiner family, it boasted rare wildlife, a primal forest, acres and acres of flowering fields, pristine ponds and, as Eddie had told him, the buried treasure of Captain Kidd. No one could go on the island unless invited. And here was Jack throwing over his chance to explore it for a dalliance with a notorious socialite who was offering up some vague idea of tennis matches and a clandestine lunch. Jack arranged his face to look worried and regretful and then turned just as Eddie pushed open the door. "You ready?" the boy asked with a sunny smile.

Eddie Grindle's face and his profound disappointment still imprinted in Jack's eye, the lie he had told his young and naive friend nagging uncomfortably in his mind, the price he might have to pay with Nettie, whom he liked and respected, the loss of face in the local community who had taken him in – all of this was washed away in that one demanding moment and this extraordinary woman.

She had taken her time coming back for him, hardly the promised hour, but by the time she did he had bathed at the pump and changed into a pair of cream linen trousers and a blue shirt open at the neck.

"A lovelorn woman must have given you this shirt, Jack. It suits you perfectly, especially with those grey eyes, and it's exactly what I wanted you to wear." She adjusted the collar just a tad and then stepped back to admire him.

Jack grinned. "This shirt, I believe, was one of the perks left behind by the stylist from *Vogue. Arrow shirts at play* was the theme as I recall."

Emmaline wrinkled her nose. "Oh, dear. A floor model. Well, never mind. We can improve on that later but for the moment you're exactly right. Now, are you ready for a wild ride?"

He offered her his arm. "Madam? Where to?"

She smiled, wagging a finger at him. "Ask me no questions."

They were off in the yellow roadster through the village of East Hampton to Sag Harbor, down Main Street over the bridge to North Haven and then onto a ferry that took them a short hop to Shelter Island.

"I've never been to Shelter Island," he shouted over the roar of the motor and the wind whipping by them. The island sat regally between the two forks of the East End. Dense woods, glimpses of water, old farmhouses flashed by as Emmaline deftly maneuvered the narrow roads.

She smiled, slowing the car for a turn off the main road to a dirt lane leading them to a deserted inlet where a dinghy was tied up to a dock. Emmaline directed Jack to a hamper and Jack dutifully loaded the heavy basket onto the dinghy and then rowed them out to a sailboat anchored in the inlet. There was no one about. He tied the dinghy to the rear of the boat and then hoisted himself aboard. She handed up the hamper and then athletically pulled herself aboard as well.

"Is this yours," he asked gesturing to the boat.

"No," she said vaguely. "But it's ours for now. Unhook me…?" She turned and Jack fumbled with the tiny series of hooks at the nape of her neck releasing the dress and revealing a gossamer thin and extremely revealing swimsuit underneath. Not the kind of swimwear you would normally see on the beach but a one-of-a-kind designer fantasy. "

He whistled. "I see you are prepared. I'm afraid I'm not…" but she reached into the hamper and tossed him a man's bathing costume. "I keep every size at Villamere. You'd be surprised how many people forget to bring their own." Opening the hamper she brought out bottles of wine, cheese, sandwiches, strawberries and taking a cloth from the bag she laid it out on the deck for the picnic. "Champagne first," she declared deftly reaching for two crystal glasses each wrapped in linen.

They drank. They swam. They nibbled at the food and all should have been sheer perfection yet Jack could feel in every passing minute the promise of the adventure slipping away as if the sun had gone behind a gloomy cloud. Yet the sun shone and the day was as fine a one as they had had all summer. At one point she napped.

He stared at the line of her legs and narrow hips, the cool, smooth skin of her arms and neck down the length of her back. He felt like touching her, stroking her like you would an exotic animal letting his eyes wander over the perfect curves as she lay in stillness. *You could paint that body; you could paint it a million times and never get the flow of it, the magic of it.*

Jack chewed at his thumbnail, a bad habit of his usually in-
voked when he was at a loss in his work. He stood hoping she
might wake but when she merely sighed and slightly shifted position he retreated to the bow of the boat. The foredeck of the
vessel was long and narrow and elegant. Aft there was a table and
built in seating for six but no cushions. He noticed the deckhouse
was locked. Jack wondered if they weren't trespassing but why
would Emmaline Hartley be trespassing anywhere?

For the last few hours he had been lost in another world, a
world of glances and moods and indifference he did not understand. After the seductive greeting that morning, and the provocative swimwear she now gave no indication that she wanted
anything other than the sun and the water and the libations.
She had stripped him bare of his expectations. What now, he
wondered?

Then, just as the sun edged the horizon, she sat up and began
organizing the hamper. It was time to go. They reversed the order
of departing. This time Jack into the dingy, then the hamper,
then Emmaline. Silently he rowed to the shore profoundly bewildered mixed with a growing anger.

Emmaline asked him to drive. He did. The evening, for now
it was well after 8 o'clock, was cool and she extracted a sweater
from her bag. Jack shivered in his thin shirt but there was no
sweater forthcoming for him from her bag of tricks. "Where to?"
he asked.

"Up to you," came the bored reply and Jack felt his anger
mount. She was playing at some mystifying game and not willing to give up and let her win he abruptly pulled the car up to
the curb in Sag Harbor. There was a dive just off the wharf – a
shanty for working guys with a pool table and dartboard where
the drinks were cheap and they made good chowder.

"All that caviar and champagne has made me hungry. Let's
have some real food," he said without looking at her as he opened
her door. He ordered a round of whiskies, two bowls of chowder
and an order of fried clams. "Darts?" he said with a challenging
look towards the board. "I warn you. I was the dart champion of

UVA." She smiled.

"Ah, the mysterious lady has a smile after all. Is it the whiskey or the fried clams?"

"It's neither, you idiot. It's you."

"Me? Listen lady, you've got me stumped. I think we would have been better off going to those mythical tennis matches."

She held up her hand. "Don't. I've behaved badly, and I hate myself but I had to make sure about you."

"You mean I'm undergoing some test of yours?"

"Actually, yes. You're game. Most aren't. I like that. I like you. My problem is I can never be sure about people. So many on the social make. It happens all the time. Too many people, too many parties. Half the time I have no idea who my guests are but now I see," her eyes took in the bar, "you really are who you say you are."

"And what's that. A down and out artist?"

"Well, that chicken coop is quite convincing," she laughed.

Jack leaned back. Women were all alike. They had their kinks and scenarios, dramas and devious means but what it all came down to was the same. Play their game and you win the prize. His anger was forgotten. She was simply the most provocative woman he had ever met.

They talked in earnest now. She asked him straightforward questions about his work, his ambitions and he found himself telling her things of real intimacy until at last he held up his hands, "Christ, I'm recounting the story of my life. This can't be of any interest…"

"But it is. I love hearing you talk. Your have the gift of story-telling. Must be those Southern roots."

Jack laughed. "Must be. Still I have no more stories to tell tonight. It's your turn."

Emmaline leaned forward never taking her eyes from his. "If it's my turn then why don't we go somewhere less crowded."

At Villamere, she stood in the moonlight in the drive and stared up at the night sky breathing in the ocean air like a greedy child and for a moment Jack again felt a turn in her mood, as if a new game might be in the offing, as if she was taking new measure but then she took his hand. Up the stone stairs, into the house, up the staircase, into her bedroom – something extraordinary had fallen into place as simply and easily as if transported on a magic carpet. Indeed. The room was like an exotic tent out of Arabian Nights. From the ceiling, folds of gold-flecked material cascaded into sheer curtains billowing against the breeze from open windows. Maybe it was the cheap whiskey or just the heavy night air but he felt drunk with sensations – the rhythmic surge of the sea, the smell of salt air, the touch of her skin against his – and as they fell onto the soft white bed, for the first time in his life Jack did not feel in possession of himself.

24

The Summer Fete
July 29th, East Hampton Village

Earlier in the summer, Jack had agreed to donate a painting to the Ladies Village Improvement Society's annual summer fête. The chairwomen herself, Celia Slade, approached him via an introduction from Walter Penn. She was somewhere in her forties leaning to plump but still showing the prettiness that must have been lovely in her youth. The kind of looks that in another era would have qualified her as a Gibson Girl and not unlike the ideal he had so relentlessly pursued at the Lyendecker stable. The day Mrs. Slade came to his "coop" which she insisted on calling his studio, she slightly ruined this ideal image he had of her by putting on self-conscious airs. She swept around the inglorious space peering at the canvases he had leaned against the wall indicating with a conspiratorial wink that though "provincial" the Ladies Fair was nevertheless THE summer event. He nodded and flashed her his most boyish and winning smile. She rewarded him with a girlish giggle.

In truth he was glad to donate a painting if for nothing else than it would be good exposure. Depression or no, these townspeople loved images of their pretty landscape and any artist with half a mind to sales knew to flatter that love of place. Accordingly he picked a piece inspired by the setting sun over Judy's lawn. It was a large and dramatic though slightly brooding painting of Mecox Bay, birds flying low, the obligatory boat in the distance all rendered in broad, firm strokes that was at once modern impressionist but still entirely familiar to the local landscape. Surprisingly Mrs. Slade rejected it, ever so politely of course, saying she felt something a little gayer would be right for the auction. Perhaps a beach scene?

And so he had given a study done at the ocean with bathers and the brightly colored beach cabanas in the background executed in a style that leaned heavily on the effects of light and shadow. And he had given it reluctantly. It was a painting he liked, one of his best of the summer and he wasn't altogether sure he wanted to part with it. Mrs. Slade was delighted and very grateful. "You can be sure this will bring in the highest bid. I shall see to it myself!" And he had no doubt that she would.

On the day of the fete, he delivered the painting to the assigned booth with Emmaline in tow who visibly shuttered when she saw the festooned scene excusing herself with an urgent errand. The notion of local life irritated her. It was as if she believed there was nothing here before she arrived each spring and nothing when she left. Jack stared after her. Three weeks into their affair and Jack was still as mystified by Emmaline Hartley as he had been the night of their first tumultuous time together. Sublimely selfish one minute in the next she could be as cuddly and sweet as a kitten but soon enough those sharp claws would emerge and a remarkably and childishly cruel Emmaline would appear.

Jack found it easy to shrug off any concern. When they were alone together the world she inhabited faded and everything else became a little vague and unimportant. In public, of course, they were simply…friends. And it was summer after all, crowded with diversion – sailing, tennis matches, club lunches–and of course the endless parties. Parties that seemed endemic to Emmaline's person – parties that even with their delightful nuances and surprising elements never seemed quite to override the essential emptiness that in her was never satisfied. There was always something more that was needed.

Jack could not help his fascination with the goings on at Villamere. The steady stream of people, the hoots and hoorays of trivial entertainment, the freewheeling and often freeloading atmosphere, the drinking, the gossip, the almost universal lack of caring deeply about anything – it was all so seductive and how easy it was to let this restless current sweep him along. The guests all talked of plays and films and fashion and parties. They told jokes and planned pranks; they were charming and gay and thought Jack was lovely and made him feel like a prince – then came the knowing looks and meaningful glances when they thought Jack was not looking as everyone tried to size up the extent of Emmaline's infatuation.

Somewhere deep down the nagging promise he had made to himself about his work nibbled uncomfortably around the edges of this indulgence but he had little inclination to stop Emmaline's insistent requirements for attention. In truth, her irreverence towards life appealed to him in some mischievous way.

The two of them were going sailing later that afternoon and the day was as fine a day as anyone could ask for. The green lawn though a bit spongy from the prior week of rain was alive with brightly painted booths, streamers made of crepe paper, artful vines and hanging baskets of bright summer flowers. With the brass band warming up on the bandstand and flags flying he saw Celia Slade in the middle of the green, a majordomo in all respects, clipboard in hand, issuing commands, her cheeks flushed. Dressed in a white cotton drop waist dress fashionable for schoolgirls in the 1920's, he could now really see how pretty she must have been in her youth. He waved and she beckoned him over peering at the painting he held as if it were a rare museum piece.

"We are thrilled, Mr. Burns, with your generosity. I adore it and I know everyone else will as well. You see it will go right here on an easel, the centerpiece of the whole auction booth." She laid her hand on his arm regally and led him to one of the larger booths already filled with *art*. Jack admired the booth and noted with an inward wince two or three entries from patrons of the Art Barn. He certainly hoped his work would bring in more money than those.

"Oh dear," Celia exclaimed. "Now where is that easel? I had it especially for you. I'm afraid the girls didn't unpack it but let me go and see. I'm so sorry…" She fluttered off in the direction of a pick-up truck parked toward the back of the green. Jack felt a little silly standing there with his painting and looked for a place to set it down. That's when he saw the boy sitting on a short-legged stool in the back of the booth. He was very still with huge eyes.

"Hello," said Jack. "I didn't see you there."

"Hello," said the boy politely. "You didn't see me because I was hiding."

"Ah, then that explains it. Are you still hiding?"

The boy stared at him for a second. "No."

"Do you like hiding?"

The boy slowly nodded. Then he smiled. "I like hiding because if you're good at it the pirates can't find you. Is that your painting?"

Jack gazed down on the canvas feeling again his reluctance to give it up. "Yep." He turned the painting towards the boy. "What do you think? By the way, my name's Jack. What's yours?"

The boy got up from his stool and peered at the painting. "My name is Lewis Palmer. How come the people don't have faces?"

"Well...I think if I'd painted in the faces then we would be looking at them instead of looking at the shapes of the people. And that's what I wanted people to look at. I was sort of hoping they would enjoy seeing the way people move and relate to one another and their surroundings rather than just what they look like."

The two of them peered down again at the picture. Lewis started to reach out to touch the painting then jerked his hand back because you were never supposed to ever touch but Jack laughed.

"You can touch it. Go ahead. The paint is dry."

Lewis ran the tip of his fingers over the painted beach scene where the water reached up onto the sand. "It's knobby," he said. "just like the sand. My father and I built a seawall out of sand last week. It was really long and we made it as high as we could to hold back the sea. But it was gone the next day."

"Hmmmm," said Jack. "It's those tides. They'll do it every time. The ocean has a funny way of coming and going, doesn't it?"

A silence fell. Jack tried to think of something else to ask the boy. He was an odd one, he thought. Enormous eyes and a sense of calm that was unsettling in a child. Dressed in a funny little sailor suit, his skinny legs stuck out from the starched shorts in a way that was almost comical and yet there was something about him that made Jack want to engage him in conversation.

"Do you draw in school?"

"Sure we do but we don't get to paint. We use crayons and big pencils and draw on paper. Miss Darlene says I draw good. She showed me how to draw a horse. Miss Darlene is from Kentucky and she rode horses ever since she was a little girl. And now Miss Darlene has a horse over at the Sherrill farm and she goes there to ride him on the beach." He liked to say Miss Darlene's name because if you said it real fast it sounded like "darling" and Lewis thought he might like to marry her when he grew up but that was silly because Miss Darlene was already getting married. That's what his mother said. She was going to marry the high school coach and then her name would be Mrs. McQuirk. McQuirk wasn't nearly so nice a name as Darlene. He looked up at Jack again wanting to prolong the conversation which was much more interesting then playing by himself in the back of the tent. "She told me when she was a little girl she had lots of horses to ride. I wish I had a horse," he said dreamily, "then I would ride up and down the street and wave to everyone just like in the 4th of July parade."

Jack nodded. "That sounds fun. Maybe Miss Darlene will teach you how to ride?"

"No. I get a new teacher when school starts again. Her name is Mrs. Fellows and she's old and mean. I won't ever have Miss Darlene again. Not ever." He said this with a certain amount of 6 year-old lament in his voice then touching Jack's painting again said wistfully, "Is it fun to paint with real paints?"

Jack laughed. "Sometimes. And sometimes it's really hard but if the picture works the way I want it do, like this one, well then, it's like magic."

"Magic?" Lewis brightened. "Like real magic?"

"Kind of." Jack allowed. "Only instead of pulling a rabbit out of a hat it's like suddenly finding something new. You see," he held his painting up, "most people want a picture to tell them a story but I don't want to tell a story, I want the person look-ing at it to tell himself his own story. That's the kind of magic

I mean." They both peered again at the painting as if held in a kind of bond.

"Here I am," sang out a voice shattering the moment. "The girls *had* forgotten about the easel but here it is." And with a flourish Celia plunked it down in the center of the table, a wooden table easel on which Jack immediately propped up his painting.

They all three stood back to admire it.

"Jack? Jack Burns? Why, honey I do declare if you aren't a sight for sore eyes." In unison Jack, Mrs. Slade and Lewis turned to see Emmaline prancing across the green in the full force of a dreadful rendition of a Southern accent, on her head a very large and floppy straw sun hat just purchased. She looked a freakish parody of the Village Improvement ladies. "I haven't seen you since the fall of Rome and here you are and here I am and, my goodness," she whirled around and spread her arms wide in an overwrought execution of theatrical horror, "what a lot of perfectly dreadful art." Then turning to Celia, she whispered as if they were old cronies, "I declare, these country fetes are beastly, aren't they. Art Tent? Oh, my dear *très pathétique.*"

Celia's face was frozen but her cheeks had turned an alarming shade of red. Jack stepped in and yanked Emmaline's arm. "Mrs. Slade, this is Emmaline Hartley and she is no more southern than you are and she is trying desperately to embarrass me. Please do forgive her."

Celia nodded vaguely took a step back completely unsure of how to handle the situation. Everyone knew who Emmaline Hartley was. To have her come to the fete was a big honor. To have her insult the fete was…well what was it? Celia felt like crying. With a few murmurings of thanks again to Jack, she scurried away.

"You were incredibly rude," Jack said watching Celia's departure and the slump in her shoulders.

"But I was nothing of the kind. I was not rude to her, I couldn't bear to be rude or unkind to people, I couldn't bear it." said a now contrite Emmaline. "I was only having a little joke at your expense."

"At my expense? Hardly. Why you knew this woman was part of the fair and you deliberately insulted her." Emmaline frowned, wafting her hand like a fan in front of her face as if clearing the air then cast her eyes down as if feeling some remorse.

"Well," said Jack relenting somewhat, " If you weren't rude then you were impertinent."

"Oh," said Emmaline now laughing. "I can live with impertinent." She hooked her arm through his possessively removing her floppy hat and tossing it carelessly into one of the trash bins. But she was rude, thought Jack, and unkind. She simply had to steamroller anyone and anything that she found tiresome and poor Celia Slade fit that bill. He took Emmaline firmly by the elbow and propelled her out of the tent.

Lewis, who had been sitting quietly throughout the exchange, watched the two strangers walk away. Grownups were awfully silly sometimes. He looked back at the painting thinking he might touch it again but instead peered out of the tent onto the lawn and squinted his eyes so that he couldn't see the features on anyone's face. It was interesting. Sort of. He opened his eyes again and saw his mother coming across the lawn. Should he tell her? Tell her that the funny lady in the big hat upset Auntie Cilly? But maybe she wasn't upset, maybe her face had gone all red because she had a sunburn. He scratched the mosquito bite on his leg.

"Celia? What ever are you doing here?" Wilma peered around the back of the supply truck parked at the edge of the green. "I was looking everywhere for you. Why Celia…are you crying?"

Celia was sitting on a low-slung crate, the clipboard lying on the grass. She *had* been crying – her eyes were red and puffy but she wasn't crying now. She was gripping her hanky and twisting it into a hard knot.

"I'm fed up, Wilma, that's it exactly. I'm simply fed up to the eyeballs with this town and this ridiculous fair. It's so…so," but she was so wound up she couldn't speak. Wilma sat down on the crate beside her.

"Tell me, dear. What in the world brought this on? You were in such a good mood this morning and you can't be disappointed in the fair. Why it all looks like something out of a picture book. I've never seen it look so pretty. You've really created a magical scene. Tell me what happened?"

Celia laughed a hard short little laugh. "Happened? I'll tell you what happened, Wilma," her voice rose in sarcasm. "Nothing – that's what has happened." Each word was said through clenched teeth. "It's 1938 for god's sake. Harry and I were only supposed to be here for a few months while *he got back on his feet*. Ha! It's been seven years. Seven long, boring, hideous years. I've begged him to find some way out of here but what does he do? He goes into real estate. In Montauk of all places. In the Depression! He's a joke, Wilma. Everybody laughs at him. He's just a big bag of wind – that's what he is and nothing more. I'm getting old, Wilma. I can feel it especially here, today, at this ridiculous fair. I can't stand it. I really can't. Who in heaven's name cares a whit about this fair, about raising money, about whether or not the auction is a success? I don't. I don't give a damn. They just laugh at us, Wilma. The summer people. We're nothing but provincial nobodies. And you know what? I agree with them." She burst into fresh tears and laid her head on Wilma's shoulder.

Wilma put a protective arm around her friend. She said nothing because she had heard it all before. Had been hearing it all their lives. Celia always about leaving town, about how wonderful the summer people were, ingratiating herself with them, fawning over them, wishing at summer's end that she too was packing up for new and exciting places. Wilma knew that whatever had upset her was probably trivial but often it was the trivial things that set Celia off the worst and the only thing to do was to wait it out.

"Look at us, Celia. Here we are sitting on a crate in the back of a truck like two hobos when we're supposed to be out there acting like grown ups. What do you think our mothers would think?"

Celia managed a half smile. "I don't know. They probably never dared to think of anything other than the next LVIS meeting. My mother lived and died for these fairs. How did they ever stand it?"

Wilma laughed. "Silly," she said.

"Willie," sniffed Celia after a long moment.

Willie and Silly, the old childhood nicknames for each other – two girls in a rowboat on Hook Pond, now middle-aged women sitting on crates in back of a truck on the village green on a fine summer day in July.

Day after day, day after day, we stuck,
nor breath nor motion; as idle as a
painted ship upon a painted ocean.

THE RIME OF THE ANCIENT MARINER

August
THE DOLDRUMS

It is a scorcher. Men take off their jackets fanning themselves with straw hats, women pin up their hair to get it off
the neck and shimmy their skirts to stir up a breeze. Along
the beaches there is no real relief. The ocean is as warm
as a bath and the hot air stirs up the sand. Adding to the
misery is the afternoon rain that does little to give relief —
if anything it makes the air more a thick moist blanket.

Just about everyone has 'had it' with the weather. 'Is this
the worst summer ever?' they ask each other over lunch,
at the clubs, in the shops. Endless rain and somehow at its
wettest on the weekends when houseguests are pacing in
frustration over missing a good day on the beach, a golf
game, tennis, sailing. Lawn parties, so revered by summer hostesses, are hurried inside as clouds and thunder
threaten the festivities. Along with the wet weather comes
a sultry humidity that wrings out clothes and tempers.
Mosquitoes and swarms of bats dive and swoop plaguing
the evening hours even if the sky clears.

The locals are no less weary of the rain. Caddies at the
club, lifeguards, sailing instructors, gardeners, party help,
tennis coaches and the shop owners — they depend on the
summer crowd and the good will of balmy temperatures.
Hot and irritable shoppers are not inclined to spend their
money, and those generous tips are hard come by from
soggy merrymakers.

A strange ennui has set in — some call it the doldrums.
And how very alike it is to the place of utter stillness off the
coast of Africa where the prevailing winds disappear be-
calming the ocean into an eerie, watery desert; where sails
hang listless in the moist air trapping any wind powered
vessel for weeks at a time in a stagnant state of inactivity.

25

Walter Penn

"You seem distracted, Jack. Everything all right?"

Jack leaned back in his chair. "Distracted by all that good food, you mean. Mrs. C should be cooking for a king." Dinner with Walter Penn was always a treat thanks to the excellent culinary skills of his housekeeper. Jack met with Walter on a regular basis and he would even go so far as to regard them as friends though he was never sure of exactly what their relationship was. One never overstepped with Walter. Through all the genial and erudite conversation and gracious hospitality there was nevertheless an impenetrable wall built up around Walter Penn.

Except when they talked about the barn – then Walter warmed like a benevolent uncle. He took enormous pleasure in knowing that the doors were open and that people were trying it out. Jack had little to report.

That day he had paused for a moment at the long worktable and looked down at the work of a girl who had been coming off and on to the barn for weeks. He had tried, tried very hard to encourage her but she seemed to have none of the "inner creative resources" Walter Penn liked to imagine inhabiting these folks from "all walks of life" – another favorite phrase of his. Here she was again painting the same blob of yellow peering over the same blue grey of water. "Hmmmm," he said giving it a doleful once over. "Don't worry about if it looks right, just feel the weight of the brush on the paper and see what it can do. Experiment." He smiled, but inside he heaved a sigh. Here was a girl with rough hands and bitten nails; a girl whose face showed the woman she would become, the outlines of a work worn life already embedded in what should have been the freshness of youth. Jack wondered, not for the first time, what the hell he was doing in this gig. Sure a few people had gotten a great thrill out of it but so what? Did it change their lives? Did it inspire them to throw over the yoke of routine and break free? This poor girl was the perfect example. What possible good could come from her futile attempts at art? Walter Penn knew nothing of these people – and it was useless to try and inspire them with notions of creating art.

The image of the girl stabbing at the paper with splotches of paint seemed somehow synonymous with his mood. If not his own work. There was nothing happening. The more he entangled himself with Emmaline the more he seemed to drain himself of any inspiration. She was a witch and he the bewitched.

He heaved a sigh. "Sometimes I wonder what the point of art is? I watch those people struggling to dredge up some inner well of talent and then I watch myself doing the same thing. It's insane. And I get to thinking the only sane person is that old beachcomber I told you about. There he is living off the flotsam and jetsam of the sea and land, feral cats as his only company, outdoors in the wind and sun and rain. I know he's just a crazy old man but I think he's got some profound answer if nothing more than to strip our lives down to the bone. Thoreau said it, 'Simplify, simplify'. If only we could."

"Agreed," said Walter tapping his napkin to his lips. "We complicate our lives without knowing it yet nothing is simple. Even Thoreau found that out. I believe he was in love with Emerson's wife? Something like that. I hear you're painting the Hartley children – that means you've come under the spell of the amazing Emmaline."

Jack grimaced. How had she wrangled that promise out of him? The portrait of Judy and Alice had been one thing – a familial duty but the three Hartley children was an enslavement. She had asked him soon after that first night and when he tried to decline she had taken his hand giving him a secretive smile. "If you're engaged in painting the children you'll be here in the house. Quite often, I would imagine. Three children is quite a commission. Be sure and charge James your top fee. He likes paying through the nose."

The children were every bit as fidgety and unruly as he had imagined they would be but inside of a week he had become a fixture in the household. He even had his own room where his easel and paints were stored along with an assortment of clothes to change into if the day stretched into the evening's festivities as often it did.

Emmaline treated him as a somewhat vague friend when in the company of her children as if she knew him and liked him but couldn't quite remember why. When James was about Emmaline was remote and formal, completely poised as if she hadn't been in Jack's arms only hours before, as if she hadn't cried out to him again and again abandoned in their voracious hunger for each other. Poise was a thing she could wrap around her like a scarf and with James she wore her scarf tightly. A man of medium height, thick-set, with an abundance of graying hair, a square strong chin and the shrewd face of a man used to getting his own way, James had little interest in Jack's presence in his house and when they spoke it was in an abbreviated sort of way, the sentences cut to the bone. "James," he said perfunctorily pumping Jack's hand the first two or three times they met. "Glad to know you." After that, he simply nodded at Jack raising a hand in an indifferent greeting. "Painting today?" "Good" "Children behaving?" "Good". He was too polite to then dismiss Jack with another wave of the hand as he might any other paid employee but Jack always felt summarily dismissed nevertheless.

James was an odd duck in Jack's book and he came away from these encounters with renewed wonderment as to what Emmaline had ever seen in her husband. The money, of course, was the only answer for it was daunting to consider how very much money was required to make her happy.

He glanced at Walter who smiled knowingly. Jack decided to chance a bit of honesty. "The children I can take but their mother is something else again. Does she cast spells?"

Walter actually laughed. "Yes. I think she does. I knew Emmaline in Paris before she married Hartley." He reached for his pipe, lit it then sat back and stared up at the ceiling.

"American girls were quite a novelty in those days but Paris is always game for novelty. And it was a wild time…I was too old, maybe too much of a prig for the scene but I got to some of the parties and I can tell you Emmaline was something to behold. She was, how shall I put it, the most captivating free spirit. An enchantress even then."

Jack laughed. "It sounds as if you were in love with her."

"Oh, yes, indeed I joined the ranks from afar. She knew how to play off of all of us but she only had eyes for an English fellow…what was his name…? One of those grand old families. Freddy. That was it, the Honorable Freddy something or other. In the end, it didn't work out."

"Why not? I mean if she was everything you say she was? What kind of man was he?"

"Well, as I recall he was a good looking fellow in that lean, hawkish English sort of way. Charming, entitled, leading a wasted continental life while he could. They were quite a pair until his family closed ranks. A girl like Emmaline without family, without money… Freddy soon saw the light though he certainly adored her. When I say men fell down on their knees for her I'm not exaggerating. She held all the cards in that face of hers and in her spirit. Her downfall was, I think, falling in love. And when Freddy threw her over, well…she was devastated."

He paused, re-lighting his pipe. After a few puffs, he continued. "That's when I got to know her best. She turned to me because I was 'old and wise,' I believe was the terminology. We spent a great deal of time together and I very 'wisely' advised her to learn how to do something, to take up an interest, break the mold, become her own woman. Something lofty like that. She had wonderful taste and style. I even offered a small position in my business which was at the time buying and selling art. I thought she would be wonderful at it."

"And?"

Walter laughed. "She met, then married Hartley in short order. So much for advice. She's restless our Emmaline, never quite satisfied, always searching. Even now she seems unable to settle down. James was, in the long run, probably a better catch than Freddy – older, somewhat tedious…"

"And he can afford her."

"Ahhh…yes…but there's more to it than that. I would never try to write off James Hartley as merely a rich catch for a clever girl. He's shrewd and no fool. Emmaline depends on James and needs him for reasons far deeper than money. She might find him a bore, she might find him tiresome to live with, she might find him any other number of irritating things but the marriage has worked out rather well and for reasons I don't think anyone really understands. It's not a traditional love match but…well, they have three children for god's sake. Something's going on there."

Jack felt himself squirm. If Walter only knew the real truth of what was going on with Emmaline. He had entered into her life on a lark, flattered she fancied him, hopeful it held promising contacts for his work, determined to hold his own and stay in control but none of that had happened. Far from helping him as an artist, she had relegated him to children's portraiture and then taken no further interest in his work. But his work was no longer in the forefront of his life either. Something else had taken hold. There were times he wondered how trapped he was – this thing was unlike any affair he had ever experienced. He had always been at ease in the world of women – womanland, he called it – where every liaison came with its own built in date of expiration. He liked clever, bright women and clever, bright women always caught on to his game and accepted it. He was no cad, holding firm in his belief that one should never make enemies of past lovers always allowing the lady to discard him. But Emmaline? She was like a puzzle that needed solving and yet he had no idea of the rules of the game. There was always something else going on – something he was not privy to too and it was unsettling.

"Yes," said Jack vaguely, wishing they could move on in the conversation. "…And the tale goes on and on and on."

Walter nodded approvingly. "I see you know your Coleridge. The Rime of the Ancient Mariner."

Jack sighed. "And its bloody albatross."

They sat for a minute in silence then Walter got up to fuss rather pointlessly at his library searching for a book he thought Jack might like. Clearly the evening was at an end.

When they stood in the doorway Walter said, "I'm giving a little talk this weekend at Guild Hall on Thomas Moran. Don't feel you have to come but if it interests you…well, bring Emmaline."

Jack couldn't help his laugh. "Of course I will. Not that she listens to me but she loves you, Walter." He turned to go then turned back. "May I also bring my cousin? You met her at Emmaline's beach party in July? Judy Tate? She is an ardent Moran enthusiast. She would love hearing your talk."

"Wonderful. I shall enjoy seeing her again." They shook hands and Walter watched Jack go down the walk to his motorcycle. Poor fellow, he thought. He's coasting on dangerous waters. He stepped outside and looked up at the night sky. Only a few weak stars peered back at him and he suspected rain was once again in the forecast.

• • •

Judy sat in the theater annoyed with Jack who was late. From the rear of the auditorium where she had taken two seats so she could keep an eye on the door, she studied the program until she thought she could recite it from memory. Seems they were to be treated not only to a "very special guest speaker, the renowned art critic Walter Penn," but a musicale as well – a recital of "light opera" featuring two ladies from the Community Theater. Judy sighed. Once again she was on her own on a Saturday night. She had expected Chip to take all or at least most of August away from his desk but Chip had first managed to manipulate all of August into only two weeks and then only into long weekends. He would arrive late Thursday night exhausted and leave on the 6 a.m. train on Monday.

"But darling, all of New York closes down in August. Surely you can't be as busy as all that? My father always took August off,"

Judy had heard the childish pout in her voice when she delivered this line not caring when Chip's annoyance crossed his face.

"It's the biggest deal of my life," he said tersely. "I have a real crack at landing this thing but it takes hours of research. I can't just loll on a beach and expect to be ready to present the campaign in September." But then he had softened. "Please try and understand, darling. I promise we'll take a real vacation when this is all over. How about the West Coast? You've never been and I know of a wonderful old inn about a hour out of San Francisco...." And Judy always fell for it. The big trip. Held out like a carrot before her ever-optimistic eyes. There had been a time when she and Chip had been the all in all to each other. Nowadays she wondered what was happening to their marriage – or what had happened to it – but her own replying thought usually was, Oh, nonsense. Nothing has, really. It's just everything dies down a little, in the course of time. You can't expect marriage to be the great love affair forever. Yet no one had been as much in love as they had been. She remembered that first year better than all the years since. They had lived in such a passionate dream, as if they were the only real people and everyone else was ... was what? Judy sat up in her seat willing herself back into some semblance of calm but sitting alone in a theater amongst strangers, she felt the familiar hard lump in her throat just as the lights dimmed and the high school students trooped out on stage.

Walter Penn's talk was exhilarating. It centered on the Moran household in East Hampton though its sweep included the whole of the man's career. There was something so poignant about the "Moran clan" as he called them – a truly happy family living in the paradise that had once been rural East Hampton. His house and studio facing Town Pond, a gondola brought over from his Venice days floating nearby on Hook Pond, his wife tending the household and garden but also an accomplished artist herself. Images of windmills and cows grazing on the village green, two beautiful daughters, costume balls and evenings of singing and tableaux vivant, the house itself a beacon for other artists from the city. All this was woven in and around images projected on a screen of Moran's work and Judy felt her heart beating in anticipation of *her* painting, the painting that had brought her to Chip that long ago day in the museum. When at last it flashed up on the screen, the beach and ocean, the turbulent clouds on the horizon and the golden light Judy felt the tears streaming down her face.

"Are you all right?" It was Jack! He had slipped into the seat beside her and she hadn't even noticed.

She took his hand and squeezed it. Dear Jack, her only real friend. What would her summer have been like without her dashing cousin? Jack Burns was the glamour in her life that seemed all but non-existent elsewhere. She wondered if the crush she'd had on him when she was 17 wasn't still lurking somewhere inside. And what of it? Why not? And then she blushed a deep crimson thankful for the darkened theater. It was true. She did harbor romantic thoughts about Jack and had secretly taken a great deal of pleasure over the fact that he had never indicated any interest in a girl this summer. *Come for dinner, Jack, and bring someone if you like.* But he never did. He always came alone.

In the lobby afterwards, Judy was surprised to see Emmaline. Of course, Emmaline *was* a friend of Walter Penn's but even so, a lecture on Thomas Moran plus the added "frosting" of local ladies singing from light opera didn't quite seem Emmaline's sort of thing but here she was and in her element too, leading them all like a merry little band of pipers down the street from Guild Hall to Walter's house where a supper party was on offer.

Emmaline sallied into the house clearly at home taking full command of the gathering in the center of the room. Judy, sipping the glass of wine Jack had placed in her hand before turning to the gaggle surrounding Emmaline, tried to look engaged. The discussion was on the latest news from Europe. The Prime Minister of England was trying his best to placate the Germans but Hitler could not be trusted with diplomacy – or so Jack was saying.

"Do you think anything will come of this? I mean could there really be a war?" said a woman, one of the singers in the program.

Emmaline gave her a withering look. "There's been a war going on in Europe for hundreds of years. This year or next... they're sure to take it up again. And as for America? You have only to be married to a man who makes military uniforms to know that America is getting ready." And this caused quite a furor of dismay amongst the singers while others nodded in sage agreement.

Judy took another sip of wine. "Emmaline has certainly got the party in an uproar, hasn't she?" Judy turned and found Walter by her side smiling.

"Do you think that's true?" she said rather lamely gesturing towards the heated discussion. "America in war?"

Walter shook his head shrugging. "I think it's very likely there will be a war in Europe but whether or not America gets in it, is anyone's guess. There are some powerful people who want to steer clear of Europe and its problems – and equally powerful who want to jump in. Ugly business no matter which way you look at it."

They both stood for a moment watching the animated group. Oh to be more like Emmaline, Judy thought, with opinions and attitude. A woman people listened to filled with wit and repartee. What she wouldn't give for just an ounce of Emmaline's flair and confidence.

Walter too was thinking of Emmaline but what he saw was a girl from years ago in Paris. Not the savvy young beauty that had so captivated the *beau monde* but a frightened girl, now two months gone in pregnancy, heartbroken and weeping in the back of his small gallery. Walter had been at a complete loss in the face of those tears but he was a man in love, passionately in love with this beautiful creature as he had never been before, nor would be again. He could offer her little but he had begged her to marry him. Enter James Hartley – a rich American tourist in Paris with money to spend. A painting, a sketch...really anything to take home a bit more original than French perfume. *For your wife?* "No," said the provincial James, so clearly out of his element, *for my mother*. And Emmaline, instantly on alert, eyes now dry, had

charmed him into buying an exquisite small impressionist painting at such an inflated price that even Walter had to blush. To celebrate his *wonderful eye for art*, a dinner invitation was proposed
and within weeks a pale but determined Emmaline emerged from
the registry office, the newly wed Mrs. James Hartley.

Walter turned abruptly as if to shake the memory out of his
head. "Would you like to see the garden, Mrs. Tate? It's rather
interesting in the night light or will we cause tongues to wag?"

Judy laughed. "I wouldn't mind setting a few tongues
wagging."

"Well then," he said with a touch of the stage villain, "may I
show you my etchings, my dear? And if we are to cause a sensation
I can't keep calling you Mrs. Tate. May I call you Judy?"

They strolled around his garden lit up here and there by candles hanging in glass lanterns in the trees and along the walk. It
was enchanting, and she said so, adding, "I think Mary Nimmo
Moran would have loved your garden. She seems a woman who
loved beauty and fun all at the same time."

"Then you *were* listening to my talk. When I dare to look out
over the audience all I can see are the people who are dozing."

"I loved every minute of it. I've loved Thomas Moran ever
since I discovered him in the Metropolitan Museum. I practically
lived in that room as a girl because of the painting of the ocean
– my ocean I called it, I guess because I've been coming here in
the summer ever since I was born. I just couldn't get over how he
captured exactly that thing I feel when I look out over that water
especially in the fall. He wasn't painting a summer ocean he was
painting something else, something…" and like the floodgates
she was unable to stop herself. It had been so long since she
talked to any one about anything she loved. Walter bent to listen
to her occasionally moving a pebble on the walk with his toe.
When she finally wound down he extended her his arm.

"I'm so glad I put that image in my presentation," he said
warmly. "And now I think our little supper is about to be served.
Shall we?"

I've bored him, she thought. I've made an absolute fool of

myself. How tedious for him to hear a schoolgirl's art appreciation prattle. She was mortified wishing she cold make a discreet
exit but he surprised her. After circulating amongst his guests
seeing that everyone got to the buffet laid out in the dining room
and had found seating at the dozen or so small tables set around
the room, he once again returned to Judy.

"If you love Thomas Moran so much," he said, "perhaps you
would like to accompany me on Tuesday to his house. His daughter Ruth lives there and she has invited me and any friends I might
like to bring to tea."

She said yes so quickly they both laughed and in that instant
Judy felt as if something very special and very new had taken place.
She said yes without considering that Tuesday was Raleigh's day
off. She said yes although she had promised Alice an afternoon
at the church fun fair with its allure of pony rides and a puppet
show. She said yes because she simply had to find a way outside this long narrow place she inhabited and onto a larger canvas where nothing was prescribed. Where there was no routine.
Where amusing herself and doing as she pleased was the order
of the day. She said yes because that's exactly what Emmaline
Hartley would have said.

26

Raleigh

"But Raleigh surely just this once…" her voice trailed off as she saw the set of his mouth.

"No, Miss Judy. This Tuesday and every Tuesday is my day. I can't change my plans." He was firm but polite and Judy backed down instantly. For all that Raleigh had been in her life for most of her life, there was much she didn't know about him and this hardly seemed the place to start. He was a devoted houseman, excellent in every way in his job, good and kind and caring to the family but he was meticulous about his day off. Where he went and what he did was his own matter. In the city of course there was no curiosity about Raleigh's day off, but out here? Judy had sometimes wondered about it. Many people brought colored help with them for the summer and surely, she reasoned, there was a place they all congregated when off duty. Where that could be was a mystery.

But Raleigh, years before, had found a solution of what to do within the confines of this very white, very established summer colony he worked in. And he had found it in the village of Sag Harbor, once a whaling port on the bayside of the South Fork now a somewhat forgotten town off the beaten track from its ocean front neighbors. Sag Harbor reminded him of a southern town not unlike the one he left so many years ago. It was old and sleepy, its rich robust prosperity born in the heyday of the whaling industry long gone; its buildings now settled unevenly into the ground with sagging roof lines and a lazy eye towards repairs. He liked walking the streets and lanes, going down to the wharf jutting out into the bay, the reading room in the local library on rainy days but most of all he loved the Oakland cemetery on the edge of the village – sheltered by large trees, cool on the hottest day and filled with beautiful stones and markers from the old seafaring days.

Raleigh loved cemeteries. They were naturally quiet with always a name worth noting, an epitaph to ponder, a story to be created around the cryptic messages chiseled into stone giving testimony to lives once lived. But mainly they were places where a colored man could walk and perhaps sit and read or eat his bag lunch without being bothered.

Every week he packed himself a lunch, selected his book and headed to Sag Harbor in "Old Woodie", the house station wagon, his for the day. He was a quiet man, as quiet as the cemeteries he liked to visit and he considered himself a contented man. Until this summer. In July he had turned 60. Time was marching on and one day he would be too old to work. He had saved his money carefully over the years and could afford to buy a house somewhere. And on this day, with Judy asking him to forego it in favor of her attending a tea party, he would be signing the contract for a small house in the tiny hamlet of Eastville just outside Sag Harbor's town limits. Eastville, once a stop on the underground railroad, was now a solid community of colored folks just like him. A place to settle. He was safe now. And the ugly past buried.

Raleigh, ever mindful, had engaged Violet Hartley to sit with Alice for the afternoon.

• • •

Arriving on the arm of Walter Penn, he in a white linen suit and a straw hat, stepping into the large room that had been the great painter's studio, his easel still in place, the room draped in heavy tapestries and crowded with objects from his worldly travels, it seemed to Judy as if she had entered into a world apart. The crowd gathered seemed each and every one like eccentric and boisterous players in an elaborately scripted pageant. Introductions were made and soon Walter was pulled away while Judy listened intently to a man explain to her the impracticality of the room they were in, indeed the entire house, which had been cobbled together from found materials.

"You see that north facing window?" He gestured. "It's from

a factory in New York and Moran put it in upside down."

Judy laughed. "I like upside down," she said flirtatiously, "don't you?"

He winked.

She saw Walter talking to a stout woman in a dress from another era and a large unflattering hat. He waved and Judy waved back. Ruth Moran herself, dressed in an old-fashioned white tea gown gliding about the room like a ghostly figure from the past. A mad tea party against which she saw her own limited life with painful clarity.

"Ah, my dear. Come sit with me. I'm worn out with all this chatter." The woman in the large hat was patting a red velvet settee with her plump hand. Judy sat primly down. "You're a friend of Walter's. Charming man. I've known him for ages. And so clever, don't you agree? Oh he does make me laugh. Do you sing?" The question caught Judy off guard.

"Me? No…no not really," she stammered.

"I love to sing but my passion is the organ. I have one in the playhouse. You must come. I've just now learned *Scheherazade*. Do you know it? Such exotic music. " And she was off on a dizzying tangent on the Imperial Russian court and their fascination with the orient.

"Ah, here you are. You do look charming in that hat." Walter arrived with a tray of tiny tea sandwiches and cups of tea. "I managed to scoff these before they ran out.

"Yes. I'm never without my hats." She turned to Judy. "I wear them indoors and out. They say I'm famous for my hats."

Walter laughed. "Judy did you know you were talking with the first lady of East Hampton, Mrs. Lorenzo Woodhouse?" He said this with a flourish and Judy blushed a deep red. She had no idea who this was but clearly she was a person one should know.

"Mrs. Woodhouse is the reason we have so many illustrious figure of note come our way.."

Mrs. Woodhouse gave out a hoot. "Well I'm not the reason for you, Walter. You got here entirely on your own did you not? This lovely young lady and I were discussing music. Isn't that right my dear?"

Judy nodded.

"I was telling her about my organ. But we needn't talk about me. You, my dear, tell me about you. Are you in the arts?"

The question came so suddenly that Judy was at a loss for words. "Uh…uh… I'm not…I mean…in the arts? I love all things in the arts but I'm…," She couldn't think of what to say.

Walter came to her rescue. "Mrs. Tate is a young mother with a little girl of four. Isn't that right, Judy? It is four, isn't it?"

"Ah. I remember that age. Charming. You can always tell in a child of four what they will become when grown. Oh, you may not recognize it then but when they do grow up, you will see it was there all along. It's such an interesting age. Of course, all of their ages are fascinating and you have so much ahead of you my dear. So much to enjoy. When Marjorie was four she performed the entire score of *Scheherazade* for us in dance, naked I might add. That's why we built the playhouse for her. A place for her to perform. She was a born dancer. More talent than you can possibly imagine. She danced with Isadora Duncan and all in her very own playhouse."

Judy looked bewildered as Walter hastily explained. "The 'playhouse' is a great deal more than a place for a child to pay in. It is a full-fledged theater built for a very talented daughter. It's quite something to see and right here in our own village. May I bring Judy one day to see it?"

"Delighted," said Mrs. Woodhouse. "Now Walter you must bear with me. I am going to play my new piece on that dusty old piano over there. Here help me out of this chair." She gave a little grunt as Walter gripped her under one arm lifting her from her settee. Judy was forgotten.

Everyone quieted down as Mrs. Woodhouse settled herself at the piano her plump hands playing the opening notes with confidence and aplomb. The music of the Russian court filled the room but Judy barely heard it. The question hung over her head. Who was she? She was 27 years old and she had nothing to say for herself. A young wife and mother with no other credentials to her name. No plans, no interests, no ambitions, no talent. She could arrange a dinner party and decorate a room. She was a whiz at bargain hunting. She could read stories to her child. She could play bridge and tennis. If pressed, she could speak a few words of Italian. She wondered if that was why Chip made excuses and stayed in New York. His days were filled with action. Her days were mired in the minutia of a mundane life. She was as interesting and accomplished as a chirping bird, unaware of the world, hopeless at politics, ignorant of things that mattered.

The recital over, Mrs. Woodhouse came back to where Walter stood applauding. "You are a marvel," he said giving her a kiss on both cheeks. Judy stood mutely by his side. Mrs. Woodhouse, flushed with pleasure, put her hands on both of Judy's shoulders. "You take care of that little girl of yours. They're gone so quickly." Her hands pressed briefly and then she turned away.

Walking back across the green Walter extended his arm and she slipped her hand through the crook in his elbow feeling a sudden and wonderful rush of warmth.

"Did you enjoy Mr. Moran's studio?"

"Yes," Judy said, " I loved it but I wish…I wish I had something more interesting to offer…I mean everyone there was so… so alive and Mrs. Woodhouse, what a marvelous character with so many interests and accomplishments and how dull she must think I…"

"Not at all, my dear friend." Walter said stopping. "I think it meant a great deal to her to meet you and hear about you. You see Mrs. Woodhouse lost her daughter in a car accident a few years ago. She drove off a bridge and drowned. I think if Mrs. Woodhouse could have anything in the world, she would have exactly what you have right now."

the air is different today
the wind sings with a new tone
sighing of changes
coming

RHAWK, ALBAN ELFED

September

THE SEASON ENDS

Some 4,000 miles to the east of Long Island, across the restless motion of the Atlantic Ocean, over dense jungle and out onto the empty quarter that is the vast Sahara desert, there is a lonely African outpost called the Bilma Oasis in Niger. There, on September 4th, a French meteorologist records in his diary an unusual shift in the wind passing over this remote and desolate part of the world.

Within a day this disturbance has moved across land out into the Atlantic to the Cape Verde Islands and over that place called The Doldrums where tedious calm and savage squalls can cause a cluster of clouds to form into a single sinister shape. Warm water, cool air, suction, spiral, a whirling mass of wind forms around an inner core. Now the Trade Winds take charge and the cone moves towards the equator. Most of these storms incubating over African waters will collapse…but not this storm. Like a racing car engine, revved up and ready to go, all that is needed is the open road across southern seas.

27

Chip Tate
Labor Day Weekend

Thank god the summer was over – almost. He had bowed to Judy's demands and taken the whole of the week off but tomorrow he would return to the city. The warm sand covered his feet, while the sound of the waves and the breeze off the ocean worked a sort of magic on the tight knots in his stomach. He could hear his daughter playing nearby with Violet Hartley coaching her in the finer points of building a sand castle. Slowly, imperceptibly his body began to soften. Was he always like this or was it only this weekend? Judy and Raleigh were back at the house preparing for Judy's big dinner party that night. Chip had all but been banished to the beach, a hamper of cold chicken, lemonade and cookies for himself, Alice and the ever-dependable Violet. Fancy Emmaline Hartley producing a child that could be labeled dependable. Chip almost smiled but inwardly the specter of the evening ahead reared its fashionable face and he groaned. Judy's party had been the topic of every conversation they had had for over two weeks. It had started as a dinner for eight, the exact number their dining room held, only to be shanghaied into a free for all with the invited guests assuming they could bring their assorted friends. Judy now thrown out of the confines of her safe and secure modus operandi determined to give one of those casual deck parties where guests balancing plates, napkins and wine glasses in hand traipsed around food tables picking and choosing buffet style. After which they were to be directed to three different seating areas concocted out of small tables, cushioned benches and ottomans draped in colorful prints. *Casual and amusing* Judy kept saying as if she had thought this up herself but Chip knew very well that Emmaline Hartley had devised this sort of entertaining long ago. Well, it was one thing for Emmaline to herd her guests in haphazard style but

Judy was not so confident a hostess. She was wound up like a top and he could smell disaster.

It was a night of firsts for Judy. Emmaline was coming for the first time to the Tate establishment as a guest. This, the last big weekend of the summer and a major coup for any hostess, let alone Judy Tate,who all summer had been pecking at the crumbs of social inclusion thrown her way from the great mansion across the road. Not only was the queen of all things chic a guest but she was being escorted by an aging actor of yesteryears Broadway season, one Grayson Blake – who was, Judy trilled, the director of a play that had just closed at Guild Hall and therefore he simply had to bring with him his leading lady. Cousin Jack was coming, two pretty young and single women from the club for him to cast an eye on, a married couple and a spare man also routed up from the club, each of whom had passed muster to Judy's exacting standards of who could and could not be paired with a Hartley, and Judy's new friend Walter Penn who was bringing a dowager from England, Lady Maude something-or-other, who had in turn pleaded that her visiting grandson and his girlfriend also be included. All of this had sent Judy to the moon in preparation and speculation even as it had settled in Chip a feeling of weary resignation.

Chip had known for some time that things were getting shaky in this great American dream life of his. It wasn't that he was ungrateful for the opportunities that had come his way, or didn't love his wife and child. In truth he hadn't any real notion of what it was that bothered him. He only knew that he felt incredibly alone.

The first big indication that he was in trouble came with the stroke. His father-in-law, Bill Delany, about the nicest guy anyone could hope for, was one minute sitting in his chair laughing at a client's joke, the next face down on the desk gurgling. Chip, in the ambulance with him, felt the poor guy clutching his hand like it was a lifeline and then later with a distraught Judy and her mother fussing and fluttering about the hospital room, saw that Delany was looking desperately at him trying to tell Chip something with nonsensical words. "Sink the umbrella…sink the umbrella" he shouted over and over again and poor little Judy even went so far as to bring in her dad's umbrella from home but Chip figured out his words had nothing to do with umbrellas.

In the office he leafed through Bill's appointment book. One name popped up two or three times, the last one being on the morning of the stroke. Chip called the number. A few hours later, having met with one Donald Pierson at Morgan Guaranty Trust, Chip felt a dread creep into his bones. Bill Delany was up to his ears in debt and had tried to leverage the beach house. The house was not in his name but Judy's and he had forged her name on the loan documents. Mr. Pierson had been very clear. They would press charges, stroke or no, unless Chip himself took on the debt. As Judy's husband he could sign on any property either one of them brought into the marriage. Chip signed. Later, alone at his father-in-law's bedside, for the few moments Judy and her mother were downstairs in the coffee shop, he told him he had met with Mr. Pierson and that all was taken care of and Bill Delany relaxed for the first time in three days and wept. He still could not speak coherently but he was now as docile as a lamb and Judy marveled at her wonderful husband and his comforting effect on her father.

That had been two years ago and since then Chip had worked double time to keep up with the loan, the mortgage on the house on Bank Street, the household expenses. Bill Delany, who would never fully recover, and Judy's mother decided to move to the farm in Connecticut and that too required living expenses though the farm itself was free and clear of debt. None of this did Chip mention to Judy, indeed anyone. To tell Judy or her mother would be, in Chip's mind, some sort of betrayal of a man he had grown to love. Delany could not be faulted for being a poor business man but the more Chip delved into his dealings, the more he wondered at the excessively generous donations to charity, especially in the face of mounting debt. Most people had cut back on giving, if not given it up altogether but Bill Delany increased his largesse – mostly worthy charities but there were first nights at the opera and museum galas that made little sense to the prudent

Chip. Mary Delany was hardly the kind of wife that needed or indeed wanted to hobnob in the haute echelons of New York society. She was as down to earth and practical as her husband was not and devoted her time and energy to the nuts and bolts of charity work with the skill, Chip often observed, of a consummate manager. Judy had inherited none of these qualities. She was her father's daughter. To Judy, money was a secondary consideration in the fanciful realm she wrapped herself in, and any reminder by him of the cost of things was either dismissed as unimportant or reason for a disagreeable scene.

So he said nothing and instead took on a monstrous work-load. And he did it without hesitation and little resentment but it meant a punishing schedule. It was a relief to send his family, with Raleigh to take care of them, to the beach for the summer. It gave him time to focus and to breathe without having to field Judy's constant demands for more of his time.

The only trouble was that when he did arrive in Bridgehampton on a Thursday night she was waiting for him with an assortment of plans and outings, parties and excursions. These he did diligently and with as much enthusiasm as he could muster but the one thing that he could not tolerate was her obsession with the Hartleys. There was nothing about Emmaline, her husband, her house guests, her parties, her whole way of life that made sense to him and this insistence that they thrill to the slightest nod from these people had all but soured Chip with life on Dune Road.

That's when the full thrust of the loneliness set in. He felt he had lost Judy to something he could not understand. He was still the same pragmatic fellow he had always been and she was a person who dealt in fantasies. Last summer it had been the new addition she built onto the house, paying for it out of a precious trust fund left to her by her grandparents. He had objected from the start, trying to explain how frivolous and unnecessary it was. They had argued off and on for months – long, pointless arguments that went round and round interminably. There were moments within those arguments that Chip had to remind himself that he loved her and that was enough to make him give in. He had a feeling if he won the argument he would find his marriage in tatters.

This summer it had been the Hartleys. He wondered what was lonelier – the long weekdays in New York without Judy and Alice or the long weekends at the beach and the requirements demanded of him socializing with their very lofty neighbors.

Somewhere in all of this he had met Maggie. Maggie O'Neill, Irish by way of Missouri – a second generation American filled with a gutsy immigrant "can-do" nature. She had become a refuge for the loneliness.

"Daddy? Come see what we have made." Alice's voice was high with excitement. "It's a turtle. See....see his legs and his shell. I made the tail," she squealed pulling his hand, pulling him out of his reverie. Chip ambled to his feet and allowed himself to be led toward a mound of sand. Violet sat complacently next to it adding a few final flourishes. She was a stocky little thing, he noticed, her bathing suit a trifle too small and once again he wondered that this was the daughter of Emmaline Hartley.

But she surprised him. "The giant turtle of Atlantis," she said with a sweeping gesture. The imperious tone of her voice was pitch perfect and she gazed up at Chip with the level eyes of a superior being as if his presence was hardly required in admiration of the sand sculpture. She really is Emmaline's daughter, he thought. Chip gazed down still holding his daughter's hand. "It's perfect, darling. Too bad we didn't bring the camera." Alice squeezed his hand and giggled.

● ● ●

They met on a photo shoot. He the advertising executive, she the stylist for one of the top commercial photographers in the city. It had been a crazy set up and had taken the crew all of one day and into the evening to get any shot worth using. The client, a tire company from Ohio, had approved an ad that promised to depict the safety of their tires. The Safety Tire – "When All Else Fails." Over and over again the models hired for the shoot were cast in dire situations – the housewife crossing the road with her groceries, the kid on his tricycle chasing a ball into the street, the man stepping off the curb while reading a newspaper – each in an oncoming line of automotive disaster if not for the Safety Tire. A good enough idea back in the art room – a complicated ordeal to shoot on the suburban streets in the outer borough of Brooklyn. Chip watched take after take and with each one found himself more discouraged, but the young stylist always bounced back replacing torn grocery bags, smashed eggs and scattered vegetables with fresh goods, placating the boy's mother with the promise of overtime fees, and fortifying the man with the newspaper with a few snorts of rye whiskey.

Chip found himself watching her more than the actual shoot and at one point suggested maybe he should have a swig or two of the rye himself lest he succumb to the oncoming disaster of the dissatisfied client. She laughed a big, generous laugh. When finally the wrap was called and the camera crew started packing up, Maggie knew of a place down by the docks in Lower Manhattan just across the Brooklyn Bridge where they could get a bowl of fish chowder, the best in the city, and a stiff drink. About five of them piled into a cab eager for the drink but only Maggie and Chip stayed at the saloon on Front Street to have the chowder.

The fact that she was from Missouri and he, Iowa, seemed to bond them and they talked about life in the mid-west and the people they had grown up with. Maggie was a photographer working as a stylist so she could meet the best photographers in the business. She was restless, motivated and sharp. And she loved to laugh with her wide mouth and eyes that went all sparkling and luminously green. Chip found himself more relaxed with her that night than he could remember being for a long time.

Soon enough he found a reason to see her again. With Maggie he could be himself, and that pointed painfully to the Chip Tate that sat high on Madison Avenue. He remembered the city he had discovered for himself when he had first come there, the people he had talked to, the awe he felt walking over the Brooklyn Bridge, the sheer fun of pointing to something on a menu written in Cantonese having no idea of what he had ordered to eat. He remembered meeting all sorts of people back then – the guys who ran the concessions out at Coney Island, the old women from the Ukraine down in the East Village, Judy back in the days when they could spend hours talking, just talking in a coffee shop all afternoon. And the museums? When had he last gone to the Metropolitan or the Modern? Where had all of that curiosity and enthusiasm gone? With Maggie he seemed to have found it again – some of it anyway. She loved exploring the city and more and more he found a way out of the office with its relentless schedules and demanding clients, and joined her.

The dinner party was over, the last guest ushered to the door with airy kisses and gushing thanks. Even Chip had to agree it had been a success. Judy's eyes were shining, her voice was light with laughter as she sat him down and insisted on just one more glass of wine to unwind.

Kicking off her shoes, she flung her arm over her eyes and fell back on the sofa like a dying diva. Peeping out from under her arm she cast him a knowing look as if they were two conspirators. Chip felt himself laugh, a genuine laugh of pleasure and for a few moments this repose of well-being was good. These moments with Judy were never long enough or often enough, but good when they happened.

"Emmaline's table looked very jolly didn't it and yours too, "she said breaking the mood and sitting up to sip her wine. "It's the last time I'll invite that tiresome man from the club though. I don't care if he is the only spare man on the entire East End. He was a colossal bore but at least he was at my table and not..." she was off in a stream of chatter. Chip nodded, smiled and threw in a few anecdotal exchanges he had had with his lot – the actress, good company despite the theatrical airs that seemed *de rigueur* and Walter Penn, a fascinating man he declared and meant it. Judy beamed. Chip had been hearing of Walter for weeks now ever since he had taken her to tea at Ruth Moran's. Judy had swooned at being in the great painter's studio and to Chip recited word for word the various conversational exchanges and *bon mots* she had overheard. Indeed, that outing had prompted quite a few more with Walter: a walking tour of Sag Harbor, a trip to an antiquarian bookseller in Southampton, a lunch party at the Maidstone Club, a concert at Guild Hall. Chip heard it all in detail yet now having met the great and wonderful Walter Penn and feeling disloyal in the extreme he couldn't help but wonder what this worldly man saw in Judy. Whatever it was, it seemed genuine and for that Chip was relieved.

Raleigh appeared with a tray and was picking up stray glasses and silverware and Judy half-heartedly got up to help him but Raleigh was having none of it.

"Sure enough," said Raleigh still impeccable in his white jacket, "you folks go on to bed. I'll tend to this." Chip pulled his wife to her feet and kissed her on the cheek. "You look ravishing, my girl," he teased. " Let's go out dancing."

Judy groaned. "Now I know how you feel when you say you're exhausted. I could sleep for days. Why don't you hustle up one of those nice girls I invited from the club and take her dancing. Jack seemed not in the least interested."

No wonder, thought Chip. How like Judy to be so naively blind to the passions that lay under her nose. Chip had seen from the onset that the evening had been layered in subterfuge. The actor, Grayson, had paid lavish court to Emmaline but had, no doubt, been duly instructed to stay close at hand until no longer needed. That moment had come just as the dessert was being served. "Oh look," declared Emmaline, "a full moon. Judy we simply have to take your canoe out on the bay. Come along Grayson and you too Jack to give us a push. " So the three of them tootled off the deck and down onto the lawn making their way to the water's edge and the canoe tied there. Only, what's this? Grayson suddenly turns back. A search for a sweater, a remembered telephone call...we'll never know but back he came and on went Jack and Emmaline. Chip, upstairs to check on Alice, caught the scene from the window. Jack and Emmaline – fully in sight from his vantage point – now kissing and grappling at one another before scrambling into the canoe and pushing off into the inky black water.

Chip hadn't meant for it to turn into an affair. Or maybe he had. The swift walk to her apartment, the climb up the stairs, the key in the lock, the dark room in which they had not bothered to turn on the lights, Maggie an eager animal in his arms. He couldn't seem to get enough of her, get deep enough into her, absorb the strangeness of her body in his arms, the fullness of her. She was new territory and at the same time she was like something long remembered and longed for. Walking home that night he had felt the weight of what had happened and the terrible cloak of guilt come over him. What in hell was he doing? What did he want? God knows he did not want to leave his wife and child. He loved them. But here he was and the scent and sensations of Maggie filled the night air around him. He vowed to leave it at just that night. A one time only fall from grace, but now watching the dark night swallow Jack and Emmaline, he found himself longing for Maggie once more, wanting to be in that darkened room with the smell of her and the twisting, teasing body so responsive to his.

"You all set, Mr. Chip." Raleigh stood at the kitchen door like a sentinel. "I'll lock up now."

"No...thank you, Raleigh. I'll lock up. I think I'll get a little fresh air." And he turned and opened the front door stepping out into the night but not before he caught the questioning look of the older man.

Chip shut the door behind him with deliberate firmness and breathed in deeply. Raleigh. That was another component in this household of his, the ever helpful, ever perfect Raleigh. Chip had not grown up with servants and in the beginning of his marriage had no idea of how to deal with the presence of another person attending him. No shoe went unpolished, no overcoat was left on a hall chair, no newspaper allowed to scatter on the coffee table, meals produced three times a day beautifully prepared and served – these ministrations astounded Chip in the beginning and had made him feel as if he were an errant schoolboy if he so much as left one untidy trail or was minutes late for a meal. And yet too soon it came to be the way of his life. It wasn't just the tidiness he got used to; to be fair it was the assurance that Raleigh was always there for Judy and Alice. This was useful, even necessary sometimes but what Chip found he could not come to grips with was the fact that Raleigh was always present. The old retainer seemed to carry his familial devotions to an extreme. At the start of his marriage Chip had tried to engage Raleigh on many occasions in conversation. These overtures were always met with polite but strained response. Where was he from? How did he learn to cook so well? What did he do in his spare time? Did he like baseball? The movies? It was as if Raleigh had no past – there was no family, no reminiscences, no photographs or mementoes in his rooms. Chip knew this because he had once gone up to the third floor where Raleigh lived at the beach house searching for a set of old golf clubs Judy thought might be stored there. Not an attic but a series of small rooms on the upper floor built for the much larger household of servants in Judy's grandparents day. Raleigh had a small bedroom and a sitting room with a comfortable chair, a good light and a bookcase filled with books. Chip had mulled over the titles – detective stories mainly but some surprisingly interesting biographies and reference books including *The Complete Works of Shakespeare*. Another small room was given over to his clothes and uniforms and a large cedar closet where blankets and linens were stored over the winter. In an alcove off his sitting room he had fashioned a sort of pantry with a small ice chest for cokes and beer and a two burner electric unit on which he prepared his morning coffee and late night snack. Raleigh, Chip saw, was fond of cheddar cheese, saltine crackers and ketchup as his larder ran exclusively to those items. A rather sophisticated Philco radio completed the domestic setting. Judy said he listened to baseball games as well as the live concerts from Philharmonic Hall in New York.

He had asked Judy about Raleigh many times but she just looked blank. Raleigh was Raleigh she would shrug. He had once worked on the railroad – a steward she thought, but her father had found him, liked him and brought him to New York to work for the family. He had been with her since she was a little girl and that's all she knew...or cared to know. Judy was like that – not really curious, taking life as it came. She was completely without guile – something that had charmed him in the beginning. Now he wasn't so sure?

Chip stood staring out into the dark. Judy was expecting him in her bed, in her arms. Tired as she was, she still wanted him. He had seen it in her face, felt it in the squeeze of his arm as she went up the stairs but he couldn't go there, into that room with all its billowy comforts and careful coordination. It was a frilly room not designed for passion but for feminine comfort. He could feel the suffocating mantle of the house falling on him and instead of going back inside he turned out into the night, down the drive and across the road to the beach. Standing on the dunes he stared out at the black sea and the white foam of the waves, inhaling the deep, sensuous, heavy salt air and marveling, as he always did, in its immensity. He had often wondered if this was what religion was about. The great universe. Only tonight it was not just the vastness of an ocean and sky but the impossible distance he felt in his life from the one person who was within arm's reach. Judy was more a stranger to him now than she had been on that long ago day in the museum. He knew she loved him but he couldn't say for sure how he felt about her, about anything. And what was love anyway? Did it even exist or was it some illusion like an advertising layout in a magazine? Out here in the darkness, he began to fantasize about changing his life, shedding all the false pretenses. He needed Maggie just as he needed Judy and Alice. And why shouldn't he have both? He thought about his father, that long extinguished man he had hardly known but from whom he had been running all his life. His car pulling out of the drive, his mother weeping in the kitchen, the smell of cheap perfume on the laundry left behind. Now he, chip off the old block, was the unfaithful husband, drifting on some powerful undertow, helpless on a dark sea.

28

Exodus
September 12th

Judy stood in the living room listening to the rain against the windows. Ever since Labor Day the weather had been dreadful. She almost wished she and Alice had gone back to the city with Chip but no; she was going to stick it out until Alice's birthday on the 21st. She would not give in to Chip's bad mood about it and determined to make these last days before closing the house for the winter as agreeable as she could. A telephone message left for Jack at the store in Amagansett inviting him for dinner had as yet been unanswered. She had even gone so far as to stop in at Cobb's farm for a chicken. He was a terrible old grump and usually Chip went to buy his eggs and chickens. She adjusted a picture on the wall moved a lamp a few inches to the right, and sighed.

Chip had left just after Labor Day in his usual mood. Somber, distracted barely speaking to her so intent he was on his big deal, the very same big deal that had plagued the whole of the summer. She had long since lost any interest in his work and only resented it. She saw her marriage, once so filled with the excitement of new beginnings, now as predictable as a grocery list. What had happened to the magic born of two strangers and a chance meeting?

They had spent their honeymoon here at the beach house – a whole month before Chip needed to return to the city to start working at the agency – it was paradise. They discovered the immensely erotic adventure of making love in the sunlight in the dunes, they swam for hours in the ocean until exhausted and drugged by the sun and the salt air, canoed into the bay after dark the stars reflected in the inky water so that they felt as if they were floating in a galaxy bubble, bicycled everywhere in the afternoons stopping at farm stands, discovering side roads and deserted bay beaches. Often in the early evening, they would fill a bucket with seawater and boil it over a fire on the beach for clams or lobsters or just a meal of corn on the cob and fresh thick cut tomatoes from the Cobb farm out toward the highway. On foggy nights they might walk the beach barefoot, half in the eddying water and white foam of the sea and marvel at the sense of being alone in the universe, just the two of them.

The euphoria of that first month changed once they returned to New York. Imperceptibly at first but Chip's success at the ad agency and the lavish attention from her parents soon patterned their lives. Chip cautioned Judy that they would have to make do on his salary and Judy approved his decision because she believed he was bringing a whole new dimension into her life, but soon enough her father had cajoled Chip into allowing small indulgences – tickets to the opera, flowers delivered weekly, wine from their personal merchant, and open charge accounts at the department stores for Judy's clothes.

And now, seven years later, that time with Chip had all but gone. Beyond the usual day-to-day coordination of married life, Chip no longer seemed to want to explore their life together and a handholding walk on the beach was about as remote as was his work. What did he do all day, she wondered? BC she called it, "Before Clients," a clever remark that once had made him laugh but now…well, now she never dared make the slightest fun of his work. Not since her father's stroke and retirement. Oh, Chip had been wonderful, just wonderful through those dark days taking charge, reassuring them all that everything would be all right, handling all the details of moving her parents to the farm in Connecticut and closing out the living quarters at the Fifth Avenue Hotel. He was exemplary in every way – a careful man, loving son-in-law and all around comfort to the grieving family, but in the months that followed things changed dramatically. For one thing their social life all but vanished. Chip was too tired. He actually groaned when she suggested dinner parties and theater tickets. For another, he was reluctant to spend time at the beach, a place he had once loved. And then there was their sex life. An act relegated to Saturday night and over before it really began. None of the long, teasing hours in bed, none of the...*Oh, stop it!*

But she couldn't stop it. She remembered their life just before Alice had been born. They had gone to see *It Happened One Night*, Claudette Colbert being one of Judy's favorite screen actresses. In the movie a rich and sassy Claudette was up against Clark Gable's rough-edged character as a journalist. Afterwards Judy had cried because she wanted to be that gutsy girl. She wanted to be impertinent and lively and out there in a world of plucky heroines but here she was with an aching back and swollen ankles. Chip soothed her tears making her a hot toddy then propping her feet up on the sofa with cushions. She was beautiful, he said, more beautiful than Claudette or any other Hollywood star could possibly hope to be and if Clark Gable ever dared to come near her, well then, he Chip Tate would give *him* something to remember. They laughed then and despite her ungainly stomach, had made love – her body hyper with hormones, her breasts swollen and so sensitive to his touch that she reached wave after wave of unbounded pleasure in Chip's arms that night. Afterwards they had walked to an all night diner over on tenth Avenue filled with workers off the docks where they ordered an enormous breakfast of greasy bacon and eggs, laughing and talking until dawn then walking to the Hudson River. Tugs and barges were already at work in the hazy morning and with her husband's arms around her, the baby thumping its own morning beat inside her, Judy believed that an angel must have been hovering nearby. How else could such happiness be accounted for?

The baby arrived on time a month later, beautiful in every way and Judy wrapped herself up in the richness of a new life. Chip delighted in having a daughter, was absorbed and fascinated with the tiny Alice. Though he had a sister out in Iowa, it was as if Alice was truly his only living relative and here at last after years on the edges of Judy's world was a flesh and blood world of his own. For a long time Alice's birth put all Judy's day dreams about wanting to be something or someone other than who she was buried under the many demands of being a mother, a wife, of making sure the people she loved most were warm and well fed and happy.

But something else was always nibbling at the edges and here with the rain at the window and the growing ennui that seemed to more and more engulf her, Judy suddenly remembered the voice of Senora. *Girls. Girls.* That vibrant little teacher as tiny as a bird that had come to her school to teach Italian tenth grade year and one of the most remarkable in Judy's life. Senora simply made you want to do things, reach for things and imagine things that you never thought you could. Senora taught so much more than Italian. She taught life, art, food and adventure away from the strict regimen of the school. Her girls, her *bella donnas*, she called them with her tiny frame, jet black hair pulled into an elaborate twist at the nape of her neck, wearing brocaded shawls and flashy earrings so that the girls secretly called her The Gypsy. And truly she was, a magical being, full of imagination and charm. Out into the streets of New York they went, to museums and poetry readings, experimental plays in the Village and once to a loft where a man in tight trousers taught them the tango. Senora taught them to cook in the Italian style, to alter their notions of dress, to read books unknown to the school reading list.

Judy was both fascinated and frightened by her. Senora was exotic, like no other adult figure in Judy's life and the doors she opened were exhilarating to Judy's young and absorbing mind yet try as she might she could never quite walk through them. And then...the next year Senora was gone. Perhaps parents were unhappy about liberating ideas, perhaps she had only been there to fill in for another teacher on sabbatical, perhaps she had been fired outright, Judy would never know but the novelty of Senora soon bowed to the customary path of growing up. Ideas, ambitions, exploration, curiosity... were put aside in favor of dances, boys, fashionable clothes, falling in love...these were the things girls cared about. These were the things that were real. And then one day she had met Chip and those doors seemed to open once again if only for a tantalizingly brief time before she had drifted back into the safe harbor of traditional life.

When the telephone rang she was miles away in thought.

"I hope this isn't too early for you?" Emmaline never

identified herself on the telephone. It was assumed you knew exactly who was calling.

"No, of course not. I was just..." but Emmaline cut her off.

"I can't bear this rain another minute. Come for lunch, will you? You'll cheer me up. You will come?"

Judy felt a rush of pleasure. Emmaline had never invited her to lunch before. "I'd love it. The rain is so..." but Emmaline kept on.

"And bring your cousin...Jack isn't it? Do you think he's about?"

"Well..." now she felt flustered. If anyone should know if Jack was about it would be Emmaline. After all hadn't he been at Villamere nearly the whole of the summer painting portraits of the Hartley children? At first she flattered herself that she had been the conduit for such an important commission for her cousin but after weeks of Jack's rackety motorcycle bypassing her drive for Emmaline's, resentment set in. She had counted on Jack to be...well, to be there for *her*. The portrait that Judy planned to surprise Chip with was so far only a sketch on the canvas, but the Hartley children were finished.

"Judy? Are you there?" Emmaline's insistent voice snapped her back into the present.

"Yes...yes of course. I was just thinking I could put in a call to Jack but in this rain and all the way from Amagansett..."

"No. Don't do that. It was only a thought. I just thought if he were lurking in the eaves. I wanted to thank him again for the gorgeous portraits of the children. Shall we say...one o'clock?"

"Yes...I'll..." but before she could finish, Emmaline issued a curt "Good," and hung up.

Jack? Lurking in the eaves?

• • •

Emmaline's idea of an impromptu lunch was an exquisitely laid table, cold lobster on a bed of watercress, remoulade sauce, Mrs. Sternhoffer's famous cheese biscuits, a sparking white wine, and a silver bowl of perfect peaches.

"I hate this time of year. Hot. Sticky. The dull end of summer," said Emmaline fretfully letting her lobster fork fall on the china plate. "The summer over, all the packing to do, getting the children ready for school. I don't know why those schools start so late in September. It throws everything off. I mean Labor Day should end the summer good and proper. All this dragging of heels and spilling over after the season." She was vague, rambling even.

"Well...I don't know. I rather like September," Judy tried gamely though she could see Emmaline was not listening to her. Fidgeting with her own fork she too was not particularly hungry but she poked the silver prongs into the claws digging out the sweet meat.

"Whatever has happened to that handsome cousin of yours?" Emmaline said suddenly.

"Jack?"

Emmaline nodded indifferently. "The very one."

"Why I would have thought you would know better than me," said Judy.

Emmaline started. "Why in the world would you say such a thing?"

"Well," Judy began, "no reason except I was given to understand he was here painting the children's portraits. I see his motorcycle here all the time." She paused, "Why do you ask?"

"Oh. Yes, but he finished the portraits ages ago. Rather amusing I think. Especially George. He got the little beast exactly right but surely you've talked to Jack. I thought the two of you were so close." She reached over and plucked the stem out of one of the peaches.

"Oh we are. Jack and I are very close." She said this in an attempt at coyness wishing it were true. "But lately he's been so busy with his work... actually I did see him a few days ago...." Main Beach in East Hampton where Judy had taken Alice and some of her little friends. Judy under an umbrella surrounded by little girls, sticky from their ice creams and just beyond the cabanas was Jack and a stunning girl with honey colored hair and a figure that had every man on the beach ogling. They seemed to be posing for someone with a large boxed camera on a tripod and both Jack and the girl were kitted out in old-fashioned bathing costumes. Judy felt Emmaline's intense gaze. "Why just the other day I saw him on the beach with some new girl and they were having quite a high time. He was dressed to look like the muscle man in the circus and she was..." Judy described the scene in detail oblivious to the look that had come over her hostess's face.

The silence following made Judy uncomfortable so she plunged the fork into the tail of her lobster and this time the meat came out in one sucking lump. Emmaline sat mutely smoking, for a long minute before leaning forward and crushing the cigarette into a crystal ashtray. An evil snake of pungent smoke kept burning. "I take it Chip has gone back to the city," she said abruptly. "I'm not nearly so lucky. James is still here."

"Yes, he's gone." Judy said wistfully. "It's work and more work. Some big impending deal. It kept him busy all summer really. He used to love the beach but not this summer..."

Emmaline gave a knowing laugh. "Ah, the hard working man. Or so they like to claim. If I were you I wouldn't leave an attractive man like that alone in the city for too long." She sat back reaching for another cigarette then thought better of it. "It's not that they mean to get up to no good, it's just that there are so many predators eager to make hay when the wife is safely tucked up at the beach." She snapped her napkin open and laid it in her lap picking up her fork and stabbed it into the tail of her own lobster. "But what am I saying? You and Chip have the perfect marriage." She was already bored with Judy and her tiresome husband. All Emmaline could think about was Jack.

She had last seen him at her end of the season party the prior weekend and they had quarreled. More than that. She had thrown him out. He had come prancing into her house, into *her* party, with a girl on his arm – a silly girl. One glance at her and Emmaline felt her talons sharpen. She was exquisite, this fresh faced girl, her skin smooth and glowing, a rush of freckles across her tanned cheeks, her lips full, her soft brown hair waved and falling loosely to her shoulders, her figure milkmaid round, a flower of a girl, sweet, just-bloomed…adorable.

Jack was a little drunk when they arrived and seeing the flare of hostility in Emmaline's face had been clever enough to steer the girl over to a cluster of men, introducing her to James and a few of his cronies so that before Emmaline could muster her counter attack, the girl was surrounded by old, titillated men making fools of themselves. Jack found it funny but Emmaline was infuriated. She pulled Jack into the hall.

"Who is she, Jack? " She said, her words light but as barbed as icicle shards. "A new *art* student?"

"No, thank God." he said grinning. "She's a model for one of the ad agencies and she's out here on a shoot. I know the photographer."

"I'm sure you do," said Emmaline. "I'm sure you know lots of girls in *advertising*." The word spat out of her mouth as if the lowest of terms. "But that is nothing to me. How dare you bring her to my house without asking? Do you think I fling open my doors to just anybody?"

Jack peered back into the room where the party was going full blast. "Come off it Emmaline. How many people here do you actually know? You said yourself your parties were mostly strangers. Cindy's a good kid. And you'll have to admit she's got the old boys on their toes. "

"May they all die of heart failure," came the caustic reply. "I mean it Jack. Don't ever presume you have carte blanche with me."

"Madam, I would never assume to presume. Not carte nor blanche nor fancy dance." He really was drunk and a sob of fury escaped her. Jack still laughing reached for her but he was unsteady and instead he pitched forward and Emmaline stepped away from him so violently that she lost her balance and fell over a small table holding a vase of flowers and now she was falling backwards and the clatter and crashing of breaking glass brought the chattering party to silence.

"Whoa," Jack yelped, stooping to assist her but then he too fell, tripping over the gauzy chiffon hem of her dress. They tangled grappling on the floor until one of the guests rushed over seizing Emmaline unceremoniously under her arms as if *she* were the drunken fool and not Jack. "Are you all right?" he asked hoisting her to her feet. Her dress was drenched in water and her hair fell in her face. She shook free and tried to regain some composure. "I'm fine," she said her voice ice. "Just fine but I can't say the same for Mr. Burns." Jack was still struggling to his feet and he was laughing as if the whole thing had been some elaborately staged pantomime. Suddenly Emmaline felt like laughing too but then she spotted the girl standing in the semi-circle of guests gaping at the scene and the ugly bile rose up again inside her. She snapped her fingers and Martin, the houseman, appeared at her side. "Mr. Burns and his companion are leaving. Please show them out." And with one last withering look, she swept up the stairs to her room.

Jack sent her a basket of yellow roses the next morning that must have cost him his last penny and a contrite note but she had no intention of letting him off that easy. She would ignore him for a few days, just long enough to let him truly suffer, then she would forgive him and in a magnanimous gesture would allow him back into her arms. But it had not gone that way, not at all. She was the one suffering. Judy Tate had given her the news she couldn't bear. He was with that girl.

• • •

But he wasn't. Wasn't with that girl or any other girl. Jack was at that very moment sitting in Nettie Grindle's kitchen with his pad and pencils drawing a portrait of Mitch.

Mitch had stood awkwardly on the step of the chicken coop late the afternoon before and tapped on the door. "Say, Jack I was thinking about what to give Nettie for our twenty-fifth weddin' and...well...I had this idea that you might consider drawing a picture for her." He seemed embarrassed.

Jack whistled appreciatively. "Twenty-five years. Not bad." He held the door open but that seemed to confuse Mitch more. "Would you like to see some of the things I've done this summer?"

"Ah...well, sir...no. Wasn't thinking of something you done. Was thinking...uh...hell, I'll just say it outright. I was thinking you might do me." Jack looked momentarily confused and Mitch stumbled on. "Thought maybe I'd ask you to draw the kids but then Jarvis being gone out West seemed like mebbe it might be me she'd like. Don't want you to think I want to be prettied up or anything, just something I can hand to Nettie. I think she'll go for it in a big way."

This might have been more words than Mitch had ever said to Jack all summer and oddly the idea agreed with him. If nothing else, Mitch might be his last chance at Crazy Tom. Enough people including Nettie had said talk to Mitch but Jack had always held that Mitch didn't like him. Leastways, Mitch had never before gone out of his way to talk to Jack and in all this time Jack had come no closer to the old beachcomber than distant sightings and the prevailing view that he should leave the guy alone. And now here was Mitch Grindle asking him a favor.

"Sure Mitch. Be glad to. It can be my gift to Nettie too." But Mitch insisted that he pay, no favors allowed. They settled on $15 but only, Jack said, if Mitch liked the finished work.

"Nettie and the kids are out to Granny Minnie's for a few days putting up preserves. Mebbe we can do this tomorrow? I got my boat in for a repair."

And so it was that while Judy and Emmaline sat eating lobster at Villamere, Jack and Mitch sat across from one another in Nettie's kitchen. Jack saw with disappointment Mitch had put on a clean shirt and combed his hair but he said nothing and sat him at an angle that caught the light coming in from the door. When he laid out his box of drawing pencils and attached a large sheet of velour to his drawing board he could see the discomfort in the fisherman's face as Mitch nervously ran his fingers through his hair. Now it stood up in clumps like the wind blowing though it.

"Great," said Jack. "So..." he picked up a pencil and sat studying Mitch who was beginning to look like a man caught in a trap. "Nettie's at Granny Minnie's huh?"

"Yeah," Mitch grunted. He had set two beers out for them and now grabbed his and took a long swig. Jack drew a line on the pad.

"Tell me about her." Jack said, looking at Mitch then down at his pad. "You can talk all you want but it helps me if you don't change the way you're sitting. If it gets uncomfortable we can break. Don't even think about me."

Mitch sat quietly for a few minutes. Then he said, "Tough old bird. My dad know'd Minnie back when they was kids. Said she always pretty much ruled the roost. Nettie's dad sure knew that."

Jack laughed. "I heard about Minnie chasing him around with a hatchet."

"And that's the truth, too." Mitch was laughing himself beginning to relax taking another swig of beer. "He was one lazy guy but Nettie and Lottie loved him." He fell silent again and started to tense up.

"So, if you don't mind me asking," Jack said, "tell me about fishing. What's it like out there?"

Mitch looked a little startled. "Well...let's see. That depends." He reached into his pocket for his pack of Luckies and sat for almost a full minute before he lit the cigarette. "OK if I smoke while you're drawing?"

"Sure is."

Mitch puffed on his cigarette and squinted at the ceiling. "First you got to figure out what kind of fishing day it's gonna be. As soon as I get to the water I can tell, not how many fish I'll catch just what kind of day I'll be fishing in. Then you got to figure where the fish are."

"I take it they're not just anywhere."

"No. They's got their places. You watch the birds. They be circling or diving. Fish come in season migrating north in the spring, south in the fall. There's lots of ways to know where they are but the main thing see, is you gotta know how best to catch 'em. I learned all I know about fishin' from the old guys on the beach. Learned by watching and asking questions."

"Old Tom, too?" Jack said. "He seems a pretty salty old guy. Did he always live on the beach?" Jack leaned into his drawing like Tom was not of much interest to him.

"Tom don't belong to us the way the rest of the folks do. Some say when the Indians got run out of Montauk he come to live down here on the beach. That was back before I was born but when I was a kid there was an old timer down this way claimed he saw Tom come up out of the water one winter day and that he'd been living on the beach ever since. That's when they did cod fishing off Amagansett. That's a hard life, hard work. The men went out on boats in tough weather. I remember the ice hanging off of wool mittens. First thing those old timers would do was take those mittens and dip 'em into the salt water then put 'em on and the steam would come out of the wool and would keep them from getting frost bite. Anyways, we kids always believed that story. Mainly, cause we learned most everything from those old guys and there wasn't no reason to doubt 'em."

Jack stopped drawing and looked at Mitch. "You really think that's true? About Tom I mean. It makes him sound like Neptune or something."

Mitch shrugged. "Don't know. There were a lot of ship-wrecks back in them days but that don't explain the magic in Tom. He pulls the most amazing stuff out of the sea. You walk these beaches and do you see much? Naw. The beaches are clean mostly. Some driftwood now and then, a few broken up shells, but Tom? Why he finds stuff that's out of this world."

Jack could see something new in Mitch's face, an expression he hadn't seen before. "So," he persisted, "do you ever talk to Tom? Do you visit him?"

Mitch shook his head. "No one talks to him. He don't like it. But whenever he shows up you know something is brewing. When I was about ten years old I was dying to get out on the water but my dad says I'm too young. No experience. And then one day Tom shows up outside our house. He give me a look and started off down the beach. I followed him and way out Napeague he walks me to a little dingy hiding out in the grasses. It had come up on shore, abandoned I guess or lost off a ship. He helped me drag it over to Napeague Bay and I started fishing for bait fish and I've been fishin' ever since. Over the years I've gotten pretty good, if the fish are there and with a little bit of luck, I can catch 'em. Once it's in your blood it never leaves you. That's why the old guys hang around the beach and on the wharves out in Montauk. Knew a fella once who was real sick with the cancer but up until the week he died he would get up and get himself over to the ocean just to make sure it was still there." Mitch was quiet now his eyes resting in the middle distance lost in thought. The only sound was the pencil scratching on the paper. Jack had started his sketch seeing a man sitting at a table, his large hands resting around a bottle of beer, his face half turned to the light, a man whose shoulders and arms were testaments to a hard working life but now he saw something else, something more… something intangible. He worked another few minutes in silence then he put the pencil down and held the paper up.

Mitch got up and came around the table. "Say now, Jack. I recognize that fellow, I think. Sure enough." He seemed surprised. "Nettie sure will be pleased."

"Yeah." Jack stared at the drawing. "I think so, too. I'm not done with it yet. I need to look at it again in another light. And I need to treat it so it won't smudge. I can even get it framed for you." Jack wanted to look at his work more, away from Mitch. He had done something new here and he needed to figure it out.

"Naw. I'll git one of the boys to make me a frame. But you take it now and I'll pick it up in a day or so. You want some stew? Nettie left me enough food for ten guys. She thinks I can't take care of myself."

Jack, too distracted to stay, thanked him and said he would have it ready the next afternoon. Mitch didn't do anything to waylay him. He walked Jack to the door and shook his hand. Jack had put the drawing back in the pad and for a few minutes they stood in the doorway listening to the ocean. "It ain't possible that a man could come walking up out of the ocean now is it?" Mitch said. Then, he chuckled and turned back into the house.

• • •

That evening a morose Emmaline sat before the mirror in her dressing room. Inside the glass with the theatrical light bulbs studding its edges like tiny balls of fire, her face stared back at her. It seemed fixed almost like a photograph and only her eyes indicated the face was alive. She examined this image with curious intensity. "Oh, my god," she choked at last, and covered her eyes with her palms.

Twelve years separated them, a yawning crevasse of time so unfairly weighted against women. He was looking forward in his life with all its possibilities and unknowns while she was looking back – a woman longing for her past, a woman staring at the truth in a mirror.

It was over. She had known from the beginning that it couldn't last, ...but why? Why did it have to end? She was going back to New York and so was he. She would go to him. Apologize. No...no. No apologies. She would go to him and tell him she loved him. Because... she did love him. She dropped her hands from her face. He had no idea she loved him! *She* had no idea she loved him! It had happened. The thing she thought would never happen again. She could have cried.

29

Urgent Weather Message
September 18th
Storm on direct course to Miami,
weather bureau advises evacuation

Judy lay awake. It was three in the morning, the worst possible time to be awake. She could hear the ocean but there was no comfort and no lulling her to sleep in the steady sound of the waves.

In the dark, with her eyes wide open she could feel the emptiness of her bed. And now she was up and downstairs pacing about her living room, in the kitchen making tea, out on the deck shivering in the cool, wet night air.

Yet despite trying to will her fears and doubts out of her mind all she could hear was Emmaline. "*If I were you I wouldn't leave an attractive man like that alone in the city for long. It's not that they mean to get up to no good, it's just that there are so many predators.*"

It wasn't work! It was another woman. The thought of it stunned her and yet it was true. Or was it? She tried to think, tried to rationalize but her brain was on fire. She needed to get out, to go somewhere, talk to someone. She would go...go... she would go to Jack. Yes. Jack would tell her she was being a fool, that she had nothing to worry about. Jack, dear wonderful cousin Jack, her very best friend. It was not yet dawn when she left the note for Raleigh, quietly easing old Woodie down the drive onto Dune Road. About halfway to the highway she saw that the gas gauge was near empty. No gas stations open at this hour. Judy bit her lip. The train! Didn't the Fisherman's Special come through at 5:15 a.m. with all those sports fishermen from New York intent on getting to Montauk and the charter boats? Judy pressed her foot down hard on the pedal and old Woodie, unused to such urgency lurched and buckled its way with only minutes to spare before the eastbound train whistled into the station.

The ride was short but Judy had been right – it was filled with fishermen, their gear piled up on seats, a boisterous bunch eager for the day ahead and she was glad to get off and away from them in Amagansett. The sun now on the horizon, she walked into the village to the general store glad to see it was open.

Herb Foss looked up with surprise. He was busy with eggs, bacon, griddlecakes expecting his usual crowd in for early break-fast but not a lady. He came out from behind the counter wiping his hands on his apron.

"Morning, miss. Can I help you?"

Judy smiled. "I would love a cup of coffee if you've got it. I haven't been up this early since…since I don't know when."

"Sure thing. We got coffee, ham, eggs, bacon, rolls…you name it. You just set right down here at the counter. You visiting?"

Judy slid onto the stool. "No. I just got off the train all the way from Bridgehampton." She laughed. "Not much of a trip but my car…well, my car had other ideas. I'm here to see my cousin."

Herb placed a steaming cup of coffee in front of her. "Cousin, you say?"

"Yes. Jack Burns. I'm his cousin Judy Tate…" She was breathless. *Get a hold of yourself* she thought. What in god's name was she doing here? "I thought I'd walk over to his house," she finished up lamely.

"Why sure thing, Miz Tate. I've put through calls to you from Jack. I know him well. He's my best customer. Sold him that motorcycle in the spring. Say, can I give you a lift to Jack's? No trouble."

Judy sipped at her coffee. "Oh, no." she stammered. "I want to walk. Thank you so much." She sipped a little more, uncomfortable in the shop owner's gaze. "You know…maybe I'll just be going. What do I owe you?"

Herb looked like he had been badly hurt. The cup was still just about as full as when he set it down. "How about we put it on Jack's bill. But now maybe I could make you some eggs…?"

"No...no...best be on my way. Thank you so much." This was madness. Why *was* she here? She pushed out of the door and almost fled down the street stumbling clumsily along until she got to Meeting House Lane. Jack's chicken coop was not far off the main road.

Judy came through the gate and then noticed the car parked to the side of the coop half hidden by a mulberry bush. It was... yes; it was Emmaline's car for sure. You could hardly mistake the jaunty yellow convertible. Emmaline must have reconnected with Jack yesterday after lunch. Emmaline must have lent him her car. Maybe that rackety old motorcycle had finally given out. Judy stood on the stoop about to rap on the door when she heard sounds coming from inside. There could be no mistaking what they were. The sounds of lovemaking. Intense and urgent. Judy stood frozen in place, her hand still outstretched to knock.

Emmaline and Jack! Of course. How could she not have known? The reality of it made her gasp.

She backed away as silently as she could cursing under her breath when she knocked a small tin bucket off the stoop but the creaking and moaning from inside did not break. She opened the gate as furtively as if a burglar. Of course, of course. How could she have been so stupid? Stupid, innocent, naive Judy. She walked without any direction. What did it matter? Jack was not her concern. He could do anything he liked and Emmaline...all those friendly overtures why they had nothing to do with her! It was Jack she wanted. Judy reached the end of the lane, saw a road leading down to the beach and she took it, passing small houses and huts and sheds until at last she was on the sand.

The empty beach stretched as far as she could see to either side of her a beautiful, infinite, timeless stretch of pale sand running unbroken for miles in either direction. If she turned to the right she would eventually, though many miles off, reach the summer colony of houses and estates, of clubs and cabanas. If she turned left there was nothing but enormous dunes and the wild emptiness leading out to the end of the island. She turned left.

Sex. That was all anyone seemed to care about. Oh they all talked a good game about *art* or *the important business deal* – they played at being clever or loyal or interested in other things but in the end it was all about sex. Nothing meant anything if you weren't embroiled in an erotic tangle of sheets. Jack, Emmaline and now Chip? Was that why he was always busy, always exhausted, never wanted her anymore? Of course it was. A sob caught in her throat. No, no, she reasoned. Not Chip, not her husband. But she couldn't breathe in the enormity of it.

She was alone on the beach, as alone as anyone could be. In her misery she didn't feel the warmth of the sun on her face as the dawn gave way to morning. It was a beautiful day. After the weeks of steaming humidity and rain, here at last was a perfect summer day – azure sky, a soft gentle breeze off the ocean, frisky little waves along the shore line, small pools left in the hollows of the sand, pipers running hither and yon, the ocean itself sparkling in a million tiny diamond lights. The warmth and beauty of it made her stop and she sat down on the edge of the shore letting the tips of the waves wash over her feet like a soothing balm.

How long she was there she didn't know, but as if by osmosis she slowly came aware that she was not alone. She got up still staring out to sea and picked up her shoes. Then, she quickly turned around. There in the dunes unseen before was a crude hut, a piece of canvas hung over the door, bits and pieces of junk were propped up against the sides of the structure – driftwood, rope, rusted and broken bed springs and pockmarked barrels. The sun sent a glare from the roof and Judy lifted her hand to shield her eyes. A man, a very old man from the looks of his beard sat cross-legged on the top of the hut, which was nothing more than a slanted piece of tin. He gazed down on her and she up to him. Judy was frozen to the spot – not afraid exactly but unable to move her body. Her hand dropped and the light glared in her eyes. When she lifted her hand again the man was gone. She took a step closer to the hut but her eyes were filled with black spots from the glare. There was nothing except a few cats pacing in front of the flapping canvas door.

• • •

Mitch Grindle was loading gear onto the back of the pickup when he saw a woman walking up from the beach onto the road. She stopped for a moment to put on her shoes and then kept on walking purposefully towards the house.

"Excuse me," she said coming into the yard. "I'm so sorry to bother you but I need to call a taxi and was wondering if I could borrow your telephone...?"

He smiled. "Can't help you there," he said. "Don't got a phone but even if I did closest taxi is over to East Hampton village and I'm not all that sure they're running now that it's September. Where 'ya headed?"

Judy thought for a moment. Where indeed? She frowned, "Well...I think...I guess East Hampton. The library. That's where I'm going. Is it far? I can walk...," although the idea of any more walking was exhausting.

Mitch scratched his head. "Say – I've got to go up town to pick up some tools. I can give you a lift. Be glad to."

"Oh thank you." The rush of relief was more than apparent. "Are you sure you don't mind? I was on the train...."

He helped her into the cab of the truck and they set off the 5 miles between the two villages. "I'm Judy Tate. I can't tell you how much I appreciate this." Mitch nodded sticking out a rough and calloused hand to shake hers. "Mitch Grindle." They rode on in silence. Once in the village they drove down the main street shaded by the giant elms that arched overhead. "It's so beautiful," Judy breathed. "I remember the first time I ever saw them. I thought I was in Wonderland, you know, like Alice falling down the rabbit hole." *Oh, god, she thought. Perhaps he's never heard of Alice In Wonderland.*

Mitch glanced up and chewed a bit on his lip. "Yep. Everybody loves them elms." At the library he parked the truck and came around to help her out. "You sure I can't take you anywhere else? Don't mind. Library don't open 'til later on."

Judy shook her head, thanked him again, he nodded and

then he drove off making a U turn in the road heading back to Amagansett. It took her a minute to realize Mitch Grindle didn't need to pick up any tools in the village.

She crossed the road and sat down on the grass embankment around the town pond watching two swans make graceful arcs in the water pausing now and then to dip their long elegant necks down to the murky bottom for a treat. It was so quiet and she flopped back onto the grass closing her eyes and letting the warm sun cover her.

"Judy? Is that you?" Judy opened her eyes and her heart flooded with relief. Walter!

If he had been surprised to see her stretched out at 8 a.m. on a weekday morning he now acted as if it were the most natural thing in the world. Judy got up brushing her skirt off.

"I'm out for my morning constitutional and would enjoy some company." He cupped her elbow and turned them both in the direction of the ocean. " At last, a beautiful day."

Judy nodded – then buried her face in her hands sobbing. Walter let her cry without saying anything offering instead a handkerchief. Crying women were not his specialty but he knew that there was usually no stopping them once they started. Somehow, instinctively he knew she was crying out of fear and not some deep loss. The Old South Burying Ground was on one side of the pond and now he led her to a stone bench placed near a grave.

When at last she had calmed down, he said. "Let's talk a bit. You can tell me what the problem is if you like…or not."

Taking a deep breath Judy rewound her story to the day before and Emmaline's comment. "She's probably right, you know. I felt it, the minute she said it. I just knew she's right. I called him last night – I called at eight, then again at ten and then again at midnight. I was too afraid to call after that. It's true. It must be true."

Walter said nothing.

"I'm hopelessly naïve. I know that," she finally said. "All my life I've been wrapped in a cocoon of protection."

"Which you enjoy, don't you?"

Judy paused to reflect on this. "Yes," she admitted slowly, "Up to now I guess I have. But then I meet someone like Emmaline and feel so envious. I would give anything to be as worldly as she is, and witty and in charge of her self. But I'm none of these things. I'm weak and dependent and…boring. No wonder my husband is looking elsewhere. I bore him. I bore myself. Surely I bore you too. Why in the world have you made me feel like a friend?"

Walter now allowed himself a wry smile. "I've enjoyed our time together. You remind me of someone. Someone I miss very much. I'd like to show you something if you're up for a little walk. It's not far and such a beautiful day. This must be an omen that all the bad weather of the summer is finally over. I think walking would do us both good," and offering her his arm they made their way out of the cemetery towards Ocean Avenue.

They reached a place called Pudding Hill and for the first time that morning Judy smiled. "Why in the world would anyone name their street Pudding Hill?"

"Well now I'm glad you asked. Gives me a chance to show off my local history. This was the site of a farm during the Revolution. The farmer's wife, Mrs. Osborne, was cooking a suet pudding when a band of hungry redcoats arrived at her door. 'Hurrah boys, said their Captain, 'We're just in time to sup.' 'Oh no you're not,' said the patriot Mrs. Osborne and she rushed from her stove with the pudding and threw it down this little hill." Now Judy laughed.

"You know so much, Walter. How did you come by that story?"

"Well, for one thing I grew up here."

"Here? Here in this house?" She pointed to a rambling cedar shingled house on the corner of Pudding Hill Lane.

"No. Not this one. That's what I wanted to show you." They walked on for a short while to Lily Pond Lane and turned into it, passing under an impressive avenue of gnarled trees.

"These sycamores were imported from France back in the 1880s. Beautiful, aren't they? I always think of them as sentinels guarding the entrance to an ancient kingdom. A kingdom by the sea as Mr. Poe said so well. I should have shown you this on a rainy day when the scent of the wet bark is pure heaven, indescribable. And...here we are." Walter stopped and gestured.

Set back from the road was an impressive expanse of lawn leading to an enormous white house floating in its sea of grass like a majestic ship beautiful and gracious with porches and towers and gabled roof tops. Built during the heyday of the gilded age, the house was a stunning testament to enormous wealth. Judy gasped in both awe and delight.

"But of course, you would have had to live in this house. It suits you perfectly."

"Does it?" Walter smiled. "I grew up in this house, lived in it until I was sixteen...but there's a qualifier. I grew up in the servants wing. My mother was the upstairs maid. My father, the gardener. My aunt Betty was...let's see, I think she was the salad maid. And her husband, my Uncle Frank, was a groomsman."

It took Judy a full measure to absorb what he was saying. Then she turned and looked at him. "I...I can't believe...I mean I don't know what to say."

He laughed. "It's a long story to be told on another day. Just know this, things are hardly ever what they seem. Life is an endless series of strange quirky twists and turns and believe me, I know. It's been the story of my life and if I've learned anything it's to try not to make sense of it all. Sometimes you have to just keep your eyes wide open and not jump to conclusions before you absolutely have to. If the worst is true, well, then listen to that tiny voice inside that wills you to keep on no matter how tough it gets."

They stood in silence with Judy staring at the house as if it was sending her a message of some sort. Finally she asked him, "Walter, why have you told me this? Why have you let me into your life? Tell me the truth."

He was silent but Judy kept her gaze steady. "I had a sister who died when I was about fifteen," he said at last. "She was a few years older than me. A lovely girl, very soft and frail, a semi-invalid for as long as I can remember. We lived behind the east wing, over there," he pointed to a corner of the house. "I adored her. She wasn't like the rest of us, never went to school, and I would push her chair down a path to the beach in the early morning when no one was about and we would play in the dunes."

He smiled, still staring at the large white house. "You remind me of her. Not as she was, but as she might have been if she had been well." Walter took her hand in his. "I think you should go home to your little girl. Don't sit in judgment until you know the facts and try not to worry. Your husband is a good man and whatever is going on will be revealed in its time. And for god's sake don't confide in Emmaline. Emmaline is not a woman to be envied for all of her outward appeal. She is someone running scared and always has been." He looked back at the house. "Life is full of surprises ...and that's exactly how it should be."

30

The Storm Turns North
September 20th

Like everyone else in town, Hannah felt exhilarated by the perfect September weather. The windows at the high school were wide open and the students paid little attention to classes. The air was euphoric, fresh and light.

After school she hurried about her errands, meat from the butcher, socks and long johns from the Army Navy store on North Main, a long list of groceries for Ma and last, just because she wanted to, a Superman comic book for the little kids. Then she turned the black sedan towards home but not before a last stop, the one she had been anticipating all day. Hannah eased her dad's car down the narrow lane off Indian Wells in Amagansett toward the barn. It made her sad to think that this was the last day. Mr. Burns had told everyone to come and get their work and Hannah was hoping she might find Mr. Burns there alone. The yard around the barn seemed deserted and she thought maybe he had gone already but then she saw the motorcycle parked under a tree.

"Mr. Burns?" she tapped at the doorsill. "Is it OK if I come in?"

Jack looked up. "Hannah, I'm glad to see you. Everyone else has been in but you. I was afraid you might forget to come and get your portfolio."

He *was* alone. She loved the way he used words like 'portfolio' around her like she was a real artist. Portfolio sounded so important even though she knew the papers inside the cardboard folder were nothing special. She had only been able to come to the barn half a dozen times over the summer and each time she had drawn the same picture – – the Fort Pond settlement. It was the only thing she really knew but she had concocted a perch up above the settlement as if she were living in the Manor House on the hill. From her perch she could remove herself from all the things she didn't like about it like she was someone from away, someone who didn't know what it was really like. She had tried to make her drawings better each time and he had helped her but they never looked as good as what other people were drawing.

The first day coming into the barn she had hung back nervous and timid but she had immediately fallen in love with Mr. Burns, a real live artist from New York and so nice she could have died. "Get to know the paint," he said with an encouraging smile and Hannah had gamely dappled some paint on the paper having no idea of how to get to know it. All she knew was that the Art Barn was different from a fish and bait shop out in Montauk and the never-ending smell of guts. Here, the smell was of old barn wood and oil paint and chalk and new paper and something that had no name – the promise of something, something fine and beautiful, something called 'potential.' Mr. Burns used words like 'potential' and 'expression' and 'exploration' like she had any idea of what they meant.

"What shall I draw?" She asked that first day.

"Draw what you like. Draw what has meaning for you. Don't ask me, ask yourself," was his unhelpful answer. When she had almost cried he patted her shoulder and said, "Try something you know. Something you can see in your mind's eye." And this had set her up in a whole new dilemma. What else did she know but the settlement in Montauk? There was little room for exploration there – fishing boats with fish guts and blood spilled all over the deck? She wanted to get as far away from that as she could. And yet in her mind she could also see everything about the settlement as if she were looking down on it from a high cliff, like maybe a lady at the Manor House might see it from her bedroom window – the boats tied to the docks, the lines of the roofs, the houses grouped around the curve of water, the sun setting in brilliant oranges over Hither Hills. She drew the curve of the shoreline with a fat black pencil he had left on the work table, then the hills across the bay, and then she had picked up a paint brush and put a large dollop of yellow on it.

Jack pointed to a brown folder. "There you go. I hope you've enjoyed coming here."

Hannah blushed. "I...I think it has been the best summer of my life," she breathed.

Jack didn't know quite what to say. She made no motion to come over to the table and get the folder so he opened it and leafed through the dozen or so watercolors. "You know you're really beginning to get the hang of the colors. And here, the out-line of the shore is very graceful."

Hannah came closer and looked at the piece of paper. "It don't look like its supposed to. I mean the bay is much bigger than that and the docks don't look right. They look like they're sticking up in the sky not down in the water."

Jack looked again at the picture and narrowed his eyes. "I see what you mean about the docks but that's just perspective. That's easy to fix. Try squinting your eyes, blur the picture a little and you'll see what I mean about the colors. I think you've done a very good job on them. The water has some really nice shimmer to it and the sun over the ridge, well...it's got real possibilities. Do you mind if I do a little something with those docks?" He picked up a pencil.

Hannah shook her head. "I don't mind. I wish you would make it better."

And he did. A few quick strokes of the black lead, a few shad-ings and suddenly they looked like real docks. Hannah was en-chanted. "I wish I could do that. I wish I could draw like you do. Oh it looks wonderful now."

Jack grinned. "Well, I've been at it much longer than you. You know what, I think I have a matt around here somewhere." He went back to the supply shelves and rummaged around com-ing back with a large sheet of stiff white cardboard. He measured the picture and deftly cut a frame for it with a sharp scalpel-like knife. Then he positioned the painting in the frame and taped it securely on the back.

"And here you are, Miss Wood. A real work of art." He pre-sented her with the painting now elegantly framed in creamy white. Hannah's mouth dropped. She was speechless.

Jack patted her on the shoulder. "I've enjoyed our time

together, Hannah. I hope you have a good school year and maybe we'll see you next summer."

"Really?" She squeaked. "Are you coming back? Oh, I hope you are."

"I have no idea," he laughed. "But I think Mr. Penn likes the idea of the Barn and will open it again next summer. He'll no doubt find another artist to help him."

"It wouldn't be the same, not if you weren't here. It wouldn't be the same at all."

"No. But things are never the same no matter what happens. Even if I do come back it won't be the same. Everything always changes."

"Not if you work in my dad's bait store," Hannah said bluntly, "nothin' ever changes there."

Jack looked at the girl and felt a sudden compassion for her. It was probably true. This girl would most likely be doing the same thing that she was doing now, twenty years hence. Only by then she would have a passel of kids. And if not working for her dad she would be working for her husband. Well, what of it? Not his problem.

"You take care, OK?" He said softly. And Hannah took up her framed picture as if it were the most precious thing on earth and looked admiringly at it again.

When she got to the car, she laid the picture on the back seat on top of a blanket and even though it was a pretty day she rolled up the windows so it wouldn't blow around. A few minutes later she was heading out of Amagansett.

The tall shade trees gave way to scrub oak and now she was on the stretch. Even with the road all to herself she drove slowly as she always did when driving back on to Montauk. To her left were the railroad tracks and beyond, Napeague Harbor. To her right were dunes and the ocean. The narrow cinder road cut right down the middle of what really amounted to no more than a wide sand bar. Hannah had made this drive so many times in her short life that she hardly ever thought about it but today she looked at the scenery around her with new eyes. Sand, dune grass, the dunes, some of them fifty feet high, each one sculpted by the wind and the water just like an artist might have done, she thought. Maybe she would try to draw the dunes someday. Not like a real artist of course, but you know, like maybe she could look at them kinda different. Lost in this thought, with her beautiful picture lying on the back seat, she got to imagining she might hang it over the woodstove but then the kids would make fun of her and no telling what Ma would say. Ma had made a terrible fuss snorting and scowling over Hannah going to the barn in the first place. She'd better keep her picture a secret.

Something on the ocean side caught her eye. It looked like a fog bank. She slowed the car. Strange. She could see blue sky on either side of this wall of white coming across the water moving fast. In less than a minute it was over the dunes and in another few seconds it engulfed Hannah and her car – a white mass so dense she couldn't see the hood in front but she could feel it. The car rocked in the impact. This was no fog, it was something else. Something alive, and it was hitting the car with small thuds like someone tossing masses of popcorn.

Hannah gripped the wheel and tried to think. And then just as suddenly as it had come, it was gone. It was a clear blue sky again but the car was covered in white – the hood, the windshield, the windows were solid with it as if the car had been frosted like a cake. Hannah opened her door and got out. Covering her car in a thick mass were white butterflies. Millions and millions of them stuck like glue – so white and fragile they came apart in her fingers when she tried to touch one of them. The radiator was packed solid with the sad, dead creatures.

She found an old section of newspaper in the backseat and brushed away the insects on the windshield and then drove ever so slowly and carefully home. When she got to the docks she just leaned on the horn until her dad and some of the guys in the store came out.

Everyone came to see the car that evening. A wall of white butterflies on the Napeague stretch – and no one knew what to make of it.

What did the deep sea say?
Tell me, what did the deep sea say?
It moaned, it groaned, it splashed and foamed,
And it rolled on its weary way.

WOODY GUTHRIE

September 21, 1938

THE HURRICANE

MASSIVE WINDS… A MEGATON OF BRUTE FORCE…
NOTHING LIKE IT…

*Teletypes throughout the Caribbean and along the
Florida mainland have been clattering dire warnings
for two days. The storm has now traversed some 2000
miles of open water floating with ease sucking up
moisture from the sea. Ships in its path report winds of
alarming force. Puerto Rico has taken a tremendous
hit. Miami, now evacuated, is a ghost town. These
were the reports coming into the Washington Weather
bureau but sometime in the early hours of the 20th
the storm turned north. By evening it had brushed off
Cape Hatteras, its path clearly heading out to sea. The
relief from Miami to Washington was palpable. This
storm, like so many before it, was following a well-trod
pattern. By turning out to sea it would dissipate and
die a natural death in colder waters.*

*By dawn the morning edition of the New York Times
was off press and on delivery trucks throughout the area.
Front page news for September 21st headlined Hitler
and his threats against Czechoslovakia with Britain
and France caving in to Hitler's demands. Buried at
the bottom of a back page is a story about the relieved
residents of South Florida. The paper praised the "admirably organized Weather Service" that had enabled
Florida and the rest of the world to be so well informed.*

*"You're up, Foster. You make the noon report today."
Will Foster clamored off his stool, upsetting a glass
holder with all of his pencils in it to the floor. "Yes,
sir," he said feeling almost as if the breath had been
knocked out of him. The noon report.*

31

Mitch Grindle
5 a.m.

He stood by his truck in the dark listening to the roar of the waves on the beach. He should get going if he was to make the docks in Montauk before the light. He liked getting there early enough to sit with some of the guys over coffee listening to the scuttle-butt but he didn't move. In one hand he was carrying the two peach pies Nettie had so carefully wrapped for him and his crew. They'd be away overnight for sure, maybe more if the fish were running. He knew she was worried. Nettie always worried when he went out in weather. And he could smell weather. The air was moist and it clung to him like a blanket, the smell in his nostrils sharp like maybe someone had lit a sulfur match. He put the pies carefully on the seat. Next to them wrapped in butcher paper was Jack's drawing. His brother who was a carpenter and worked on the docks repairing boats and traps would make a frame – his brother who had dragged him to a high school dance years ago.

Mitch knew Nettie was the one for him from the first minute he laid eyes on her at the Fall Swing. She was a senior that year and he was already twenty-four years old and had been on the water full time since he was fifteen. He hadn't wanted to go to the dance – *kid stuff* – but Ray insisted and as Mitch stood around on the edges of the darkened gym which had been decorated in, of all things, an 'underwater' theme with large cut out fish painted silly rainbow colors, lots of crepe streamers and a big hull of a boat dragged in from somewhere filled with 'pirate treasure'. *Yeah, sure.*

Nettie and Lottie sang that night and they came out on the stage dressed identically in fishermen slickers with big brimmed storm hats singing a lively little song about the sea...*By the Sea, by the sea by the beautiful sea...* and Mitch's breath caught in his throat and his heart thumped so hard he thought he might faint. They might be identical twins but he had eyes for only one of them. It was like she glowed, like some light came off her skin and her hair. He had never seen anyone like her.

It took him five years to convince Nettie to marry him and by then he was almost 30 and had his own boat and was making good money. Rum running didn't hurt his pocket either. He and just about every fellow he knew with a boat had done the run from the offshore yachts sitting just outside the limit. Mitch only did the small stuff. A few runs here and there, the extra bucks were plenty welcome and he used that money to improve his house hoping to impress Nettie but there were a lot of fellows after the Kitchin girls and Mitch didn't know the finer points of how to win a girl's heart. Nettie was always sweet with him but he could tell she didn't love him, not like he loved her. And then one miraculous day, she did. He never knew why, only that one day she looked at him with that shine in her eyes and said, "Yes, I'll marry you."

That had been really something. Going to the little chapel in Springs, watching Nettie come down the aisle on her father's arm. That was the year his brother bummed up his back and couldn't work so Nettie and Mitch had taken on his traps. Every morning before light they would set out in the boat, Nettie saying it was like Christmas every day because you never knew what was in the traps – lobsters, fish, skate, horseshoe crabs, even old junk. Once they hauled up a pair of men's long johns that were so big you could of put three men in them. And they had got to laughing about it until they were near out of breath. The men on the dock said they thought a bunch of crazy summer people had been out there. And that made Nettie and Mitch start in all over again.

Those were the best times, him and Nettie out on the water, alone, with no one and nothing but themselves even when she was big as a balloon with Jarvis. After that she had to stop of course. And in a way that was maybe the start of their real married life together. Jarvis. A son born almost to the day nine months after the wedding. Oh, my, hadn't he taken a lot of ribbin' on that. But proud to bursting. Nettie had wanted to name the baby after Mitch but Mitch didn't want that. He wanted him named for his father, a man he revered, so Jarvis it was but somehow his son had not grown up to be what he expected. Nettie adored that boy almost to distraction. Even after the others came it was always Jarvis this, Jarvis that yet somehow Mitch and his son were at odds. Jarvis hated the water, and cried, bellowed even as a kid at having to go near the boat, terrified of the waves. He hated the smell of fish and soon enough that meant he hated the smell of his father. And that turned into a generalized kind of hostility so that nothing Mitch did or said found favor with Jarvis. Pretty soon it was easier for Mitch not to talk to him rather than put up with his guff. Still, it weren't right and it bothered Mitch. Bothered him more now that Jarvis was gone than before.

He stood by the truck looking up at the heavens. The stars shone but were hazy and wan. The ocean was rolling in fast. Could mean a blow off shore. The first thin grey line of dawn was on the horizon. This was always a mysterious time for him. The coming of light, the night transformed into something fresh and new. He thought about the butterflies plastered all over the girl's car and Nettie's reaction when he come in last night and told her. *Why Mitch, you don't say. Butterflies. Imagine.* Nettie didn't like unexplained things. She liked for thing to be set out plain and simple. He had to get going. But something made him stop and head back into his darkened house. Nettie would have gone back to sleep by now. She got up with him every morning but as soon as he left she would head back to bed able to get an hour more sleep until time to get the children ready for school. He stood awkwardly in the house feeling like he wasn't supposed to be there. The clock ticked and he saw it was after 5 o'clock. He started again for the door but turned instead and went into the bedroom where the soft snore of his wife told him she was sound asleep. Sitting carefully on the side of the bed he stared down at her. Nettie stirred but gave no sign of waking. "I love you, Nettie," he said softly feeling instantly foolish, hoping she wouldn't wake and find him there.

And then he was gone.

32

Wilma and Celia
11 a.m.

Celia Slade beeped the horn of her cream colored Pontiac in front of her best-friend Wilma's house on Huntting Lane. As ever, Wilma was prompt. She waved to Celia from the front door and then went back to the kitchen to make sure her note to Margaret Day and the lunch instructions were still propped up between the little china rooster salt and pepper shakers Lewis had given her for her birthday. He had been so proud of them each one wrapped in Kleenex tissues with a red satin ribbon. Wilma knew he had brought them at the LVIS Fair on the jumble table for she had put them out herself pricing them at 5 cents. Should she call Margaret and remind her to be prompt in picking up Lewis at school? No – Margaret had never let her down. Jim was silly to worry but then Jim was not silly, never had been silly. She pulled the cloche hat firmly on her head and hurried out and got into the car. At last on this long awaited day in September, the two not so young matrons were driving to Southampton in anticipation of a wonderful time ahead. At least so Wilma thought.

"Jim says to be careful on the S bend in Wainscott," Wilma said dryly as they pulled away from the curb.

Celia giggled and then for the hell of it gave the horn on the car two sharp hoots. "And I say, 'Jim, stuff it'."

"Celia, I'm shocked. Behave yourself." Wilma settled comfortably in the roomy car as Celia roared away from her house barely slowing before turning onto Main Street. It was a beauty of a machine and by far the most elegant automobile Wilma had ever been in – – the leather seats matching the pale cream color of the finish. She wondered how Harry could afford the car and hoped, like so many other things in her friend's married life, that the car would not be taken back for lack of payment. Harry Slade could get himself into more precarious deals than anyone could imagine and never once had he admitted poor judgment. You had to hand him that, she had once commented to Jim but Jim had exploded in righteous indignation. *Harry Slade is only a hair's width this side of the law,* he had stated grimly. *Mark my words, Wilma. Just mark my words.*

Celia drove the powerful car with expert control and at the same time a sense of abandon so that if Wilma hadn't known her so well, she might have thought herself in reckless hands. As they turned down Main Street under the canopy of elms, Wilma noted the end of the summer wilt in the leaves even more so this year after such a hot, humid and wet summer. The ground was porous and saturated from the excessive days of rain and even this last week of dry air and sun had done little to temper the sodden ground. She could see in the leaves the damage that had been done but no one else seemed to notice, least of all Celia whose general lack of interest in trees, the village, and LVIS was absolute. As Celia turned onto the Bridgehampton Road to Southampton thirteen miles away, Wilma eyed the sky. No rain yet but the air was heavy and clammy.

"You won't believe what happened this morning, Celia. There we were, the three of us having breakfast when out of the blue the window in the kitchen blew out. Just like that." She snapped her fingers. "Almost as if we had thrown a rock at it. I can tell you we were shocked. There is simply no explanation for it."

"Uh, oh. Jim must have re-written your policy on the spot," Celia laughed. Celia had never much approved of Jim Palmer. A stuffed shirt with no amusing conversation was her assessment, and the ins and outs of selling insurance actually gave her a head-ache. "Whatever do you suppose caused it?" she said not really caring.

"I have no idea and neither has Jim. It was like…It was like a sort of omen…like a warning."

"A *warning*? God, Wilma. That sounds very theatrical. Are you sure you weren't dreaming?"

"No. Of course not. We were having breakfast – scrambled

eggs and toast. Jim was in a fuss over the milk delivery being late. If I were dreaming, I would certainly dream something more interesting than that." They both laughed but then Wilma frowned. "It's got me all unsettled. Things don't happen for no reason. I mean, what could have caused it? Jim thought maybe a bird had flown into the window but there was no bird. And the window blew out, not in. Poor little Lew, he was so frightened."

"Well," said Celia, losing interest, "so it goes. I'm sure Jim will get to the bottom of it. He always does."

They drove for a few minutes in silence and Wilma noticed for the first time how Celia was dressed. She was wearing a bright red suit with a little feathered hat perched on the side of her head. The outfit was, to Wilma's eyes, ridiculously girlish but that was Celia, always a little overdressed and sparkling. She would stand out like a peacock at the lunch. Ah, the luncheon. Wilma was glowing with anticipation. "Lawrence Pinckney is the arborist for Central Park. Imagine it Celia, all those extraordinary trees from all over the world." Wilma had read Pinckney's book *Trees and Shrubs in Public Places* almost as many times as Celia had read *Pride and Prejudice*. She could see Celia had little interest in what she was saying but knew Celia was always game for an adventure and these days Southampton and a lunch at the invitation of one of its preeminent hostesses qualified as an adventure.

When they got to the bend in the road in Wainscott, Wilma stopped talking about trees and Lawrence Pinckney long enough to point out the "S" bend to Celia. "Jim says more accidents have happened here than any other place on the road." And Celia laughed and pressed her foot to the pedal taking the turn as if a racing driver. Then, and without preamble, she abruptly pulled the car over to the side of the road letting the motor idle. She turned to Wilma and there were tears on her checks.

"Celia, what's wrong? Why are you crying? Oh, dear. Celia whatever can be the matter?"

"I'm not crying because something is *wrong*. I'm crying because I'm so happy. Oh, Wilma, Wilma, Wilma – you will never guess in a million years what I'm about to do."

Wilma looked at her warily and braced herself.

"I'm leaving, Wilma. I'm leaving Harry, I'm leaving East Hampton and I'm going to New York. My bag is packed in the trunk. I'm driving us to the Southampton station and I'm catching the 1 o'clock train. Oh, Wilma – I never thought this day would come but I'm finally getting out for good." She reached over and gave the dumbfounded Wilma's hand a little squeeze.

"Celia." Wilma's voice was apprehensive. "What are you talking about? Leaving? Leaving Harry? What are you saying?"

"I'm saying, my dearest friend, I'm meeting someone in the city. Not someone, *the* one. Do you remember that big party at the Maidstone Club in August? It was for that new play at Guild Hall. You didn't go but I certainly did and that's when I met him. He was the director. His name is Grayson Blake. Isn't that a lovely name? And we…well, we just couldn't take our eyes off one another. He and I…well…we…," she giggled. "God, Wilma I never thought it would ever happen to me again. I've been feeling so old and dowdy lately but Gray has made me into a new person. He loves me and I…I love him. Oh I do love him." Celia clutched her heart.

Wilma sighed. "Celia, you can't mean this. You're going off with a man you met a month ago? You know what the summer crowd is like. You can't possibly know him very well…. a few parties? Have you told Harry…?"

"Only you, Wilma. You are the only person who knows. Harry will know soon enough. I'm sending him a telegram tonight. Oh yes, he'll be shocked and furious and all of that but it's not as if Harry's been a saint these past years. Those endless business trips? And Grayson…Gray and I have met on a number of occasions at parties and for walks and…" she giggled again. "You know, it's not always the young people in the dunes. Oh, Wilma, you have no idea of what it's like to feel like an attractive woman again. Attractive? No, beau-ti-ful." Her eyes were twinkling and Wilma thought she might burst into song.

She waited a few moments, willing herself to be as gentle as possible but frankly she was annoyed. Here they were embroiled in yet another hair-brained romantic notion of Celia's and today, of all days, Celia decides to bolt. She didn't dare look at her watch but much more of this nonsense and they would be late for the luncheon. "Celia, what about the children. Are you sending them a telegram too?" She could feel the tone of stodgy indignation creeping it.

Celia looked momentarily confused. "Of course not. Don't lecture me, Wilma. The children are almost grown...I've done everything for the children. They're well taken care of and I'm not abandoning them. Just as soon as everyone gets over the shock, well then...but what about me? Am I taken care of? Has Harry ever done anything but fail time and time again trying out his endless schemes on my money! Our life is a mess, Wilma. Can you honestly say you even like Harry?"

It was true, Wilma thought, a little bit of Harry went a long way but Wilma didn't say that to Celia and never would. She started to say something else but Celia rolled over her in a wave of despair. "No one likes him and now I don't either. I've put up with him, been embarrassed by his boorish behavior, his overly familiar ways and dreadful lack of any kind of ...of...class. He's a big blowhard. And now, at last I have a chance again, a chance for something bright and fun and meaningful. When you meet Gray you'll understand. He's worldly and fine and a real gentleman...." At this juncture Celia broke down in tears again sobbing for all her might. "Why can't you be happy for me."

Wilma fumbled in her handbag for the hanky she always carried. "Celia – I have always wanted you to be happy. How could I not after all these years? But this is something else again. This isn't daydreaming and fantasizing, this is breaking up your marriage, leaving your children and your home. What about your father? He'll be heartbroken. Are you sure of this man? I mean a few summer parties? Does he know you're coming...?"

Celia blew her nose into the hanky and straightened her shoulders. "Of course he knows. I've got a room at the Waldorf and he's meeting me there. Of course he knows I'm coming." Then she turned on the ignition with a deliberate hand, and said, her hands on the wheel with grim determination, "I've never been so sure of anything in my life."

Wilma and Celia now stood on the platform of the station in Southampton. The wind whipped around them in an alarming fury and the sky had turned an ugly ochre color but Celia had regained her girlish bravado. "When I met Grayson I had all but given up. Of course I gave up on Harry years ago but that night at the club with the band set up on the terrace it was a perfect setting for romance. I don't even remember who introduced us but it was like magic. We talked and we danced. It was the loveliest evening. He asked if he could see me again and I said yes. And that was it."

"It? Did he know you were married? With two children?" Wilma held onto her hat in the ripping wind.

Celia ignored her. "He loves me. And I love him." The upshot of it all was that she had used the luncheon as a ploy to get away. "I'm never sure whether or not Harry will be out in Montauk. Like there's any point to opening that real estate office of his. Such a stupid idea. He thinks he can be the next king of development. What a laugh that is. Nothing has sold in Montauk for years and yet Harry acts like he's sitting on a gold mine." They heard the train whistle down the tracks and Celia clutched at Wilma's arm. "You understand, don't you? I have to go. I just have too," she pleaded. "I asked Gray to meet me at the hotel this evening. I told him it was important. I'm sorry Wilma. I'm using you to run away but I can't stay in that house and live that lie any more. I just can't."

The train appeared in the distance. "Take the car and park it in your drive when you get home. It's mine, not his. That's one thing Harry will never get. He loves that car – certainly more than he loves me." The train steamed into the station. Celia gave her one quick hug and then she reached for her bag and climbed on board. Through the grimy windows, Wilma could see only the bright red of Celia's hat.

33

Lewis Palmer
Noon

Lewis sat miserably at his desk, his teacher drumming her fingers on the book she was reading.

"You're sure Miss Day knew to pick you up at noon, Lewis?"

He nodded. She had asked him that before and he had heard his father telling her the same thing when he brought him to school that morning. He hated it when grownups made you repeat things all the time. Mrs. Fellows was not nearly so pretty as his first grade teacher Miss Darlene. Mrs. Fellows wasn't pretty at all. She wore thick stockings and clunky shoes and she smelled like throat lozenges. That was a funny word, lozenge. He said it over and over until it didn't sound like a word anymore but some sort of gurgle.

"You hoo," He could hear Margaret all the way down the hall. He scrunched deeper into the desk but Mrs. Fellows jumped up and went to the door. She hooted back. "We're down here."

"Hello Margaret," said Mrs. Fellows when Margaret came in the classroom.

"Why, Barbara. I haven't seen you in an age. I like your hair." Margaret sang out.

Mrs. Fellows probably never had compliments much, Lewis thought, because she was old like Margaret. He watched as Mrs. Fellows touched her hair and smiled.

"Lewis and I were waiting for you…Mr. Palmer said you'd be coming for him. What a day. Looks like a real storm coming our way. And the wind…are you sure you want to be out in this weather?"

"Oh, we'll be alright. We've only got a few blocks to go," Margaret said brightly in that same singsong sort of way. "Come along, Lew," she held out her hand and gave him a big smile.

She had lipstick smudged on her teeth. Lewis ducked by her out into the hall.

The walk home was indeed windy, real windy, and Lewis felt like if he could hold onto something like the lamppost with one hand that the wind might pick him up and whirl him off his feet. When they turned down Main Street Lewis checked the posters across the road in front of Edwards Movie Theater. Tom Mix was playing on Saturday and he wished he could go. Charlie Dunn was going and so was the new kid whose name he couldn't remember. Lewis didn't like Charlie or the new kid. They pushed him at recess and Charlie stole his red pencil, the one Mr. Marley had given him when he went in the newspaper and smoke shop with Father. Father was always going around to the shops and he was real friendly with all the shop owners because he sold them insurance *policies*. His father was always trying to talk people into improving their policies. Lewis didn't quite get what insurance was. If you paid Father money he would give it back to you if your store burned down and then you could build a new one but that didn't make any sense. That would mean you would *want* your store to burn down, didn't it? Say you had an old, creaky store like Mr. Niccolo who had a shoe repair shop in a tiny shed out back of the post office. If Lewis was Mr. Niccolo he would want that shed to burn down and then he would get a nice new proper shop like the new...Margaret tugged him down the street. Shop owners stood in their doorways, "Looks bad..." they said or "big blow comin'...or "you better get on home...."

"Lewis. Lewis! Stop daydreaming and take my hand, " said Margaret and Lewis was glad when they got inside his house because he was tired of the wind but he would have been gladder if his mother were there. Definitely. The shattered window in the breakfast nook, the one that had broken all on its own this morning at breakfast, had been fixed with a piece of cardboard and tape but now all the windows in the house seemed to be rattling and shaking. Margaret fixed him his lunch, which was what his mother had left for them – – a tomato sandwich with lots of mayonnaise, which he liked but now it was kind of soggy, and vegetable soup, which Margaret had not warmed properly. She didn't eat the lunch and they sat in silence while he ate listening to the wind.

It made a real spooky noise like there was a ghost in the attic.

Lewis suspected there was a real live ghost in the attic anyway because at night when he was in his bed, after mother had given him a last hug and kiss, he could hear things up there. Creaky things. Once he had told Father about the ghost but he was having none of it. "Lewis," he had said in that way grown ups did when they had an opportunity to teach you something that was good for you, "this is an old house and the wood makes noises all the time because it expands and contracts but you only hear it at night when everything else is quiet. There are no such things as ghosts!"

But Lewis didn't believe him. Besides Father got to sleep with Mother so no wonder he didn't know about the ghost. Now his soup was really cold.

34

Walter Penn
12:15 p.m.

Walter wondered if it had been wise to walk out in the face of this severe wind and was actually glad now that he saw how strong it was blowing that Mrs. Cunningham had refused to come. She was a funny old bird, cranky and devoted all at the same time. They suited each other; he had always liked strong-minded women. He knew people must think he was homosexual or the more vernacular 'queer' a term he disliked for it removed from everyday language one of the most useful and satisfying of words. In that sense, he *was* queer if it meant unconventional. The truth was he was in love with art, with inspiration and the outer limits of the artistic vision. And he saw no reason nor had he any inclination to tarnish that love with the other kind – unbridled lust, heartbreak and the sexual obsessions of people adrift on the tides of their passion. But hold on, he *had* been in love. He had been in love with Emmaline who had set off alarming and crazy impulses in him. He had begged her to marry him and let him be the father of her child but instead she had nabbed that oaf of a man. And that had been that.

He stood on the bridge over Hook Pond and surveyed the water teaming in the wind. He wondered why he had told Judy Tate the story of his humble beginnings. It was not like him to talk about himself but she was such a funny little thing, like a child so eager and yet so lost. He was a sucker for lost people having been one himself he supposed. That boy was still in him, still in awe, still obsessed over a gondola.

He could see it now. Thomas Moran's Venetian gondola afloat on Hook Pond complete with high back woven seats and a great curved nose at the bow painted deep reds and blues. He used to go down to Hook Pond every time he could just to look at it transforming the ordinariness of the pond into something out of a dream. One day a woman came up behind him and stood with him. Then she asked if he wanted to go for a ride. And simple as that, his life had changed forever.

• • •

"Yes, missus. Yes. I would like to go for a ride."

"Well, then alright." She was a pleasant looking woman and had a very pleasant way about her. She was carrying a large satchel, which he would later learn held her etching tools but now he watched her intently as she maneuvered the craft into the shore and then folding her long skirts around her she waded a few feet into the water and nimbly climbed aboard not in the least mindful of wetting her shoes. He managed to hoist her heavy bag aboard and himself all in one go.

"Well done," she smiled. "My name is Mary." She held out her hand.

Walter wiped his hand down his trousers and shyly held it forth. "My name is Walter."

"Now then Walter. You sit there and I'll be the oarsman. It's tricky at first and takes a bit of knowing how. Someday you can try but for now I will be the captain of our fate." She laughed and not entirely sure why, Walter laughed too.

The gondola was long, the rear of it flat so the oarsman could stand and navigate but curling in the front in an elaborate curl like the toe in Aladdin's slipper. And that's how Walter Penn, age 10, felt. He was no longer a boy on his way home from school but an adventurer straight from the pages of A Thousand and One Nights.

That was the start of it. She told him she was the wife of the artist Thomas Moran. Later, she invited him to meet the great man and soon after their house in the village became his second home. It was a house filled with magic.

When Moran was working, he was never disturbed but in the evening and on the weekends, the house came alive with parties and parlor games, the studio full of artists from New York, cousins, friends. Mary was a superb hostess, entering into every quadrille and costume party yet the woman to whom he owed everything, was not Mary the hostess but Mary the artist. She did something called 'etching' and Walter soon became her helper. He carried her bag, he showed her places she might find interesting as subject matter, he sat long hours with her, never tiring, fascinated with watching the intricate process of drawing on a sheet of copper with a steel needle. Then when done, he helped spread the copper plate with ink to fill in the etched lines and learned under her careful tutelage how to transfer the engravings to paper. Once she handed him the plate and said he was to make his own mark on it, a drawing of his own midst hers. And he had, a few tentative strokes in the corner of the tall grasses around the pond. She had smiled when she saw them – "beautiful," she said, "no other grass like them and do you see here what is hidden in the grass? A muskrat. You have helped him to hide. What shall we call our work of art, Walter? How about...Muskrat at Hook Pond."

• • •

The thundering sounds of the waves on the beach brought him back into the present. She loved storms. She would have captured this one in all its glory, filling the sky with the turbulent clouds so that you could almost see the wind.

She taught him many things and who knows what would have come from it if Mary Moran had not caught the yellow fever. It was 1899 the year Teddy Roosevelt bivouacked hundreds of soldiers from the Spanish American War sick with the fever out on Montauk. What a sight it was. Miles of white tents, flags, horses and Red Cross doctors and nurses and, of course, the sick and injured soldiers and their flamboyant leader. They had been forbidden to go out there but he and his pals had hitched a ride on the train and hidden in the hills just to see that great spectacle. Had it been he who had carried the sickness back to East Hampton?

Walter closed his eyes for a moment. He could still remember the pain of her death. She had been so good to him, had taken such an interest and made him feel like he was worth something.

She had taught him to dream. And then she had died.

He stared down from the bridge at the pond. Cattle Bridge it had been then, an old wooden structure so beautifully rendered in her etchings – now a stone crossing for the convenience of golfers at the Maidstone Club. The wind was really kicking now and he pulled the hood of the anorak tight lowering his head against the stinging salt air and almost turned back towards home but he wanted to see for himself, and for her, the magnificent waves caused by a storm somewhere out at sea.

35

The Birthday Party
12:30 p.m.

Judy heard the knocking thinking it was the wind. The wind was getting fierce and the children had long since come inside. It was bedlam, as she knew it would be. There were eight children in all, and a baby too. She had invited a young mother from the club at the last minute, never expecting she would tote her four-month-old son along but so she had.

And, oh yes, there was the clown. Judy had seen him first from the back of the room at the club one Saturday morning. A small man with grey hair brushed so that it stuck out from under his clown hat. He had thick eyebrows and a big, grey handlebar mustache. The children loved him and he was doing all sorts of quite thrilling magic tricks and silly honking things with bells and whistles. She had asked the concierge at the club to arrange for him to come to the birthday party, only the clown who arrived at her door had not been a jolly grey haired man, but a boy – granted a teen-age boy but a boy nevertheless. He was wearing the same costume but up close it was as fake as could be, the grey hair and mustache of the cheapest stage material. It turned out he was the son of the clown seen at the club. His dad was not feeling well, he said, but Judy sensed that dad had found a more lucrative offer that day for his talents. Well what did it matter? The children were clearly delighted and he did seem to know a few fancy tricks. She could see the glue on his lip where he had pasted on the mustache and figured he was still too young to shave.

She looked at the clock in the hall and wondered if it might be better to call the parents and have them come early to pick up the children. The storm was really howling and it occurred to her that storms often meant flooding on Dune Road. Two of the children, a boy and his twin sister, had been dropped off by their father a full hour earlier than she had expected them. "Hope you don't mind. We're sailing today," he said with a mock salute, "heading out from Sag to Robbins Island. Can you believe it? Our seventh anniversary." He laughed putting two hands around his neck. "Hey, you two. Be good and have fun." He bent to a hurried hug with his children anxious to be off.

"You're not worried about the rain?" she said at the door.

"If I worried about rain I would be in the nuthouse after this summer. We've decided to love the rain."

Judy wondered about that 'love the rain' line now. Then she heard the knocking again only this time louder, an urgent knocking. Raleigh was in the kitchen and Judy opened the door to a rain soaked and clearly distraught Emmaline Hartley, her hand at her throat as if she couldn't breath. Finally she grasped Judy's arm. "Is your telephone working?"

Judy nodded. "Yes. Of course…I was about to call the parents to come for the children early…at least I think it's working." She went to the telephone on the table in the hallway and Emmaline followed still clutching at Judy's arm. Judy reached for the receiver and saw that her hand was shaking. The telephone was dead.

Emmaline groaned. "Oh, god. Judy, you've got to let me have Raleigh… to drive us to the doctor …or the hospital. It's James…he's had some sort of attack…it might be his heart… I rang the doctor over an hour ago but he was out on his rounds… his wife said she would send him just as soon as she could but…" she was gasping now. "The telephone went out…" and then she did a most unusual thing completely out of character for cool, sophisticated, worldly Emmaline Hartley – she sat down on the stairs and began sobbing, horrible, choking sobs.

Judy, stunned, jangled the telephone one last time. There were shouts and squeals coming from the living room. She felt helpless but Raleigh was by her side in an instant and before she could quite sort out what was happening, he had taken charge getting rain gear out of the closet, helping Emmaline into an oversized slicker that was Chip's, telling Judy the cake and ice cream were ready to serve and that he would be back as soon as he could. With that he and Emmaline made their way in the rain back across Dune Road and up the drive to the Hartley's house.

Judy had a time shutting the door against the wind. She was anxious. Nothing seemed right. First the pony that wouldn't get in the truck. Then the wrong clown. An escalating storm. The telephone gone dead. Now a medical emergency. And Raleigh was gone. As she turned back towards the living room the lights flickered, went out, came back on, flickered again and then went out for good. The entire house seemed to fall into a gloom as if nightfall. What little light came through the windows was an eerie, sickly green. The children too seemed to be aware that something was wrong. They had stopped watching the clown pulling silk scarves from a hat and were looking at her.

A small hand slipped into hers and Judy looked down into the cool, steady eyes of Violet Hartley. Violet as official "helper" had so far been wonderful organizing a treasure hunt, cajoling poor tempers, doling out the party favors but now she seemed as vulnerable as the little ones.

"Why was my mother crying?" she asked.

"Oh, darling…I think this storm is upsetting everyone. She needed Raleigh to help her and I'm sure it's all right now. Sometimes you just can't help having a good cry even though it's usually not very serious. Let's see if we can wrestle this party into some sort of shape. The clown seems to be overwhelmed and I think the cake is ready." She could hear her voice climb into the squeaky high register of creeping panic realizing that she was alone in the house with eight children, a young mother, a baby and a teenage clown. All alone.

At the Hartley's, Emmaline had pulled herself together explaining to Raleigh the situation. *Perfectly normal one minute – slumped over the next.*

Raleigh took a look at the grey pallor of James Hartley's face. His lips pale and quivering. "I'll bring the car to the front, Miz Hartley. We best be goin'."

"James, everything is all right. Raleigh is here and we're driving you to the doctor. Come on, everyone, it's alright now."

James was sitting in a wingback chair but he looked pale and confused. Nine-year-old Peter was holding his hand. The house-keeper, Mrs. Sternhoffer, her coat and hat on, was sitting in a straight back chair in the entrance hall a grim and terrified look on her face.

Raleigh was familiar with the house from helping to serve at a number of parties and walked through to the kitchen more suited for a fancy restaurant than normal household needs but then the Hartleys entertained on a far grander scale than any restaurant. Beyond the kitchen was the garage. Of the three cars available, Raleigh could see immediately that only one was right for the trip, the 1933 Pierce-Arrow, a black beauty of a machine, large and comfortable and heavy like a tank but as easy to drive as a child's toy. He had driven it only once before, chauffeuring the Hartleys to a round of parties in Southampton. The car was sheer magic with its wide running boards, its sleek black lines, the leather interior and beautiful wood fittings, a thing to behold but as he slid into the driver's seat Raleigh was thinking only of the Pierce Arrow as a perfect emergency vehicle.

Soon James, Emmaline and Peter were settled in the back of the car leaving a place for Mrs. Sternhoffer in front with Raleigh but at the last minute she froze in panic and would not leave the house. Spume from the ocean, now whipped into a frenzy, blew against the windows. Mrs. Sternhoffer, hypnotized by the sounds of the water against glass, wailed as Raleigh tried to get her to her feet. She gripped the arms of the chair as if holding to a lifeline. Peter came back in the house to help, then Emmaline, but no amount of cajoling or commands seemed to penetrate the wom-an's fear. At one point Emmaline shook the petrified woman's shoulders but to no avail. They had no choice but to leave her moaning in the chair in the hallway.

The car moved slowly out of the drive and down Dune Road. Raleigh was amazed to see a crowd of about fifteen people stand-ing on the top of a dune watching the ocean. They were gesturing and even laughing as the black car rolled by. Just short of the end as he was about to turn onto the paved lane that began the three miles into town a rush of green churning sea water crossed over the dunes directly in front of the car causing Raleigh to slam on the brakes. Then another…and another and the dune seemed to dissolve as he tried to ease the car forward. Sand and water swirled around the tires, then it was over the running board. The motor sputtered, caught again, then sputtered and died.

Raleigh jumped from the car and found himself knee deep in rising water. "It's no use, we got to get out of here and get up to higher ground," he shouted.

Emmaline shouted something back at him but her voice was swallowed by the wind. The look on young Peter's face was one of sheer terror but Raleigh managed a smile and nodded to him as if they were long standing partners in rescue tactics. He gestured to Peter to help his mother and father and the boy sprang to the task. Together they forced the back door of the car open, the water sloshing over the luxurious upholstery, and again, supporting James on either side, he and Peter and Emmaline struggled through the water until finally they got to a higher portion of the road.

There was no turning back. Dune Road was awash in murky churning water. Stumbling down Hedges Lane, the wind pushing at their backs, stinging sand and debris hurtling past while overhead the wires pitched a high piercing whine, Raleigh could see that the sky had turned an eerie greenish yellow like the yoke of an egg gone bad, unlike anything he had ever seen.

Twice they stopped to give James a rest, trying to shield themselves against the rain behind tall hedges. The few houses they passed were dark and deserted summerhouses shuttered for the winter. A mile more and they would be on the highway but a mile was a long way with a sick man Raleigh knew and in this weather he wondered if they shouldn't try to shelter in one of the deserted houses. They were all soaked and confused. He would go much faster if alone. At least in a house they would be dry and maybe a telephone hadn't been cut off for the season.

Then, as if out of a dream, a car, a lone car drove down the lane. Before they could even think to wave it down, it stopped, and like the welcoming arms of a comforting friend, the driver reached behind him and opened the back door. First James was put in the back seat and then Peter, then Emmaline. Raleigh closed their door and walked behind the car reaching for the outside handle on the passenger side of the front seat. The driver, a thin and pallid man who seemed ridiculously over-dressed in a pinstriped suit complete with vest, gold watch chain and bowler hat abruptly reached over and locked the door. "No niggers ride in this car," he said firmly and then he gunned the motor causing the car to skid sideways. Raleigh leapt backwards to avoid being hit.

Emmaline gasped. "You can't do this. Do you hear me...let him in the car RIGHT NOW!" But her words and tone made no impression on the driver. "If you don't like it, then get out." He said without qualm. And he slowed the car.

James was gasping now, his lips an ugly blue. Peter stared dumbfounded at his mother. Emmaline started to say something but, instead, leaned back in the seat and closed her eyes. Through gritted teeth, she groaned, "the hospital. We need a hospital."

Peter twisted around in his seat and peered out the back window. Raleigh was just standing there, his white jacket plastered to his body in the driving rain. His chestnut face shining wet. He was ankle deep in water and for as long as Peter could see him, his image getting smaller and smaller as the car accelerated, he didn't move.

* * *

"Do me a jig, boy. Do me a jig."
He could hear the voice clear. Its ugly menacing tone just as it had been those many years ago.

Raleigh felt the strength go out of his legs and he lurched to the side of the road through the water to a fence post grabbing onto it. He shook his head, shook the water from his eyes but the voice was still there and now he wasn't on the road but back in time twenty-five years, in the bar car of the Silver Cannonball the sleek bullet of a train with an observation dome and lively club car. And he was tending bar as the train sped through the low country of South Carolina. Early on it was a boisterous, happy crowd until later when it turned sour.

"Din' you hear me boy? I said 'do me a jig' one of them jungle bunny jigs. Come on out from behind that bar and git over here." Raleigh feigned ignorance. He grinned and kept on polishing the glass in his hand. "Yez, sir, boss. You want another?" The man was florid, his face a dangerous red and he was very drunk. The bar car had grown quiet. Raleigh could see that it was empty of most passengers this late, it was just him and these fat cats on their way to Miami. He had been here before, they all had, all the porters and waiters and bartenders. Don't act out was the consensus. Keep the aggravation inside. Nothing good comes from retaliation. Just swallow it man, do what they say, keep your job.

Raleigh was good at masking his feeling but the turmoil inside was something terrible. Just swallow it man, do what they say, keep your job. Only this time he couldn't. His grin faded and he kept on polishing the glass gripping it to keep his hand from shaking. What happened next happened so fast that Raleigh could hardly piece it together afterwards.

A man, unnoticed before, appeared from one of the banquets and put his hand on the drunk's shoulder. "Hey, now. Take it easy friend," he said. The drunk wheeled around in a fury and smashed his glass in the man's face cutting him just above the eye and now there was blood gushing from the cut. Raleigh came around the bar grabbing some of the towels so he could help the fallen man but the drunk was flailing away now at Raleigh who put up his hands to ward off the blows. The man was insane with anger punching and screaming profanity while his cohorts had backed away from the scene not bothering to help the fallen man bleeding on the floor. Raleigh tried to duck the worst of the blows but then saw that his hands were around the drunk's throat, his hands were not his hands and the rage inside him welled up so that the hands tightened. The drunk started choking and gagging and suddenly he pitched forward falling and passing out on the floor. Only he hadn't passed out. He was dead.

Raleigh froze stupefied starring down at the man whose face was blue. The other passengers now very aware of the situation and perhaps no more than strangers to the dead man exited the car and only Raleigh and the man who had come to his defense were left. Still bleeding, that man now rolled to a sitting position and Raleigh knelt down with the towels. The injured man waved Raleigh away as he slowly got to his feet mopping at the blood on his face.

"Don't get blood on you. I'm OK, but you better get out of here, my friend. It's not a deep cut. Just a lot of blood. Get off at the next station."

Raleigh started to back away towards the end of the train. Then he stopped. "Naw, sir. If I run, I'm a dead man too. I ...I killed him." His voice mystified in disbelief.

The white man looked at him hard then he shook his head. "No. He had a heart attack. I saw. He was beating on you and you were trying to help me..." he turned and saw that the car was empty. "No telling what those other fellows saw and what they're going to remember in the morning. Get me some ice and leave it on the counter. Call the Conductor. I'll take it from here. It was a fight between me and him. And that's that. You never touched him. Remember that." The train was slowing down for the Jacksonville station.

They took the dead man off in a hearse and took Bill Delany off in an ambulance but not before he told the police that there had been no other witnesses and he, Bill Delany, had provoked the argument. "The man was drunk and obnoxious and I told him so." When questioned, Raleigh said the white men had fought and that's all he knew. Raleigh was left to clean up the mess before the early breakfast crowd came in just before Miami. By then his hands had stopped trembling but in his heart, he knew he was a killer.

Fearful of reprisal, but terrified to quit his job lest that cast suspicion, in the weeks that passed he got himself assigned to the kitchen where as cook he could remain hidden from the white passengers. How could he know that Delany's testimony at the inquest in Jacksonville had been accepted on face value. Delany was, after all, related to a prominent Savannah family and his word was never in question. No one seemed to recall the ugly baiting of the black porter.

It might have ended there but Bill Delany wanted the porter to know he was in the clear and sought him out. He was easy to track down, the name Raleigh stood out. A few weeks later he found a confused man terrified of repercussions. Delany offered him a job in New York and Raleigh never looked back. He came into the Delany household a quiet and dignified man of 35 and there he had stayed for 25 years. Grateful, respectful and private, he fulfilled his duties with unfailing loyalty to the man who had rescued him from a certain ugly fate.

• • •

Judy. Alice. Raleigh shook himself out of stupor and turned back down the lane determined to get to the house on Dune Road.

36

Crazy Tom
1:00 p.m.

Jack stood in the doorway of Nettie's kitchen. There, not ten feet from him, was Crazy Tom. Jack barely breathed so as not to startle him. With his long white beard and tattered clothes he seemed more a ghost than a flesh and blood man; yet here he stood in Nettie's kitchen as real as you please. "Ol' man up to he trickies t'day. You best git." His voice was high and the words came out in a singsong sort of way with an almost indecipherable accent but Jack got the gist of it.

Jack also saw that the clock so revered by Mitch and Nettie was laying on the kitchen table and that he had come upon the old man wrapping it carefully in a blanket.

"Where's Nettie," he asked pleasantly but the old man didn't look up and didn't answer, continuing on folding the heavy wool around the clock. For a minute Jack thought that maybe he was stealing it but no, this was not the action of a thief, more like a mother wrapping her infant deliberate and with care. Jack stepped into the room but when he did Tom stopped what he was doing one hand held frozen in mid-air. It was a signal, a warning stronger than words for Jack not to come closer. After a few minutes in which they were both motionless Tom finished wrapping the clock securing it with a stout twine. Tom looked up but not at Jack. He stared at the opposite wall.

"Ol' man gotta blow. Ol' man can't rest 'til he blows it out. Missus gone to her momma. You go now." The sing in his voice was caught in the pitch of the wind.

Jack backed slowly out the door and once on the road the full force of the wind pushed him up through the dunes, sand stinging the back of his neck and coating his hair, down the lane to his coop almost as if an unseen but commanding hand was propelling him away from the ocean. He felt disoriented like in a dream wandering from place to place and not knowing why. He sat on his sagging bedstead staring at the wooden slats of his ceiling and wondered what was happening to his life. A whole summer gone – teaching art in a barn, a few half-hearted attempts at painting the way he wanted to paint, rolling around in bed with a woman he couldn't begin to understand much less have. Her behavior the other night had upset him far more than he would have thought. Her babbling on about loving him. What did that mean? Nothing. She only loved herself. She had turned him into a summer fling and he should have left long ago. He was broke. He looked around the coop hoping for an answer but all he saw was his own heaped up mess of clothes and half finished canvases. He couldn't explain this eerie sense of foreboding. He would go back to the city and get the big job and spend the rest of his life mocking up ads for billboards. Why not? Why the hell not? The air was heavy and the wind ominous and the coop claustrophobic.

Get out, get away! Once on his motorcycle he felt better, empowered, and gunning the motor, he had an idea of riding full speed maybe all the way to New York. He was sick of this place, this summer, these people. And to hell with this storm. He would outrun it. Turning onto the main road, he saw that the Amagansett school, a new brick building and the pride of the community, was letting children out. He saw Eddie standing with one of the teachers and then Eddie was jumping up and down waving to him. Reluctantly, he pulled over. "What's happening?" he asked the teacher standing with four or five of the students.

She glanced at the leather helmet he wore and the dust jacket. "We're sending the children home because of the storm. We're ending classes," came the curt answer.

Eddie was by his side, his hand on Jack's arm tugging at him. "Hey, Jack! Ma's down in Springs with Granny Minnie. You think you could ride me down there? Can't leave on my own." Eddie's eyes were pleading.

Jack felt the frown on his face and was about to shake his head but the look on Eddie's face stopped him. The kid was afraid.

And that wasn't like Eddie at all. He put his arm around the boy's shoulder. "Ok, ma'am?" he turned to the teacher. "I'm a good friend of his family and I can ride him down to his mother in Springs." He flashed a concerned furrow of the brow. "Sure looks like a bad storm."

She was a nervous woman unsure of herself in this situation. The fewer children she had to deal with the better. She nodded and gave Eddie a quick hug. "You OK Eddie about this?" but the boy had twisted out of her grip and was already climbing into the sidecar.

37

The Storm
2:00 p.m.

Chip jolted awake and for a moment had no idea where he was. On a train? Then he remembered. He was on the train to Bridge-hampton on a Wednesday in the middle of a heavy work week. And why? He stretched out his arm, the skin tingling with a million tiny pinpricks. He had been dreaming and in the dream Judy was standing just ahead of him smiling with Alice in her arms. And he had been so glad to see them. Like he had been gone and was seeing them for the first time in a very long time. He had tried to reach out to her but he felt paralyzed, immobile.

Inside the train it was dark with only a dank grey light from outside to see by. He looked at his watch. They should be coming into Southampton now. Torrents of rain beat against the windows and he could make out nothing, but the train was rocking violently on the tracks and it was at a dead halt. The other passengers were in various states of distress but Chip sat stoically in his seat. "What in the hell is going on?" he said to no one.

"Dunno," a man sitting in front of him turned in his seat. "This storm seems to have slowed us down. We're nowhere near Southampton. I'd say we're outside of Patchogue."

At that moment, a conductor appeared with a lantern wearing an enormous black slicker wet with rain. "Folks. Sit tight. There's a tree across the tracks and the men are working on it. Word is, the storm is worse up ahead. We may have to terminate in Patchogue."

A collective groan went up from the passengers, but at just that moment, the train lurched forward and the lights, with much flickering, came on. The conductor passed quickly through to the next car. Chip settled back willing the train to pick up speed. They stopped in the Patchogue station for a long time, then slowly it pulled out to the audible relief and some cheering of the passengers.

Chip closed his eyes: Westhampton, Hampton Bays, Southampton, Bridgehampton. He had done this trip every week for the past seven years. Seven years! It didn't seem possible. One day you're a hapless guy alone in the urban wilderness and the next you're a Madison Avenue executive with a beautiful wife, a child, a townhouse, a beach house and–

Chip didn't dare to complete this sentence. A mistress?

The train inched its way east, and now the wind had joined the rain in some frenzied dance outside the windows, blasting them as if a fire hose had been turned on full force. Water seeped in through the vents, through the doors at either end, through the windows themselves, and he could hear a high-pitched howl outside. The further east they went, the worse it got. Judy. Alice. The thought of them on the edges of the ocean in weather like this rocked inside his brain.

In the winter, Dune Road flooded in nor'easters, and the very few residents who happened to be there in the cold months were evacuated to the high school. Yes. He had definitely heard that. Thank god for Raleigh. Raleigh would know how to get through a bad storm. Surely Raleigh would have driven them into town.

The train pitched one last heaving lurch and then shut down like a dying behemoth, its lights out for good. Except for the piercing howl of the wind, there was silence. In the gloom, the passengers all looked at one another. The man in front of him said, "Looks like this is it. I wonder where we are."

They all waited with the train rocking violently until someone ventured to the door. "Looks like we're near the station," he called back. "I can see a light."

And with this came voices from outside. A crew of linemen were shouting at the passengers to disembark. They did, some trying to bring their suitcases with them only to have them wrenched from their hands by the wind the minute they stepped down from the train. They formed a line, clinging to one another bent over like beasts until reaching the tiny Hampton Bays station.

There, they were told the tracks were washed out up ahead. Chip looked around and caught the eye of the man who had been in front of him. "I've got to get to Bridgehampton. Do you think there's a taxi?"

Yes. There was a taxi or at least there was a driver willing to take them but the fee was exorbitant. Chip didn't care, pay him what he wants, he said, but the man from the train was trying to haggle. Then another man and a woman said they would share the ride if only they could get as far as Southampton. It was settled, and the four of them piled into a Ford station wagon and off they went down Route 27, debris smashing into the side of the car as they inched along in the rough murky light.

They had just made it across the spit of land between the ocean and the bay to a place called Shinnecock Hills when the driver pulled over to a road house and said he could go no further, he could no longer hold the car on the road, he could no longer see the road, and his car was getting battered by all the flying debris. They would have to take shelter here, in the roadhouse.

Charlie's Dry Dock was on the edge of a marina on Shinnecock Bay and was aptly nautical with portholes for windows and ships wheels hanging from the ceiling rigged up as lamps. Charlie himself was standing behind the bar, which was lit with candles and a few kerosene lanterns since the electricity had gone out over an hour ago. He was polishing glasses as if it were the most normal day of the year.

"What'll it be, gents and lady?" he bowed to the one lone woman in their group. "Bad storm, eh? But I seen worse. It'll pass soon enough."

They all dutifully sat at the bar and ordered drinks. Chip looked at his watch. It was half past two.

"Yep," said Charlie, setting bourbon in front of Chip. "I seen lots worse down in the Carib-be-an. I was on a cargo ship down that way back in '28. Now that was a storm. Took out most of Puerto Rico and most every boat, too. We was lucky not to have drowned. Them's real storms down there. Hurry-canes. What we got here is one of them hurry-canes for sure."

"Hurricane?" Chip looked at the man. "You mean this storm is a hurricane? Like tropical hurricanes? They don't come this far north … "

"Sure they do. Not often, but they come."

As if on cue, the storm seemed to escalate making the shutters of the roadhouse bang and rattle with alarming ferocity.

"Ever hear of the 1815 September Gale? Took out the whole standing forest on Long Island. Took out the farms and the top-soil and destroyed almost every building and near all the livestock. Big loss of life, too, but that was back when there wasn't many out here. Hurry-canes like that come once in 100 years so, they say. Naw – this here storm ain't gonna do … "

His words were lost. At that moment, a huge surge of ocean water broke through the narrow strip of land just west of the roadhouse. The roadhouse, on higher ground, stood shuttering and shaking only a few yards from the torrents of seawater. The force of it caused every bottle of liquor to fall from the shelves into a crashing heap of glass and booze on the floor.

Chip and the others flung themselves on top of the bar. Outside, boats moored in the marina were now upside down up on the road. Chip felt a frigid fear grip his whole body. All he could see was Judy holding Alice in her arms.

A Coast Guardsman stood in the door to Charlie's, shouting at them to get out. "It's not safe. Get to higher ground. Evacuate now!"

Chip could hear the water rushing like Niagara somewhere near the roadhouse but in the grey, teaming rain he could see nothing.

They scrambled back out to the car only this time they had Charlie with them and they were squeezed in tight. Inching toward Southampton as the hurricane now escalated into its full fury.

• • •

The Garden Club luncheon was held in a fashionable club just west of Southampton Village. The single story building was modern by local standards with a circular lobby and glass domed ceiling so the light shining through gave the whole interior a sense of being airborne like a comic book space ship.

Wilma arrived at the luncheon just as the main course was being served, having missed the reception and first course. She sat numbly at the table with her name scripted on an embossed cream-colored card, mumbling something about 'car trouble' and drank a cup of coffee with a trembling hand.

She didn't hear a word Lawrence Pinckney had to say. All she could see was Celia's glowing face and that funny whimsical red hat as the train pulled out of the station. Wilma may not have been worldly but she wasn't stupid. She could read between the lines and she knew that this Grayson fellow had no idea that Celia was leaving her husband and coming to him. He probably thought she was coming in to shop. It was all too laughable if it hadn't been so serious. Imagine letting a summer dalliance turn into such a debacle. She should have done something more to stop her! But what?

Behind the lectern were tall glass windows framing a stone terrace at the center of which was a willow tree, its long weeping branches hanging to the ground. As Mr. Pinckney spoke, the willow's delicate branches danced in wild mayhem. The lights flickered and then came back on. Then the rain began, at first in gusts and then torrents beating against the glass. Mr. Pinckney raised his voice to be heard over the drumming but it seemed no one was listening to him anyway; every eye was riveted on the increasingly violent action of the willow tree.

Suddenly the branches lifted straight up into the air as if given an electric shock and the tree was torn from its roots and flung against the glass doors shattering them into a million pieces. The women screamed and the lights went out. Chairs were pushed back, some overturned as everyone scrambled to get out of the room.

Wilma felt as though she were in some sort of bad dream. Nothing was making any sense: first, the shattered window at breakfast; then Celia's confessional, the train steaming into the station; the rain, the storm and now they were all being herded by the club manager and waiters into the central room away from the windows. She could feel the building groan and shake as though as fearful as the people in it. Overhead, it sounded as if heavy furniture were being pushed and shoved across a bare floor, yet there was nothing overhead but the roof–a glass roof at that.

Wilma clutched at her purse and felt something sharp in her palm. She looked down at the keys to Celia's car. She was gripping them so hard they had cut into her hand. The car keys made her think of Lewis and now she was bolted into the reality of what was happening. She had to get home.

Lewis. Oh my god. Where could he be? She couldn't see the tiny hands on her gold watch but Margaret Day would have picked him up from school long ago. Margaret Day! Ridiculous, hapless Margaret Day.

Oh, she should have listened to Jim. The thought of Margaret taking care of Lewis in a storm like this was maddening. Were they in the house? Were they alone in the house? Very likely. Jim was in Sag Harbor. Maybe he was back by now. But no. Hadn't he said he was going to meet a colleague for lunch? That was Jim all over and again. He never met a friend. He met colleagues.

Wilma had never felt such despair–leaving her child with that silly woman. She had to get home. And now she turned determinedly to head for the door and the parking lot, but she was being herded like cattle with the others into a passageway that led from the kitchen to the main part of the club.

"The glass roof, Madam, the roof," shouted the club manager, a small round man with a pencil-thin mustache. He was surprisingly strong and determined in his round-up of the ladies. There was no leaving now.

• • •

"Will you look at that?" Margaret jumped up, peering out the front window toward the street. Lewis rushed to the window but he couldn't see anything except the top of the trees blowing so hard the trunks were half bent over.

"May I go upstairs and play with my toys now?" he asked. But Margaret gripped his shoulder and didn't seem to hear him. She was now at the front door shouting to two high school girls who were trying to walk down the street. They were laughing at the how the wind kept them from making much progress.

"You there, Betty, Janet. You girls go next door and get my mother and bring her over here. You come in, too. This is looking bad." Margaret's voice was high and squeaky.

The girls did as they were told, and soon enough, old Mrs. Day and the two girls were gathered in the living room. Margaret had shut one of the heavy sliding doors that separated the living room from the dining room, and the darkening sky cast the room in gloom. The girls giggled nervously saying they thought they ought to get on home, but old Mrs. Day snapped at them.

"You girls stay put. This is no time to be running around."

Old Mrs. Day was really, really old and bossy, Lewis thought. Betty and Janet sat on the sofa doing as they were told, but Margaret didn't stay put. She kept disappearing into the dining room and Lewis could hear the sideboard cabinet door being opened and closed. Then she would come back in the room looking at them like she had forgotten they were there.

"You girls turn on the lights and play a game of cards with Lewis," old Mrs. Day insisted, but the lights would not turn on.

Lewis wished again for his mother. Why did she have to go hear some boring man talk about trees? Trees were trees and there was, in his opinion, nothing more to be said about them. He went to the front window and looked out again. Maybe his father would come home. But didn't he say he was going to Sag Harbor today? Lewis couldn't remember the conversation over breakfast, he could only remember the window exploding all of a sudden and for no reason.

He stood at the window. The storm and rain and wind were howling like the loudest train, louder than a train. The tree in the front yard, the big oak, was moving, moving towards the house.

And before he could say anything about it, one of the girls, Betty, let out a shout.

The oak tree fell. It made an awful sound, a big crunching sound as it hit the roof, and now Lewis could feel himself starting to cry. Big boys don't cry, his father always said. Lewis bit down on his lip.

They all stared up at the ceiling but nothing more happened. Margaret gripped the sides of the big armchair and sort of pushed herself up to standing. Then she kind of did a little sideways dance back into the dining room and now he saw what she was doing. She was holding his father's bottle in her hands, the one he got out when special people came to the house, and she was pouring the dark brown liquid into a glass. He wanted to tell her she shouldn't do that, even though he wasn't supposed to ever tell grownups what not to do, but then Betty, or was it Janet, shouted out again.

"*Oh my god!* The tree is falling through the house."

They could hear it crunch, crunching like a big angry animal breaking through the roof and attic. Then it would stop. Then it would start again, breaking through the ceiling of the second floor rooms. Lewis could hear things shattering and crashing upstairs and he worried about his toy soldiers.

Old Mrs. Day sat in her chair looking kind of confused. Her mouth was open and he could see a little drool, just like a baby, coming out of the corner of her mouth. She was real old.

He looked around for Margaret but she had not come back from the dining room. Betty grabbed Lewis and dove under the big refectory table, Janet right after. They heard one more ear-splitting crunch and all the plaster in the ceiling fell in big chunks, the glass chandelier in the entrance hall crashed to the floor sending a cloud of plaster and broken glass everywhere. Rain poured down the stairs. The girls were sobbing now but Lewis could only stare out from behind the thick legs of the oak table. He looked from the giant hole in the front hall, to old Mrs. Day gripping the arms of her chair to Margaret who appeared to be taking a nap on the dining room floor.

• • •

The surf was now running through the bottom of the house, all white water. Judy had shepherded the children to the second floor when it first started seeping under the doors but now it was more than a foot high. Upstairs, she and the young mother with the baby had got all the children on the bed where they sat like so many little wide-eyed souls not comprehending what was going on. The clown sat miserably on the small stool Chip used to shine his shoes.

"I think I might try to get on home, Mrs. Tate," he said weakly.

Judy just gave a short laugh. "Not an option," she said. "No one can go out in this. Wait until it blows over."

Judy took a deep breath trying to keep calm, but inside, she was churning in frustration and anger. What a time to have Raleigh gone and for whom but the ever-demanding Emmaline! Her eye caught the look on Violet's frightened face.

"Oh, honey. Don't be scared. I'm afraid the party is ruined but we'll just have to have the party up here. Yes, that's it exactly. The party is now in the boudoir." She made an exaggerated gesture. "I'll just go downstairs and salvage what I can. This will be fun!"

And rushing back down the stairs to get what food and party favors she could gather up, Judy waded through a foot of water to the kitchen. With a tray of cupcakes in one hand and a pitcher lemonade in the other she headed back down the hall and was almost to the stairs when the front door ripped from its hinges and a wave of seawater four feet high broke through the house hitting her full force. Food, favors, pitcher were knocked out of her hands crashing first up against the wall and then coming back at her as if shot out of a cannon.

Judy clung to the stairs' newel post. From the top of the landing, she could hear her daughter crying for her, and she saw Anne, the young woman from the club, looking ashen at the top of the stairs holding the baby.

"I'm all right," Judy laughed and waved. "I never thought I'd go swimming in my own house. Don't cry, Alice darling. See Mommy is fine, just fine." She got to the top of the stairs dripping wet. Anne gripped her arm.

"God, Judy I was so frightened. We've got to do something. We've got to get help." Anne's eyes filled with tears and her voice choked.

Judy gripped her arm. "Don't!" she said so sternly it surprised her. "Don't let the children know you're scared. I'm scared too but there is no way to get help. We just have to wait until the water goes down and the storm passes."

Anne looked down at the seawater now on the third stair. "Oh my God, the baby's formula. I left it down there. Here hold him. I've got to get it." She thrust the infant into Judy's arms and was down the stairs wading through the high water into the living room.

From the kitchen Judy heard a deep gurgling sound and realized that the refrigerator was now toppled on its side. She shook her head in disbelief and then turned away and took the baby back into the bedroom. She needed to get out of the wet clothes but first turned to the large window intending to draw the curtains so the children wouldn't be more frightened than they already were.

Dear God, what if the window blew out? She had just put her hand on the cord when she saw it. Unreal. Impossible. A wall of green water was rising up over the dunes. Not a wave, not like anything she had ever seen in her life, but a sheer thick wall of water. A sickening bile of fear seized in her throat. She backed away from the window gripping the baby so tightly it began to wail.

"Children," she screamed in a voice that came from somewhere else, a voice loud, controlled, and insistent, like a growl that seemed to be coming out of her gut and not her mouth. "We're going to the attic now. NOW!"

Violet Hartley, who had been sitting at Judy's dressing table fingering the perfume bottles, got up immediately. The clown gasped in fear. Judy screamed for Anne down the stairs. Then came the impact of the water on the house. In an instant, as if it were made of nothing more than spun sugar, the entire living room, her beautiful room, ripped from its joinery and disappeared into the bay.

There was no Anne. There was nothing but a gigantic hole where the room had been and sickly green and white seawater surging up the stairs.

Judy ran to the stairs where the children were all huddled, many crying. "Hush now chickens, this is a bad, bad storm but we're going to be

alright. We just have to get up the stairs now, all the way up. Violet, GO! And you, too," she said to the clown. "Take their hands, carry them, get them up there, *NOW*." Again the voice from deep in her gut filled with authority and command.

Only once, as she was pushing the last little boy ahead with Alice clinging to her skirt, did she look back. The water had reached the second floor and she saw her daughter's bedroom, the lovely pink gingham bedroom, the white wooden furnishings trimmed with tiny flowers–those little posies and butterflies she herself had so lovingly painted when Alice was a baby–she saw them now crashing violently into one another and splintering like matchsticks, the windows of the room blown out, the wallpaper bulging with blisters, the toys and stuffed animals, the fairy tale books and china dolls flying and churning.

• • •

The trees were blowing in a violent rage and the air screamed out above like yowling cats. Jack was having a hell of a time keeping control on the motorcycle as they rode down Old Stone Highway to Springs. He stopped once to get his goggles on and give Eddie the spare pair, and as they came down the steep hill, the wind seemed a little less ominous once they were away from the ocean. But when they got to the little triangle of buildings around a small green patch that was the heart of the community–a chapel, a community hall, a pond–the storm began to reassert itself.

The motorcycle was buffeted all over the road with limbs of trees and other debris flying by, and Jack could see it was dangerous to keep on. They ditched the cycle then started down the Fireplace Road, his arms around Eddie, the two of them bent over against the wind.

About fifty yards on, they saw an old man sitting on his porch as if there were hardly a breeze. Eddie nudged Jack. "That's Old Man Burl," he shouted. "He ain't very nice." Jack knew they couldn't get to Minnie's walking, so he took Eddie's arm and approached the old man.

"Hey," he shouted over the wind. "We're trying to get to Granny Minnie's. This is her grandson. His ma's up there. You got a car?"

The man looked at them still rocking in his porch chair. Then he leaned his head away from the wind and spit a long brown stream of tobacco. Some of the juice caught in his beard. He reluctantly raised his hand off the arm of the chair and signaled they could come up on the porch.

"Mebbe. I know'd Granny and I know'd this fella. Who the hell are you?"

Jesus. These people were impossible, thought Jack, but he shrugged and held his hands out palms up. "I'm just trying to get the boy to his Ma."

The old man spit again and got to his feet. "Let's go," he said. "Got me an ol' truck out back."

The truck gave new meaning to the word 'old' with its rusted metal wheels, coiled springs jabbing upwards in a torn seat, and holes in the floorboard so you could see the ground beneath. But it roared into action and made it up the road, both truck and driver oblivious to the maelstrom around them.

When they came around the last curve, they could see the bay whipped into turmoil with high, ominous waves furled by the wailing wind. Burl snorted. "For my money, the ocean done come over Napeague. Don't get no waves on the bay like them. Them's ocean waves." He spit juice again out the window mercifully on the downside of the wind.

Just as they turned through the gate to Granny's farmhouse Jack saw what appeared to be an entire barn fly overhead and then crash into a tree, breaking it all to bits.

"Jesus," he said throwing a protective arm around Eddie. This was serious.

"You'd better come in with us," he shouted to Burl but the old man was already in reverse gear.

"You git now." Was all he was inclined to say, his truck already backing down the dirt lane.

Nettie was at the door and pulled them inside, all three of them leaning on the door to get it closed.

"Good God almighty," she said kissing Eddie on the top of his head. "Thank the Lord. I was beside myself thinking about the kids. Surely they'll have the sense to keep the girls up to the high school." She lifted the baby– June, born in June, now five years old, but still called baby. "My god, this is a bad one. I've never seen anything like it."

Nettie was pale with worry, the lines around her mouth pulled taught. "Mitch went out this morning," she said. "But he knows better'n me about these storms. He's probably still at the docks. He wouldn't go with this comin' in and Mitch sure knows his weather. He knows how to call 'em." But there was a hint of uncertainty in her voice.

In the corner of the house, Lottie was huddled with Granny Minnie. "Sit with them, Eddie, take care of your sister. I swear we should think about going down to the cellar."

The walls and roof were vibrating wildly as if a rocket that was about to take off for the moon, and then before anyone could comprehend it, the entire front porch–furniture and swing, the old wash tub, the stack of wood, the butter churn, and shelves of Minnie's preserves all carefully lined up and labeled for sale in Herb Foss' store–ripped away from the house, instantly gone.

"Look there!" shouted Eddie and they could see a corner of the house straining to come loose of the foundation. The old joists, unprotected now by the porch, rose up and the wind rushed in blowing everything into a turmoil of crashing, careening chaos.

Books flew from shelves, china and glass crashed to the floor, chairs overturned.

They all jumped, trying to catch falling plates and crockery, to pin down chairs and the rugs, shouting at one another to watch out, when suddenly they all stopped in unison, even baby June who had been wailing for her mama. All of them stopped. It was a sound, a new sound coming from outside, so strange and terrible, it froze them all in place. A long, loud, deep moan, as if some enormous monster were lying in unendurable pain just outside the door, bellowing to the universe.

It isn't the wind, thought Jack, his whole body pressing against the blue china cupboard he had been trying to keep from falling. His ears were so filled with it he felt he might be hallucinating. Was it the sound of the world coming to an end?

The moan now entered into his body and twisted down his spine and he felt it take possession of him. Nettie's scream brought him back into the room. She was pushing Eddie and June, her mother and Lottie ahead of her, and screaming for Jack to head for the back porch and the door that led down into the cellar. Jack let go of the cupboard, which did not crash to the floor but sort of danced about the room like some clumsy animal desperate to get out of its confinement. He was crawling now behind Eddie and the others with Nettie crawling behind. They got to the cellar door on the back porch, a single wooden door almost flat against the floor, opened it and Lottie and Jack went down the ladder first so they could help June and Minnie down, then Eddie, then Nettie. down into the dark earthen root cellar.

Just as Nettie was half way down, she reached to pull the door after her, but it ripped from its hinges. A corner hit her on the forehead and she was bleeding, and now Jack was taking off his shirt to wrap her head. With no door to shut over their heads they pulled as far back into the cellar as they could to avoid the rain but almost instantly there was a tremendous crash. The old iron wood stove, a giant of a thing unmoved from its spot for more than 80 years, scooted across the kitchen as if nothing more than a light table, and colliding against the kitchen wall and ripping a hole as it slid onto the porch, it pitched over and came to rest fully on top of the opening to the cellar, giving those inside protection, and at the same time, imprisoning them in the dirt hole.

Jack's knew logically that the wind could never move such a thing much less fling it against the wall; it was an insult to every rational notion about weight and velocity. But now, as he peered up from the root cellar, he knew pure fear for the first time in his life. His spine turned to ice; his whole body broke out in a sweat; he couldn't move. The fear was literally sucking the breath out of him.

It was Eddie, only Eddie that penetrated this wall. Eddie clung to his mother. "Where's Dad? Where's Dad?" he shouted though his words were whipped away in the howling scream overhead. Nettie held him close, but Jack could see the expression on her face. If Mitch Grindle was out in this storm, he was lost.

• • •

Judy looked around the room. They had always called this the attic, but it was really a series of small rooms built long ago as a servants quarters. As such, Judy had never much ventured to the third floor, but even in the chaos of the moment, she could see how nice Raleigh kept it. She placed the children on the sofa and the big easy chair.

Oh god, if only he were here now. Raleigh would know exactly what to do and how to do it.

Somehow the smallness of the room gave a sense of protection and comfort. She commandeered Violet and the clown to strip the bed in the next room of blankets and coverlets. It was not cold but the children were crying and Judy knew wrapping them would calm them. For a brief moment, her instinct had worked and all was calm. Judy wiped her face—was it sweat, seawater, fear?

"Where is Mrs. Tremble?" Violet asked her. She was holding the baby. "I brought the baby's formula up with me. I told Mrs. Tremble that but she didn't listen."

Judy stared at her for a moment and then at the baby having no idea of what Violet was talking about. Then she forced a small laugh. "Why she decided to swim to the next house to get help. You know as well as I do, Violet, the Glenns have a lovely big boat and I'm sure any minute they will come sailing up the stairs and take us all into town."

The children giggled. They liked the idea of a boat sailing up the stairs. Judy took the baby holding it close to her, her other arm around Alice. Violet gave her a withering look of disbelief, but Judy stared her down.

"Be a good girl, Violet, and help me with the little ones?" Violet's face was solemn but determined. She instantly bent down and picked up a little boy, who was now sobbing and hiccupping a whimpering cry for his mother.

"A boat, Benny," she said. "A big boat with lots of nice things to play with. You'll like that I know you will." And Benny wrapped his small arms around Violet, now his lifeline, and lay against her with a sigh. Judy marveled at Violet, a child so cool and self-possessed far beyond her twelve years.

"Who knows Row Your Boat?" Judy called out. "If we sing it, really loud then the big boat will find us. OK? Here we go."

They sang, tiny voices hardly making a dent in the din of the howling storm, but they sang and sang until Judy abruptly changed the song to Twinkle, Twinkle, Little Star.

• • •

She sat very still in the hardback wooden chair. A nurse had offered her an upholstered chair in the waiting room but Emmaline did not want comfort. She wanted something rigid, something to help her collect herself. And Emmaline Hartley very much needed collecting.

It had once been an old house converted to a hospital with add-on wards on both floors. Unused to this kind of homespun medical facility, Emmaline wanted nothing more than to get James out of Southampton and back to New York. She had delivered all her babies in a private hospital on the Upper East Side, more like a hotel where a bedroom and sitting area for guests was the standard. The nursing staff provided therapeutic care and also served refreshments to her visitors. James had engaged Delmonico's to bring in her meals.

Emmaline looked around her, hard wooden benches, a frightful linoleum floor flecked with a pale sickly green pattern and walls a bilious matching color defying any imaginable sense of proper decor for a place to heal people. She had always loved pretty things, soft colors that evoked harmony. Why even as a girl she could walk into a room, any room, and know instantly what was right and wrong with it.

An image of that hideous little house she and her mother had lived in forced itself on her and Emmaline shivered. *That house.* You could refashion hand-me-down clothes, you could make sure that no one knew you were a scholarship student, the poor relation to a more affluent branch of the family, but you could not hide the house or make it over into anything other than what it was: a featureless row house on an indifferent side street.

That piece-meal life of her girlhood was something she had put far behind her. Why in God's name was she remembering it now? Shivering again, she sat numbly with her sweater hung on the back of the chair to dry, her hair still damp from the rain and her shoes soaked through.

The ride to the hospital had been a nightmare, the three of them stuffed in the back of the odious little man's car and James turning an ugly shade of purple and though she had only been here for an hour it seemed like whole days had passed since this morning.

God, this morning. Up at 7 to have a quick cup of tea with her departing son George. James in his paisley dressing gown, a fully cooked breakfast before him, including calf's liver, which always made her feel ill, advising his son on the merits of making the lacrosse team. Both Peter and Violet were still asleep.

Emmaline herself had hastily dressed in a blue skirt and cotton shirt for the day's packing ahead. She had been the one to

drive George to the station in the runabout. Standing on the platform, George allowing her one kiss and then hopping on the train
with a final jaunty wave looking so very grownup in his somber
school uniform. He was such a handsome boy and after a summer
of sailing and tennis, he was a picture of health, his brown hair
bleached in streaks by the sun and too long by school standards.
Her floppy eldest child, confidence gleaming in his eye, but then
George was the confident one, and the naughty one. She smiled.
The prankster. How very like his father. She tried not to think of
Freddy, and over the years, mostly succeeded. But here he was
again in that careless wave of her son, in the same mischievous
eyes. And there she was again back in that never-never land of
Paris and youth and love.

Emmaline stood on the platform watching the train disappear down the tracks. Love. The word hung in her mind, a heavy
reminder of Jack and the awful scene of two nights ago. Arriving
there after midnight, not knowing whether or not he would even
be home, or alone, but he had been mercifully both, sitting out
on his front stoop smoking a small Cuban cigar – something she
had never seen him do.

Clearly he was not pleased to see her, declining her offer to
go for a ride in the night air. Instead they had gone inside the
coop, which was in terrible disarray, almost a mockery of all the
beauty and order she kept in her own house. As a peace offering,
she handed him a small package wrapped in linen and watched
his face expectantly as he opened it. It was an exquisite sketch of
two women in a café in Paris done around 1900. The artist was
unknown but clearly gifted and Jack had much admired it over
the summer.

"I want you to have it," she said over his reluctance to accept
the gift, "because you love it. And because I love you. I love you,
Jack. I just never knew how much until now. Please don't turn
away. Please tell me you love me as I do you?" She was fawning
in a way that was not attractive and she knew it.

Jack was embarrassed and tried to stop her from saying more,
but Emmaline couldn't stop. She could hear her whimpers and

pleadings and see the growing alarm on Jack's face. Or was it disgust? She had played this scene before on a long ago day in a loft bedroom in Paris, and it had not worked then any more than it was working now. Oh why couldn't she stop?

Freddy had fled that squalid little scene of hers, but not Jack. He was angry, she could tell, and all her talk of love turned to indignant jabs and nitpicking, escalating into a full blown row when she saw a woman's under garment half hidden beneath the bed. It had ended in an impassioned almost violent sexual struggle along about dawn. Nothing had come to anything—not the sex, which failed to satisfy either one.

No, she could not debase herself again and go to Jack. There was no place to go except back to Dune Road where a tedious day with Mrs. Sternhoffer and the packing awaited her. Emmaline determined not to think of Jack, not to think of anything at all, plunged into the task, but then, the children, Peter and Violet, on a runaway sail.

Like second and third children everywhere, Peter and Violet were not as special to her as George was. How could they be? Peter was a serious fellow always questioning as if somewhere, somehow the correct answers were at hand and Violet was the practical one, her father's image and personality.

Well, at least they looked like Hartleys. But George as he grew older took on more and more the ghostly image of Freddy. Of course, James knew the truth but he had married her seemingly without reservation. Your child is my child now, he had said after that hasty little wedding and he had meant it. They had never spoken of it again, and when George had been born, James had accepted with aplomb all the hail-fellow congratulations on his first-born son. She closed her eyes again and the image of James slumped over the lunch table reared in ugly detail. Emmaline rubbed her hand across her eyes, rubbing them in a way that was strictly forbidden by her beautician: "Tap, never rub, Madam, it will stretch the lids. Tap, never rub."

She felt a snorting guffaw ripple up through her throat knowing what she looked like now. Here, in a third-rate hospital ward, her husband dying or dead for all she knew, wet clothes, wet hair, oxfords on her feet. Well, what sort of outfit did one wear to the hospital when your husband was having a heart attack? She must think about that one.

She could hear rain pelting against the windows, blown almost horizontal by the wind, and poor gentle Raleigh left there in the road. That insidious little man and his stupid prejudice. If only she could feel superior to him, put him roundly in his place, but he had not been so awful once the issue of *a Negro in his car* had been solved. He had driven as fast as he could in that tin can of his, buffeted by wind and water to the tiny hospital and even helped James into a wheelchair. And she had thanked him, oh more than that. She had thanked him profusely as she stood dripping wet in the emergency lobby with Peter staring at her like he had never seen her before.

They took James to the second floor, and here she had been for an hour not knowing what was happening. The relief of getting to the hospital and turning him over to medical care had faded in the waiting and now she felt the sharp edges of worry creep into her. James mustn't die. The thought of it actually made her flesh crawl with fear.

The head nurse was busy and unable to give her any report other than to say they had put him on oxygen and the doctor would be out soon to talk to her. But the doctor had not come out and only the nurses intent on moving patients down to the basement were about.

"Everyone must go to the basement," said the head nurse in a voice that was used to being obeyed. "Mrs. Hartley, this is no ordinary storm. The hospital can't be responsible for—"

"I'm not going to any basement," she said imperiously. "I am staying here until the doctor tells me what is happening with my husband. Peter. Peter, you go with the others." And he had. Without so much as a backward glance.

The corridors were empty now. She was dying for a cigarette. Like a fool she had left her handbag behind in the rush to get James into the car, and that silly housekeeper carrying on like that. Well, she was in a fine pickle now alone in the house in this storm. Jack had made such a lot of fun of Mrs. Sternhoffer and could mimic her dead on, accent and disapproving look to hilarious perfection. She smiled thinking of Jack and then she frowned. She had not known how to make him love her. As with Freddy, she knew how to play the game, but not how to win it.

The noise from the rain and wind was like a shrieking, wild harridan piercing her already aching skull like a drill. Emmaline stood up and started down the hall. Surely, the nurse would have cigarettes. Then she saw her, a tiny figure lying in one of four beds in a ward. She looked to Emmaline like a child.

She went in and saw in an instant that the child was a young girl, a young, very pregnant girl clutching the sheet in terror sobbing silently, her enormous belly barely concealed.

Emmaline approached the bed. "Don't cry," she said. "Are you all right? Do you need a nurse?" But the girl only sobbed more and then she cried out something that Emmaline couldn't make out. It sounded like a name. The girl said it over and over until Emmaline realized that she was not speaking English, but, yes, unmistakably, she was speaking French, a very crude French, a dialect.

"Maman, maman, maman," sobbed the girl.

Emmaline leaned down. *"Avez-vous besoin d'une infirmière?"* Emmaline repeated her question from before. The girl stopped crying and looked at Emmaline in astonishment. Emmaline leaned in closer to the bed. "The nurse will be here soon. They are taking all the patients to the basement."

She stopped not knowing what else to stay but the girl stared at her then she clutched at Emmaline's hand. The pain on her face was ugly and grim to see. *Oh my god, she's having the baby, right now.* Emmaline tried to disengage her hand but the girl's grip was like iron.

Emmaline reached with her other hand to the nightstand where there was a washcloth and a small bowl of water. She dipped the cloth and began to pat the girl's forehead, all the while asking her in French if she was all right. The girl began to relax as the wave of pain rolled away. Emmaline removed her hand from the grip and stroked the girl's hair back from her face.

"*Je m'appelle Emmaline. Et vous?*" The girl didn't answer but Emmaline glanced at her hand and saw a wedding ring. Well, at least she had that, she thought. "*Où est votre mari? Votre maman?*"

Tears came into the girl's eyes and haltingly, slowly she answered. Her husband had gone to see about his truck, worried about it in the storm. Her mother was in Nova Scotia. She had been in the hospital for three days and the baby would not come.

"*Je m'appelle Milly.*" She whispered so that Emmaline had to lean down and have her repeat it.

"Why are you alone?" Emmaline asked. "Where is the doctor?"

And for that matter, she thought, where is the goddamn nurse? Emmaline looked at her watch and saw that it was three o'clock.

The girl cried out as another wave of pain hit her and Emmaline, not knowing at all what to do, kept pressing the cold cloth to her forehead. Then she remembered a little song they used to sing in Paris. It was a song about three small rabbits in the moonlight who end up drinking wine. It was a bawdy song but she remembered it word for word.

"*Au clair de la lune, trois petits lapins,*" she sang, and she saw the girl start to smile.

A nurse appeared in the doorway. "We've got to get her downstairs. You'll have to help me. I'm all alone. They've taken your husband down, Mrs. Hartley. He's stable now but they have him on oxygen. I can't make her understand. She was hysterical when we tried to take her before so we thought we'd wait for her husband. She doesn't understand anything we say. It's these people that come down from Nova Scotia to work. They don't bother to learn our language. They expect us to take care of them—"

"She's terrified," said Emmaline sharply. "And she's about to have a baby. Good god, woman, do your job and stop nattering about learning English." Turning back to the girl, speaking in French "Your husband is downstairs with the others. Don't worry. I won't leave you until we find your husband."

The nurse unlocked the wheels on the bed. Emmaline held onto Milly with one hand, pushing the bed with the other. They had no sooner got through the doors when a piercing unholy scream tore at the building and in one giant roar the entire roof of the hospital blew into the wind.

• • •

She is flying. Everything is flying—bed pans, trays, sheets, chairs, and though she tries to hang on, she feels herself being picked up in the rush of the wind and now she is hurled against something hard and, like an old rag doll, she comes to rest on the linoleum floor, the floor she so hates for its ugly color and design.

She must get up, she must not lay her head in this ugly green speckled dreadful place, but when she tries to move, she is unable to do so. They are looking at her now, the nurse and the poor little girl from Nova Scotia who is having the baby. She blinks against the rain. The girl smiles and whispers something and her face seems so familiar like an old friend she recognizes from long ago. She can't make out exactly who this kindly person is, but no matter, because Emmaline has two very important things she must think about.

The first is the costume she wore to the Bal Blanc in Paris the summer of 1922. Such an extravagant party and everyone must wear white. She has no funds for a gown, but she is clever... and there she is standing at the top of the grand staircase wearing a tennis skirt with white canvas shoes and a white halter top, her long tan legs and arms shown to perfection, her luxurious dark hair held in place by a white sun visor sparkling with a thousand tiny sequins, and in her hand, a white racket studded in paste pearls. The effect? Absolutely astonishing. But there is no time to linger here, to listen to the applause because she must think of James.

James, with his overlarge head and paw of a hand. His lack of grace and his corny stories. His face gone grey at lunch and the look

he had given her, that fleeting look, and she, him, as if everything they had ever been to one another, or had not been, now vanished into one silent exchange that said everything that needed to be said.
    He'll wonder where I am, she thinks. He'll worry about me.

Death comes then. And all that Emmaline Hartley has ever thought or felt or cared for evaporates and is gone forever.

• • •

Thirty-foot waves, green and monolithic, roared onto shore and broke on top of everything in their path: houses, dunes, roads, people. Raleigh held tight to a telephone pole to keep from washing away, but the real hazard now was the wreckage being hurled by the wind turning cedar shingles or a stray lawn chair into a deadly weapon. With the water rising, he held tight, trying to think.

It was impossible to get back to Dune Road, impossible to get back to Judy and the children. He was sick about it, sick in a way he had not felt since that ugly incident on the train. He had always been able to do something, handle the situation, get the job done, but not then and not now either. He could see little in the gloom, but instinct told him he couldn't stay where he was. For one thing, the lines were snapping over his head and he was afraid he would be electrocuted when they hit the ground. For another, the water was coming in waves and each one getting bigger and more deadly. He would not be able to cling to the pole much longer, yet he couldn't move either, paralyzed in indecision.

Across the road, was an open farm field with a small wooden windmill, its arms careening wildly like a child's whirly-gig. Raleigh was transfixed, watching a swan careen through the air completely out of control. It smacked against the center post of the structure impaling itself, its wings broken and limp. Yet with each subsequent gust, the swan—was it alive still?—would spin around like a wheel of fortune. The sight made him suddenly and violently ill and he vomited.

He knew there was a house behind the giant hedge. Maybe he could wade through the water and get to it, get inside, away from the water and wind. Just then, another wave smashed over him and Raleigh lost his grip, the torrent of sea like a roaring river washing him down a long driveway as it ran towards the bay. He swept by the house unable to find anything to grab onto, but not before he saw three terrified people clinging to the rail of the back porch.

The wave rolled on to the bay and Raleigh was able to at last find a footing near a boathouse. Boathouse! If there was a boat inside, here might be a way to ride out the storm. He struggled to open the double doors and saw that they were padlocked. He turned back again, and through the gloom, he saw the three figures struggling toward him in the knee high water, waving and shouting.

"Jesus," he muttered. It was Sarah, Jessie, and Dudley, servants in the Windermere house. He flattened himself against the boathouse, which gave him more stability in the wind.

When the trio reached him, they fell on him as if he were some sort of rescue squad. Dudley, in his twenties and strongest was practically carrying Sarah while Jessie clung onto his jacket. "Man, oh, man, I'm glad to see you," he shouted. "I got the keys to the boathouse."

Inside it was dark and dank and, though some respite from the storm, the sound of the wooden slates shuttering and moan of the wind was little comfort. They climbed up a small set of stairs to a storeroom above and the four of them sat panting from exertion and fear. Sarah, in her sixties was trembling uncontrollably. "I can't swim," she wailed. "I can't swim."

"You ain't gotta swim, Sarah. Raleigh's here. He's gonna get us outta here. Hush now." Jessie put her arms around the older woman, but she too was hollow-eyed with fear. "Whatta we gonna do?" She wailed looking at Raleigh.

"Where are the Windermeres?" he raised his voice over the din.

"Gone. Mr. Windermere loaded up his wife and kids in the car when this started to get bad. Said he'd be back for us but that was two hours ago."

Raleigh could feel the walls of the boathouse shaking. They had all been left behind like so much useless debris. "We've got to get back to the house," he yelled. "It's the only strong place. This building's gonna go."

"Naw, man." Dudley shouted back. "That's why we was on the porch. All the windows blew out. I got cut bad and I say we gotta get outta here."

Raleigh now saw that Dudley's arm was wrapped in a towel with an apron tied around it. Saw, too, that blood was beginning to ooze.

Raleigh shook his head. "There's nowhere to go."

Dudley looked at him incredulously until it began to dawn on him that Raleigh was right. Reluctantly, he nodded assent and they got Sarah to her feet and Jessie, too, making their way back down the narrow stairs to the floor below. Just as they began wading to the door, they heard a roar and the ground underneath began to shake uncontrollably as the floorboards buckled under their feet. The boathouse was breaking up around them.

With Raleigh and Dudley both lifting Sarah up, and Jessie clinging behind, they got away from the structure and waded back to the main house and up the back stairs to the kitchen door. The door was locked. The two women stood down a few steps clinging onto the rail while Raleigh and Dudley tried to batter down the door using a metal chair on the porch. The waves were coming fast now, and then, with a frightening grinding sound, the stairs caved in. The last the two men on the porch saw of Jessie and Sarah were the soles of their shoes.

Dudley was hysterical now and Raleigh not far behind. They could not see any trace of the two women in the grey foam of water. Instead, the roof of the now shattered boathouse bumped up against the porch and Raleigh shouted for Dudley to jump on it. Raleigh grabbed the roof peak holding it with all his might and Dudley leapt onto the boards.

In an instant, they were hurled into the maelstrom each clinging to the meager raft. Another wave and they were catapulted into the bay, only to be sucked back toward the shore where, as the water receded, the roof sank into the mud. They clung on waiting for the next wave, terrified, not knowing if it would carry them again into the bay or crush them to pieces. It came with a force so powerful, the roof and the two souls clinging to it were driven into the deeper waters of the bay. They heard a giant roar and looking back Raleigh saw the Windermere house explode and all that was in the house – furniture, beds, sheets, pictures – sailing into the wind.

Only inches from one another, they could not communicate in any way. Raleigh could see the wound on Dudley's arm, the towel and apron long gone and a deep ugly gash now exposed to the elements. There was nothing he could do. At one point, Dudley slipped off the roof but then surfaced and caught hold of Raleigh's foot until he could finally climb back up.

Doors and limbs from trees flew overhead like weapons of war. Giant sections of houses roared by. Whole cars floated in the surf until the wind got behind them and churned them over and over like breaching whales. They could see nothing else, no shore, no person, no light. There was no hope of rescue. It was as if he and Dudley were the last living beings, and this was the end of all time.

• • •

The cellar was long and narrow and had once been a small dug-out for storing root vegetables, but someone had thought to extend it like a tunnel back under the house, lining the walls in brick, though the floor was still hard-packed dirt. Against the walls, rough-hewn boards held up by stacked brick supports comprised shelves for storage. There was an old lantern and matches which Jack promptly lit, but rather than a comfort, the weak light only outlined the misery of the five people who were trapped underground.

"Don't know if it has much oil," Granny said tersely. "Can't think when I last used it."

Jack shook the lamp and could hear only a small amount of liquid in the bowl and so extinguished it. "We'll need this later," he said. "Is there any other way out of here?"

Granny shook her head and Nettie confirmed it. "Dad dug this out and put up the brick walls but he only extended it about 8 more feet. I think the plan was to extend it the full length of the house but dad wasn't much on hard work."

Lottie snorted. "He cussed a blue streak having to do this much." There was a little light coming in from the opening where the stove had landed and they could hear the storm howling and nothing more.

"Well, we'll just wait it out and then figure what to do. At least we have plenty of food." Jack could see in the dim shadows shelves filled with jars of pickles and jams, dried onions and a large basket of potatoes. There was no place to sit and so everyone squatted down on the ground, June sucking her thumb and clinging to Nettie, Eddie in between his grandmother and aunt. Only Jack remained standing, glancing every now and then at the great iron hulk that covered the doorway overhead. If he had a shovel or a pick he could smash the floorboards around it. He peered through the dark up the stairs and could feel every muscle in his body tight with the sickening fear of a man trapped, imprisoned.

There was no point in talking. Each one of them seemed to retreat into their own thoughts. Even baby June was nodding her head in a drowsy stupor. Nettie stroked June's head and was grateful the child could sleep. She looked through the darkness and could just make out her son; the misery on his face told her he was thinking of his father and she wished she could reassure him, touch him, stroke his head like she was doing for June. But Eddie never let her hug him anymore. He was trying so hard to grow up and be like his dad. She took a deep breath. Mitch was a careful man. He wouldn't go out if there was danger. She said this over and over again until her head throbbed more from the desperation than from the blow to her forehead, but it did nothing to dampen the dull ache in her stomach. She looked over at her mother but the old woman had her eyes closed not in sleep but in some sort of resignation. Her sister's face was in deep shadow. Nettie leaned her head against the brick wall and felt its chill.

Waiting. Waiting it out. Waiting for Mitch to come home. She was an expert at waiting.

• • •

Judy could feel the house shaking under the second then third impact of water coming fast now one surge after another as if the whole of the tempest was coming just for her.

Dear God, dear God she prayed, *these children can't die here, now, like this.* From where she sat she could see the stairs and she could see the water that engulfed the entire second floor moving their way. There was no place else to go; there was nothing she could do.

The entire house now rocked. Its wet walls weary from so much pressure seemed to give up hope of holding fast to the foundation. It was unthinkable–the Atlantic Ocean a wall of water. She closed her eyes, cold with fear, unable to bear looking at the children, who whimpered and huddled on the opposite bed.

Another giant wave hit the house and Judy thought she would scream, but instead, like a charged bolt of lightning, she remembered Chip that first time they had been together in the house. That warm, delicious time of being loved and loving so strongly that you felt you were in control of all the world.

"A strong house," Chip had said that. "Built like a fortress."

And she had told him about her grandparents, who had built the house back in the 1890s when there were hardly any houses out here on Dune Road. She remembered her grandfather. Such pride in his Scottish roots and a stern, unforgiving man but solid and surely he would build a strong house. Nothing so frivolous as a floating living room.

Oh God, please let the house stand, Judy prayed, though it was not God she saw but the image of her grandfather with his firm, steady, fearsome gaze that then morphed into Chip's face–and that same steady gaze but a face so dear to her that she almost cried out to him. His face swam before her and in its presence she felt herself take in a deep breath of air past the lump in her throat, past the sickness in her stomach, and a warmth spread through her as if a warm cloak had been wrapped around her. This must be what it's like to die, she thought.

Then Violet started another song, "Oh Mr. Sun, Sun, Mr. Golden Sun," and Judy opened her eyes, as if she had been deep in a dream, to the small worried, tearful faces that were staring up at her. She felt the floors and walls shuddering, but miraculously she felt her fear dissolving like sugar in a hot cup of tea. She smiled and hugged Alice, then bent down and hugged each child in turn, all the while singing, "Oh, Mr. Sun, please shine down on me." And now she was laughing like the whole thing was a game. She felt like a fortress, she, Judy Delany Tate, felt like she was 10 feet tall and stronger than any wall of water. The house *was* solid, and she *would* save these children.

She gestured to the clown. "What is your name?" she shouted reaching for his hand. He gripped it and she could feel he was surprisingly strong despite his stature.

"Billy. Billy Carlton."

"Well, Billy, you and I and Violet are going to work some miracles here. There's a ledge outside of the dormer window and if we have to, we'll crawl out there and up on top of the roof. Don't be afraid. We have to make an escape plan. If the house goes, we will float with the roof. Violet you start ripping these sheets and tying them together so we can wrap them around the children if we have to go on the roof. Billy, I want you to find something that we can use to bust out the window." She pointed to a small door that led to a storage closet. "Maybe old golf clubs…"

Billy nodded, relieved to have something to do. He made his way down the passage just as another huge body of water crashed into the house tearing a gaping two-story hole in the east wall.

• • •

How long they were there, Wilma didn't know. An hour seemed like a day. And still the storm got worse. In the kitchen corridor, a hallway smelling of old food from the garbage barrels, the women were crammed, some clutching at one another, others seated on the floor in a daze, still others, like Wilma pinned against the wall in a frozen stance. At some point, when it seemed it could get no worse, a group of five wet and beleaguered people arrived from the outside. The women inched down the corridor to make room and Wilma found herself next to a man who was shivering uncontrollably. She took off her coat and draped it around his shoulders and he nodded at her gratefully.

"How did you get here?" She shouted over the din.

"We were in a taxi. I was on the train but it stopped in Hampton Bays. We made it as far as Shinnecock Hills but had to move on. I think the ocean broke through to the bay. You can't imagine what it's like out there. I never thought we would make it. It's like the end of the world."

Wilma could hardly breathe. "I'm so worried about my little boy."

He looked at the floor and nodded. "Where do you live?"

"East Hampton. We drove over this morning and everything was fine. It wasn't even raining. I've got to get home."

He shook his head. "My god. You'll never get that far. All I have to do is get to Bridgehampton. My wife and daughter are there."

They were silent, each lost in worry. A tray of desserts lay on a rolling cart next to Wilma and she reached over and passed one to the man still shivering with her coat around his shoulders. A raspberry tart, she noted and the man seemed grateful for the food but there was no comfort in the shaking of the building and the sound of the torrential rain and screaming wind.

Time passed, and somewhere around 5 o'clock, it seemed as if the storm was lessening. By six there was definitely a sense that it might be coming to an end. Wilma was still gripping the car keys and now she turned to the stranger next to her.

"I have a car outside if it's still there. I'm going to try and get home if you want a ride."

He didn't wait to answer. He sprang into action. "Come on then," he said taking her hand. "Let's go."

Over the protests of the club manager, they pushed past the others and made for the door. Outside Wilma gasped in disbelief and felt a lump of utter despair rise in her throat. She could not believe what her eyes were telling her. Trees were uprooted everywhere. Across from the club, a row of modest village houses that had once been pristine testaments to the care of their owners were now in various states of abject destruction, some without roofs, all without windows, many with whole sides blown off. But it was the trees– uprooted, snapped in two, lying atop the houses–that took her breath away.

"Dear God," she gasped. "We've been through a war." And she would have stood there frozen if the man had not taken her hand.

"Where is your car?" he said urgently.

Wilma shook her head trying to clear it. She looked over the parking area, itself a tangle of limbs and debris, and by some miracle, Celia's beautiful car was there as she had left it, covered in branches and mud but still in one piece. She pointed to it.

"There. If we can get it started and out of here, maybe–"

The car started up after a few coughs and sputters and with the man clearing debris Wilma carefully backed it out of the space onto the road. Once underway, they were almost jovial, like two bandits making a getaway.

"My name is Chip Tate," he said. "If you can get me as far as Bridgehampton I will be so grateful. We live on the Dune Road."

"Wilma Palmer," Wilma said, gripping his hand briefly.

It crossed her mind that Dune Road was not a place you would want to be in a storm like this coming off the ocean but she didn't say anything. She concentrated on driving, inching the car down Main Street, stunned to see the devastation around her–storefronts smashed by cars blown into them, a restaurant cleaved in half by a fallen tree, cars crushed by debris or blown upside down, the eerie desolation of a town that only hours before had been in the fullness of its day. They didn't speak again until Wilma had turned onto the main road towards home.

"Thank God it's still light enough to see. Oh, my God. Look at that. Look at the hospital."

The two-story building was almost a shell. The roof was off and one side was partially exposed so that you could see into the rooms as you would look into a doll's house. She could see beds and chairs dangling from the wreckage.

The trip from Southampton to Bridgehampton, normally a 12-minute ride, took them well over two hours with Chip jumping out of the car every few minutes to clear branches or to direct her around fallen trees. Once, he waded into a depression in the road filled with water to see how deep it was, and together they determined whether or not the car could make it through. In Water Mill, she could have wept to see the old windmill smashed like a child's toy on the Village Green, but they passed through and kept on their way to Bridgehampton.

Chip expressed worry about her going on alone. East Hampton was surely impossible, he said, but even if she did make it, it would be hours given the state of the roads, and he wouldn't be with her to clear away the wreckage. He begged her to stay with him but Wilma shook her head.

"I know these roads and I know every side road. I've been driving since I was fourteen years old. I'm going on. Good luck to you, Mr. Tate. I hope you find your wife and child safe. I'm sure you will. If there's one thing I know about the people out here, they will work to the bone to help a neighbor."

Chip got out of the car and watched as Wilma maneuvered it past the War Monument and out of the village.

For the next four hours Wilma battled her way home. There were stretches on the road that were mostly clear as if the storm had swept them clean, and here she throttled the gas pedal down amazed at the strength of the car. Other places were near impassable. She came to one section where all the telegraph poles were flat across the road and she saw cars tangled in their wires. She had to drive off the concrete into the mud to get around them. At one place the mud was so deep she didn't see how she got through but when she did she sat gripping the wheel for a few moments thanking pompous, braggadocio Harry Slade for buying such a powerful car. Outside of Wainscott, she was in water up to the running board for a mile. In the headlights, she could see hundreds of dead ducks from a nearby duck farm, their white bodies upside down in the murky water.

It was dark. She saw some people by the side of the road and pulled over but they shook their heads at the offer of a ride. They were heading the other way. "You'll never get through," said one of the men. "East Hampton is all down and Montauk is cut off. The ocean broke through at Napeague."

"I don't care about Montauk," Wilma snapped. "I only want to get home. I've got to get home." And on she went, until at last in the gloom and pale illumination of her headlights, she saw she was almost into the village, only a quarter mile left to go before the turn by the pond and so relieved she was that she didn't register the giant elm that lay across the road. The car was half under the tree before it smashed to a halt, the windshield glass breaking into a million tiny shards. Wilma fell against the steering wheel and it knocked the breath out of her.

When she could draw a breath she tried backing the car out but the motor turned over once then died, and along with it, the headlights. Wilma opened her door and got out into the night. There was still a gusting wind but the air was warm and overhead were a million stars as if the storm had washed clean the sky and polished the stars to a jeweler's shine. She brushed off the glass as best she could and started walking.

When she got to Town Pond and turned down Main Street she almost collapsed at what she saw. Her eyes had grown used to the dark and she could make out that the avenue of elms, the giant elms, her elms standing strong for over 200 years, were down. The earth's giants unable to hold in the wet ground from

the months of rain, now toppled with their enormous roots upended, naked like ghostly limbs in a horror movie.

Wilma kept moving. When she couldn't duck under the fallen
trees, she climbed over them, at least twenty of these monoliths
before she got to her street. Climb up, sit on the top, slide down.

She saw the Dowlings lovely white house, dark with most
of its roof gone, and she felt sick. Where was Celia now? That
man, Chip something-or-other, had said he'd heard the train to
New York had derailed outside of Ronkonkoma. But she couldn't
think of Celia now. She could only think of Lewis and Jim. Maybe
Jim had made it back – Sag Harbor was only six miles away. Jim
would have come back at the first sign of the storm. Yes. Yes. But
still she could feel her heart beating in her throat and she was
almost strangled in the fear.

When at last she came to Huntting Lane, she picked her way
around all the debris and then stood some seven hours after leaving Southampton in front of her house – the oak tree with its
wide sheltering limbs now lying like a dead animal cleaving her
home in two, the porch caved in, the windows broken, and all so
horribly quiet.

Even so she didn't hear the men come up behind her and
jumped when one of them touched her arm. "Wilma? Wilma is
that you?" It was Sam Johnson a neighbor and volunteer fireman.
She gasped and then felt hot tears start down her cheeks.

"Oh Sam. Oh Sam, my god, do you know what's happened
to my little boy?" She started toward her house but he stopped
her.

"Don't!" He said so sharply she stopped and slowly turned
to him. "You best head up to the high school, Wilma. Everyone
is there. Doc Dowling has his hands full. They've taken everyone
to the gym. Come now. I'll walk with you. Main Street is torn up
pretty bad but the guys have already started clearing the worst of
it. You can come with me."

Wilma nodded as if in a dream and let herself be led down
Main Street, past White's Drugstore, past the newsstand and
Epstein's Dry goods, past the shoe shop and Edwards' movie

theater and all the places that were part of everything and everyone she had ever known, now dark, smashed and broken.

Only the school seemed untouched by the storm. A heavy
red brick building, it had come through almost intact. It was dark
but she could see the pale lights of lanterns coming through the
gym windows. Sam got her to the door, then he patted her hand.
"I hope Lewis is OK, Wilma. Go to the gym. They have a list of
who's there."

"And who isn't?" Wilma asked. Sam looked miserable.

"I really don't know, Wilma. But they've brought everyone
here–"

He faltered. Wilma straightened up.

"Thanks, Sam. I'm OK from here." She walked down the hall
towards the gym.

• • •

"There's no more Dune Road, Mr. Tate, and no way to get out
there if there was. I'm sorry, sir. You best get over to the church.
They've got coffee there and people coming in from the storm.
Maybe someone's got more news than we have." The police officer was polite but harried. They had set up an emergency station
at the soda shop and were trying to field questions from every
direction. People were frantic to get home, to find family, to hear
information. No one wanted to go sit in the church; they wanted
to do something.

All the main water pipes had burst and there was no electricity, but the counter man was cooking on a gas grill making grilled
cheese sandwiches as fast as he could to send over to the church.
The police had set up a long table blocking off the booths, trying
to direct people into one place. On the table, a lined yellow pad
listed the names of people who had sheltered at the church. There
were no Tates on the list.

Chip was pressed into duty to deliver the latest batch of sandwiches to church and he did so. The smell of toasted butter and
melted cheese, normally a welcome combination, now made him

feel ill. At the church, he saw there were people sitting or lying in the pews, some hurt, some–

But no, they wouldn't bring the dead in here, he reasoned. He looked around for someone to hand the food to. A woman approached him and thanked him. Blankets had been brought over from the dry goods store. A Bunsen burner held a large pot of coffee. She started to lead him there but he clutched her arm.

"I've got to get out to Dune Road to my wife," he said urgently. "Someone must know what's happening out there?"

She was apologetic. "I don't know. You might try the police?"

But he shook his head. "I've tried, they sent me here. I've got to get out there."

A man stepped in and put his hand on Chip's shoulder. "Mr. Tate? I'm John McCord, the minister here. I recognize you and was always glad when you could come to services with your wife. Why don't we sit down for a few minutes?" He led him to a pew away from the others. "The only way out to Dune Road is by boat. The roads are all blocked, but locating a boat that can still float won't be easy. All the lines are down but we got word from a fellow over in Sag Harbor on a ham radio that the Coast Guard is sending cutters out from the city. I'm afraid they won't be here until morning but it's too dark now to do anything anyway."

"No. NO, it's not too late. They're still bringing people in. I've got to get out there. Surely the rescue effort hasn't stopped just because of the dark? This is when they would most need us." Chip groaned and put his head down in his hands. He couldn't bring himself to ask the next question but he did. "Where are they taking–taking–?"

The minister nodded. "All able-bodied men and women have been searching for the dead and injured since the storm passed. As victims come in, they bring the survivors here and the dead over to the golf club on Ocean Avenue. You can go over there if you want to, Mr. Tate. I'll go with you if you like."

Chip shook his head. "I'll wait for the Coast Guard. I couldn't bear it if they were there. My wife was giving a birthday party for our little girl and a whole bunch of kids. I don't know how many. I'm sure they didn't stay out there in a storm. She had our houseman with her. He knows what to do in an emergency. He wouldn't let them stay in a bad storm. I'm sure they're OK. I can't believe–." Chip knew he was jumping all over the place. He couldn't stop himself. He couldn't think straight.

"Is your man a colored man? Older?" McCord asked. "They brought in two men about an hour ago. Seems they rode it out across the bay on top of a roof. Come with me."

His face was blue with bruises, his hands torn and bleeding through the makeshift bandages and he could barely speak when Chip leaned over him lying in one of the pews. "Raleigh. Raleigh," he gripped his shoulder. "It's me, Raleigh. Oh, god, what happened? Can you talk? Raleigh? Where are Judy and Alice? Can you hear me?"

Raleigh nodded weakly and tried to speak. Chip leaned in close to him but all he could make out was the word *alone*.

"Who, Raleigh? Who's alone? You were with Judy! You must know what has happened to them?" He was practically shouting.

"I don't think he can talk now, Mr. Tate," said the minister. "I'd let him rest. He's not doing so good as you can see. He came in with another man who's not much better off, but maybe–"

They went around to another pew and Chip peered down at a man he had never seen before. He, too, was badly beat up, but he was young and stronger and able to talk a little.

"Raleigh, he was stranded on the road out front of the Windermere's where we work. We was trapped until Raleigh come, and then Sarah and Jessie, they got taken by the water. Raleigh, he grabbed hold the roof and we rode it out. We made it. I never think we do it. I said my prayers like it was over but we made it."

Chip couldn't piece the story. "Why was Raleigh on the road? Was anyone with him?"

"No, sir. He was alone. The folks left him on the road. Those folks he was driving left him on the road in the storm."

Chip felt an electrifying shot of adrenaline. Here at last was some news! Driving. Raleigh was driving them out. They must have gotten away. But where? Where would they go? It took him a full minute before the story began not to make sense. Judy would never push Raleigh out of the car. Judy was a nervous driver at best. In a storm with kids? She would never have driven herself. And even if she had, she would have come here, or someplace close to it. The roads were near impassable. She would have had to come here unless she had gone to a house on the way. In his mind, he mentally drove from Dune Road into town, three little miles. There were houses all along the route. She could have stopped anywhere.

Where in God's name were they?

38

Granny Minnie's
6 p.m.

It was over. They could hear it was over. The howl of the wind, the downpour of rain gone. Gone from Long Island, but not gone. The fastest moving hurricane ever recorded had moved across the breadth of Long Island in three hours and was now wreaking havoc across the Sound where, with all communications wiped out, there had been no way to cable or call the mainland to warn that the killer was coming. Long Island had been battered by the powerful frontal winds and storm surge of the hurricane. The deadly backside, with winds more powerful, more vicious, more destructive than those that had flattened the East End, were now roaring down on Connecticut, Rhode Island, Massachusetts, and Vermont and they too, had had no warning. In the cellar at Granny Minnie's, no one had spoken for the better part of an hour but now, in the diminishing sounds from outside, everyone seemed to stir. They could feel the storm passing. They could feel the worst was over. Now what? Jack once again lit the lantern and immediately wished he hadn't.

The light illuminated the brick walls, loosely fitted with a porous mortar, now dripping streams of water. Eddie got up from where he was sitting, the seat of his pants wet. Lottie let out a wail; she was suddenly ankle deep in water. Water was seeping into the cellar from the ground up, from the walls in, the earth so saturated from the heavy rain it could hold no more. Nettie looked at Jack and in an instant they knew, they all knew that here was an immediate and insurmountable problem. With no place else to go, the water rushed in the cellar as if filling a well. And they were trapped.

For one wild moment, Jack thought maybe the water, if it rose up to the top of the cellar, could move the iron stove that sat like the sealed lid of a pickle jar over them, float it off, and release them into the air above. But that would mean it would have to rise at least a foot or more over their heads. They were going to drown. Drown like rats. No, he thought, the panic rising, like puppies tied in a sack and thrown into the pond. He had seen that once as a boy. The old man with the burlap bag, the whining and tiny yips from the hapless pups, the heavy rock tied to the sack marking a line in the dusty road leading to the bridge over the pond. The sight and sound of it had stayed with him for years and with the water now rising up his pants leg, the image was as fresh and awful as if it had been yesterday and he understood why the horror had stayed with him all this time–because he had seen his own death in that sack. Were we born with the knowledge of how we were to die? His mind was racing. What is it like to die by drowning? The lungs engorged by water, exploding, bloated, the mouth greedily trying to suck in air.

"Listen!" This from Granny Minnie. Jack opened his eyes not realizing they had been closed. "Do you hear?"

They all strained to hear. "What is it, Mom? What do you hear?"

"Don't know. It's something. It's a horn. Like a car. Don't you hear it?"

The water rushing into the cellar was all Jack could hear but Eddie then piped up. "Yeah. I hear it too. Like someone's leaning on the horn. "Hey, hey," he started to shout.

Then they all started shouting, shouting like mad people until Jack called out to stop. "Stop for a minute. Do you still hear it?" Eddie got up on the top stair and pressed his ear against the iron underbelly of the stove.

"No," he finally said, dejected. "I don't hear nothin' now." Tears flooded his face in frustration. He suddenly punched the iron lid, screaming in rage until Nettie waded to him and pulled him down into her arms holding him with all her might and he, her.

June started crying and Lottie held her up away from the rising water. Jack clenched his teeth not wanting to cry out. The helplessness was like a scream with no sound.

Granny Minnie reached out her hand, old and knurled like a claw, to Eddie but it was not to comfort. She jabbed her finger on Eddie's arm and she was smiling. "Hush, boy. Quit your hollerin'. There's someone there."

Sure enough they heard a shout from above. No mistaking or tricks on the ear. It was Old Man Burl.

• • •

"Mommy, mommy," Lewis flew into her arms. And Wilma sank to her knees, all the strength gone out of her. She held her son so tightly he began to squirm. "Ow, too tight, Mom." And Wilma let the sob in her throat come out in a great, gasping series of chokes, not realizing until that moment how much fear she had been holding in. A young woman, one of the teachers, yes, now she recognized her, Lewis's First Grade teacher, Lucie Darlene put her arms around her and helped her to a chair.

"It's OK, Mrs. Palmer, Lew is fine. Just fine. He had a big scare with that tree falling on the house but he's fine. The girls took care of him and brought him here as soon as they could."

"The girls?"

"Yes. The babysitters? Betty and Janet? High school girls. They were with him."

Wilma hugged her son again. "I–I don't know. Margaret Day was taking care of him. Margaret was his sitter."

"Well, as best I can make it out, the girls came in the house when they couldn't get to their own homes and they brought old Mrs. Day over from her house next door and then Margaret fainted or something and the girls got themselves and Lewis under a table in your living room when the tree fell. They stayed there until the storm passed and then the girls got him out and over here. Only–" she stopped and glanced at Lewis. "Lew, honey, go get your mother a glass of water. I think she might like that. They have the water and donuts over there, see?"

When he was out of earshot, Lucie Darlene leaned down and whispered to Wilma. "Old Mrs. Day didn't make it. She was dead when the rescue people went in. Died in the chair she was sitting in. Not from the storm. A stroke they think. They had to leave her there."

Wilma looked around and saw dozens of people she knew lying on the floor or huddled in small groups. She knew she should try to help but she couldn't move. Jim. Where was Jim? She looked back at Lucie, "Have you seen my husband? Jim? Jim Palmer?" But Lucie shook her head.

"I don't know," she sighed. "I've been here the whole time but I saw my fiancé about an hour ago and he said they were bringing in four more. Seems a whole bunch of people went down to the dunes to see the waves and got caught in the surge. The doctor has his hands full with bad cuts and we ran out of bandages hours ago from the school infirmary. It's been pretty bad."

"Do you have any names?" Wilma asked.

"Only those four," Lucie said. She took out a piece of paper, school-paper-lined, and Wilma took it closer to the light. *Oh no,* she whispered – *Walter Penn.*

Lewis brought her a glass of water and a napkin filled with donuts but she only drank the water. She was so tired she felt she could sleep standing up but now Lucie was leading her over to a makeshift bed, which was really only a few blankets on top of a mat the boys used in gym for wrestling. But Wilma lay on it like it was the finest down feathers. Lewis cuddled up against her, his little body so warm and secure, and Lucie assured her that when any word of her husband came in she would come and wake her.

Wilma yawned in a way that did not fill her lungs so she knew the tension was still inside her but Lewis fell instantly asleep in her arms. She held him as if he were a priceless gift laying her cheek against his hair but though she was in a state of complete exhaustion her mind was fully alert.

• • •

It was a long night and dark with no moon and no light from street lamps or houses except for the flickering lights of candles in windows and the flashlights and kerosene lanterns of those out trying to reach people. Chip sat next to Raleigh throughout the tedious hours, drinking coffee and watching the old familiar face willing him not to die, willing him to open his eyes and tell him that Judy and Alice were safe somewhere, but Raleigh slept and never spoke again that night.

As more survivors came in, Chip would jump up asking over and over again had any of them come from Dune Road. There was another man in the church as frantic as he. His name was Donaldson–Chip couldn't remember his first name–and his two teen-age daughters were missing, having been out to visit a friend and her baby at their ocean front house. Now it was confirmed the baby's mother had drowned and so had their neighbor across the street. The baby had not been found. There was no sign of the girls.

Chip had seen Donaldson before at some of the dances at the club but they didn't know one another. Come to think of it, Chip knew very few people out here. He had made it some sort of point not to know the club crowd. And why? Because he, Chip Tate, had all the answers when it came to whom he saw and what he did in his free time. Poor Judy, married to such a sourpuss. Hadn't she even called him that–not in anger he remembered–but trying to cajole him into wanting to go to the dances, wanting to go to the cocktail parties, wanting to relax and 'have fun'. *Don't be such a sourpuss, darling. We'll have fun.* He should have been here. He should have taken the time to come to Alice's party.

Christ. Did it take a hurricane to make him come to his senses? They were his life, that tiny bundle in Judy's arms four years ago. And now, in the darkened church on this hard worn pew, he remembered coming into the bright room in the hospital, himself unshaven and smelling of all the cigarettes and cups of coffee he and those other men had shared through the night, each of them waiting, waiting to hear about their wives, their babies, and nothing else then nor now meant anything to him. And then seeing Judy and the tiny wizened Alice peeping through the swaddle of pink blanket and his joy, unbridled, unadorned.

If she were dead but no, no, he wouldn't think of that. He should have been a better man. He had betrayed his wife and his daughter in such a clichéd way it made him cringe with the thought of it. Why was he doing nothing? Why wasn't he taking some action? Yet here he sat listening to the other distraught man, who, like him, was begging anyone who came in for news.

He could stand it no longer, and sometime in the night, he wandered out into the street so dark he could barely make out the steps from the church to the walkway, marveling at the mild, clean smelling air after the sickening reek of fear and injury and coffee and grilled sandwiches inside.

Had he detected sympathetic glances his way? Did they know something he didn't? There were too many rumors, too many stories peppered with words like "crushed," "washed out to sea," "drowned," "lost." Too much disbelief and horror. Too much whispering and shushing and weeping. He would ask no more questions. He would wait for the dawn. He would go out there and see for himself. He would not hear the fate of his wife and child from strangers.

• • •

When he saw his sleeping wife and child, Jim Palmer did something he had never done before. He leaned against the wall and sobbed. Wilma heard the sound in her sleep and came awake to see her husband slumped against the hard wood of the gym bleachers. She got up and went to him.

"Jim, Jim dear, it's alright. We're all right. I was so worried about you." She put a protective arm around his heaving shoulder, leading him out into the hall where they could be alone. She put her arms around him, just as if he were Lewis having a bad dream and stroked his head until at last he seemed to quiet and then she led him outside where they sat huddled on the stone stairs of the school looking out onto the main street of their town. In an hour, the dawn would come, but now the stars were out and a gentle warm breeze, still gusting every so often, played around their bodies pressed close together. It was hard to see the damage to the trees and the buildings and that was just fine as it was soothing not to see.

At first he found it hard to talk, but holding her hand and wiping his eyes with the other, slowly the story came out. He had heard the wailing wind from inside the hardware store in Sag Harbor and then watched the windows break as he crouched down in one of the store aisles. He saw cars upended into trees and trees upended and shot through buildings. Boats from the harbor were shoved up onto Main Street. When the steeple from the Whalers Church toppled, an icon of over a hundred years in the old seaport town, he had thought she must be dead somewhere on the road between Southampton and home. And his boy? Where was he in this storm?

Yet, he couldn't get home. When the storm passed, he had tried to drive but couldn't start the car, he had flagged down anyone on the road but there was no road passable and so he had walked the full ten miles from Sag Harbor and just when he got to Gingerbread Lane, the first recognizable turning into the village of East Hampton, a pickup driven by a man who had only a week before filed a claim Jim was inclined to turn down, pulled up and given him a ride the few remaining blocks to the high school. He had walked into the school, a man paralyzed by the fear of having lost his wife and son.

But that was not the end of it. He talked about his father and his death when Jim was fourteen years old, about his mother who had never recovered, and how she never quite remembered anything as it should have been after that. Birthday presents in the wrong month. Easter eggs on Christmas, money from the small insurance policy that never made it to the bank, school uniforms lost at the cleaners because they had gone to the dump instead, new knick-knacks for the house she had "found"–only Jim knew she had stolen them from the shops. It had been up to him all those years to keep it straight, to see that bills were paid, to intercept monthly insurance payments and make the deposits, to return items to the store owners. And he had done it all, had taken it all on and thought he was OK. And all these years he had kept it well in hand, learning his trade, making careful decisions, thinking ahead. Careful, careful in every way – making sure there was no room for anything to go wrong. And then the storm.

Wilma said nothing letting him talk it through. The fear bubbling up inside of him, all that he had kept buttoned up for all these years, the terror at losing the only two people on earth who meant a damn to him.

Finally he stopped, and the two of them sat holding tight to each other. They had been together for twelve years, she had loved him, lived with him, had a child by him, and had grown into a middle-aged woman with him, but in all that time and until this moment she had never really known him.

39

Chip Tate
September 22nd

True to the report from the ham radio operator, the Coast Guard and their cutters arrived in the early dawn. When the rescue boat set out at the head of Mecox Bay, Chip was on it.

They hadn't been gone long before they saw a small rag-tag group waving from the shore. Among them were the two Donaldson girls in muddy clothes with bedraggled hair and faces, arms and legs scraped by stinging sand but they were otherwise fine and deliriously happy to be rescued. As the cutter turned back to the main shore, the girls chirped out their story. They had left the friend with the baby as the storm got worse, determined to get home so daddy wouldn't worry. Their car had shorted out in the flood on the beach road and they had waded on foot to higher ground and started to walk.

"We had only gone a short way when we realized we had left the keys in the ignition so we started back and we saw the wind pick up the car and throw it up onto the sky and then into the bay. We kinda knew then we were in for it, but there was no place to shelter until we found an old fishing boat turned over in the dunes so we got under it and then we saw these other people coming down the road trying to get to safety so we got them under the boat too. I don't know how it held, the waves came over the dunes out into the bay and we thought it would take us out too but it didn't. When it was over we were all so wet and hungry and cold, but by then, it was dark and we couldn't see how to get out so we had to stay under that boat all night." And then they giggled and hugged each other and hugged the people they had huddled with through the long hours of waiting. "It's over. It's really over," they kept saying.

So, thought Chip, Donaldson has some good news coming his way. His girls are alive and well. Once the survivors were safely off the boat and wrapped in dry blankets, the Coast Guardsman pushed off again, saying to no one in particular, "They were lucky. Most of the casualties are coming from people out on the ocean roads."

The cutter crept on across the bay. The debris in the water was astounding and made for slow going – floating cars, pieces of furniture, beds, tables, sofas, sections of roofs and halves of houses, dead dogs and hundreds of dead birds. The biggest worry was the fallen telephone poles and wires – if they got caught in the boat's propellers the boat would be useless so there was much stopping and long poles hooking lines away from the boat. The sight of all the destruction made Chip's small hope fade.

He had clung to hope all through the night sitting alone on the church steps until finally he had gone back inside to find that Raleigh was awake and calling for him. Chip went to him immediately and reached for his bandaged hand. "They're out there alone. Miss Judy and all the kids. Ain't no one with them."

"But Raleigh what happened? Why did you leave?" He tried to keep his voice calm.

"Ms. Hartley," Raleigh whispered. "She needed me to drive her and her husband to the hospital. He was bad off, heart attack I think, but then, then the car got washed out and I tried to get them to a house but another car came and they, they left. By that time the storm, wouldn't let me get back." He stopped, breathing hard, clearly distressed. "I tried."

Chip patted his shoulder keeping his voice low and steady as he reassured Raleigh that all would be OK but inside he was raging. *The Hartleys.* Always *the Hartleys.*

The cutter was now approaching the opposite side of the bay and Chip's eyes swept over the spit of land that had once been Dune Road. Little remained. Finally, he saw his own house tilting into the sand, one whole side of it torn away, the rooms from the ground to the attic exposed in the ugliest of ways, but he could still recognize the wall paper of the upstairs bedrooms – pink candy stripes in Alice's room, a deep periwinkle blue for the bedroom he and Judy had shared for so many years. He jumped off the boat and waded in. All was empty and silent except for the lapping of the water on the shore.

• • •

"The sun rose this morning on the saddest sight we have ever seen." declared the *East Hampton Star*. Everywhere, in the villages and on the roads people were standing in disbelief, picking their way around the debris, searching for friends, making sure neighbors were all right.

At one farm, the entire brood of chickens were smashed against a wire fence. The sight of dead farm animals and injured dogs was heartbreaking. Information about anything was slow in coming or impossible to get. Out in Napeague, the flood over the stretch had made Montauk an island. With no word whatsoever from the people there, some were saying Montauk had blown away. The Montauk school kids who had stayed overnight at their school in Amagansett stood helpless on the road out with no way to get home across the flooded land, listening to the rumors with growing despair over the fate of their families. When someone brought a tractor to the edge of the flood plain and they saw how the doctor and some firemen and a nurse were on it hoping to get across the floodwater, two of the high school boys grabbed onto the back and now all of them were splashing after the tractor determined to get to their homes and their people.

• • •

Chip stood on the beach blinking in the bright sunlight. It was a warm day, the water glistening, a blanket of tiny jewels, and the ocean now comfortably back in its bed picture perfect. Though the bay was clogged with the storm's havoc, here on the ocean, the beach was swept clean. The clarity of the air made it possible to see for miles in either direction.

Chip was unable to think, to react. There was no one left here. Not a sound, save the lapping of the water. Not a soul but the cutter now in the distance. He knew it would hit him soon but now all he could do was walk. And so he did. He put one foot in front of the other and started walking not looking at anything, but walking the clean, clear beach straight into the rising sun.

He did not hear it at first but then it came again: a voice, a woman's voice calling to him. Stopping, he slowly turned towards the dune or what was left of it. He saw someone waving to him and then he saw others all waving. He raised his hand to his eyes. There, walking through the sand looking as if they had stepped off the pages of the Swiss Family Robinson, was his wife, his child holding her hand, a baby in her arms, and around her, a group of children and a teenage boy dressed like a clown.

Chip sank to his knees. He couldn't breathe, terrified it was some sort of hallucination, but then he heard her laugh, that breathless laugh and Alice's high pitched, "*Daddy!*" He did not feel the tears down his cheeks, only the incredible sweetness of a miracle.

40

The Worst Storm On Record!

The headlines nationwide were devastating. Killer Storm. No Warning. Deaths Mount. Hundred Million In Damage. Tidal Wave Destroys New England Coast. The impact of the waves on the land were recorded by seismographs in Alaska some 5000 miles away. And in Washington, the Weather Bureau was taking no less a beating than the storm itself. Only one forecaster had warned his colleagues and he had been ignored. A densely populated part of the country had been given no warning of a deadly storm and had paid the price. Some 800 people were dead. The loss of property, incalculable. Even the very shoreline of the Eastern United States was irrevocably changed.

The Weather Bureau maintained its position, that the storm appeared to be following a predicable path and was headed out to sea, further pointing out that, if the storm had continued toward Miami as originally feared, it would have found the city a near ghost town, prepared as never before. But all that was of little comfort to the thousands who had not been prepared. Inside the Bureau, a shake-up of command was in process, army meteorologists were brought in, systems overhauled. The head of the Bureau, Victor McGraw, a man who had devoted his life to the weather, was unceremoniously retired and one Will Foster, the only one to predict the storm's path was raised to the level of weather analyst.

The *East Hampton Star,* by the miracle of a generator that had worked through the night, published their weekly newspaper only one hour late on Thursday. There had been little to no time to check stories for accuracy, so they brought out another edition on Friday. The stories they carried were awesome, heartbreaking, unbelievable, funny, and terribly, terribly sad. Everyone had a tale to tell marveling at how scared they had been, how close to death they had come:

"Why, if my head had been two inches more to the left, that shingle would have killed me. Instead it embedded itself in the side of my car."

"I watched them cows get swept into the bay. They's goners, I says, but hold on, you won't believe it. Five hours later, they come back to what was left of my barn for milking."

The dead, of course, could not tell stories. And the list grew every day. Some, like Walter, had been caught in the surge of water, swept into the maelstrom and drowned, others crushed or battered by the missile like debris, still others lost without a trace.

"There were kids on that bus, and when it got to the middle of the causeway, a wave just took it out. All of them kids gone, just gone."

A high number of deaths were the household help who, like Sarah and Jessie, had been left behind to manage on their own while the families they worked for escaped. Some met death on a fool's errand. A woman paid two teenage boys to go out to her house on the beach to rescue her dog. They drowned. Others survived against all odds. The Hartley housekeeper, Mrs. Sternhoffer, too terrified to leave the house when she had a chance, had finally crawled into one of the two remaining cars in the garage. The house was destroyed but oddly the garage remained intact, as did the cars. She was rescued–in shock, but alive.

Two elderly people in Westhampton had been carried twenty miles clinging to the roof of their house only to be gently set down in a field that belonged to their daughter and her husband. Their next-door neighbors were swept out to sea and not a trace left of them or their house. The fates of many fishermen were unknown.

Most people had simply hunkered down and prayed. Trees on roofs, cars blown away, storefronts blasted to smithereens were soon routine tales, but some stories were exceptional.

"Damnedest thing," Jack said sitting in Herb Foss' store telling his story for the umpteenth time. "I thought we were sure to drown in that cellar. There seemed no way out and no one to help and then Old Man Burl shouted down through that iron stove.

Seems that after he'd dropped Eddie and me off at Minnie's, Burl tried to get back home but he didn't make it much further than the bend in the road. The wind blew that old truck of his on its side and Burl decided it was as safe a place as any to ride it out. When it was over he blew on the horn hoping we'd come out of the house and when we didn't, he came looking for us."

"But how did he get the stove off the cellar?"

Jack laughed. "Easy. Rose and Pearl. Two of the biggest, shaggiest, dumbest looking pair of oxen I've ever seen. Storm hadn't fazed them. Burl was pasturing them in Granny's meadow so he hooked them up and easy as you please they dragged that stove off like it was nothing more than a bale of hay. We were chest high in water by that time."

Everyone marveled; it was a good story, one of the best. But in the back of the store, Nettie sat twisting her handkerchief in her hand. There was no word about Mitch and she was hanging on a thread.

"They found that other boat washed up in Connecticut," Lottie told her, sitting with her all that week. "Those men were fine. Mitch and his crew will show up, too. I just know it." But she didn't know it, and every day that went by, hope for the *Kitchin Girl* and her crew grew a little dimmer.

Jack did not go to Emmaline's funeral, held in New York and headlined in all the newspapers. BEAUTIFUL SOCIALITE KILLED IN LONG ISLAND HURRICANE. The memory of their last time together was still raw and disturbing to him and when he saw the photograph of her family, of James and the children leaving the church their faces downcast, he knew he had been right to stay away. She belonged to her family and not to stray lovers, despite all that she had proclaimed. He had stared at the photographs of her in the news–a young Emmaline photographed in Paris by Man Ray, the fashion icon Emmaline in a satin gown, the imperious Emmaline behind sunglasses on the terrace of the now gone Villamere.

Nothing whatsoever left of the grand rooms where so much nonsense and revelry had taken place, nothing but clear sky where her bedroom had been. It all seemed so unreal to him and though he tried to feel something, some emotion, something profound, he only felt numb.

• • •

East Hampton's Presbyterian Church was packed. Not with luminaries from the art world, that would come later in New York at the Metropolitan Museum, but with the everyday local people who had followed Walter Penn's life with pride and who now would bury him as one of their own.

The speakers told the story of the boy who had stumbled out of an ordinary life and of the woman who had inspired him. Yet even as Mary Moran had been the one to start him down the path that had taken him so far, it was the townspeople who had provided the wherewithal.

When Walter had been accepted at Harvard, a first for a local boy, the word came that despite the full scholarship, money was needed for books and travel so from dozens of pockets in town– from clergy, shopkeepers, teachers, and dairy farmers–Walter Penn had set out on his journey with the love and well wishes of his town in his pocket. The Harvard degree led him to Oxford, and then to employment in a London publishing house that specialized in fine books on art and for whom he traveled to France and Italy. A few years later, he decided to try his hand as a dealer in contemporary art, opening a small gallery in Paris. He did well, very well. New York took notice and he sailed back to America and the Metropolitan Museum.

These were the facts of Walter Penn, but his spirit? Jack spoke about the Art Barn, the physical place where Walter had put to the test his faith in the artistic potential of every man, woman, and child.

"He believed," Jack looked out over the many familiar faces in the pews, "that art was a life force. Out here, to many people, life is about the sea and the sky and the salt air. It's about tradition and history, about the old ways of doing things, but to Walter it was also about magic, about a gondola on Hook Pond and the beauty in everyday objects. It was about seeing with new eyes and discovering, through the simple act of going inside an old barn and picking up a paint brush or a charcoal pencil, something new about yourself, something new about the place where you live, something new about the sea and the sky and the salt air. Walter Penn was to me, a visionary. And he brought his vision home to the people and the place he loved most."

• • •

Celia Slade returned home four days after the storm. Her train had been derailed only 30 miles outside of New York and she, along with dozens of passengers had waded through oily water and treacherous debris to an abandoned brick factory where the rising water turned the factory into an island on which the people were trapped. She was pale and weak when an ambulance brought her to East Hampton and seeing her children and Wilma waiting for her at the Huntting Inn, where so many who had lost their houses were boarding, she turned her head into her pillow and wept.

In that unforeseen way that happens in extreme conditions, heroes are often born in unlikely people. Harry Slade became such a hero. No one before had much liked him. Harry Slade was too big for his britches and puffed up with self-importance, but these were the very traits that were now credited with saving dozens of lives.

Harry had been alone in his improbable real estate office in the empty, six story building in Montauk. With few, if any takers for property in Montauk, Harry had been napping, feet up on his desk, when the storm hit. He roared awake and out into the tumult, driving to the train station hoping to get to East Hampton. When he saw what was happening to the fishing settlement, the water flooding the docks, the tiny shacks collapsing into the wind, the people scrambling up to the road, defenseless in the storm, Harry turned his car toward the Manor House, picking up half a dozen women and children. Once there, it was Harry who got the custodian of the hotel now closed for the season, to open up and provide shelter. It was Harry who made trip after trip for as long as he could battle the elements, down to the settlement carrying carloads of women and children up to the Manor. It was Harry who broke open the pantry and storage closets and made coffee and provided dry blankets to the drenched and terrified people – and it was Harry who, days later, greeted that tractor that finally made it across the mile of Napeague stretch where the ocean had cut Montauk off from all communication. He was a hero, no doubt about it and now everyone loved Harry, and the word about his quick thinking and take-charge larger-than-life personality caused a big stir.

But even heroic Harry couldn't steal the limelight from the lone woman out on Dune Road, where every house had been all but destroyed, where even the Hartley mansion was hardly more than a shell, and yet, she alone had saved the lives of eight children. And a baby, too. This was front-page news in New York. The Birthday Party heroine. The photograph in the newspapers showed a diminutive Judy Tate looking like a child herself so delicate and pretty, yet here was a woman who had kept the children safe, singing nursery rhymes and planning to use her very own roof as a raft, securing the children with makeshift ropes from sheets and towels even as her house was being torn out from under her.

"Were you scared, Mrs. Tate?" asked the reporter.

"I was. Yes, scared in a way I can hardly describe but the best thing about fear is it makes you smarter than you are." Judy smiled. "Believe me, I'm no heroine. I hung on because the house hung on. I sang because the only other thing to do was scream and who but the wind would hear me. But mostly it was the children. You hang on for them. What else is there? When the worst of the storm passed and the water receded, I wanted to get the children out of there, away from the house as fast as I could. Half of it was gone and I thought it might collapse altogether. We slid down the staircase, mostly gone but piled high with sand and started walking. There was nothing left of the road and nothing much of any of the other houses, but I thought if I could just get us as far as the turn towards town we might find help.

"And did you?"

"No. There was no one. It was dark and no lights, no sound but the ocean still pounding at the beach. I could see the bay was impassable and I was scared of all the fallen power lines. It's not easy to walk with little children...and a baby." Judy voice trembled, her eyes filled with tears. The body of the baby's mother had been found under the smashed wreckage of the once beautiful living room. But then she looked over at Chip who was hovering nearby and took a deep breath. "We made it to the end of Dune Road and miraculously there was one house still standing on Hedges Lane. Made of stone. Like in the Three Little Pigs nursery tale. It had been closed down for the summer so we had to break in."

"Break in? How?" he asked, all the while scribbling in his notepad.

"Oh, I took a stone and smashed the front windows." She said this so sweetly he looked up in surprise. "When we finally got everyone inside, we built a fire in the fireplace with books and small pieces of furniture. The children were wet and cold so I wrapped them up in the curtains. And wonder of wonder, there was a tin of saltines in the kitchen. We dined on that. And then– and then, it was morning."

They were sitting on the terrace at Walter's house as the guests of Mrs. Cunningham. The reporter thanked her and shook hands with Chip who walked him to the door. When he returned, she was standing inside staring at a painting hanging on the wall.

"Chip, why were you on the train?"

"What?" He was confused.

She turned to him. "I'm asking why you were on the train the day of the storm. We talked that morning and you said you couldn't come out, but you did. Why?" She was looking at him intently with those wide blue eyes of hers, only they were no longer the eyes he knew.

Chip couldn't look at her, and for a moment, he couldn't think of what to say. It seemed to him that there ought to be some way to unravel what had happened. He was too pragmatic to believe you could turn back the clock but it seemed perfectly plausible that he could work his way back to the moment when things had started to go wrong.

"I was coming to tell you–to tell you I–I had met someone. Her name is Maggie." He could barely stand to look at her, but he did. Her expression was unreadable.

And then in the relief of having it out, he started talking. About her father and the financial situation and how he had tried to manage it without upsetting Judy or her mother. About his loneliness, about his need for a friend, just a friend who wasn't caught up in the merry-go-round of fashionable parties and obligations and how he had met Maggie on a shoot.

"It was nothing in the beginning, just a friendly face in the crowd but then–" He sighed and looked at her miserably. He stumbled on. He had no idea that one could fall into something so fast. One day he was meeting a friend for a drink and the next it was something more. A lot more. He told her how sorry, more than sorry, how fearful and scared he had been, but that he was glad she knew and how he would devote the rest of his life to making it up to her. "I don't love her. I never did. I can't even remember now what it was all about. I thought I had lost you to something I didn't understand. I thought when I met you that I could step out of myself and into a different world, into the life you wanted and needed but I let you down. I don't want to lose you."

Judy listened, and when he had stopped, said nothing. For a long time, the two of them were suspended in the silence. Then she stood up. "I want to see my house."

Chip waited. "I'd like to go, too."

She nodded collecting her handbag and the keys to Walter's car, putting on a sweater and calling out to Mrs. C that she was going out. Outside, the sounds of hammering and sawing and the roar of motors on giant-sized rigs with wrecking balls swinging to bring down houses beyond repair drowned out any other talk. But Judy drove purposefully out of the village toward Bridgehampton and Dune Road.

• • •

"Can I help you, ma'am?" The County sheriff held up his hand and Judy rolled down the window of the car.

"Yes. Thank you. I want to go out to see my house." She pointed down Dune Road. There was a barrier across the road.

"Sorry. No one goes. Say now, aren't you the birthday lady? The lady that saved all those children?" Judy felt her face redden. "I guess I am. At least that's what I read in the papers."

"Sure. Sure, I saw it just the other day. Say now. You were a mighty brave little lady."

Now it was Judy's turn to hold up her hand. "Can't I go out to my house? I can walk. I did it before."

He scratched his head. "We've had bad looters out there. Maybe more like treasure hunters hoping to find something from the Hartley house. And some of those structures aren't safe. Not much clean-up out this way yet. But I guess," he looked at Chip in the passenger seat, "I guess if he goes with you it'd be all right. Seeing as you are who you are."

Judy and Chip stood for a long time looking at the house, torn and ragged and probably beyond repair. She spotted something half buried in the sand a few inches from her foot Reaching down she picked it up. It was a fragile teacup made of the most delicate porcelain.

"Look at this," she said holding it up to the light. "Not a scratch. And look at that." Beyond their house was Villamere with its once grand terrace, its lovely rooms, the exquisite furnishings, now only partial remnants of walls and skeletal windows giving it the look of an ancient castle in ruins.

"It doesn't make any sense", she said more to herself than to Chip. "One minute you're going about your day, throwing a birthday party for four-year-olds, and the next–"

She kicked at the pile of sand at her feet. Why? She asked herself again for perhaps the millionth time. Why was she alive and Walter Penn dead. Why Emmaline Hartley and the baby's mother both dead and in such frightening ways. And now–she couldn't bear to look at him–why had the man she trusted and loved turned away from her? Was it her fault, was it his? Her heart ached for him, for the burden he had carried, for her father and mother. And yet, for herself, she felt numb. Did she love him still? Could there ever be forgiveness? There were no answers, of course, and no one to turn to. And here she was. Here she was now. Here in this sharp cloudless autumn day with a warm breeze around her, alive.

"Let's go down to the beach," she said. "I don't want to look at this anymore."

Walking across the road and over the dunes, Judy kicked off her shoes letting her feet wiggle in the warm sand.

Chip watched her then pulled off his own shoes and socks. His bare feet on the sand had a calming effect. The tension of the last week had been brutal. "Judy? I think we should–"

"Talk?" she answered.

He nodded carefully. "We don't have to but the fact that we don't talk at all has me in knots. I've had to listen to you talk to reporters, read about you in the newspapers, but I need to hear about it from you. You did the impossible."

Judy gave a kick to the mound of sand at her feet. "And how could sweet, mild, docile, dependent little Judy ever manage such a thing?"

Chip started to protest but Judy held up her hand.

"Don't pretend that isn't true. I thought the same thing. I thought we were going to die up in that attic and I prayed for someone to come and rescue us until I realized that I was that someone. It was a revelation. And I mean that for real. It was like a bolt of clarity bigger than anything I have ever known. I was the one in charge, and for the first time in my whole life, I felt–I don't know how to describe it–I felt strong. I know it sounds crazy but it was like the house and I were one thing. That house was holding on. And I was holding on." She stopped and gave a quick intake of breath. "Being brave, saving lives, figuring out a master plan isn't something you think about. It comes from a place I never knew I had. And it was bigger and more powerful than those waves."

She waited a moment. "It was like coming awake fully without cobwebs or dreams, and let's face it, I've been dreaming for a long time. All along, I've been waiting for my life to begin as if it were a movie. That day in the museum, when I saw you standing in front of *my* painting, I felt like an actress walking onto the set, and it was magical. You were magical. But I don't know how much of it has been real." She took his hand.

"Do you remember the first time we made love on the beach? I do." She led him to a sheltered place in the dunes, away from the wind, with the sun shining down and the sand warm from it. "It was on our honeymoon. You were such a stuffed shirt about it." Still laughing she removed her skirt and sweater, and then her underclothes until she was naked in the light, stretching out her arms to him. He fell into her with an unbridled urgency, wild and fearful at the same time. He wanted to crawl inside her head. He wanted to feel her, get closer to her than he had ever done before. He wanted her to love him as she once had, and he felt an almost desperate need to hold on to her.

They lay quietly in the sand. He could not see the look on her face but if he had he would have seen the light shining in her eyes.

"What I found up in that attic, Chip, with all those children, with wave after wave destroying our house, was me. And you know what? I rather like her. This me person. I haven't gotten to know her well yet, I just know I don't want to lose her."

"And I don't want to lose you," he said.

"But we *have* lost each other." Her voice was clear. "I don't know where or when it all started to come apart but I know that I lost you a long time ago." She started dressing again brushing the sand from her arms and legs.

He felt the knot tighten inside him. "What happens now?" he finally asked, his voice low almost inaudible.

"I don't know." She took his hand and held it to her cheek. "And that's the truth. We begin again, I suppose is the right answer, but I'm not sure. We can't go on in this marriage. I do know that." She kissed his hand and let it go. "We'll just have to see what happens next, but for now, I think have a good idea. Let's get Alice and go for a chocolate malt."

Chip laughed. "OK." He got up, brushing the sand from his clothes, making light of it all, but inside he felt a lead weight sink into the pit of his stomach. He hated the truth of what she said. He wanted to believe it would come to good in the end, that he and Judy would find in each other everything they needed and wanted. But who really knew?

41

A Final Farewell

In the church in Amagansett the eulogies were about a man of few words, about a man who took care of others before he took care of himself, a man who loved his family and was proud to make his living on the water.

"He quit school at sixteen to fish full time," said Captain Billy Taylor, the most senior of the fishing community. "He learned from his father and grandfather about tides and wind, where to find weakfish, bluefish, and striped bass, how to operate traps and haul seine. He learned the ways of the ocean and he understood as much as any man, the danger. Mitch Grindle was about skill, strength, knowledge, and tradition.

"We know he must have put up a strong fight, a game fight against this storm, but it was man against the elements. And this time, man lost.

He doesn't want us to cry over him," Captain Billy concluded. "All's we can do is pick up the pieces. And keep on fishing."

But they did cry. His children cried. Lottie and Herb and the hundreds of people who crowded into the church, spilling out onto the front, many sitting on top of a large tree trunk felled in the hurricane, they cried because they loved him. They cried because they would miss him. They cried because he was the best fisherman.

"*Why, he could drag a dredge down a driveway and come up with a full load of fish,*" they said.

But mostly they cried because Mitch Grindle was never coming home.

Nettie did not cry. She sat very tall and very still in the front pew surrounded by her children. She listened to the eulogies with a steady and dry eye. Only once did she falter and that was when the choir sang the old seafaring hymn with its final words sinking deep into her aching heart. *Oh, hear us when we cry to Thee/For those in peril on the sea!*

Mitch had not been found, nor any of his crew. The *Kitchin Girl*, the hull of her anyway, had washed ashore on Block Island with no trace of the souls on board. Mitch, her Mitch, was somewhere out there, forever lost at sea.

And now on this day, the day Nettie had prayed so hard not to come, they all came to Granny Minnie's farm after the service, the men setting up long tables in the front yard and the women laying out their trays and baskets and pie tins and covered casserole dishes. Here they gathered, this tightly bound community, the old families who had worked generation after generation the land and sea.

Nettie circulated among them and everyone remarked at how well she was holding up and how beautiful the service was and how sorry, so very sorry they were. After an hour or so of this, she took Jack's arm and asked him to come and sit with her inside. She sat and rocked in the rocking chair for a while in silence. On the mantle was Jack's portrait of Mitch. Nettie did not take her eyes from it.

"I remember one day back before we was married, Mitch came over the bay to this house in that old skiff of his. It was the sorriest lookin' thing and I never understood what he loved about that boat, but it was his first, got it off an old timer when he was about ten years old, and Mitch was so sentimental about things like that. So here he came like he always did and I was standing at the window right over there." She waved her hand to the window that looked out over the water. "Mitch had been courting me for a long time but I didn't want a fishing man. I had my sights set on more of a town life. Lottie was about to marry Herb and I thought I fancied a man like that who kept regular hours, come home clean smelling at the end of the day, and Herb was a lot of fun. Mitch, well, Mitch was serious. I could never get him to do anything, go to any of the parties, wouldn't hardly even go to church dances or picnics. But there I was standing at the window, and there he was hauling his boat up on the beach so careful like, putting the oars just so and finding the right sized rock to hold his line. And when he turned and started walking toward the house, well, who can explain a thing like this, it was like a bolt out of the blue. I was just filled up with love. That's how it was. I was filled up with love for him. I knew that minute, just as sure as I've ever known anything, that this man walking towards me was *my* man. And when he got to the steps of the porch, I opened the door and went out to him."

Nettie stopped for a minute swallowing hard as she gripped the hanky in her hands.

"I stood there looking down at him, he stood with one foot on the step looking up to me, and I said, 'Mitch Grindle, I want you to ask me one more time to marry you but I can tell you right now the answer is yes.' And you know what that man did, he just let out a breath like he'd been holding it in for a long, long time and then he smiled the biggest smile I'd ever seen on him. Oh, he was beautiful."

Outside, Jack could hear the murmur of the gathered people, their voices rising and lowering almost like a chorus. It seemed right to him that he should be sitting here, looking out over the bay, the sound of the water and the movement of the leaves in the trees and the quiet sound of the rocker against the wood floor here in the gathering dusk.

· · ·

The old beachcomber Tom had not been seen, though his cats came back to the shack, most of it buried in the sand, and hung out there for weeks after. Some said he must have died, been taken by the sea, others said, "Nah, not Tom. He's around."

Nettie and the children were settled in at Granny Minnie's but Nettie still got up early like she'd always done with Mitch. The first thin light was just coming over the water and Nettie went out on the newly built porch breathing in the early air. It was a still morning, the birds not yet in song. A sudden breeze came up from the water and danced around her for a brief few minutes before settling back again into the stillness.

Nettie stood quietly watching the sky turn into the pale pink of dawn. When she turned to go back inside she noticed a small bundle at the edge of the porch. It was a blanket tied with twine. Inside was Mitch's clock, the two brass keys, one for the time and one for the chimes, still hanging from the hooks inside the glass door.

THE WIND SCUTTLED. *The leaves on the ground swirled in circles – a sudden gust blew them down the street past the movie theater, past the drug store and the hardware. It blew them up to the school where students were just getting out of classes for the day. It blew loose papers and caps and the boys ran after them laughing.*

It blew the little children home along the side streets and up the back stoops of their houses. The wind blew into the warm kitchens filled with baking smells. Outside on the clothesline, shirts and socks and night-gowns danced wildly in a silly kind of jig.

The wind blew stronger and the trees now swayed and twisted, billowing out in one gust, sucking in on the next. Women opened doors and shouted to their children to come in but their words were flung back at them. There was a popping sound and no one knew what that meant.

The wind had a mind of its own – it was no longer playful but threatening. Clothes ripped from the lines and blew helter-skelter – some of them flat against back yard fences, others up and away and out of sight. There was a moment of near panic – hands to the throat – oh, god, what's happening…again…not again.

And then, as suddenly as it had come, the wind left and the air stilled. You could hear the children shouting and mothers calling to them and dogs barking up and down the street. The wind spiraled up into the stratosphere. The sun sank and the houses and lawns were bathed in a soft golden light. Night came into the now still quiet air and the stars shone polished and clear the way they do in September skies.

wind

Author's Note

The Great Hurricane of '38 still casts a spell over the Eastern seaboard and, while those who lived through it are getting scarce, it is always uppermost in everyone's mind during hurricane season. No storm since can be compared to it. My fascination with it began from the very first time I visited East Hampton in 1970, not so much for the immensity of the storm but for the fact that it came without any warning whatsoever in the middle of the week on a day like any other. This to me was the real story and the seed of this novel.

I am deeply indebted to the many factual books and firsthand accounts of the storm and thank LTV, the local East Hampton television station that houses over 25,000 tapes of local lore. From these video recollections (many voices now gone), I heard vivid accounts. Foremost, Captain Milt Miller, Sr., and Richard Hendrickson, a lifelong East End weather watcher who died in 2016 at the age of 103. Thanks, too, to the East Hampton Library's Long Island Collection for access to their bountiful archive. Two books were inspirational: *Sudden Sea,* by R. A Scotti, and *The Great Hurricane of 1938,* by Cherie Burns. I am grateful to Lew Zacks for his first hand story experienced as a seven-year-old child, to first reader, India Richards, and to Ruth Wittman, Kirby Williams and Mary Croghan who read it with fine copy editors' care. And speaking of readers, I am particularly grateful to the talented and encouraging women in my writers group who have shepherded this novel for many years – Susan Duff, Hope Harris, Leah Sklar, Tamar Cole and in particular to artist Charlotte Sherwood, who created the brilliant maps and drawings. Special thanks to my agent Paul Bresnick who has stuck by this endeavor since the start and to Mary Kornblum for her creative design and care for this book. And to my daughter Lily who has always given me tremendous support (and most lovingly, in this publication year, twin grandchildren – William and Hunter). And of course my great thanks to my husband, Bill, who never allows me to put my writings in a bottom drawer.

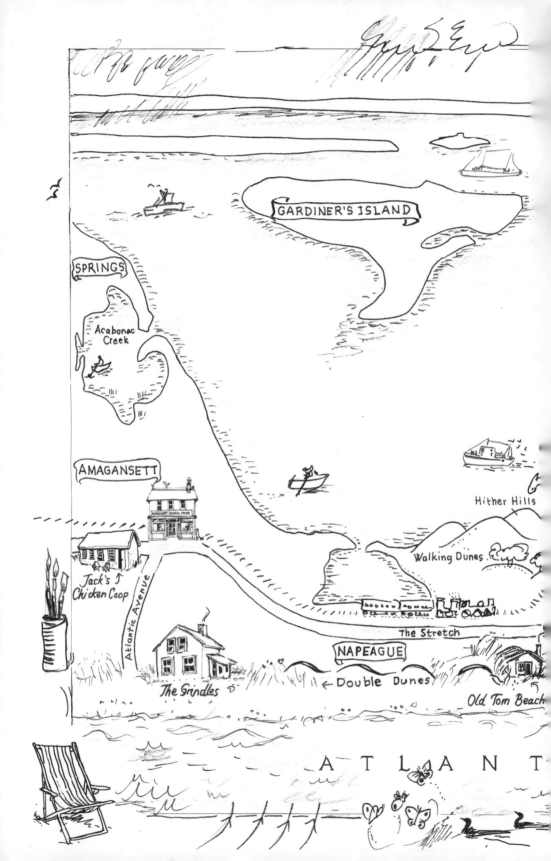